Desert Angel

A Family Justice Novel

Suzanne Halliday

DESERT ANGEL—A Family Justice Novel
Copyright © 2015 by Suzanne Halliday

All Rights Reserved. No part of this book may be reproduced or transmitted in any form or by an means, electronic or mechanical, including photocopying, recording, or by any information storage and retrieval system without the written permission of the author, except where permitted by law.

This book is meant for mature readers who are 18+. It contains explicit language, and graphic sexual content.

Edited by www.editing4indies.com
Book Cover Design by www.ashbeedesigns.com
Formatting by Champagne Formats

ISBN-13: 978-1514142967
ISBN-10: 151414261

Dedication

This book is dedicated to every reader who enthusiastically embraced Family Justice.
Every word herein is written with love and a heart full of gratitude.

I never dreamed with Cameron's story, when those complex, endearing Justice Brothers were first introduced, how exhilarating and challenging this ride would be.

From the bottom of my heart, I want to thank you for loving these characters as much as I do.

Suzanne Halliday

Chapter One

"You're about the only person I know who can turn a simple steak dinner into a nonstop—and *very* boring—comedy routine. Can you stop with the moo-ing? Please?"

"Why the hell should I when I know it annoys the shit out of you? Someday that eye-rolling head shake of yours is going to freeze in mid-motion and then, dude, *I'll* be the one laughing!"

Alex couldn't help it. He rolled his eyes, shook his head, and added some smirking side shade at the end for shits 'n' grins. It was always like this when he and Parker Sullivan got together. More than just the oldest of friends, they'd known each other far too long for superficial bullshit.

And, as his sexy-as-fuck Irish goddess, the one he was blissfully engaged to, would say, this was the *sit down and be serious* portion of the program.

Thinking about Meghan, Alex shifted uneasily in his seat. Something was up with her but figuring out what was as elusive as stumbling upon a leprechaun. In the desert.

Their meal was cleared away, and the two friends were enjoying a glass of Port before falling face first into their dessert. Parker chose a slice of creamy cheesecake that was the size of his fat head and would come out on a platter instead of a plate, drizzled with a local favorite . . . saguaro syrup. The man had an insatiable sweet tooth.

"So," Parker drawled in that laid-back way he was so good at. "Ready to let me in on what this get-together was really all about?"

After refilling his glass from the hoggett decanter to his left, Alex passed it along to Parker. The unusual Port ritual had always been a part of their shared history. He blamed his family's wine-making heritage and the Sullivan's close relationship to the Valleja-Marquez clan.

"How 'bout we make a toast first?"

Parker did that other thing he did so well—blank stare Alex with a crooked smirk. *Jeez. Some things never change.*

"You mean like—*Here's to our women and horses—may both be ridden hard and put away wet.*"

Cue the eye roll. Alex tried not to snicker, but it was no use. Running his fingers through his hair and not caring that with that one movement, he'd made a mess of it, Alex muttered, "Man, you are fucking hopeless," while his friend grunted his agreement.

"*Pfft,* just coming to that conclusion now? You really are one dumb motherfucker, Marquez."

Holding his glass slightly aloft, Alex enjoyed the clear tawny color of the exceptional wine for a brief moment and then tipped his glass in a toast.

"To friendship. The ones that last."

"Hear, hear," Parker concurred. "And may I add that I'm damn glad we both made it."

They sipped their Port in companionable silence, Alex organizing his thoughts and Parker waiting him out. In that regard, his friend had an edge. Patiently waiting, letting the silence build . . . wasn't that a lawyer requirement?

Across from them, an older couple appeared to really enjoy their dinner. Alex noticed them right away. They were hard to miss. Instead of sitting across from each other, the elderly man with the distinguished air sat close to his beautiful gray-haired companion while the woman beamed.

He liked the way their heads moved close when they whispered to each other and how the woman's shoulders shook when she laughed.

To say he'd been shocked when the old man's hand drifted to the leg of his companion was an understatement. When he spied the old codger slowly pulling his lady's dress up and slide his hand beneath,

Alex nearly choked on his food.

God. He hoped that he and Meghan were like that fifty years from now. Still with the naughty talk and forever with his hand doing things in public that made her blush. But he had to stop daydreaming and remember why they were there.

"Look," he finally said, leaning forward, elbows resting on the table as he toyed with his glass. "There's something I want to talk to you about."

"You're not going to start whining about that fucking prenup again are you? 'Cause I'll tell you what, buddy—we may be the oldest of friends and all, but putting my neck on the line with your woman is asking too much. She scares the piss out of me when she gets going." Parker chuckled.

"Jesus! When did you become such a pussy? Isn't putting it all out there what you badass lawyer types get paid to do?"

"Tell me something," Parker countered with an evil sneer. "When was the last time you didn't fold immediately when Meghan made that face at you? And don't play stupid, man. You *know* what face I'm talking about."

"You mean the one that sends my balls running for cover?"

They laughed quietly, each smirking at the other. *Women.* The great equalizers.

"Actually, I want to talk to you about the wedding."

"Ah! The royal event? Big church, white dress, Uncle Eddie doing the sacred anointing thing? Is that what you dragged me here for?"

Alex groaned at the description. But he left out the horse-drawn carriage, fifty-two gun salute, and the Irish flash mob doing Celtic dances along the avenue. Shuddering at his fanciful thoughts, he silently prayed that he'd just made all that shit up. Maybe it was time to start paying attention to the planning.

"Yeah, *that* wedding. And nobody dragged you anywhere, you cheap son-of-a-bitch. Promise of a free meal and you'd be anybody's friend."

"Suck my dick," Parker taunted as he knocked back the end of his Port.

"Not even negotiable."

The waiter appeared with Parker's ginormous slab of cheesecake and Alex's bowl of ice cream. He liked cakes and treats as much as the next guy—but ice cream? *Fuck.* He dreamed about the stuff.

Sweating his balls off in an unforgiving and inhospitable country where he had to spit sand out of his mouth each night, his fantasies about vats of the ice-cold treat were a regular occurrence. To this day, he never passed up an opportunity to indulge. In fact, Alex treated a bowl of good ice cream like a lover. Savoring every lick, he took his good ol' time with each spoonful, even moaning when the cold sweet cream melted in his mouth.

Parker sat with his knife in one hand, the fork in the other, resting upright in his grip. He looked like a caveman using utensils for the first time. Never failed to get a laugh. But it was the ridiculous and very exaggerated Cookie Monster voice that easily cracked Alex up.

"Me like cheesecake! Listen," he chortled, leaning his ear toward the dessert. "It say *eat me!* And eat begin with E and me begin with M . . . as in M*mmmm.*"

That shit would never get old.

They said nothing for a couple of bites before Alex went back to their conversation.

"So, here's the thing, fuckface," he said taking a deep breath. "There's some tradition that says the groom needs a best man. Bunch of bullshit about having a second, in case of cold feet."

Parker made a strangled sound and quickly reached for his glass of water. After a quick recovery, he smirked and mumbled, "Holy shit."

With the hint of a smile, Alex shook his head and sat back heavily.

"Crap. Like asking Meghan to marry me wasn't enough. Now I have to grovel to your sorry ass as well."

"Hold on! Hold on!" Parker wheezed with laughter. Putting his utensils down, he wiped his mouth on a napkin then reached across the table and took one of Alex's hands.

Anyone watching would assume they were a fucking couple. He wanted to throttle the asshole.

Grinning broadly, Parker snickered. "Okay. That's better. *Now* ask me and make it good, Marquez. It's not every day a guy gets asked to be in a wedding."

Alex's eyes widened at the jest, which was said just loud enough for the two tables nearest them to hear. One of the female patrons looked at them and made that *Oh, how romantic* expression.

The fucker. Okay. Two could play that game.

Clearing his throat dramatically, Alex sandwiched Parker's big paw between his hands and squeezed. Hard.

In a voice equally as loud and attention getting he said, "Parker Sullivan. Will you do me the great honor of coming with me to Boston and standing by my side at the marriage altar?"

It was a priceless fucking moment made even better because Alex knew damn well at least one cell phone camera had captured the proposal.

Parker burst out laughing, followed quickly by Alex who nearly fell over from the absurdity of the scene they were creating.

"This calls for champagne!"

"Why? Because I'm paying for it?" Alex drawled.

"You can afford it," Parker said *tsking*. "And you knew I wasn't a cheap date when you asked me out."

Within minutes, they were toasting from a bottle of Perrier Jouët Nuit Blanché Rose. Two grown men sipping from a pink champagne bottle. This was why he put up with Parker all these years. The man had a unique sense of the comically absurd.

"So, is that a yes, dude?"

Half his glass of champagne was gone before Parker answered. "Of course, it's a yes. On one condition."

"There's a condition? Are you fucking kidding me?" Alex groaned.

Cocking his head to one side, his old friend smirked. "I argue and make deals for a living. What the hell did you expect?"

Alex chuckled but fixed his companion with a searing look.

"Well, okay . . . but if the words *droit du seigneur* come out of your mouth, I'll drop you where you sit."

Parker inhaled another huge forkful of cheesecake and grinned at Alex like a mindless idiot. "God. I like having the upper hand with you. The possibilities are endless."

Shaking his head, Alex raised an eyebrow. "Don't flatter yourself, counselor. There are two more buttheads like you who can just as easily fit into a tuxedo."

"Perhaps," Parker laughed with a wink, "but I'd wager that a certain Boston Bombshell knows all about this little tête-à-tête and would have your balls if you fucked it up."

Sliding a spoonful of vanilla ice cream into his mouth, Alex had to stifle a smile. *She would, indeed.* Putting the spoon down with an exaggerated sigh, he ran his fingers through his hair and smirked.

"Okay. What do I have to do? Beg? Get down on one knee? I'm sure the other diners would love that," he said, looking around the room.

In a crisp, no-nonsense, *I have your ass over a barrel* tone, Parker laid out his terms.

Seriously, Alex thought. *This is why I love this fucking guy.* It had always been this way with them. Half cheesy, half poker-face with a large dollop of comedy thrown in for good measure.

"I will happily come to Boston and do my very best to cause as much mayhem as humanly possible if you agree to come out of retirement and get back in the saddle with Desert Thunder. Not all the time—I know you like to think you have an important job, *as we all do,* but at least once or twice a month."

So . . . that was the deal? Play with a motley band of old heads? Sure. Why the fuck not? Meghan would get a kick out of it. And the truth was that he missed playing live. Missed the camaraderie that came with a bunch of grown-ups living out their rock 'n' roll fantasies in a booze-soaked honky tonk because, well—because they could.

Decision made, he stuck his hand out and declared, "Done!" in a firm voice.

"Hot damn," Parker murmured. "A bloody steak, the best Port in town, cheesecake to die for, pink champagne, and the return of Thunder Foot. *Winning,* man!"

Alex blew out a breath and chuckled at Parker's use of the band nickname he was known by. "Fucker."

Making quick work of his softening ice cream, he was surprised when Parker commented, "Thought you'd ask one of those Justice fools you babysit. Or your uncle. All kidding aside, man. I'm honored."

"Drae and Cam are in Dad One and Two mode. And Uncle Calder? Jesus. He's got his head up his ass over Tori's mom. Damn lovesick fool. I swear to Christ if he doesn't make a move soon, I'm gonna throttle his sorry ass."

"That bad, huh?"

"You have no idea," he snickered. "Nothing worse than a grown man mooning over a woman."

Alex felt the silent chill that descended upon their table at his off-hand comment.

"Uh, I was wondering," Parker asked with what Alex supposed the man thought was believable nonchalance. "Will, uh . . . I mean, will Angelina be in Boston?"

Angie. Alex's little sister. The depth of her one-time adoration and hero worship for his friend was well known. It was more than strange that they were so distant from each other now.

Alex shrugged. "Will she be in Boston for the wedding? Of course, man."

Watching that tidbit of information sink into Parker's thick skull, he waited a few beats and added, "Matter of fact, she's coming here. Soon."

His old friend paused and glanced around the room for a few seconds at everyone and everything except Alex. Then, on a growl that came out sounding cautious, he asked, "Here? You mean, *here* here?"

"Yep. She's coming to help Meghan with the wedding. It's what she does, after all," he added tactfully. "Plan events."

Parker's eyes clouded, and he glanced away. "Right."

"Will be good for her," Alex added in a rush. "Mom says she's been a right royal pain in the ass since she ended her engagement."

Hmmm. If he wasn't mistaken, the mention of Angie's on-the-way-to-the-altar farce made Parker turn positively white.

"I'm sure Meghan will be giving you a call when she gets here. Family dinner and all. Give Angie a chance to catch up with old . . . *friends.*"

"Oh, uh . . . yeah. Cool. Look, dude, I'm stuffed. Think we should call it a night?"

Wow. For quick turnarounds, this one was epic.

It sure did seem like Alex's suspicions about his old friend and sister having at least flirted with a relationship were on target. Since it happened when he was a billion miles away trying to stay alive and get home in one piece, he didn't have any hard facts—just a sixth sense. Parker's shocked reaction to learning Angie was coming here now certainly got him thinking.

Chapter Two

ANGELINA WAS COMING HERE? To Arizona? *What the fuck, man?* He hadn't seen that coming. He never dreamed her coming home was any sort of real possibility.

Gripping the steering wheel, Parker tried to focus on the road while his mind careened all over the place. Quickly touting up a hundred potential scenes made possible by Angie coming home, he cringed. Estranged as they were, none were comfortable and all involved an Armageddon-like potential he wasn't happy about.

The Sullivan and Marquez families had been closer than close for decades. All of Parker's memories included Alex, who was one year behind him and very much his partner in crime. Alex Marquez was his right-hand, the second-in-command—his co-pilot and the friend he counted on to ride shotgun.

Alex's cool as shit parents, Uncle Cristián and Aunt Ashleigh, were his parents' dearest friends. The two families had a bond that went back. *Waaay back,* meaning Parker's memories also included Alex's two sisters.

Sophia, two years younger than Alex, was a straight-laced over-achiever with high aspirations. He liked Soph—everyone did, but it was her baby sister, Angelina, who captured his attention from the start. Heart, mind and soul. In fact, Parker couldn't recall a time when the girl hadn't fascinated him.

Boys being boys, it was hard to ignore the arrival of a pink bundle of chubby delight when Alex's baby sister invaded their world. That was how he remembered her. Soft, wonderful Angelina. Alex adored his unexpected sibling, which made having her around easy. She was a mischievous imp as she grew and more likely to cause a ruckus than sweet, sedate Sophie. And he liked her. *A lot.*

During his college years, as Angie went from little girl to breathtaking young woman, the fascination with the girl who was technically off-limits had messed with his head. Their family's close-knit bond and the significant age difference between them confused Parker.

He remembered how close they became once she was off the Marquez leash as a young, carefree college student. Those thoughts were *always* his undoing. Sweat was pouring off his neck into the collar of his shirt as the five-star meal he'd consumed churned in his gut. It took a damn lot of energy to compartmentalize and cut off an entire part of his life, but it wasn't like he had much choice. His thoughtless transgression when they parted ways had been so monumental, he couldn't see how they could ever get past it. He kept all those feelings locked down tight so he wouldn't go mad.

Lights drifted by in the darkness along the winding drive to his home on the outskirts of Sedona. He could do the drive on automatic, which was probably a good thing in his current preoccupied state.

He knew that Uncle Cris and Aunt Ashleigh were staying at the Villa while Alex and Meghan honeymooned but he assumed Angie and Soph would return to Spain after the wedding to hadle the vineyard. Thoughts of the Marquez Winery reminded Parker that every summer, his folks traveled to Spain for an extended visit with Alex's parents. Always full of news and gossip when they returned, he'd have to sit through the obligatory sharing of the vacation pictures and the enthusiastic re-telling of every moment spent at the opulent Valleja-Marquez hacienda enjoying the splendor of the massive casa grande and winery with its ancient cellars brimming with history.

He'd had to endure watching the beautiful young girl he'd unintentionally betrayed change into a breathtaking, accomplished woman—one who he had no doubt hated his fucking guts. Knowing he deserved her hostility for having been a dick didn't lessen how he felt.

The moment Alex and Meghan got engaged, he knew his days of avoiding the biggest mistake he'd ever made were numbered. He'd been mentally preparing himself for having to see her at the wedding. Mostly, he'd hoped to stay out of the line of fire. Keep his damn head down and try not to be a complete ass. The very last thing he expected was an extended visit. Here, in Arizona, no less.

Angie. *Fuck.* Even after all these years, he worried about facing her. As time went by, he'd grimly shut all his feelings and memories of her away. Pushed them deep where they hid in his soul. But there was also that other thing that wouldn't go away or stay in the shadows. The wanting. The yearning for Angelina Marquez that lived in every atom and cell of his being

Navigating through the dark streets, Parker also thought about Alex. When his friend had very nearly come home from the war in a goddamn body bag, he'd vowed to make their friendship a priority in his life. Closeness like the one they'd been blessed with didn't come along every day.

And now that Parker was back in Arizona for good, he made even more effort to stay close to his old friend while carrying this enormous secret inside him. That no matter how hard he tried, he couldn't forget the fresh-faced beauty who happened to be his best friend's little sister or her profound effect on his psyche.

"Hey, baby. Wake up." Running a knuckle down the side of his fiancée's face, Alex enjoyed the sight of the sleeping beauty before him.

She was adorable—curled on her side in the corner of the big sectional sofa in the family room with her hands tucked beneath her chin as the TV flickered, his beautiful Meghan looked so peaceful.

Stirring from his gentle touch, she blew out a sleepy puff of air. He knew when her eyes opened that first glance would be full of love and happiness. But it wouldn't take long for the hint of shade to appear. He didn't know what was going on with her, but he knew something was making her . . . *well, shit.* He didn't know what it was making her. Sometimes she seemed sad. Or bummed out. And for no good reason. Mostly, he didn't understand, and it was making him uneasy.

"*Mmmmm,*" she moaned as her back arched and her legs straightened.

He liked watching the riot of her auburn curls winding across the creamy skin of her neck and shoulders. She was wearing a flimsy nightshirt and a pair of baggy pajama pants covered with clouds, moons, and stars. The real celestial bodies though were her magnificent breasts. The thin t-shirt material of her sleepwear did little to conceal their ripe beauty. Alex could barely control the searing jolt of fierce desire that ripped through him, landing with a burst of heat in his groin. He gazed hungrily at the perfect nubs that tempted him through the semi-sheer fabric. If his dick got any harder, he was going to have trouble functioning.

Meghan's hands slid beneath her head as she turned fully and did one of those arching stretches that made his mind go kind of blank. Was there anything sexier than a beautiful woman slowly waking up? He didn't think so. When he saw the necklace she wore, with the little hearts he'd given her the night they got engaged, he found the sense he needed to focus.

His Irish goddess needed him to do what he did best. For all her ball-busting ways, she was her most grounded when he took control. When Meghan surrendered to him, let him be her Alpha, there was a simple perfection to their partnership. Something was troubling her. It was up to him to help her through whatever was going on. He stretched her. She smoothed his rough edges.

"Hi," she sighed, the sleep clearing from her gaze.

Alex smiled. Reaching out he cupped one of her breasts and through the thin fabric, thumbed the hard nipple that peaked at his touch.

"Hi yourself," he drawled. Rolling the tight nub between his thumb and forefinger, he watched her face as she shuddered and murmured huskily.

"I missed you." Lifting her hands, she ran her fingers into his hair and rubbed his scalp.

Reacting like a dog getting a complimentary ball scratch, he quivered when she clutched at his hair. Alex chuckled lightly, working the nipples on both breasts while she clung to his head and squirmed.

"I was only gone a couple of hours," he chided. "And unless I'm losing it, didn't we make love before I left? That *was* you, wasn't it, who rather sternly accosted me in the shower and demanded my cock."

The instant pout almost unraveled him. She honestly looked like a naughty child.

"But you didn't. . . . well, *you know*," she whined.

To his amazement, she looked genuinely distressed. It was impossible not to grin as he remembered their soapy coupling. Her need had been great, so he'd brought her quickly to a moaning climax with his tongue, and when she immediately demanded him inside her, he'd complied. After that, she pretty much went wild in his arms.

For his part? *Shit. It was all good.* He thoroughly got off on satisfying her lusty demands. Ferociously responsive, he'd tried teaching her how to control the arousal, but there were times when he only had to nudge her inner primal goddess before she'd lose control.

Afterward, she'd been mad at him for not coming inside her. Alex liked Meghan's greedy side. It turned him the fuck on. Stoking the fire, occasionally, like earlier—he withheld that final moment. When he'd pulled out of her, his cock had been hugely swollen with unfulfilled need. A little orgasm denial only made the anticipation for next time stronger.

Alex was an intensely sexual being. It was just who he was. And Meghan was such an extraordinary woman that being with her unleashed his primitive side without fear or holding back.

His woman was pissed off because he'd made her come. *Twice.* But he hadn't satisfied his desire and her petulant frown told him she intended to even the score. It certainly did not suck to be him at this moment.

Tugging at her breasts, he pinched both nipples until she moaned loudly, enjoying the way her fingers dug into his head.

"Alex."

She arched her back some more. Pushing her breasts into his waiting hands.

"What do you need, baby?" he asked.

"Kiss me," she begged while her hands tried to force his head to hers.

Alpha front and center, his mind commanded. Remind her who she belonged to. Meghan's need to please him was his ace in the hole. She had this way of letting her desires be guided by his. He was a lucky motherfucker.

"No." Abruptly standing, he began unbuckling his belt, enjoying the way her green eyes flared. She hadn't expected him to deny her.

"I have a much better use for those sweet lips," he growled.

As sleepy understanding lit up her face, he knew a primitive satisfaction that could not be contained.

With a few unhurried movements, Alex yanked on his zipper and pushed his slacks and briefs down his thighs. Meghan's rumbling sigh when his sex sprang free made him snicker.

Helping her sit up, he put a finger beneath her chin to draw her gaze away from his swollen cock and slipped his thumb into her mouth as her eyes met his.

"I couldn't wait to come home to this mouth," he told her boldly. "All through dinner, all I thought about was you sucking me. What it feels like when you moan as I slide across your tongue."

She moaned. He leered. *Bull's-eye.* It was like hitting her sweet spot and watching her slowly unravel.

Keeping his eyes locked on hers, a rush of staggering lustful need shook Alex when she treated his thumb to a naughty demonstration that held so much promise.

"Do you know why I didn't come earlier?" He asked the question quietly and saw the flash of uncertainty. Defined it instantly.

Sitting back slightly with her hands in her lap, she became very still. He recognized the body language. The deeply erotic and sometimes kinky way their relationship developed had taken both of them by storm. But more so for Meghan who had never experienced such intense intimacies before him. There were still times when she was unsure. Hesitant. He had to help her step outside of her head, leave all the noise behind, and delve deep into her body.

"Was it because I lost control?" she asked in a hushed voice that said a lot about her surprising insecurities.

"No," he answered with a slight frown.

"Oh, well good," she whimpered, sounding quite relieved. Shrugging, she lowered her eyes and admitted, "I don't know what happened. It's just that when I came into the shower and saw you, I couldn't stop. I, um . . . you know. I needed you so bad."

"And I enjoyed every fucking second of that need, my love," he assured her. Cupping her chin, he forced her to look at him. "Meghan.

I will have you learn this lesson or I swear, we'll do this over and over until you get it."

She was so still.

"I didn't come because watching you take your pleasure was about the hottest thing I've ever witnessed. Enjoying your orgasm without expectation was . . . *powerful.* Feeling you squeeze my cock just blows my mind, baby. I love how responsive you are. Sometimes, I just want to get off on getting you off."

He saw the realization break across her features.

"My pleasure is your pleasure," she whispered.

He reached out and touched the heart necklace. "Mine."

"Yours," she replied.

Each time they replayed this moment, he found new ways to love her. What they were saying had powerful implications. It was the moment when he controlled and she submitted, and when she commanded and he surrendered. It was perfection and completion all at the same time. It was what defined them.

She ran her hands up the outside of his thighs and ended by firmly clutching his ass.

Staring him down with a look that demanded satisfaction, his naughty-as-fuck goddess purred, "Mine."

Uh, fuck yeah. "Yours," he growled. "Now suck me, woman. Show me how much you missed my cum."

Alex wasn't disappointed when she took the slow route from his ass to his manhood, taking him in her hands and slowly caressing with a thrilling thoroughness that rocked his world.

In a gruff voice, he commanded, "You will look at me when my dick is in your mouth. I want to see your eyes, Meghan."

A sly grin hovered at the corners of her twitching lips as she tried to bite back one of her mischievous giggles. Giving him a naughty wink, she subjected his throbbing staff to a thorough stroking and drawled huskily, "You do know how much I like doing this to you, right?"

He wanted to laugh. This was one of their games. She was trying to assert her desires. *Witch.* The clever tactic was an endless source of humor for them and she did it, he knew, almost always just to get a response from him. Meghan liked it heavy-handed sometimes. He was happy to comply.

Grabbing a generous handful of her sexy curls, he pulled her head back forcefully. The surprised squeak didn't stop his naughty fiancée from biting back a smile.

Snarling playfully, he held her eyes and said, "It's damn good that you like it, baby because, once we're married, I expect to fuck your mouth whenever I want."

Taunting him with those wicked green eyes, she purred, "You mean like in the limo? Or the barn? Or the tech cave? Or the truck? Or the . . ."

He cut off her litany of the places where she'd taken him in her mouth by simply grabbing his cock and guiding it against her lips.

"Shut the fuck up and suck me."

Her mouth opened on a gurgle of laughter that turned into a groan of desire as he used the hand fisted in her hair to move her head in position to accept the entire length of his throbbing erection.

And then she looked at him and never looked away.

Chapter Three

"**A**RE YOU GOING TO TELL me what's bothering you, or do I have to fuck it out of you?"

Meghan stirred from where she lay sprawled across Alex's big, wide chest but that was all she had. A weak stir. Boneless in the aftermath of a ravenous coupling that left her covered in sweat, her hair plastered against her head and neck as shuddering after-quakes continued to assail her body, she couldn't move. Let alone think.

He wanted to know what was wrong. She should have known he'd eventually demand that she talk to him, even though Meghan had no idea what to say. Or where to start.

Seriously, she thought. *What in the hell is wrong with me?*

They'd pretty much sucked, licked, and fingered their way from the family room where he'd found her when he came home, across the wide, open foyer, and up the majestic staircase. There was something especially salacious about the near savage way he'd taken her on the steps with her knees spread wide and ass up in the air as he pounded into her from behind. She thrilled to the sound of his primitive grunts bouncing off the old whitewashed walls. Meghan was sure she'd never walk up those steps again without remembering.

Next came a ritual that made her feel so . . . cherished. The one where her demanding and controlling Major gently washed her body from top to bottom. It was all so solemn and reverent—the way he cared for her as he lavished attention on every inch of her body, swiping a damp cloth in sensuous arcs across her skin and murmuring words of love and praise for how well she pleased him.

When he was finished, she was so turned on and aching that it was a wonder they made it to the bed. But they had and he'd given her a sort of carnal high with his exuberant lustiness. And now, when she was pretty much incoherent and exhausted, he wanted her to talk? And make sense? He was joking, *surely*.

And then her conscience made an appearance. There *was* one thing she better tell him. Rolling off her fiancé's muscular torso, she slid down his side and lay against him, held in place by his arm.

In that deep, sexy teasing voice, Alex muttered, "You're quite beautiful after I've had my wicked way with you." It was all kinds of alpha sexy when he used his other hand to brush some sweaty tendrils of hair off her face. The things this man did to her . . . Meghan shivered on a choppy sigh.

"Okay," Alex grumbled. "Tell me what's happening inside your head. I need you to let me in."

"I know," she sighed. "I'm sorry. Please don't think I'm *trying* to keep anything from you. It's not like that."

She fidgeted a moment and hung her head then sucked in a deep breath and met his gaze.

"You know how we talked about trying right away for a baby? After the wedding and all."

She felt him tense. His voice was hushed and heavy with emotion when he asked, "Have you changed your mind, Meghan? Is that what this is all about?"

Shimmying closer, she flung a leg over one of his thighs and pressed against him.

"Well, kinda . . ." she muttered.

He sounded heartbroken when he murmured, "Can you tell me why? Do you not want my children?"

Oh, my god. What? What had she said to make him think that?

"Oh god no, Alex! That's not what I meant at all! No, no, no, no." She grabbed his face in her hands. "I can't wait to be pregnant. It's all I think about most of the time."

She shook her head and rolled her eyes. "Well, that and the wedding."

"So, I don't understand. You've *kinda* changed your mind? What the actual fuck does that mean?"

She could feel the tension radiating off him. Meghan swallowed the lump of dread forming in her throat. All she could do at this point was hope he didn't freak out.

"Um, well . . . you see—I didn't begin a new pill pack after my last cycle."

She waited and held her breath while the ramifications of her confession sank in. A long, silent pause ensued and then, without warning, he flipped her onto her back and lodged his beefy body between her legs.

"Are you saying we're making babies now?"

"I don't know if it works like that," she hurriedly told him. "I mean, it's only been a couple of days. I suppose, if you wanted, I could start again and just go forward like I missed a couple of pills. Take some precautions. Stuff like that."

"Absolutely not!" he barked.

"Then, you're okay with this?"

"Are you fucking kidding me?" Alex laughed. "You just made me a very happy man, Meghan. I dream about seeing you big with my child. When you get pregnant, I'm going to drag you with me everywhere I go so people can see your belly and know it was me who did that. Seriously, babe—you have no idea what having a child with you means to me."

"Really?" Her voice cracked as a wave of love for the big man pinning her to the bed washed through her.

"Yes, really. And no, I'm not mad. I just wish you'd told me what was going on in your head, but it's not like we hadn't already decided we wanted kids right away. Shit, honey. Next to saying vows together, making a baby with you is nothing short of sacred. I mean—we've been making love for hours. I need to know that there's even the remotest of possibilities that I'd be planting my seed inside you."

Fuck. Could he be any more perfect? Sacred baby-making? Plant his seed? Did it get any better than this?

Pulling up her knees, she wrapped her long legs about his hips and tightened. She had to give him credit—he didn't even hesitate. With one achingly slow thrust and grind, he plunged inside her and joined them in the most basic of ways.

Wrapped around each other, they shuddered and moaned in unison. It was always like this. Each time she welcomed him into her body, the physical and emotional communion consumed them.

Shoving his hands beneath her ass, he rocked shallowly and ground their bodies together. A fullness that made her toes curl had Meghan whimpering as currents of exquisite pleasure raced through her body.

"This is how we ride, my wild Irish beauty. Feel me inside you? When you come and your pussy squeezes the shit out of my cock, I'm going to fuck it deeper."

Oh. My. God. Maybe this making babies thing was the sexiest thing. *Like ever.*

Kissing her wildly, Alex built a steady rhythm that got her clit throbbing and her sex aching with need. She was so wet, so turned on, that with each forward thrust, her juicy pussy made sounds that caused them both to moan and grunt. The way he moved her ass with his strong hands so each stroke sent her closer and closer to the edge was pure Alex. He knew what angle of penetration would have her melting down and used it to his ruthless advantage.

"Baby," he groaned. "Let me feel you come."

Meghan undulated and clutched at his hard heated cock with muscles made tense from exquisite arousal. One of his hands slipped between their bodies as his fingers sought her swollen clitoris. Rolling the tiny pearl between his fingers, Alex slammed into her over and over. The pleasure he gave was indescribable and the orgasm that thundered into her pelvis made her cry out with wonder. As her body contracted over and over, she could feel every inch of him buried deep inside her.

"I love when you get off," he moaned. "That rush of wet heat drenching my cock. *Oh, baby.* I want to fuck you like this all night long, but I have to come now. Your pussy . . . it's too much. Too much."

His words enflamed Meghan. Grabbing onto his flexing buttocks, she urged him on, rising up to meet him on each fierce downward thrust.

Grunting, he told her in a demanding growl, "Fuck me, baby. Harder. Harder!" And she did. Until her body shook and quaked from the ferocity of his lovemaking. He wasn't kidding about planting his seed as deep and completely as he could.

Crying out, she stared at him in wonder when he bellowed loudly, and with his cock buried balls deep, she held perfectly still while he emptied into her. She felt every throb. Each pulse as his flesh jerked and surged. Seeing him, his neck arched and mouth open on a rumbling primal groan, sent her flying.

They stayed joined for a very long time. Alex kissed her face, her neck, and nibbled on her ear while she stroked his back and gently ran her fingers across the ridges of scarring on his hip and upper thigh.

"Alex," she murmured. "I've been thinking . . ."

She heard his short sigh and smiled.

"You think too damn much, lady," he grumbled. "What else could possibly be on your mind now that we're in baby-making mode? I mean, shit, babe. Isn't that and the wedding enough?"

It wasn't all that hard to keep her Major on his toes. She was one lucky gal. Even the slightest suggestion that something was on her mind had him prepared to move mountains to make her happy.

"Oh, hush," she giggled playfully. "Why is it always the man-growl with you? Huh? If you'd just let me finish before going all He-Man on me, then maybe you'd be surprised at what I have to say instead of dreading whatever you think is coming next."

His deep chuckle curled around her nerve endings. "Are you trying to school me, woman?"

"Well, somebody has to keep that enormous alpha ego of yours in check."

Rolling them to the side, he pulled her leg high on his injured thigh and rocked against her, keeping them intimately connected.

"This oughta be rich," he drawled as he lightly smacked her ass before caressing the curves he never failed to worship.

He had no idea, she thought.

"With Angie about to arrive that pretty much sticks a fork in our privacy, wouldn't you say?"

His grunt was so damn cute. Alex liked being able to have her on every surface and against every wall and piece of furniture. Not just in the hacienda, but in every nook and corner of the Justice compound.

"You liked wagging your pretty bottom in my face on the steps, didn't you?"

"Shut up," she gurgled, as a burst of laughter broke free.

He snickered as he *tsked.* "What did I tell you about that? Every *shut up* from your naughty mouth gets you five spanks. Are you *trying* to wind me up? If you are, just say so and over my knee you go."

"Hmmm. What number are we up to in this spanking scenario?" Meghan felt the skin on her ass prickle at the thought of what he did to her when his big hand went to town on her naked flesh.

"That last infraction brings the current total to twenty-one." He drew back and landed a hearty whack on her butt that made her sex clutch his embedded cock. "Now, it's twenty but I'm making a change. Here on out, I prefer two smacks—one for each beautiful cheek—to deduct a single point." She groaned at his devious scoring tactic. "That way it'll keep you honest"

Squirming wickedly against him, she made a pout with her lips and growled, "Shut. The fuck. Up."

"Twenty-five it is, my lady, but I don't think a good spanking was what you had on your mind so spit it out before you earn yourself a blistered ass."

Meghan placed soft, unhurried, open mouth kisses on Alex's sexy chest. "Before your sister gets here, there's something I want to do."

"Mmm hmmm," he moaned. "Whatever you want, baby. Just tell me . . ."

She nodded and smiled. All she had to do was ask and he'd be all over her in a Boston second.

"I want you to strip me naked, downstairs. And blindfold me."

He pulled back and looked at her. "I like where this is going so far."

"Shut up," she giggled.

"Thirty. Naked and blindfolded. Then what?"

"Then, Mr. Thunder Cock, sir, after that, it's alpha choice. You can tie me up, tie me down—whatever speaks to the moment. Surprise me."

"Hands behind your back?" he asked silkily.

Meghan shuddered slightly. He had a need to push this particular limit of hers. Although frightened by the loss of control, she trusted him enough to give in to this command and control fantasy. She was, in fact, starting to crave the experience of placing herself totally in his hands.

That was what this request was all about. An absolute expression of his domination over her. She'd be sightless from the blindfold. Totally naked. Helpless if he bound her hands behind her. His to do with as he pleased—in every sense of the words.

"Yes," she answered softly.

Alex's sharp inhale let her know how deeply her acquiescence to his desires affected him. Her calm consent spoke volumes to the depth of her commitment to him.

"Thank you, baby," he murmured before kissing her passionately. There really wasn't anything else to say. She knew he'd come up with a sexy scene worthy of the trust she was showing him.

"Come on, fuck goddess," he drawled, pulling out of her body and scooping her into his arms. "There's a tub waiting to be filled with hot water and a shit ton of those bubbles you like so much."

"I can walk," she told him in a rush as worry about her weight putting a strain on his old injuries made her pause.

"Yes, but when I carry you it says something you need to hear. You are mine, Meghan. Completely."

Well, alrighty then. Looks like it was bath time in the Marquez household.

Chapter Four

THE DRIVE FROM THE AIRPORT to the Villa was a ride Angie knew quite well, and thankfully, it was long enough for her to take a stab at getting her emotions under some sort of control. It had been more than two years since she'd felt the Arizona sun on her face. Two long years since she'd come home to the States.

Stretching her legs out straight in front of her, she enjoyed the roominess of the luxurious limo that she learned from Meghan had been an impulse acquisition. Knowing her older brother the way she did and after having gotten to know her future sister-in-law pretty well over these past few months, Angie didn't have any trouble whatsoever conjuring up all sorts of naughty scenarios possible in the limo's private interior.

Hmph, must be nice to have a man who was willing to explore the temptations of civilized debauchery within the confines of a real relationship. She had that once upon a time or, at least she thought she had, until an unexpected and particularly painful reality check had set her straight.

And, of course, *that* thought brought memories of Parker Sullivan screaming full tilt boogie into her head. *Pfft.* Why the hell not? After all, he was the real reason she'd avoided coming home. Pretending otherwise would be more deceit than denial.

As soon as Alex announced that he was getting married, Angie knew the years of staying away were numbered. She hadn't been wrong. And now, here she was, on a brilliantly bright day traveling along the deeply rural ranch roads and by-ways of her beloved Arizona. She was . . . home. *At last.*

Angie sighed dreamily. When Meghan asked for her help as event planner for the O'Brien~Valleja-Marquez nuptials, it was a dream come true. Sure, she did events, launches, and all of the PR for the Marquez family vineyard and winery and had entertained aristocrats and farm workers alike but a society wedding? Woo-hoo!

Thanks to Meghan's phenomenal vision for the uniquely old-fashioned sacrament that would join their two families, Angie had been given the rare opportunity to design an event blending two cultures that could not have been more different.

She giggled and shook her head, reaching up to snag a long strand of soft dark hair that she twined around her fingers as she thought about the proud Irish family from Boston who boasted generations of community minded folk. Angie loved Meghan's gruff but loving policeman dad who unabashedly adored his only daughter. As the wedding plans took shape, she'd had countless conversations with Paddy O'Brien and Maggie, his wife. They were the real deal, those two.

The old, stately Boston church where her Uncle Eduardo would officiate the marriage ceremony was the epitome of romantic settings. The stained glass windows were magnificent and the dark wood overtones along with the gray stone walls were the perfect canvas for a planner's dream location.

Out of an abundance of respect for Meghan's family, the Marquez clan was bypassing Arizona entirely in favor of congregating in and around Beantown in the weeks prior to the big day. And it wasn't going to be just her parents and sister, either. All of the Valleja-Marquez cousins, aunts, and uncles were going to attend. Their side of the church would be overflowing once all the family friends and those important to the winery and vineyard were added to the mix. It was going to be one hell of a party.

Her eyes turned toward the window and she gazed at the distinctive Southwest rock formations out in the distance. The low shrubs running alongside the road were every imaginable shade of an earthy tone beneath a brilliant, cloudless blue sky—a far cry from the lush, verdant Spanish hillsides where she'd been hiding away.

A sharp pain tore through her—tears suddenly stinging her eyes. *Shit.* She missed this. It was her home, after all. But did she belong here after all this time? Could she stop running long enough to let her beloved Southwest creep back inside her soul?

Parker. Oy. Every question she asked or memory she had involved him. Was it the desert she missed and yearned for, or was it him? Was this her home or was it simply where he was? Truth was . . . she didn't know anymore.

Wasting a year of her life engaged to Ronaldo Esperanza had shown her that saying she was over Parker and meaning it were two entirely different matters. The business-like way she and Ronaldo decided to marry had been as passionless and humdrum as the underlying relationship.

In a last-ditch desperate attempt to wipe Parker out of her heart and mind once and for all, she'd sold herself on the cheap. Not her finest moment. Once the engagement was official, she'd dragged her feet about everything. She didn't want a ring, but he demanded that she wear his grandmother's ruby—a big, ugly hunk of junk she hated.

Aldo also expected her to immediately set up housekeeping with him, away from the winery where she maintained a private apartment in an old two-story gatehouse she shared with her sister, Sophia.

Angie didn't want to play the role he was laying out for her and objected at every opportunity. She was a modern girl and a career-oriented woman who wasn't about keeping house and burping babies. At least, not with him. She had a degree in International Business, spoke three languages, knew her way around royalty, and would have made a kickass diplomat. She was well versed in modern wine-making and helped run a centuries-old vineyard and winery that supported a highly respected family label.

Cooking dinner and doing laundry for a man who basically sat on his ass all day while schmoozing on the phone just wasn't going to happen. His proud, aristocratic family needed the infusion of new Spanish blood that a marriage would bring. The Esperanzas might need her, but she sure as shit didn't need them. Once she came to her senses, it wasn't long before she admitted to barely being able to tolerate Aldo.

What had she been thinking? Simple answer. That entire year that she played the fiancée had been a direct result of feeling rejected by Parker for a second time. When his dad, her Uncle Matt, had had a heart attack, her parents immediately flew back to the States with Angie in tow to be with their friends. For two long weeks, while Angie anxiously hovered on the sidelines, Parker ignored, avoided, and generally blew off any contact with her. Not even a glance down a long hallway. There had been nothing.

As the car made a familiar turn and started down the long drive to the Villa, Angie fidgeted like crazy while her conscience snickered. Okay. *So maybe there was a glance.* Well, actually more than a glance. More like an ocular screening worthy of the Feds.

She'd seen him through the glass of a hospital door when he'd been deep in a conversation. Angie felt a gentle thrill race inside her recalling how he'd looked. He was so big. And oh, my god, those shoulders—that face. His posture had been straight and rigid. He had looked sad and to her remembered horror that sadness had her considering going to him so she could lend him some strength. But she had come to her senses and ran—remembering that he wouldn't welcome her comfort.

Rattled by the flood of memories and anxious to put her feet on the desert ground, she gathered herself—eyes drinking in familiar sites. Ah, nothing like that feeling of coming home and . . . *wait* . . . what the hell was that?

Craning her neck when the car eased by, she saw another big sign. A construction entrance? What the hell? That certainly wasn't familiar.

And then there it was, the winding driveway with the majestic Valleja-Marquez Villa at the end. It was so postcard Spanish hacienda perfect that she laughed and clapped her hands together with unashamed glee. Home. She was home!

As the big car came to a slow halt, she was ready to bolt the second she could. When she sensed that the car was in park, Angie was off and running.

The Villa!

Oh, my god!

The trees, the flowers. It was all just so damn beautiful. And the smell. Goddamn, she loved that smell.

She raced toward the timeworn archway with the distinctive iron gates that to her knowledge had never been closed. Angie wanted to hug the trees and caress every bloom. Smiling, she turned her face to the sky and breathed deeply. Everything was going to be all right. She was older. Wiser. Would make better decisions this time around. It was time she sorted her shit out, and coming here was the only way that could happen.

Her reverie was stopped by the sound of the massive wood door to the main house opening and then she was running at full speed. Alex! Oh, my god! It was Alex!

Launching into him at the last second, he caught her in an exuberant embrace and swung her around like she was a rag doll.

"Baby girl!" her brother boomed with glee. "Welcome home, darlin'."

Angie couldn't help herself. They'd all come so perilously close to losing him. In the years since, some of that anxiety had lessened, but the intense love she had for her complex older brother was overwhelming. Letting him crush her in a fierce hug, she clung to his shoulders and thanked the angels for saving his life.

"Alexander," she choked out with a final squeeze before he let her go. Getting a good look at him up close, Angie burst into giggles at his bemused expression.

"What? Have I grown antlers or something?"

Angie was stunned by how happy he looked. He was relaxed and smiling. Okay, he was still Alex but a lot less of a mess. His hair, which always bore that freshly rumpled look, was now cut in a way that made the disheveled mess into an actual style. In short, Alexander Marquez looked like a content man. She saw no hint of the devastating injuries that ended his military career. Instead of pain and frustration in his eyes, she found joy. Her heart was full to bursting. *Meghan.* She brought him back. Oh. My. God. Where was the woman she owed everything to?

"No antlers, brother. I'm just so happy to see your moldy old ass."

"Says the sassy bitch who's staring at thirty," he taunted. "You're the one getting older, baby girl. Not me! I'm getting better with age."

She slapped him on the shoulder and tried a shove, which only made him laugh. "Angie. *Baby.* It's good to see you."

She beamed. Alex—her hero.

"Not a baby anymore according to you! And for the record, thirty doesn't scare me at all. In fact, I'm thinking about getting a tattoo to mark the occasion."

He burst out laughing. "Oh shit, Ang! A tattoo? Mom will fucking kill you!"

"*Hehehe.* Not if she doesn't know," she chuckled.

Grabbing her hand, Alex barked, "Come on," and yanked her along as he made his way through the large foyer and headed toward the kitchen. Keeping up with him was immediately a problem. With each big step he took, she stumbled with two or three.

"Whoa, big brother! Slow down, okay? These boots were made for *walking,* not running."

"Oh, my bad," he murmured as he slowed. "But come on, hurry the fuck up."

Good grief, the asshole was actually tugging on her arm. "What's got your shorts in a bunch?"

Wait a minute! Was that a pile of sugar donuts piled high on a stoneware platter? Angie twisted in Alex's grasp, pointing back over her shoulder.

"Were those donuts?" Angie's sweet tooth was legendary. She'd never met a sugary treat that she didn't immediately fall in love with.

"Later," he drawled, pulling her along. At the big rustic doors that opened onto the private patio, he finally stopped and let her go. Smiling as he pushed open a door, he told her, "Get ready," then guided her through the archway.

The enclosed patio surrounded by garden walls and the backside of the family villa was another picturesque-perfect spot that held many happy memories. Of her aristocratic grandparents who brought the crumbling villa back to life and the countless times they'd all gathered in this very courtyard. Her parents, Uncle Eduardo, Sophie, Alex. It was familiar and heartwarming to be there again.

Standing near the fireplace with a nervous looking half-smile was someone who Angie knew immediately. She heard Alex proudly announce, "Angelina Marquez, this—*this* is the love of my life. Meghan, come here, baby. Meet my little sister."

And just like that, Angie felt herself mentally handing off the *baby* endearment she was used to and finally becoming just the little sister.

As Meghan came forward, Angie was a little stunned. They'd video chatted a thousand times, shared endless pictures, so she'd know her brother's fiancée anywhere. But seeing her in person for the first time? Holy shit. No wonder Alex was practically aglow. He got himself a bona fide beauty with curves that went on for miles and a face framed by a riot of rich auburn curls. She was tall and gorgeous—the perfect fit for Alex.

"Angie," Meghan said warmly. "Welcome home. I'm *soooo* glad you're here."

She glanced briefly at Alex and exploded with joy. The way he looked at Meghan was just so freakin' adorable.

Walking into the woman's embrace, they hugged like sisters, rocking back and forth, laughing happily.

"Damn, Red," Angie giggled quietly so her brother wouldn't hear. "I love you already but seeing that shit-eating look and him all but chest thumping his satisfaction? Priceless, lady. I'm in your debt forever."

Meghan sighed and snickered at the same time, whispering, "He's a handful."

Leaning in for a two-cheek kiss, Angie murmured, "You're going to have to share your secret with me. That's a happy man, Meghan."

Boom! And just like that, it was two gals knee deep in a gab sesh and Alex was essentially forgotten. Looping her arm through Angie's, Meghan started walking them into the house while her brother stood aside looking adorably baffled.

"All the cases and packages you sent are in your suite. Ben will bring your bags up, won't he, sweetheart," she said to Alex as they passed by. It was a statement not a question and Angie nearly fell over laughing at how domestic these two were and how clearly Meghan ruled the roost.

She had to admit. This kind of surprised her. Alex was always the leader of the pack and had the military record to prove it. To say he liked control was the mother of all understatements. It had taken less than thirty seconds to realize that where this fantastic lady was concerned, her brother was in total crap-your-pants style awe.

And then Meghan did something that brought their completely charming relationship into focus. Sliding from Angie's arm, she backed up a few steps and wound herself around Alex. The rather possessive way he grabbed his fiancée's ass was pretty damn telling.

"Thank you, baby," she overheard Meghan purr just before they fell into a steamy kiss that was so mesmerizing it was difficult to look away. One hand grabbing ass and the other gripping the back of her head—Angie rolled her eyes at the sight. Now, *there* was the Alex she knew.

"Oh Christ, bro. Let her up for air, would you?" Angie sniped with feigned exasperation. "And let go of the leash too. I promise not to let her run into traffic, okay?"

"Shut the fuck up, you little rugrat," he chortled once he tore himself away from Meghan's mouth.

"How come you get to say shut up?" Meghan sighed.

"'Cause I'm the M-A-N, that's why!" He laughed as he swatted his woman's butt. "You girls run along and go play with your Barbies. I'm headed out to the construction trailer."

"Yeah, I saw that," Angie squeaked, remembering what she'd seen on the way in. "What's going on, Alexander? You making some changes?"

"You could say that. Look, we'll catch up and share newsletters at dinner, okay? Meghan's been jumping out of her skin with excitement for you to get here so in the interest of peace and harmony . . ."

Angie snorted at the comment.

"As I was saying before the heckler in the peanut gallery added unwanted sound effects," he said with a shake of his brotherly head. "With a nod to peace and harmony, you two get the rest of the day to lose your shit over all this girlie stuff. Fun now. Get down to business later."

Kissing her quickly on the forehead, Alex lingered quite a bit longer on Meghan's lips, then said. "Later," and strode from the room.

Meghan's sigh as she watched him go clutched at Angie's heart.

"Okay, bride, so show me the latest pictures from your dress fitting. I have a trillion questions and want to show you some awesome ideas for attendant gifts."

"Thank god you're here, Angie. I'm drowning under the weight of all the wedding details."

Looping their arms again, she shrugged like all this was no big deal. "You relax. Enjoy being engaged. Let me take over, okay?"

"Gladly," Meghan hooted. "Come on. Donuts first. Ria left a whole bunch."

Playfully pushing her new sister out of the way, Angie taunted, "Donuts? Dibs!" and went dashing into the house as Meghan's happy laughter split the air.

Chapter Five

"Wow. This is a lot to take on, you guys. Do the 'rents know about this?" Angie asked Alex.

"Absolutely." He was quick to assure his sister. "Just because I have legal control of the property doesn't mean I'd do anything without Dad's approval. This is Valleja-Marquez land. By shifting things around and moving the Justice areas further from the main house, we'll be preserving our privacy. Less blending of the two. With the family expanding, it was time to draw a line between work and home."

"And Meghan," Angie gasped. "Oh, my god, Red. What you're doing is off-the-hook, lady!"

Meghan did a quick half-shrug, dropping one of the miniature buildings back onto the table where the working display of the new compound layout sat. It was like her very own dollhouse only with roads and benches, an outdoor pavilion, and a parking lot.

"Tell her the rest, darling," Alex encouraged with a smile and a nod.

"There's more?" Angie chirped. "How the hell do you even have time for more?"

"She never does anything half-assed. One of those hard-working New Englander traits."

Shut up, she mouthed with a pout, earning her a salacious leer and the mouthed reply of *five* as he held up the fingers on one hand.

"Ignore him, Red," Angie sneered. Sticking her tongue out at Alex and wrinkling her nose, she said, "What the hell else could there possibly be after all this?" She waved her hand at the impressive model and shook her head in wonder.

Alex childishly stuck his tongue right back out at his sister then started babbling to her. Meghan thought about her brothers and their own unique dynamic. She understood Angie's relationship with Alex.

"Remember that rundown luncheonette on the old county road out on the other side of the interstate? The one with the fake desert windmill?" he asked Angie.

"Sure, sure. Busty's. God, Mom loved that place, remember? Is it still open?"

Smiling broadly, Alex came to Meghan's side and drifted a possessive hand across her butt and up until ending at her waist, which he squeezed softly. She felt a familiar warmth spread through her. He was proud of what she was doing.

Kissing the side of her face, Alex answered Angie's questions and quickly filled in the blanks.

"Open and Busty still runs the place! She's something of a legend now—must be at least eighty. Right, hon?" he asked.

"She'll be eighty-four this year," Meghan chortled. "And I seriously heart her! I mean, c'mon! With a name like Busty Winds, what isn't there to love? The pictures she has on display of her doing burlesque in Vegas before the dawn of the showgirl era are mind-blowing."

Angie agreed. "Probably why Mom liked that place so much. Some aging pastie-twirler telling tales about gangsters and movie stars? Right up her alley," she snickered.

"Well, wait for it, little sister, 'cause you haven't heard anything yet!"

Meghan fidgeted. She was uncomfortable taking the spotlight. Sheesh. Anyone in her position would be doing the same thing. Alex nudged her playfully. "Go on, baby. Tell her. It's not like it's a secret!"

He had a point. And come to think of it, maybe she should be picking Angie's brain for ways to get some media attention for the project.

"We heard that Busty wanted to sell the land adjacent to the luncheonette. That area is off the beaten path and nobody was interested. Then we started throwing ideas around." Meghan paused to smile warmly at her fiancé. "What this area needs is community outreach. We thought a multi-purpose center for families with an emphasis on veterans and active military would be a win-win scenario. Busty could be the food vendor, even do catering. Think of it as an updated version of a community center. For families."

"Meghan's been involved with a military spouses project that offers support and resources for service families on active duty." Alex beamed at her, and she swore her heart fluttered. "She teaches yoga as a stress reliever."

"Good lord, Red."

A quiver of emotion in Angie's voice made Meghan look at her sharply.

"Can I help? I mean, what do you need?"

Meghan was somewhat stunned. Angie actually sniffed. And reached for her hand, squeezing her fingers. She was the center of a Marquez sandwich with Alex plastered to one side of her and now Angie on the other.

"When Alexander was hurt," Angie said quietly, emotion clogging her voice, "the support Mom and Dad got from the groups assisting families of the wounded was phenomenal. And now, even from our outpost in Spain, the vineyard is involved in military outreach. The Spanish forces fought with the coalition."

Meghan understood. It must have been frightening for Alex's family. That awful time was when she first came to know Major Alexander Valleja-Marquez. He had been a physical and spiritual mess. Their letter exchange during his long convalescence gave her a rare glimpse inside the mini-universe of pain, fear, and loneliness that marked the end of his military time.

"I want to see a place where families can go that is packed with all sorts of organic, holistic stuff. You know, whatever nourishes the soul. Not just entertainment. Anyone can build a community center with game rooms and big screen TVs. I just want everything to be positive. There's far too much toxic negativity to go around these days. It's hard enough for families as it is."

Meghan abruptly stopped talking and looked away blushing. She was starting to sound like one of those new age-y life coaches—preaching about spreading love and acceptance. Alex, always alert to her every mood, chuckled softly and squeezed her waist.

"Okay, enough with the serious talk," he drawled. "My bride and my little sister are in da house." Smacking Meghan on the butt, he pushed her toward the hall and shooed Angie along as well. "This calls for a drink."

They shuffled from Alex's study into the big family room and made for the built-in bar where Meghan quickly set up camp behind the polished wood. Pulling a bottle of Jameson's from the shelf, she slapped it dramatically on the bar and smirked at her fiancé.

"Oh, my god," Angie cried. "So this really *is* a thing?"

Pouring a healthy splash of the fragrant amber liquid into a large tumbler, Meghan played her part with teasing perfection. She didn't care what anybody said. This would never *not* be funny.

"Glenfiddich is for pussies," she purred. "Angie?" she asked politely, holding the bottle aloft in invitation.

"Oh, absolutely, Red! I've even been practicing so I can keep up with your family of Irish hooligans!"

Meghan poured them each a drink as she openly snickered at Alex. "What about you, Major?" she cooed with a purposeful smirk.

"You know, it's just not fair," he muttered. "First, I lose half my damn closet. Then I keep finding hair ties in the weirdest places. Like inside my socks."

Meghan's feminine giggle complemented Angie's wide-eyed smile.

"And my whole crew. A bunch of flaming fangirls every time you make an appearance. It's fucking ridiculous."

Alex made sure to interject just enough long-suffering sighs to make his whining completely adorable. Pushing an empty tumbler on the bar toward Meghan, he growled, "But taking a man's favorite pastime away just for the sheer hell of it? That sucks, ladies."

A sound came out of Meghan's mouth, a word she bit off before it was fully formed, and then she grinned from ear-to-ear. "Bite me," Meghan chuckled.

Alex roared with laughter. "Choked on a *shut up,* hmmm? Still holding at thirty-five. Smart move, love."

With Alex's glass now filled, Angie held hers up for a toast. "Obviously an inside joke and no . . . I definitely don't want to know what's holding at thirty-five. To Alexander and his beautiful bride-to-be and hopefully another generation of the Marquez dynasty! *Salud y amor y tiempo para disfrutarlo!*"

Angie enjoyed the burn from the Irish whiskey as it spread warmth throughout her body. She hadn't been kidding about practicing. With her life in Spain taken up by the vineyard and family label, she'd grown accustomed to endless samplings of the wine and sherry associated with the region. Throwing down with hard liquor rarely occurred. Neither did enjoying an ice-cold beer on a hot desert day. Two things she was looking forward to during this visit.

Eyeing the happy couple, she loved the unique vibe rolling off her brother and his lady. It was so unexpected and charming plus her sister was going to fall over laughing when Angie confirmed that, yep, the Jameson Glenfiddich rivalry was for real.

"Health, love, and the time to enjoy. I like that," Meghan told her with an enthusiastic nod.

Alex snorted with amusement and rolled his eyes at Angie. "My bride thinks she has to learn Spanish in a hurry." He *tsked* and quirked a half-grin. "Someone needs to tell her that we aren't exactly a bilingual family."

"Speak for yourself, Alexander!" Angie yelped. "Just 'cause you were lazy about language doesn't mean we all were."

Something that smelled seriously amazing wafted from the kitchen and immediately got her stomach growling. She'd been traveling for days and was looking forward to a relaxing meal that didn't involve container food or throwaway utensils.

Angie was relieved when Meghan led the way into the much cozier and smaller family dining area rather than to the formal dining room. Exhaustion was starting to get the better of her and all she wanted to do was kick back and relax.

"I made a brisket."

Alex's playful laugh split the air. "You *so* did not!" His mock-stunned expression struck Angie as truly funny. "Ria barely lets you put butter on toast," he taunted a clearly exasperated Meghan.

"Major Marquez!" she barked at him. "Shut . . ."

"Eh, eh, eh," he *tsked* with a wink and shake of his head. "Forty? You want to try for forty? Better curb that tongue, woman!"

"You two are so weird," Angie chuckled. Raising an eyebrow, she looked back and forth between them and pulled a comical face. To Meghan, she drawled, "Hon, whatever y'all are tallying, forty sounds like too many!" And to Alex, she sniped, "And you, brother? You look entirely too pleased with yourself."

Throwing them a saucy wink-smirk, she set her tumbler on the table and eyed the place settings. Four?

"I thought you said Calder wasn't here," she muttered as Alex slid by.

"He's not," Meghan complained. "And maybe that's a good thing because I think your brother was about fed up. Calder's been impossible since Stephanie left. We thought he'd go after her, but . . ."

Alex interrupted gruffly. "Fucking whiny bitch, that one. Ran off to the mountains. Something about getting his head together."

Angie was amused by the snark in Alex's tone. But then again, she'd never witnessed her handsome uncle in a tailspin over a woman. *Sheesh.* Stephanie Bennett must be one hell of a lady.

"Okay." Angie shrugged. "So if Calder's M.I.A., who's the fourth place setting for?"

"Hello, Angel."

Angie didn't need a mirror to know her eyes just bugged out of her head and she'd turned a sickening shade of white. *Parker.*

Across the table, Alex was motionless, watching her intently, while Meghan looked an awful lot like someone trying to ignore the elephant in the room.

His voice coming so unexpectedly and catching her off guard had wound around every nerve ending in her body rendering her stupid. Pivoting slowly, her breath stalled by surprise, Angie turned and came face-to-face with the one person in her life who didn't fit into a category. He had been her friend. Her stand-in brother and protector. Her Prince Charming. Her first lover. Her first heartbreak. Her greatest sadness. And by her own doing, someone she hadn't spoken to in a very, very long time.

And holy fucking shit. He'd always been the cute boy. Then the good-looking rebel. And Parker Sullivan had pretty much written the book when it was his turn to be the serious, hungry professional. But the drop-dead gorgeous one hundred percent man in front of her was a big time grown-up. And shit! Had he always been so ruggedly hot? The man staring her down was a far cry from the conservative lawyer she'd known.

And just like that—a thousand flashes of memory lit her up. All of her and Parker naked and entwined. Considering all the things they did together, naked was the thing they did best.

Dammit. And just like that, she dropped a stitch and couldn't get it back. *Fucking jet lag.*

She had a choice. She could fold like a cheap suit or act like this moment was no big deal and hope it was enough to save face. Some part of her wanted to strangle Alex for doing this to her on the first night she was back. *Asshole.*

Clearing her throat, she forced a smile to her lips and met his gaze. "Hey, Parker."

"It's been too long," he murmured.

She opted to let that comment slide. "I expected to find you in black robes by now," she offered more sarcastically than intended. "No judgeship yet?"

He snickered as his eyes bored into hers. "No robes. Still just an unrepentant ambulance chaser."

The part of Angie that was fried from travel and overexcited from being home just couldn't stand there and trade quips and one-liners. Not with nothing but whiskey in her system. Not if she wanted to get through the rest of the evening with some shred of decorum.

"Um, will you guys excuse me a minute?" she asked in Meghan's direction. "It's been a long day for me and I think some fresh air would help. Give me a few minutes, Red, and I'll lend a hand in the kitchen, okay?"

And on that false note, Angie smiled tremulously at everyone and headed for the patio.

Chapter Six

"Uh," Meghan moaned. "What was that?"

If there was an easy answer to that question, Parker wasn't aware of it. He'd never known Angie to fold and run—it wasn't her style.

"Dude," Alex growled. "What the fucking fuck? She was fine, then you show up, and suddenly it's chilly in here? Care to explain?"

"Am I missing something?"

Parker swallowed at the dark scowl Meghan shot his way.

A perplexed Alex headed for the door. His gruff, unhappy tone felt like a punch to Parker's gut. "I'll talk to her."

"No," Parker interjected, holding up his hands to block his friend's path. "No. This is between me and her."

"You want to tell me what the hell is going on, Sullivan? Or do I have to smack it out of you?"

"Alex," Parker implored testily. "Give it a rest, okay?"

His friend instantly bristled and looked at him like he was sizing Parker up for a body bag.

"That's my fucking sister, man."

"Gentlemen," Meghan, the referee, cut in—trying to defuse the rapid escalation of tension in the room. But she also looked like she wanted to smack the shit out of him, which made Parker flinch and swallow harder.

When the stern-faced Irish beauty glared at him, honest to god, it was like having a bucket of ice water thrown in his face. *His buddy had his hands full with this one,* he thought. Christ, but Meghan O'Brien, soon-to-be Marquez, had a no-nonsense way about her that made his balls shrivel

Parker was astonished when she suddenly softened and put her hands on the snarling bear standing next to her.

"He has to go, darling," she murmured to Alex. "Let Parker handle this."

He didn't miss the unspoken conversation that went on between the two. Though Alex looked unhappy about it, he backed down after fixing Parker with a hostile frown.

"Dinner is in ten minutes. Understand, shithead? Ten fucking minutes and then I take matters into my own hands."

Parker practically sprinted down the hallway in pursuit of Angelina. Ten minutes to repair years of damage? Shit.

He found her instantly because he knew exactly where to look. Ever since she was a little kid, whenever she came to the Villa, she eventually found her way to her very own hidey-hole. A big, wooden double-seater swing set in a tiled alcove draped with climbing vines and blooms. It was her favorite place to disappear and had been since she was a kid so she wasn't all that hard to find.

His angel saw him approaching. He could tell by the way she appeared to draw inward—become smaller. The sight made him feel like a dick.

Leaning casually against the end of the swing, Parker was surprised at how calm his voice sounded when, in fact, he was freaking the fuck out inside. "Want to start over?" he asked quietly.

Oh, my god. Angelina. Right there. An arm's length away. And she was even more striking than the last time he'd seen her in the flesh. The years had been good to her. Though the young, gangly girl with the braces and the impish grin was long gone, the beautiful woman he fell so desperately in love with was achingly present.

Her hair was still long, and the features on her face, so familiar and haunting. He'd know her anywhere–especially since she'd been frequenting his dreams for longer than he cared to admit.

For a tantalizingly brief second, he considered dropping to his knees and prostrating himself as he begged for forgiveness. Desperate for some form of penance to make up for his part in destroying their friendship.

And then she lifted her eyes as an unsteady and visibly trembling hand tucked the hair behind her ear. When he felt her sapphire gaze on his face, he prayed to all that was holy that whatever came next wasn't the beginning of the end of his world.

But she didn't say anything. Silence hung all around them. Parker's hands clenched tightly at his sides when the sparkle of tears rimmed the eyes staring back at him. The emotion in the air was thick and heavy.

"I take it they didn't tell you that I was coming for dinner." It wasn't a question. Her reaction to his unexpected presence was tearing him up inside. Did guys cry? Nobody he knew ever admitted to crying, but right then, he was sure that was where he was headed.

Her slight head shake said it all. Hadn't been expecting to see him and wasn't happy about it. *Fan-fucking-tastic.*

Knowing that Alex was counting back from a thousand, and likely to come thundering in at any second, rattled Parker's cage. He needed to pull this shit show back from the ledge and do it quickly. And after that, he should probably figure out what the hell he could do to repair his relationship with Angie.

But right here, right now, he had to smooth things in a hurry. Maybe a touch of mockingly sarcastic humor would help. Sort of darkly acknowledge the fucked-up-ness of the situation and pray it acted as a pressure release. Buy a little time. The sort of thing he did in front of a judge all the damn time.

"So . . . I should take from your silence that you're still mad at me?"

Now, that wasn't so bad, he thought. A straightforward admission that he'd been a dick. She should be happy with that, right? At least as a start, anyway.

His first inkling that he was way off base came when she shot to her feet and rushed toward him. In the muted light, she looked like an angry wraith, her dark hair flying, eyes glittering with something he couldn't name. *Holy shit.*

Unease gathered at the base of his neck. The cold, heavy squeeze of anxiety knowing he'd miscalculated made it difficult to breathe. She looked like she meant to do him bodily harm.

"Mad at you?" Angie hissed as she bore down on him. "*MAD* at you?" she yelled with rising emotion.

"Guessing . . . that's a yes?" he ventured cautiously.

Coming to quick halt mere inches from where he stood, a visibly pissed off Angie adopted a combative pose that was very much meant to make it seem like she was getting up in his face. She was spitting fury and looked like she was going to rip him a new one, a thought that only ended up turning his sex to stone.

Her fire turned him on. Always had. Unexpectedly finding himself on the receiving end of her fierceness awakened the sleeping giant inside him. Everything about her body language, expression, and tone warned Parker that she was set on stun and he was directly in her line of fire. The thing was though, watching her get ready to tear into him made whatever decision-making he imagined was necessary a lot less involved.

It hit him like a lightning bolt. *Angelina Marquez was his. And she knew it.* Maybe not before they came face-to-face, but she knew it now. She also wasn't happy about it, which was why she ran. And looked like she was going to do everything she could to build a wall of anger between them. *Good luck with that.*

Okay, Angel. Let me have it. Give it your best shot.

Hands-on-hips, she tossed her hair over her shoulder with a jerky headshake then tilted her chin up so she could fix him with a salty glare. He wanted to laugh but thought better of the suicidal response. She'd flay him alive if he so much as cracked a grin.

"You think not speaking for years is because I. Am mad. At *you?*"

Maybe the edgy disbelief in her voice should have clued him in, but the truth was, with her so tantalizingly close, all his mind could grasp was how fucking awesome she smelled and how ridiculously sexy her sapphire eyes were when she was spitting mad. The rest? Parker was a clueless idiot.

He shrugged and tried to act like he was all unruffled and composed when nothing could be further from the truth. "Well, would explain why I haven't heard a word from you or seen you in forever."

The minute the words left his stupid mouth, he knew he'd stepped in it. Big time. What the hell had he been thinking? It was as if all sense deserted him and he conveniently forgot that he had been the asshole in their relationship and was one hundred percent responsible for why they no longer had even the shell of a friendship. *Fuck.*

"Oh, right," she spat at him. "Yeah. That was *all* me." Playfully smacking her temple like she was an idiot, she drawled, "Well, duh. Of course, it's my fault. I mean, it's so annoying isn't it, when you're babysitting and the little kid you're forced to hang out with is a . . . what did you call me? A nuisance?"

Her caustic glare was enough to give him a permanent sunburn.

"This is ALL you. *You* did this," she growled as her hand shot out and two fingers stabbed him in the chest. Hard.

"*You.* All you."

And then she shoved him with both hands and ducked around his off kilter body as she made a quick dashing getaway—leaving him standing there with his mouth open and his stomach in a knot.

Chapter Seven

THE MINUTE PARKER VANISHED AFTER Angie, Meghan turned on Alex.

"When the hell were you going to tell me that putting those two together in the same room was going to be a problem?"

He didn't say anything right away, which only made his feisty Irish lady go mental on him.

"Oh, my god," she squealed. "You're at it again, aren't you? Alex," she threatened with a warning bite in her delivery, "enough with the matchmaking. Didn't what happened with Calder and Stephanie teach you anything?"

Grabbing her by the waist, he spun his outraged fiancée toward him until she collided with his body then quickly took control of the situation by helping himself to a handful of her magnificent ass while grinding his pelvis into hers.

"I'm right about Calder, and you should have a bit more faith in me, woman."

"How do you figure that?" she quibbled.

"For your information, my lady—Calder going to Aspen is just a pit stop. He's already got one foot in Atlanta and it's only a matter of time before he gives in and goes to claim what belongs to him."

Meghan frowned and made that half-smirk he loved. "Victoria knows nothing about any so-called *foot*," she drawled, "being in Atlanta. She says Stephanie is putting on a happy face but so far, there is no sign that your uncle has come to his damn senses. I'd say that makes your success rate pretty low."

He snickered, enjoying how she managed to keep him on his toes with her balls out attitude. Submit to him—she most certainly would—but first, she was going to shoot off a whole litany of comments and innuendos.

"You know," he drawled while kneading handfuls of her ass, "we may be in the only room in this whole Villa where you haven't been tied to some furniture and fucked."

"Alex," she gasped. "*Shhh!*"

"Hey. It was your idea after all. Too late to feign shyness," he taunted.

Her eyes flared and she sank into him with a deep sigh. Lowering hers for the briefest moment, she blushed sweetly then met his gaze head-on.

"Yes, well . . . where I envisioned a single scene, you made it an all-day affair."

Alex chuckled at the erotic memory and leaned in for a nuzzle. She'd wanted to take advantage of their limited privacy before the wedding, and he'd pretty much taken that ball and ran with it. For a hundred-yard touchdown.

The light bondage games they indulged in that he knew she enjoyed offered endless scenarios. When it came time to pick one or two, he'd opted for seven full innings of sexy playtime. Per her stated desires, she'd alternately been bound, blindfolded, and completely sensory deprived with earplugs. A little at a time and all at once. He'd bathed her. Fed her. Teased, fingered, licked, and fucked throughout an entire day.

Recalling the curvaceous beauty tied to a chair in his office, completely naked while he pretended to work, made his cock throb. During that scene, he'd left the blindfold, and instead of the earplugs, he'd filled the room with a Pink Floyd song he'd told her was like an instant hard-on for him.

She sat there, listening and anticipating what was coming next. Watching her nipples pucker, seeing her squirm knowing that she was making the leather seat wet as her excitement built had been deeply satisfying. So too had keeping her hands bound when he pushed her down onto the thick carpet and taken her on her knees.

Coming out of the sexy reverie he grunted, "Maybe, if I'm lucky, Angie will knock Parker the fuck out and they'll both storm out of here." He bit her gently under her ear then quickly licked the same spot. "Then I can lay you out with your hands and feet tied to the table and have a private feast. Something sweet, sticky, and delicious."

Alex delighted in the shudder that rolled through Meghan's body. He knew that if he continued on, whispering wickedly about her luscious body, he could make her come with just his words. She was that responsive to him.

"Baby," she whimpered while clutching at his shirt. "Please tell me you know what you're doing. I like your sister and I know how close you are to Parker."

Alex sighed. "I'm working off instinct, honey."

She looked at him skeptically.

"Tell you what," he urged her with a conspiratorial wink, "when they come back, you watch. Look past the surface stuff and you'll see. There's something going on with those two. I don't know what, but it's there. You know that part of Angie's story where she goes to college in D.C.? Well, Parker was the designated family protector while she was spreading her wings. But since then? It's like they never met. It's weird."

"So what? You're forcing the issue by throwing them together? I don't know how smart that sounds."

"It was Angie who suggested she come here now. To help you with the wedding. She knows Parker is part of our life—part of Family Justice. I just figured . . ." He shrugged. "Well, you know."

Meghan melted against him and offered her mouth in a sexy, wet invasion of tongue and lips that stole his senses.

"Yes, I do know," she murmured into his chest when the kiss ended. "You want everyone to have what we have."

"Is that such a bad thing?" he asked. "Look at us . . . it staggers me sometimes. I used to see Cameron and Lacey and think, *why can't that happen to me?* And then with Draegyn and Tori. Those two are a fucking handful and will supply plenty of fireworks in the years to come but seeing the energy they create? That shit doesn't come along every day."

"Energy," she murmured thoughtfully. "Yes. I know exactly what you mean."

Something flitted through her expression so fast that he almost missed it, but they didn't call him the big daddy of the family for no good reason. Alex might not know exactly what that was all about, but he was smart enough to capture the look in his mind so he could go back later to figure it out. He wasn't considered a master tactician without cause.

If Alex had learned just one thing in his time with Meghan, it was that what was said about women being unpredictable, able to stop on a dime—was absolutely true. His woman excelled at the quick about-face.

"I like when you grab my ass," she said while wrapping her arms around his neck.

She was fucking perfect.

"I know," he growled playfully.

She nuzzled her nose against his cheek and breathed hot kisses onto his skin. Putting her lips close to his ear, Meghan sighed, and then murmured, "And Major, I have total faith in you."

With her fingers speared into his hair, she pressed against him and did a naughty shimmy. "Please tell me you know that."

He squeezed her ass but good, until she yelped with surprise.

"Mine," he growled deeply.

She pouted like a pro and gave him a dirty look. "And just because I didn't actually make the damn dinner doesn't mean you have to go telling people that!"

Put in his place, Alex roared his approval. Well, she certainly told him!

"Oh, for god's sake," a cross sounding voice cut in. "Get a damn room, okay?"

Angie couldn't believe what was happening. Parker was here, with his head so far up his egotistical ass that it was ridiculous.

And her brother and his woman? *Fuck my damn life,* she thought. Why'd they have to be so . . . *ugh*. There weren't words to describe

Alex and Meghan. Every phrase she entertained became an understatement.

Coming upon the couple wound together in a serious embrace took all the wind out of her sails. Sensing that Parker was a mere step behind her, she couldn't believe her shitty luck when she quite literally crashed headlong into someone else's intimate interlude. "Oh, for god's sake! Get a damn room, okay?" she grumbled quite loudly.

Sulkily pushing past Alex and Meghan, Angie reached for her tumbler and knocked back a healthy mouthful of Jameson as Parker rounded the arched doorway. Dismissing his presence with a grunted "*Hmph,*" she plopped inelegantly down in a chair.

"So . . . are we having dinner or is it pistols at dawn?" Alex asked in a voice dripping with sarcasm.

Meghan, looking bemused, scurried away saying she would pull dinner from the oven. Before disappearing into the kitchen, she called out, "Darling, get Parker a drink, would you."

Oh, great. The idea of playing nice made Angie want to scream. Maybe a temporary escape was possible.

"Uh, need help, Red?" she blurted out.

Her chair scraped along the tile floor when she stood and before she moved another inch, Parker was right there, doing that gentlemanly thing. Taking control of the chair, he placed a hand below her elbow for support as she stood. It was a simple, helpful gesture—he would have done the same for any female needing assistance but when his hand cupped her arm, she felt like a balloon with all the air being let out.

"Actually, I'm good," Meghan quipped with a wave of her hands. "I've got this, Ang. You hang out with the guys. Ask Alex to tell you about the new Justice dog program. We're trying to saddle Parker with a Lab puppy, but so far, he's resisted!"

Meghan's laughter continued to ring out after she'd left the room.

"Oh god, would you two give the puppy thing a rest?" Parker groaned. Pushing her chair under the table, he was the epitome of a chivalrous man—considerate and attentive.

His treatment felt familiar, reassuring, and normal. It struck her that it had been a very long time since she had been alone with the older brother she worshipped and his dashing best friend. Being included in their brotherly dynamic was the greatest compliment they could give her. *These two shitheads were her family,* she thought.

Watching silently while Parker and Alex tossed off one-liners and insults with an ease that spoke to the depth of their bond, she took a minute to internally marvel at how fucked up the last ten minutes of her life had been.

Here she was standing alongside a man she honestly thought she'd never speak to again as if nothing unusual was happening when five minutes prior she'd almost torn his face off and the five minutes before that, she'd been so overwhelmed at seeing him in the flesh that she had to run away.

Brought out of her contemplation by a grinning Meghan carrying an enormous stoneware baking dish, she refocused as everyone took a spot at the table and Red drawled, "Delete all previous mention of a brisket." With everyone's attention on her, Meghan boomed in a funny Irish brogue, "Ah, a shepherd's pie, it is then," she *tsked* with a laugh. And then rather pithily in her usual no-nonsense way added, "And a note from Ria saying she remembered the dish was a particular favorite of Miss Angelina's."

"How terribly sweet of her," she remarked when all eyes turned her way. "It's the little things that count, sometimes," she added with some hostile side shade Parker's way that was unavoidable. "I miss our family cookouts," she told Alex with a wistful smile. "Remember? When we camped, Mom always made shepherd's pie with our leftovers. And over a campfire! Amazing." She chuckled.

"Hey," Parker exclaimed. Stretching an arm out, he grabbed the back of Meghan's chair. "Alex, remember the summer we went camping in Colorado and the night our moms got shitfaced and we ate that amazing pot of beans?"

Alex barked a laugh and nodded.

"You were too young to remember this, Angel," he chuckled, "but dumbass over there," he said with a dip of his head in Alex's direction, "and I were fourteen and fifteen so for us, seeing our parents tie one on out in the woods and watching them get silly was quite entertaining."

Meghan exploded with a hilarious giggle-snort. "Been there! Done that," she yelped with glee.

"I can't wait to party with your parents," Angie told her with relish. "No, seriously. Your mother is fucking hilarious."

"Anyway," Parker continued, "there was Aunt Ashleigh and my mom making a simple pot of beans-n-weenies over the campfire. First, there was a metric ton of bacon followed by another half-ton of local handmade hot dogs thrown in the pot. I remember 'cause Dad insisted the scent of the meat was going to attract animals. He and Uncle Cristián tormented our moms with the threat of bears looming behind every tree."

"Oh, my god," Alex chuckled. "I remember that. It was fucking hilarious."

"Soph, of course, was all of about twelve and already so serious that we started calling her *hospital corners*. She was writing down the recipe as they went along, saying it was for a school project. The beans were added along with a hunk of brown sugar the size of a softball and the pot was set over the fire to cook. Alex's mom suddenly dumped a container of pineapple chunks into the pot and from there a legend was created! Was the best damn beans-n-weenies ever!"

"I've seen that recipe card," Angie said excitedly. "Sophie is so organized. She has this huge box of loose papers and stuff ripped from magazines of all our family recipes. She called it Hawaiian Cowboy Goo."

"Well, I thought it was amazeballs," Alex chimed in. "Of course, we *were* operating with a serious case of the munchies."

Parker drawled, "It was the Colorado Mountains, after all, and we were set-up on the edge of some old stoner campground so my wing-man and I were pretty buzzed."

Angie giggled when Meghan jerked upright and snarled at Alex. "Excuse me?"

Watching her big brother grin like a lunatic at Red made Angie laugh.

"First and last time," he chuckled with a straight face.

"Uh-huh," she bit back.

"Actually," he laughed, "it was a summer of many firsts."

An interesting interplay of silent communication bounced back and forth between Alex and Parker—obviously a shared memory from that summer. Meghan also noted this unspoken interchange and raised an eyebrow at Angie.

God. What she wouldn't give to be the fly on the wall when *that* conversation fired up. Poor Alex. She didn't envy him the cross-examination coming his way.

After that comical waltz down memory lane, they ate in companionable silence mixed with smatterings of polite, politically correct small talk while Alex and Meghan refereed and kept the conversation going. It actually wasn't all that bad. Once she recovered from the shock of having to deal unexpectedly with Parker, she'd calmed down.

Of course, she also managed to check the man out from head to toe several times—she hoped without notice by anyone. Holy god, he was hot. When the hell had that happened? She was used to big men. Alex was the size of a football player and her dad wasn't exactly small. But the man sitting between her and Meghan? He was huge. Or the room was overly small. One of the two.

After a bit, their dinner discussion turned to the wedding plans. Seemed like a safe topic until Meghan dropped a bombshell.

Angie was in the process of forking a large pile of food into her open mouth when she saw Meghan reach for Alex's hand. Something was up.

The two smiled broadly in her direction, and from the periphery, she saw Parker put his fork down and wipe his mouth with his napkin before dropping it on the table. Anticipation hovered in the air around them.

"Angie, honey," Alex began. "Meghan has something she wants to ask you."

Glancing wide-eyed at Meghan, she quirked a fleeting half-grin and murmured, "Anything, Red. Ask me anything."

Meghan smiled warmly and she saw her squeeze her brother's hand before she spoke.

"Angie—I love your brother more than you can possibly imagine. His happiness, his well-being—they mean everything to me. Becoming his wife is something I take seriously."

She smiled. *Awww, how sweet is this?* Tears of happiness gathered in her eyes. "You're going to be an awesome Marquez, Red," Angie squeaked, overcome with emotion.

Meghan choked back an emotional gasp and said, "You have no idea how much hearing that means to me."

Oh, wow, Angie thought. *Alex is so damn lucky.* His bride actually gave a shit about the prospect of becoming a member of their crazy family.

"To that end," Meghan continued rather solemnly, "it would mean the world to me . . . I mean, to us," she emphasized with a nod toward Alex, "if you would bless our marriage as my maid of honor."

Maid of honor? *What?* Had she heard right? Oh, my god! This was really happening if the hopeful, nervous expression on Meghan's face was any indication.

"You guys!" she yelped in shocked disbelief. "Oh, Red!" Angie choked out as she jumped from her seat and ran around the table just as Meghan rose.

Grabbing her in a fierce bear hug, Angie laughed joyfully. "This is fantastic! Thank you so much."

She heard Alex snicker. "I take it that was a yes?"

Angie was exploding with happiness. Her parents would be so touched to hear this bit of news. They were already charmed and impressed by how magnificently Alex's choice of a bride was handling herself. Having Meghan ask Angie to stand by their side as she wed Alex was an honor she did not take lightly.

Wiping away an emotional tear, Meghan hugged her one last time before running into Alex's waiting arms. "You two have made us so happy," she gushed.

You two? *Huh?* Angie felt confused.

Looking sideways at Parker, she immediately noted the way he'd paled and how his mouth seemed stuck in an open position.

When Meghan all but purred with satisfaction and burrowed into Alex's chest with her arms around his waist and a contented grin, Angie felt the floor drop out from under her.

"Looks like we have our maid of honor and best man!" Alex drawled.

Angie's jaw joined Parker's in a freefall. She had *not* seen that coming.

Chapter Eight

Completely in awe of what he was seeing, Alex excitedly proclaimed, "This is incredible, Drae," when the whole thing came into focus. "What the hell was this room before?"

"Fuck if I know. One day all the girls descended out of nowhere and dragged me here . . . said, will this work?" Looking around at the space, his friend shrugged. "I said yep, and next thing anyone knew, a project had been born!"

Alex laughed at the apt description of what dealing with the women of Family Justice was like. Meghan was the battering ram. She simply ripped down walls to get what she wanted. And Tori? Shit. She might be little, but she was the scariest one of the bunch. That woman could talk circles around anyone. Fuck, man. Sometimes she won because her ridiculous grasp of arcane facts pretty much beat every argument into the ground.

And then, of course, there was Lacey. She was sweet, young, bright-eyed, and completely authentic in every way. The first of the Justice wives, she couldn't fathom the glass half empty notion because, after all, to her, the glass was half full. Period. Her simple belief in all that was good, right, and true was what changed everything. For all of them.

"Crazy women! They caused all kinds of hell in the construction office the other day. Something about solar lights." Alex shook his head remembering the dust-up their interference had instigated.

Draegyn snorted a laugh, which got Alex laughing along. They went back a long way, he and Drae. Theirs was a unique friendship, born before the firestorm of an ugly war and made closer through long years spent building a business together. They were more than friends. Draegyn St. John was hardwired into Alex's conscience—his own personal Jiminy Cricket. The wise partner along on the adventure.

"Well, bro, the good news is that it doesn't take much to soundproof a room so here ya go, Thunder Foot. One music studio as requested. Plenty of room for a stadium-size drum kit, a grand piano—whatever you need."

Alex was suitably stunned. A studio. And shit but it was impressive. The walls and ceiling were covered by unusual carved foam that created different hued waves making the room look like it was alive. Huge framed landscapes were hung here and there—all photographs of the surrounding countryside. There was a comfy seating area and even a small wet bar. And it was soundproof, huh? Suddenly, he could think of some additional uses for the room. Lately he'd gotten insatiably greedy for the screams that he got out of Meghan when their playtimes were especially intense. He wondered if the door locked.

"Dammit, man," Drae groaned, his hands on his hips and head bowed. "I fucking hate you for putting that picture in my head."

What the hell was he bitching about?

Drae's hand came out with a key dangling from his forefinger. "Of course, the goddamn door locks, you old pervert."

Alex took the key and snickered. "Was I that obvious?"

"Yes," Drae mocked. "Yes, you were. And since I live in constant fear of finding unlocked doors when you're around . . ." He shuddered dramatically. "I made sure this one has a double lock."

The memory of Drae returning to the Villa unexpectedly to find Meghan trussed up like a virgin sacrifice in the stable's tack room swirled in the air around them. Ever since that day when Drae had freaked out and Alex and Meghan fell over laughing, the incident had been a constant source of amusement.

"Oh, and by the way," Drae snickered as he drawled, "I found a box of carabiners. Tactical issue stuff. Installed a bunch of 'em carefully hidden in the walls and ceiling. Pretty clever of me, I think," he jeered. "It's up to you to find them."

Carabiners? What the hell did something like that have to do with . . . oh! *Duh.* He got it. Not bursting out with a hearty laugh wasn't an option.

"You're never going to let that go, are you?" Alex chuckled.

Drae grinned broadly. "Nah. That shit's comedy gold."

"Oh, you mean like giving Meghan a hank of bondage rope for Christmas?"

"Dude," Drae sneered. "The look on your face was fucking priceless. I know you tried to act all big daddy-like, but I saw what you were thinking. You were sizing that poor girl up and wondering if you had enough rope."

"Watch it," Alex muttered.

Drae laughed and motioned him over to check out a control panel by the door. "Relax, Major. No disrespect intended. And, for the record, once my other half got wind of that damned rope . . . well, let's just say it comes in many colors."

The lighthearted moment faded as Drae went into specific detail about all the technology he had installed. This was Alex's passion. Bring electronics of any sort into the discussion and he was sporting half a chub.

Happily pushing buttons and relentlessly swiping his fingers on the panel's screen, he found himself chatting away. He tested every feature available and immediately began thinking of ways to improve and expand all the bells and whistles.

"Hey, did I tell you about the email I got from Brody? I'll tell you what," Alex exclaimed, "plugging him in and making it official was a smart move. I like his vision. What he wants to do with the animal program and the veteran's outreach is way beyond anything our old asses would have thought of."

"And speaking of old ass," Drae drawled mockingly. "I'm pretty impressed with a couple of the recruits Cam singled out. Sent me a bunch of resumes to look at. He really had his shit together on this. Everything seems to be coming together nicely, don't you agree? And Brody being on the ball, too?" Drae air-played a home run complete with sound effects and a final jump onto home base. "Winning, man! Now if only Calder would get his shit together."

"Have you heard from him?"

Drae snorted and shook his head. "Heard from him? No! Why? He's *your* uncle, and if that was just some coy way of asking about Stephanie . . . just cut to the chase, okay?"

Leave it to Drae! Grinning, Alex shrugged. "Man, all the lines are so fucking blurred lately. It's weird, isn't it? My old friend becomes your mother-in-law and now my uncle, who's also our business associate, is moping over Tori's mom. What a tangled web."

"I'll give you that it's all fucking weird," Drae drawled. "Oh, and my wife has wisely chosen not to tell Stephanie that Calder has retreated to the mountains."

Alex considered this bit of news. They were all tiptoeing in one way or another around an unexpected romance that surprised everyone but Alex the matchmaker. Calder and Stephanie's attraction was passionate and intense. They were also both pigheaded as all hell and painfully set in their ways. It was hard to watch and not interfere.

"Well," Alex calmly volunteered, "Tori's being smart and just between us? Aspen was only where he went when he left here. It isn't where he's going to end up though."

"*Hmmph*," Drae grunted. "Are you saying you think he's going to take his head out of his butt and go to Atlanta?"

"You don't?" Alex countered smoothly.

Drae snickered. "I've known your uncle a good long time. It's a bit disconcerting to have a guy who you've hung out with, sometimes naked, often howling at the moon, and usually drunk as shit, be *shtooping* your wife's hot widowed mother."

Alex roared. *Shtooping!* Classic St. John.

"I mean, shit, Alex. I don't know whether to high five the guy or pull him aside for a stern chat!"

They both nearly collapsed in laughter. Wiping away snot and tears, Draegyn choked on his last couple of laughs.

"And yeah, man. I think he'll go after her, and while we're sharing, here's more food for thought. Victoria mentioned that her mother started making noises about selling the Atlanta condo, so if Uncle Calder is going to make a move, he needs to do it soon."

"Understood."

Punching the light timer, they exited Alex's newest playroom and made their way back to the main portion of the old hacienda.

"Have you checked in with Lacey today?"

Alex couldn't help the smile that lit up his face. Of course, he'd checked in with her. It was their custom that whenever Cam went out of town they'd video chat over coffee in the morning. And now with a baby on the scene? Alex was a hundred times more big daddy where Cam, Lacey, and Dylan were concerned.

"She's good." He chuckled. "Played Peek-a-Boo with Dylan on her iPad. That boy has gotten so big and ornery! Can't believe he's sitting up and already starting to get in trouble."

Also a proud father, Drae was quick to reply. "Daniel lights up when Dylan's on the scene. I predict many years of fuckery ahead from those two. There's nothing quite like having a partner," he reminded him.

Alex thought about Drae's comment hours later when he was taking a work break and Cam drifted into his thoughts. He missed his brooding, intense brother. Because the wedding and compound expansion was taking up all of his time, and with Drae still in the initial rush of first-time parenthood, Cam had really stepped up and kept the agency running. Doing the work of three had him constantly on the go, and for the last several days, he'd been in Texas meeting with prospective associates and some important south of the border clients.

The past year had been a hell of a ride for all of them, starting with Cam, who'd been the first to fall. Lacey's arrival at the Villa had been just one of many changes that would come their way. Along the way, Cam became the go-to guy for all matters in the husband and father department.

Was kind of ironically fitting in a way, considering the backstory of the man known as Cameron Justice. Orphan, foster kid, teenage hooligan with a badass reputation and an attitude to match got his ass handed to him but good during a couple of tours in a war zone. Damaged and cynical Cam seemed like the least likely of the three of them to embrace love, settle down, and be a family man.

On the other end of the spectrum were he and Draegyn—both privileged trust fund snots from affluent families who never had to worry about anything. Drae had been expected to submit to a politically and socially correct business merger carefully disguised as a marriage. As a result, it seemed highly unlikely that he was all that interested in happily ever after.

So, Draegyn had pretty much fucked his way around the globe, relying on an aura of danger and sophistication that made the ladies line up for a chance to sample the man's famous seduction first hand.

Shit, Alex thought. He'd been shaking his head over Drae's exploits for years. But just as with Cam, legendary ladies' man Draegyn St. John crashed and burned in spectacular fashion once a little witch with a very smart mouth gave him the *what what.*

And now here he was, right on Cam and Drae's heels, completely and utterly obsessed, infatuated, crazy about, gaga over, and down on his knees in lust and love with an amazing Irish goddess.

Meghan.

A shot of excess energy propelled Alex up and absently prowling the room in an effort to block the tiny flame of worry that thinking about his fiancée sparked.

Something had changed over the last ten days, but he couldn't really explain what that meant. Nothing specific or glaringly obvious had happened that sent up any red flags. Mostly, he was operating on a feeling. And not even a clear-cut feeling. This felt more like a nagging in his gut that he couldn't pin down. Something was going on with her, but try as he could to find clues, he kept coming up empty. In fact, watching her tap dance around doing an *Everything is Awesome* routine was part of what was bothering him.

That was probably why he'd been feeling melancholy about Cam's absence from the Villa. Fearing something was off with Meghan was making him edgy. He really wanted to talk to Cam and get his input.

Aw, fuck it. Not even Cameron's quiet intensity and great advice was going to make any difference. He needed to hear from Meghan what was going on. She'd already confessed to impulsively stopping birth control. Excited by the little bombshell, he used the making babies ploy to get inside her twenty-four seven, so *Nah, that wasn't it.*

The only way to get a handle on what was happening was to go to the source because he took seriously the well being and happiness of the woman he intended to marry.

Chapter Nine

WHAT WAS IT ABOUT THE Arizona sunshine that always made Angie feel like no matter what was going on, everything would work out? Maybe it affected her so because it was something she closely identified with her childhood. In her world, a sunny day was a blank canvas of endless possibility.

She'd ridden out on horseback into the desert early, plodding along, sometimes breaking into a short trot—and for a time, the clamor in her mind and the heaviness around her heart eased off.

When she was a kid, she couldn't wait for the weekend. Not because she didn't like school. On the contrary, she'd always been an excellent student, but from her earliest memories, Angie recalled being at the Villa with her grandparents at every opportunity.

She, Alex, and Sophie had grown up in a sprawling ranch-style home near Sedona. Her grandparents had a house nearby but once the Villa had been completely renovated and updated, the enormous grand hacienda and the thousands of acres of beautiful southwestern heaven had immediately become Marquez home base.

A smile tugged at the corners of Angie's mouth remembering the summer she'd been allowed to work as a stable helper. She'd been eleven and thought going to a job a couple of days a week was the gateway to instant adulthood. Boy! Had she learned a lesson!

This was Arizona, after all, and that particular summer had been hotter and drier than the waiting room to hell. Spending long days sweating her ass off in a barn full of animal smells and running around outside in the brutal sun kicking up dust from the hard, dry-packed ground was far from the glamorous imaginary world she thought would greet her as a budding grown-up. But it gave her a chance to wander out into the desert on her own every day to exercise the horses. It was during that oddly transformative summer when she'd developed a real affinity for this little corner of Arizona.

If the last week had shown her anything, it was that this instinct to connect with her roots was as strong as ever. It was harder and harder to deny that she belonged here.

Pulling her mount to a halt, Angie slid from the saddle, dropped onto the canyon floor, and took a long deep breath. Flinging her arms wide, she burst out with an earthy coyote howl that ended on a laugh when she got nudged from behind. Turning, she stroked the horse's neck and let the mare put her face close to hers. They were sharing a moment.

"Next time, I'll sing," she mumbled out loud. The horse whinnied and shook her head—which Angie took as agreement. Along with being in the desert, Angie's second guilty secret pleasure was music. All music. Any music.

A definite advantage to having baby boomer parents was their eclectic musical tastes. Throughout her childhood, she'd been exposed to it all. Rock 'n' roll, musicals, theater, jazz, classical, church hymns, cowboy tunes, motown. You name it. Each of her siblings played at least one instrument. They were a musical bunch. Not quite the *Sound of Music* family but close!

Angie's specialty was anything with a string. She played the guitar, violin, banjo, and had attempted to master the harp with little success, but that hadn't stopped her from trying. She could make music on a zither, a ukulele, and a mandolin. She could also belt out a tune as capable as any of those kids on *Glee*.

Singing in the middle of the desert without anyone around for miles was just the coolest thing ever. Any kind of music, especially live music, out in nature was something that actually moved her, even as a youngster. She remembered singing *Afternoon Delight* a cappella with her mom and Soph during family car trips.

The heartwarming memory suddenly blasted into a zillion pieces when *boom,* another memory filled her up. Parker played the guitar. He sang, too. Played the piano, as well. And the harmonica. *Goddammit.*

Rubbing her face affectionately against her horse's muzzle, Angie sighed repeatedly.

Yeah, she played the guitar all right. And had taken lessons because that was what Parker did. If he had played the bassoon and thought marching bands were cool, she would have, too.

Angie realized a long time ago that her infatuation with the older man shaped the person she became. Would she like different music, maybe prefer being a vegan to an unabashed carnivore if it weren't for him? It was hard to say since their lives had been so intertwined from such an early time.

I mean, shit! She ended up studying international affairs and going to college in D.C. because that was where he was. From the moment Parker landed at the Department of Justice, she'd begun researching colleges in the East. There had been a lot going on with her family during that time and being the youngest meant that nobody was really paying attention to what she was up to. Not with Alex in Afghanistan, Sophie starting grad school, and her parents' sudden decision to move to Spain taking center stage. Hell, she could have sat at the dinner table and announced she was going to clown school and nobody would've blinked.

So, she went for it. Balls out. Her folks thought she applied to a handful of Ivy League schools, but the truth was she'd only ever submitted a single application and that was to Georgetown University. In her teenage mind, once she hit eighteen and was an official ADULT, all she had to do was be around Parker and he'd magically fall under her spell and they'd live happily ever . . . oh, *whatever.*

She snorted louder than the horse and kicked up some dirt with the toe of her booted foot. *What a stupid kid she'd been.*

Sure, she'd been accepted to the college of her dreams. She'd even moved into a small studio apartment in an old building that catered to students because she'd convinced her parents that being in a dorm would lead to too much distraction. The truth was that argument had nothing to do with grades or studies. Angie's fertile imagination had worked up some cozy, private love nest scenario where she could show the charming lawyer how awesome life would be if they were together.

"What a fucking joke." She groaned aloud.

From the moment she was on her own in the nation's capital, Parker became her de facto protector. He showed her the ropes, taught her how to get around in the city, where to buy groceries, places and areas to avoid. Day one, he rather arrogantly planted his flag in Mount Angelina and declared himself king of the hill. *Shithead.*

And so it went for two whole years. She threw herself into the Georgetown experience, determined to get the most from her time at the prestigious old school and who was with her the whole way? Right by her damn side? Parker.

Over time though, their friendship started to change. They were in a unique situation, bonded by family ties, more than comfortable with one another, and most importantly, out from under the restraints of having family around. Completely off in a world of their own, Angie and Parker pushed the boundaries at every turn.

Flirty looks. Tongue-in-cheek text messages. Casual touches on an arm, a hand low on the back, playful nudges. Hello hugs and good-bye kisses that were right on the line. Naughty chats late at night.

He always managed to be around whenever she went out. Watching her. He said he was just keeping her safe while she had fun, but to Angie, the interest felt more possessive than protective. That was where she made her mistake.

It was probably inevitable that they'd end up having sex. Hell. Angie all but served herself up to him on a silver platter.

But she'd been overwhelmed by his enormous sexual appetite and unprepared for what that kind of intense physical involvement would do to her spirit.

On a soulful high, her head swimming with romantic fantasies fueled by the gritty sexuality her dominant lover unleashed, it had come as a severe shock to her system to hear him describe their involvement as an uncomfortable nuisance. She hadn't been the same since. In that one horrible moment, her whole world had been wiped out.

He thought she was mad at him. Who the hell was that man kidding? Mad. That was what he came up with? She whimpered softly and grimaced. Looking at the rocky formations in the landscape glowing vividly red, Angie blew out a harsh sounding sigh.

His calling her position one of anger only magnified the fact that for him, their intimacies had been a blip on the radar and nothing more. And that, she realized with blazing clarity, was what the real problem was.

She'd come home to find out if it was time to return and decide once and for goddamn all what her true feelings were for her brother's best friend. It hadn't taken long at all to find definitive answers to both those questions. The joke was on her. It had taken all of a nanosecond to realize that she was still in love with him. Had in fact been in love with him from what seemed like her very first breath. The soul-deep connection was disconcerting.

"Oh, my dear sweet baby Jesus," she moaned into the vast silence. Bending over, she grabbed her knees while her head exploded as a firestorm of confusion crippled her.

Believing Parker to be her one true love, it came as a blow that he apparently wasn't on the same page and had blown off their involvement as something to be mad about.

Truth was, she'd been crushed. And not just because her lover had declared their liaison to be unsatisfactory, but because . . . *well, hell*—because it was Parker and their relationship had been so much more than just a few weeks of naked Olympics. Or so she'd thought. It had destroyed her foolish romantic heart to overhear his harsh opinion spoken so rudely.

She'd cut him off rather ruthlessly after that awful day when everything changed. Denied all contact until he gave up trying. Never in her wildest dreams had she imagined him being such a dick, but even so, her mind refused to accept the notion that he'd used her for the sex. Confused, hurt, tormented, and in an emotional freefall from losing her anchor and best friend, she'd simply turned all that emotion into action and focused on getting her degree. Fuck him. She'd show that bastard someday what a mistake he'd made. Thing was, that day was here, but all she wanted to do was curl up on his big lap.

Angie straightened and looked out at the beauty around her. Tugging the horse's reins, she brought the mare in and easily hoisted herself onto the saddle. Ready to head for home, she paused one last time to enjoy the moment then urged the horse forward.

Unfortunately, she in no way felt like she had any control or shame where that man was concerned. Especially not after the scene she'd caused at dinner the first night she arrived. Damn the Jameson. Alex was right. Meghan could pound that shit like water and walk away laughing.

Note to self, she mockingly thought. *Don't compete with an Irishwoman when whiskey is present!* Great, only this was now and that had been then. Then, as in *before* she understood that slamming back an endless parade of drinks while retaining her dignity, was not in the realm of alcohol soaked possibilities.

She didn't want to think about the scene she'd caused. It was positively cringe-worthy but continuing to walk on eggshells wasn't working. She'd hidden away the following day claiming she needed to adjust to the time and climate changes. Was a pretty good excuse for holing up in her room. Even the housekeeper, Carmen, stayed away.

But she had to grow the hell up and take this one on the chin. Shit, she was old enough to know better, but the truth was, she'd fucked up. Plain and simple. Everyone did from time to time, right?

That was the real reason she was riding alone in the desert—to clear her head. She was here to help Meghan—not make a fool of herself in front of the boy who'd broke her heart.

Thing was, he wasn't the boy her seven-year-old heart adored. He was a grown man, and she'd been out of her mind to think she could calmly handle being around him again.

She heard his husky growl in her head and shuddered. *Hello, Angel.* Calling her by that name meant she'd been doomed from that moment on. Or maybe she was damned? *Hmmph.* Doomed. Damned. She shrugged. What difference did it make? Either way, she'd been screwed.

After dinner was cleared and they were gorging on dessert, things got weird and they got weird fast. Emboldened by her whiskey buzz, she tried to be all European sophisticated, an act she failed at quite miserably. Angie was a lot of things, but a trendsetter was not one of them.

At some point, she got all high-and-mighty about something. Alex had probably been egging her on in that big-brother-knows-everything way he had. High and mighty led to pithy. Pithy segued quickly to unleashed snarky and the snarky, unfortunately, ignited her inner bitch. Only this bitch was hammered.

Oh fuck. What the hell had she been thinking? Traveling for an entire week, hopscotching from Madrid to London to New York to Arizona. That first night she hadn't even unpacked yet. She was still partially in airplane mode so drinking her ass off and thinking that was going to help had been the height of lunacy.

For some insane reason, she'd blathered on and on about Aldo and their doomed engagement. Not a shred of fucking reality or truth made it out of her mouth, a fact that made her uneasy. Basically, she explained away their breakup as a simple matter of bad timing.

In her alcohol-blurred recollection, Meghan and Alex said next to nothing during her cosmopolitan rant while Parker turned every shade on the color wheel from seething blue to angry red and outraged purple. She'd said awful things that tasted bitter in her mouth—but that hadn't stopped her from throwing down.

After Alex and Meghan had said good night, she remembered stumbling from the room only to find a scowling Parker hot on her heels. They'd gotten into a nasty row at the foot of the stairs. Angie grimaced remembering the angry exchange.

He'd scolded her like she was a kid. Said getting wasted and going on and on about her love life was disrespectful to her brother. He'd been right and since she'd been lying about all of it anyway, that only made her feel worse. But she couldn't admit that to him. Hanging on to her pride was a struggle around Parker on a good day. Dammit. Why did talking to him have to hurt so much?

He railed at her about behaving like a snotty Euro-socialite and wondered where the real Angelina was.

She'd lost it in rather spectacular fashion, waving her arms, hopping up and down like a crazy person moving from the floor to the first two steps—up and down and up and down. What was it she'd thought before? That she was older, wiser, and would make better decisions this time? Yeah, that didn't even last through one night. The truth was, she had no idea what she'd even said. Drunken explosions were like that.

What she did remember was Parker yelling and her wanting to cry. She didn't want him to yell at her. Why wasn't he happy to see her again? Why didn't he love her? Why? Then finally, like a plug was suddenly pulled, she'd hit maximum overload and just like that, she'd slithered to the ground in a drunken blackout.

There was nothing after that. She'd simply woken up late the next morning feeling like she'd been run over by a herd of buffalo only to find that she was half-naked and safely in her bed.

How embarrassing. She'd tried to remember but the harder she tried, the more it seemed a given that he'd scooped her drunk ass up and gotten her tucked safely in her room. The clothes she'd worn were draped over a chair, her favorite ankle boots nearby. She had been too wasted to be that organized.

Finding herself wearing nothing but a bra and panty set had seriously rattled Angie's cage. Knowing he'd undressed her, she didn't know whether to be outraged or excited, especially when she fixated on his reaction to stripping her down to her lingerie.

And that right there was the real reason why she was plodding along on a horse out in the desert. A week ago, it hadn't seemed possible that the situation between them could get any worse, but boy, had she been wrong about that. She'd really fucked this up and had to get her shit together.

Now if only she knew how . . .

Chapter Ten

ALEX WENT LOOKING FOR MEGHAN the first chance he got. He'd been dragged from their bed by an early call and hadn't gotten a chance to start the day the way he preferred—with her writhing on his cock while he played with her breasts. By the time his business was concluded, she'd risen, showered, and gone to start breakfast.

Quickly following suit, he raced through his morning routine, still buttoning his shirt when he hurriedly left the master suite hoping to catch her in the kitchen.

Damn. She was gone. He'd missed her by mere minutes. She'd left a note stuck to the fridge that said *Yoga* with a cute drawing of a lotus flower for emphasis.

There wasn't anything to do at that point. He knew better than to interfere when she was in the zone so he grabbed a mug of coffee and headed to the tech cave. There were a couple of things he needed to do and check with Tori about.

He gave her ninety minutes then headed across the compound to the cute southwestern style bungalow that she'd had custom designed into a yoga studio and meditation retreat.

He still hadn't figured out what was eating away at her and then last night she went slightly batshit when some sort of problem came up with her dress. The freak-out was minor and very short-lived—Meghan wasn't a drama junkie—but it reminded him that she was under an enormous amount of pressure. Just because he was a guy and had no fucking idea what any of this bridal shit meant didn't make her worries any less valid or troublesome.

Coming prepared with a surprise might help so he'd had Betty working the phone and the internet for a couple of days, putting together something special for his stressed out bride-to-be.

At the bungalow, he made his way quietly onto the wraparound porch and glanced in a window before rounding for the door. What he saw stopped him in his tracks.

Okay, something was definitely up, and dammit, he needed to know what.

Aarrgh! She was beyond her limit. Dropping onto her knees like a puppet whose strings were cut, Meghan slumped, her whole body limp and useless. Thinking maybe pushing so hard wasn't such a good idea, she eventually rolled flat on her back, arms and legs outstretched.

"Relax," she whispered out loud. "Breathe."

In and out. Slowly. Mindfully. She breathed deep. For long minutes, she tried to bring her thoughts back when they wandered, but the unseen forces battering Meghan's mind and spirit were too strong to control. Or ignore.

She was worried twenty-four seven and not about the wedding itself. Her mother and Angie were doing all the real work. No, what was nagging at her day and night was something else. Something she was having a hard time putting into words.

Meghan lay there on the studio floor with her eyes closed and tried to calm the anxiety. She heard a noise and in the next heartbeat felt his presence. He was there in the room with her. She didn't have to open her eyes for visual confirmation. His effect on her was palpable.

She heard the quiet snick the lock made when he shut the door followed immediately by the distinct sound of the shutters closing.

Her stomach fluttered with anticipation. He hadn't dropped by to look at silverware patterns. Gracefully rising, she stood and admired the handsome giant moving around her studio. Alex never failed to take her breath away with his brawny masculinity. Not one of those guys with the carefully styled hair and at least some awareness of fashion, her Major was a bona fide absentminded mess. If their life were a comic book, he'd be the Nerd King and she'd be an Irish version of a very sexy Jessica Rabbit.

He was so commanding that the minute she was in his powerful presence, all the chatter in her head quieted. Just by *being,* he cut through all of it. This unique facet of their relationship fascinated Meghan. He led. She followed. Without question or inner murmur.

But at times, she didn't feel like waiting and following took too much time. Sometimes, like now, she couldn't be the obedient submissive when her passions took over.

She didn't exactly jump on him but came damn close. All Meghan knew was she desperately needed that inner noise and turmoil to relax its grip. Losing herself in Alex's arms became as necessary as taking her next breath.

"I missed you this morning," she murmured. Wrapping around his big, sturdy body, she felt the heat coming off him and sighed.

He groaned. "You know I don't like it when you leave our bed unsatisfied, my love."

She smiled shyly and nuzzled into his neck. They had an agreement. She wasn't to leave their bed in the morning without permission. Actually, it wasn't so much an agreement as an edict made by her domineering lover. She'd struck gold with her hunky bad-boy Major. His day was entirely shot to hell unless he had seen to her pleasure first thing. And by pleasure that meant anything she wanted. A back rub. A screaming orgasm. A foot massage. Hell, he would've lain in bed with her and read *Green Eggs and Ham* if that was what she needed from him. *Ah, the shit she had to put up with,* she thought, giggle-snorting against his skin.

His arms tightened as she relaxed against him. *Mmmm.* Rubbing on his hard, wide chest felt delicious and he smelled so damn good.

And just like that, her pussy clenched with need. No, really. Actual *clenching.* The sort that triggered a husky moan to rumble from her throat.

Ordinarily, she didn't call the shots. Another one of their so-called unspoken agreements, only a bit more basic and in your face than the others. This one was all about roles. When it came to what went on in private between them, Alex was very much the sexy, caring dominant. Right now though? She was greedy.

"Kiss me, Major," she demanded.

He didn't hesitate at her gruff command, holding her face in his hands and taking her mouth with a hunger that thrilled Meghan.

Their tongues tangling, Alex devoured what she gave. His voracious sexuality consumed her, and in moments, she was panting with need and completely out of control.

She wanted him. Now. As in right fucking *now*.

Her hands were everywhere—undoing the buttons of his shirt, gripping his waist, kneading his muscular back, and massaging his scalp.

His hands settled on her ass, grabbing her forcefully and hauling her into intimate contact with the prominent bulge that told her of his desire. Her yoga pants offered little hindrance to his wicked fingers as they massaged and kneaded the globes of her butt.

Their kissing became wild and fierce. He sucked her lower lip into his mouth, and right before releasing the soft flesh, he bit her. She gasped with pleasure, wanting more.

He performed a similar action on her ear. Drawing the fleshy part of her earlobe into his mouth, swirling his tongue and sucking lightly. She shivered with delight as her pussy pulsed with need.

And then he bit her ear and tugged on it with his teeth, growling deep and low. She moaned when he licked the skin just below her ear and nibbled, occasionally sucking and finally biting the shit out of her neck and shoulder. That was it for Meghan.

"Alex," she moaned. About to tell him of her desperate need, he cut her off with an earthy grunt.

"Let's go back to the house. I have a need for you naked in my bed with your hands bound while I pleasure your body."

No! That was not what she wanted.

Okay, I should probably take that back, she thought. I did want that. But right this second? Him. Inside me. *Now.* Not twenty minutes from now after we'd wandered home.

Writhing against him, Meghan became desperate. Tearing at his clothes in blind haste, she struggled to get past the barrier and connect with skin.

She also tried to send them both to the floor, but he was having none of it. Worked up and frustrated, Meghan wasn't going to have any problem begging for what she wanted.

But she hadn't gotten a chance to plead. Grabbing her aggressively, he walked them to the nearest wall and slammed her up against it—hard. Gasping with surprise, she locked eyes with his and cowered at the grim expression coming back her way.

"We seem to be at an impasse," he growled.

Biting her neck just below her chin, she whimpered softly.

He moved his mouth close to her ear so she felt his warm breathing on her skin. "You want me to fuck you and I want you to tell me what the fuck is wrong."

Oh, shit. He knew her too damn well. Meghan wanted to howl with frustration. How could she tell him what she didn't really understand?

Was that a bucket of ice-cold water she felt slither along her nerves? Well, that was what it felt like. Shit. Talk about a buzz kill.

Pushing out of Alex's arms like doing so was no big deal, she shrugged and tried to make a half-hearted jest.

"Yes, well . . . I don't think we have enough time for either of those options."

Turning, she gathered up her water bottle and an Adidas jacket and made a wry face. "Anyway, I'm due at Lacey's to . . . uh, meet with the girls."

He didn't even try to disguise the shocked expression on his face. She wasn't acting like herself, she knew that, but he'd tapped into something she wasn't ready to discuss.

"I'll text Ria later about dinner. Let me see what everyone else is doing, okay? Cam will be back tomorrow so I'm sure Lacey isn't thinking about cooking."

Meghan was babbling and knew it; she didn't know how to just run away because doing so wasn't in her character. She wanted to reassure Alex, but she also didn't want to get into it with him at the moment.

He was looking at her with such intensity she was sure he was using his x-ray vision or something.

Maybe he understood or maybe he was just really good at reading her vibe because he eased off and gave her the space she needed. But not without getting the final word.

"To be clear," he drawled in that clipped tone he used when her Major was large and in charge. "We *will* talk, Meghan. I'm letting you run but make no mistake, you just admitted there is something wrong and I won't be denied."

"I know," she choked out.

He took a step forward but Meghan knew if he touched her she'd fall to pieces. Before he could, she backed away and broke eye contact.

"Gotta go. See ya!"

Feeling like a thief running away in the night, she ran from the studio, grabbed a cart, and headed for Cameron's cabin while seeing nothing but the shocked and angry expression on Alex's face as she took the coward's way out.

Watching Meghan's hasty retreat in dismay, Alex wondered what the mother fuck had just happened.

She ran. He couldn't believe it. Weakness and self-doubt? Christ! This was huge. She was normally a force of nature. Nothing rattled her. She liked to say that was because she'd been a teacher for so long. *Never show fear in front of a room full of tweens.* But after meeting her family, he knew that ball-busting thing was in the O'Brien DNA. For her to fold so quickly . . . well, shocked didn't quite cover how he felt.

He was also pissed off. Not at her. Hell. Never at her. No, he was angry at whatever was making her unhappy. Meghan and unhappy were two things that should never occur in the same thought. He couldn't have it. She was his everything, and as far as Alex was concerned, she should never want for anything. Never worry. Never feel unsure. He'd promised her father that he would see to her every need and he took that shit seriously. If something was wrong—which it so clearly was—then he wasn't taking proper care of her.

Dammit. What should he have done differently? Should he have dropped her to the floor and fucked her doubts away? It was what she'd been aiming for. He wasn't daft. He knew desperation when he saw it.

And that was why he'd tried to slow her down. Not pull back but just take a breath. Suggesting they returned to their bed would give him time to try and dial back some of the desperation. He didn't want to be her fear habit. Something he knew well from his military days. Obliterating whatever was bothering you with alcohol, sex, food . . . whatever. Didn't matter. What did matter was the underlying cause. He wouldn't allow their intimate life to be corrupted by doubts and fears. They'd come too far for that.

But when he'd challenged her, she'd stopped on a dime and shut down. It was the first and only time Meghan had ever come even remotely close to saying *no,* and he did not like the way that made him feel.

Thankfully, it wasn't him she was rejecting and that was the only reason why he wasn't chasing her ass down right this second. She was saying no and running from whatever was eating her up.

He'd let her have the afternoon with the girls. They were good for Meghan. Maybe the ladies could help her find her center again. *Bitches need other bitches,* he laughed to himself while making a mental note to thank Tori again for turning him on to the awesome expression that seemed to come in handy for all sorts of things.

Chapter Eleven

"When does the hubby get back from Yuma?" Tori St. John asked.

Angie liked the little whirlwind who somehow managed to bag an arrogant, over-sexed alpha. The new mommy, who packed a serious amount of wallop in her tiny frame, was, at present, an adorable mess.

Lacey marched through the room with her beautiful son slung on her hip. She dropped the stack of baby blankets that she was carrying next to Tori, who was trying to build a sleep nest for her snoozing baby.

The simple domesticity made Angie smile. These women were so cool. She felt an instant kinship with them. The wives of Family Justice. Alex's second family.

"*Mmm,* Texas kicked his butt. Too much time in a suit and tie. You know Cam." Lacey chuckled. "At least the stop in Yuma wasn't so formal. Those Border Patrol guys and the Marines at the air station roll out the guy carpet, if you know what I mean."

Tori gurgled with mischievous laughter. "Oh, you mean like tittie bars and rattlesnake shots off a hooker's ass?"

Lacey's pursed lips and mocking eye roll said that was exactly what she imagined went on.

Meghan snatched Dylan from his mom's hip and danced away grinning. "I bet if we checked her cell phone, we'd find that she and Cam FaceTimed last night from whenever he got back to his room after dinner until they fell asleep together. That man is too besotted for tittie bars or hookers!"

"If he wants to keep all his body parts intact, he better not be drinking snake bites or whatever you said off some poor woman's butt."

"Rattlesnake shots, darlin'," Tori jested. "And only you, honey, would call a hooker some poor woman!"

"Shut up, Victoria," Lacey snapped. "I understand how someone ends up in that position. That's all I meant."

After tucking a dozen blankets around her sleeping baby so he couldn't move nestled in the soft cocoon on his back, Tori jumped up and bear hugged her sister-in-law.

"Sorry, Ponytail," she muttered. "Sometimes I forget."

Angie watched the emotional interplay with interest. She knew a little about Lacey's backstory. How she was abandoned by her only parent, abused for years, and eventually ended up a runaway living on the streets who survived by ingenuity and luck. Sobering stuff.

"Yeah, well when I turned up here, I had a backpack stuffed with second-hand clothes and nothing else. I know about choices. If Cameron hadn't rescued me . . . who knows what might have happened."

"And look at you now," Meghan said with an abundance of praise and encouragement. "Married, a mommy, and in college! You're kicking ass and taking names, Mrs. Cameron."

"College?" Angie quipped. "Are you crazy?"

"It's mostly online courses." Lacey shrugged and looked a little embarrassed. "What a difference a year makes, huh?"

Meghan blew a loud raspberry onto Dylan's neck, which got him giggling and waving his arms.

"And speaking of a year," Tori chuckled as she watched Alex's fiancée love up the adorable little boy, "don't you guys have an anniversary coming up?"

"Oh, my lord, I can't wait!" Lacey gushed happily. "We're going to Vegas for a long weekend. I'm going to see my first concert!"

Tori groaned loudly and rolled her eyes. "What happens in Vegas . . ."

All three women cracked up as did baby Dylan.

"What'd I miss?" Angie asked.

Meghan handed Dylan back to his smiling mama and then high-fived Tori. "Oh, didn't you know?" she teased. "Vegas would be where the legendary Draegyn St. John awoke one morning to find himself married to a sharp-tongued wench after a night of drunken frivolity."

"*Whaaat?*" Angie barked on a full-bellied laugh. "Victoria! Oh, my god! For real? I knew you guys eloped, but holy hell! What is it with these Justice men? Unbelievable," she muttered, shaking her head and giggling.

The smirk on Meghan's face reminded Angie of something. "Oh!" she shrieked. "And, by the way, what the hell was all that keeping count crap the other night, Red? Please don't tell me you actually let my brother have the upper hand."

Quiet snickers met her comment then all eyes landed on a blushing Meghan.

"He likes to think he's in charge," the embarrassed woman mumbled, which was met with more raucous laughter from Tori and Lacey.

"All right. That's enough," Meghan told them sternly.

Angie liked hanging out with Tori, Lacey, and Meghan. They were funny, smart, and dynamic. She felt completely at ease and like she belonged there with them. Another checkmark in the Arizona win column.

Helping herself to the pitcher of ice-cold lemonade Lacey had plunked down on the coffee table, Angie topped off her glass and fixed Meghan with a mocking grin.

"Since we're talking about my brother, pass on the details, okay? There are some things a little sister does not need to know! But if his domineering ass is keeping some kind of score, I suggest you learn the art of the deal."

"Sheesh," Lacey laughed. "Sounds like a TV show." Breaking into a fake announcer's voice, she boomed, "New on this season of Justice TV for Women is the groundbreaking series . . . Art of the Marital Deal."

Pretending to shove a microphone in Angie's face, she asked, "Joining us today is Angelina Marquez, international deal-making expert. Tell us, Miss Marquez, exactly how does this work?"

Ah! This was fun. "Simple really," she quipped. "Men see the world as a scoreboard. They need to know what the stats are at all times. It's how they navigate."

Angie grinned as the women nodded and chuckled at her playful description.

"So, fine! Let them keep track if it makes them happy. But you can keep things interesting by taking advantage of a score stacked against you."

She let that comment sink in until she saw Tori's head snap up, her face lit with humor. Angie wasn't in any way surprised that naughty Victoria got there first.

"Oh! You mean like demerit bargaining? You know!" She laughed, looking at all of them for agreement and understanding. "Demerit bargaining! Like . . . take five points off if I make nachos and let you watch the game without interruption! Get it?"

Meghan burst out laughing. Apparently, baby Dylan also thought it was hilarious, which only got Lacey giggling like crazy. Yeah, they got it.

"Hey, Ang," Tori drawled. "Speaking of demerits, I hear you've got an epic shit ton of them stacked against a certain rebel lawyer who shall remain nameless."

Angie gasped. "What?" she shrieked. "Who said that?"

"No good?" Tori squeaked. "Oh shit, Angie. I'm sorry. I mean," she paused and looked at Meghan and Lacey for help, "everybody knows you're pissed at him or something. Hell, Carmen mentioned that Parker has been avoiding the Villa and Draegyn, well . . . he's dealing with Alex's side of things."

Meghan rushed over and put an arm around her shoulders for a quick hug. "It's okay, Angie. You're among friends here. And just so you know," she said with a nod to the other women, "what we say during ladies' time stays off the record. Fuck! If we didn't have each other as a sounding board and for support, it would make dealing with our men impossible. Understand?"

"Parker Sullivan is a boob," Lacey blurted in a sanctimonious sounding voice that got Meghan and Victoria falling over laughing.

"Direct and to the point!" Tori yelped gleefully.

Angie couldn't help but laugh along. "I can't imagine any way he could bargain his way out of the serious deficit he's earned. Some points are permanent."

"Angel, honey," Tori drawled. "You have come to the right place to talk about permanent points."

The skin on the back of Angie's neck prickled, hearing Victoria refer to her as Angel, but instead of squirming at the reminder, she felt warmth circle in her belly.

"Each of us here," she continued, gesturing with her head to the others, "can tell you plenty about that. It's something we've all faced."

"Sometimes," Lacey chimed in, "you have to zero out and start fresh. Not all *uhhh* . . . demerits are equal."

Angie was humbled by who she was in the presence of. The men these women were referring to weren't your average run of the mill guys. She'd heard stories of their wartime exploits and she wasn't stupid. They each bore scars and not just the external kind like her brother carried. Their women had to be strong enough to accept that. Suddenly, she felt like an idiot bemoaning some hurt feelings when they had real shit to contend with.

"Alex says you hardly ever come home. Is that because of Parker?" Meghan asked.

Angie nodded hesitantly. It was the first time she'd admitted Parker was the reason for anything.

Lacey plunked Dylan into an impressive baby apparatus that looked like a mini circus. The happy baby scooted around in his spinning seat and ended up staring at her with a slobbery grin. Damn, the kid was cute. He had dark hair like Daddy but his eyes? They were all Lacey. She and Cameron certainly made beautiful babies.

Kissing her son on his head, she looked at Angie. "Alex treats Parker like a brother. He's part of Family Justice. I'm surprised they're that close if you and he are . . ."

"Nobody knows," she was quick to assure Lacey.

"In the interest of full disclosure, let me jump in here and say that the Major knows *something*. He just doesn't know what." Meghan's knowing nod spoke volumes.

"Well, he'd certainly have more than a clue after the scene I caused the other night."

Tori looked at her excitedly. "A scene? There was a scene? Irish!" she squealed at Meghan. "You're holding out on us."

"Shush, Tori," Meghan waved at her dismissively. "Hush. I want to hear more about how nobody knows. Doesn't know what exactly?"

she asked pinning Angie to the spot with a penetrating stare.

"Can I tell you something without you freaking out or running to my brother?"

"Unwritten rule number four-oh-seven. Unless there's danger or safety is an issue, we never tell."

Angie said it quickly. Like ripping off a Band-Aid, she wanted to make it painless and as instant as possible.

"I'm thinking about moving back to Arizona. Permanently."

Meghan blinked heavily like she was trying to translate a foreign language. Lacey said, "Oh, wow!" while Tori clapped quietly with a huge grin spreading across her face.

Shrugging self-consciously, she went back to observing Dylan's antics. "Like I said, I'm just thinking about it. Lots to take on board, you know?"

"Oh, my god!" Meghan yelped. "You could help with the expansion! We're going to need a PR person. Hell, we need one now, don't we, Tori?"

"Are you kidding? Shit, Angel! That would be epic! I know he's not here now, but your Uncle Calder just signed on the do R and D for Justice. And with the compound under construction, now would be the time to build you a bungalow somewhere around the Villa. Come on, senõrita! Join the club."

"Whoa, whoa, whoa, ladies," Angie laughed. "I said *thinking!* Y'all are gonna have me moved in and buying bath towels before I've even thought it through."

"Do you sing? Or play an instrument?" Lacey asked out of the blue.

Astonished at the unusual question, she barked, "What?"

Meghan giggled.

"We have this karaoke thing we do. It's loads of fun, and I thought if you sang then you could join us," Lacey clarified, studying her carefully.

"Whiskey Pete's," Tori drawled.

"Are you fucking kidding me," Angie asked. "You sing karaoke at that shithole?"

"Yeah," Meghan cut in. "We were going to go check out the competition tomorrow night. Gotta keep one step ahead." She laughed.

"We call ourselves, Ass, Boots, and Sass." Tori pointed at Lacey who wiggled her butt. "She would be the ass."

Meghan was chuckling. "Irish over there wears the boots." Tori laughed with a jaunty salute. "And I, of course, bring the sass."

"I fucking love you guys," Angie crooned with delight. "Yes, I sing. And I can play the guitar. I've never done karaoke, but I'd love to try."

"Hey!" Lacey cried to Meghan. "Have you taken Angie out to the spot?" She looked enthusiastically at her and smiled. "It's where we go sometimes to practice," she clarified with a serious expression. "Out in the desert."

Meghan smiled. "No, but now that I know you have a musical background like your brother," she told her with a wink, "I'll be happy to introduce you to our special spot."

Wow, Angie thought. *Singing in the desert.* The universe was throwing all kinds of signs her way.

Chapter Twelve

"You know, it actually *is* a whole hell of a lot easier to ignore an elephant in the room over the phone than in person."

Parker knew it was just a matter of time before Alex said something, but he was content to wait him out. He preferred for his friend to ask all the questions 'cause there was no fucking way he was volunteering dog shit. The truth was bound to come out eventually, but until it did, he was walking on eggshells.

"I'm not sure what you're referring to," he answered. They were wrapping up a long call about the endless legalities of the Justice expansion and all he wanted to do was get off the phone and go back to sulking.

He and sulking were old friends now. Ever since Angie came back, all Parker ever seemed to do was work like a madman and sulk. No in between. Basically, it felt like he was circling the drain.

"For the record, shithead," Alex snapped. "I resent being forced to ask, but since you seem to be on your period all the fucking time, I'll be the one to man the fuck up. When were you planning to tell me that my sister was going to shit a literal brick when you turned up? I asked you to be my best man, you fucker! If something was going on with you two, didn't you think I should know this before you two started a fist fight at the altar?"

Jesus. Nothing like laying the whole case out there in the opening argument. Maybe it was Alex who should have been the lawyer because, at that moment, Parker didn't know what the fuck to say.

"*Uh,* what has Angie said?"

"Really?" Alex griped. "Answer a question with a question? What the fuck, Parker? Can you take two seconds please to remember who the hell you're dealing with?"

"Look, Alex, I know we need to talk."

"Do you?" he asked none too nicely. "Because you're putting off an awfully strange vibe for someone who is supposed to be my oldest friend."

Damn. Now what did he say?

"I, *uh* . . . think this might be your sister's story to tell. That's all. Really."

"Swear to Christ, dude, if your shit starts affecting Meghan, I'm going to kick your fucking ass."

Well, fuck. This got messy fast. "Do you think it would help any if I tried talking to Angie?" Shit. He'd do almost anything at this point to try and fix this mess.

"How the fuck do I know?" Alex barked. "Depends on what you did to her, I suppose. And what the hell with all the Euro-drivel about that douche nozzle she was going to marry? All of that seemed directed at you, fuckface."

Even over the phone, Parker didn't miss the cold chill in his friend's tone.

"I could use your help here, man," he admitted.

"You aren't going to tell me, are you?" Alex muttered angrily.

"I need to talk to Angie. Alone."

There was a long pause and then Alex told him, "I'll see what I can do. I'm trusting you, Parker, because of who you are, but if you do anything to hurt my sister . . ."

"I know," he assured Alex. "And if it helps any, I'd take a bullet for her."

"Strong statement."

"Agreed."

"*Hmmph.* You're still a dick."

"Takes one to know one."

Alex paused. "Oh, did I mention? We're all piling on at Pete's tomorrow night. Carmen and Ria are treating the girls to a babysitters' night so they want to go see who's on the microphone."

"Will she be there?"

"You've met my sister before, right? Spotlight. Microphone. Music. Hell yeah, she'll be there."

Meghan felt wretched by the time she got home. Not even hanging out with the girls and spending time with her baby nephews had taken the sting out of her earlier reaction to Alex's demand to know what was wrong.

She'd done a terrible thing by running from him and worry had been eating at her ever since.

The house was quiet, and the minute Meghan stepped through the front door, she smelled something wonderful coming from the kitchen. She was so spoiled these days. Carmen and Ria, Alex's longtime housekeeper and cook, ran the Villa and oversaw the practicalities around the compound. Betty handled the business office and Ria's husband, Ben, was the resident master-of-all-trades.

Her life had certainly changed since that day more than six months ago when she knocked on the front door of Villa de Valleja-Marquez for the first time. It was bizarre to have someone else handle the cooking and the grocery shopping. Just as crazy as dealing with a housekeeper who sometimes picked up after one of her and Alex's naughty romps and who also did their laundry without comment. Meghan's never-ending wardrobe of sexy lingerie had to raise an eyebrow or two.

Climbing the distinctive wide stairway to the second floor, she made her way quietly to the master suite. The entertainment system was on and she just barely made out the sounds of some hard rocking oldie coming from the speakers. She smiled. Only Alex would relax to AC/DC. Meghan flipped the system off figuring the second she appeared, he'd be finished with the relaxing portion of the day anyway.

Glancing into his side of the wardrobe, she spied his usual clump of clothing piled haphazardly on a bench. A half-empty tumbler sat nearby that she sniffed and smirked at. *Glenfiddich. Bah!*

He was in the shower. The spicy scent of his bodywash wafted from the steamy enclosure and acted on her like a hypnotic suggestion. Hurriedly removing her clothes, which she added to his piled clump, Meghan grabbed a hair clip and used it to secure the thick, long curls she piled into a messy bun on the crown of her head.

Plodding on silent feet, she entered the shower room and approached the large glass enclosure, admiring the sexy silhouette her handsome Major created. He was so damn gorgeous it never failed to take her breath away. Even the scars that marked one whole side of his magnificent body were beautiful to her. They were the marks of a warrior. Reminders of another time.

It was a struggle not to flatten him to the wall and climb on board. Impale her body on the proud cock she saw bobbing under the streams of water running off his massive torso. "May I join you?" she asked in a small voice.

He turned slowly under the wide shower stream and looked at her. By the time he finished his leisurely inspection of her naked body, she was trembling and very aware of another kind of wet at the juncture of her thighs.

Without saying a word, he just nodded and opened his arms. Meghan didn't hesitate to walk into his embrace. When Alex touched her, she felt all her worries melt away. Nothing else mattered but this. She adored him with all her heart and soul.

"I'm sorry for running away," she murmured as water rained down on them.

He didn't say anything, which threw her off. She expected him to use the advantage of her apology to demand that she tell him why.

Instead, he casually turned her so she was facing away from him and reached for her shower pouf. Holding it out, she picked up her wash and responded to the silent command, dribbling some onto the scrubby.

He stroked it across her shoulders and up and down her spine as rivers of fragrant bubbles caressed her wet skin. Washing her with ritualistic thoroughness, he murmured quietly the entire time, telling her of his unconditional love. How he'd protect her and that she was never alone. He would always be there. Always love her. Always take care of her.

She'd come prepared to apologize and beg for his forgiveness. But Alex had a different agenda. He made her sit on the tile bench and put her foot in the middle of his chest so he could stroke the wash up and down her leg. By the time he massaged her foot with the sudsy pouf, whatever he was saying got lost in the steam. Meghan was seriously turned on and struggling to stay ahead.

After he finished with the other leg, she wasn't entirely sure she could stand again. But he made her, so she trembled and leaned with her back sliding against his wet chest. And then he started on her front and *oh, my fucking god.*

Each of her breasts was lovingly washed, massaged, and kneaded. His husky groans and her hushed whimpers mixed in the steam. Meghan's stomach rippled when the sudsy pouf teased her belly button and when he knelt in front of her, the way he stroked her hips and thighs, and the way his eyes burned with lusty appreciation, took her to cloud nine.

When he ran the pouf up the inside of her thighs and teased her mound, she arched into his touch and let her head fall back on a groan. That was pretty much the end of bath time.

Quickly rinsing them, Alex turned off the shower and wrapped her in a big fluffy towel. His tender care didn't end there. Wearing an expression of intense concentration, he proceeded to dry her from head to toe, gently removing every last droplet of water from her skin. When finished, he stepped back and admired her naked flesh. Instinctively, she straightened and thrust her chest out, knowing how pleasing he found her breasts.

Twining his fingers through hers, he took her to their bed. Meghan couldn't help but thrill at the sight of his proud cock jutting away from his body as he walked, knowing she was the reason for his excitement.

Laying her down gently, as though she was a frightened virgin and this was her first time, he stretched out on his side beside her and stroked the tips of his fingers against her skin.

She had to say something. Her conscience was killing her. "Do you forgive me?" she asked quietly.

Gently rolling a puckered nipple between his fingers, he tugged until she groaned and looked at him.

"What do you think?" he asked.

An unexpected sob tore out of her throat and a single hot tear leaked from the corner of one eye. "Alex," she cried as all the emotions she was carefully guarding burst free. "Please tell me you still love me."

"How 'bout I show you?" he asked in a husky voice.

Several orgasms later, she lay quietly in his arms and enjoyed the sweet aftermath of an erotic high.

He'd once again orchestrated the perfect way to deal with what was right in front of them. By not overreacting and giving her some time and space to figure things out, he'd shown her by his actions that she truly was safe in his care. When she was ready, she'd talk to him, and though he hadn't said those exact words, she knew that was what this tender, exquisite loving had been about.

"New rule," he drawled as she snuggled deeper into his side.

"Mmm hmmm," she sighed.

"If we're making babies, there can't be any secrets between us."

I wonder how long it took him to come up with that angle, she thought, *because it was a damn good one.*

"I'm not keeping secrets from you," she assured him as her hand moved across his muscular chest.

"Call it what you want," he complained, "but however you put it, something's making you unhappy and you know I can't have that shit, Meghan."

"I'm sorry." Her lips pressed to his skin. M*mmm.* Even his sweat tasted wonderful.

"Have I done something? Don't *not* tell me if I've been a dick because you want to protect my feelings. Just tell me, honey."

Shit. He wasn't going to let it go this time. She groaned and sat up, pulling the sheet across her chest. She didn't think having him distracted by her tits in his face would be helpful.

He lay on his back and watched her intently. She wondered if he knew how reassuring she found his attention. Whenever he focused solely on her, her heart nearly burst with love.

"Marriage is something sacred." She sounded a tiny bit like her old teacher self, addressing a room full of distracted teenagers.

"If you're backing out of marrying me, I'll tranq-dart your sexy ass and make Uncle Eduardo do the deed while you're unconscious."

Meghan laughed at the absurdity of the scene he just described but knew deep in her heart that he was completely fucking serious.

"I'm standing my ground, buddy." She giggled, stretching her leg out to kick him playfully with her foot. "And besides, you told my brothers and my dad that you'd make an honest woman of me now that I've been defiled by your wicked ways. So, unless you want a Boston beat down, I expect you to show up on the appointed day and time and swear before God and our families to love, honor, and obey."

"Who the hell said anything about obey?"

"What?" she snickered. "There was a meeting of the Alpha Bad Boys Club and they decided to strike the word obey from the vocabulary?"

She loved that he smirked right back at her. "Fuck no! There's going to be plenty of behaving and submitting going on, but it's kind of one-sided, don't you think? That obey thing is all you, my gorgeous Irish fuck goddess."

"What am I going to do with you?" she teased. "You better watch that kind of language around my mother. She's got quite an opinion these days about the whole dominant and submissive thing, and you know I hate those labels. And I told you. Ever since she read that damn book, she thinks she knows fifty fucking shades of everything. The last thing I need is her commenting on our bedroom activities."

He chuckled. "Understood. Now . . . please continue."

And so they'd arrived at that moment when she had to try and explain something that kind of defied any sort of rationale. A paradox. An absurd contradiction, a little like Sammy Hagar.

"Marriage to me is more than an excuse to throw a big party. When I said yes to being your wife, I was making an inviolate promise to put you before everything, even myself if need be."

Alex reached and brought the hand wearing his ring to his mouth for a soft kiss that made Meghan tremble.

"I make that same promise to you as well, my love."

Unf. She loved him so damn much. "I know. And all of this," she said moving her hand between them, "everything that goes on between us in private, it's all part of that sacred promise."

Chapter Thirteen

At first, he wasn't sure where she was going and was a bit stunned by how serious his fiancée was being, but as her thought process unfolded, he was starting to understand.

This thing between them was strong. Powerful and intense. What they'd been through to reach this moment could not be understated. She fought for him when he was at his lowest, even after he pushed her away. Alex wasn't whole without her and together they generated enough heat to power half the state.

The passion fueling their relationship was part of this sacrament they were entering into. Meghan was so different in her outlook on just about everything. He enjoyed that about her. She wasn't stuck in her ways and had an almost empathic connection to every living being she came in contact with.

For her, *of course* getting married would actually be the solemn occasion it was meant to be rather than the sideshow to a lavish party. He should have seen this coming.

"What can I do?" he asked softly. He felt her body language ease slightly but she kept chewing on her lip—a sure sign of hesitation.

"I know this sounds crazy," she began. "But I've been thinking a lot about energy. The kind we create with our actions."

She was absently twisting a corner of the sheet in her hands, and Alex wondered if she could look any more adorable.

"The energy you and I create is . . . *powerful.*"

He liked that she smiled shyly and lowered her eyes when she said it. Powerful, indeed.

"Anyway, when we make those vows, our energies will be joined forever."

"I love the way you put that." And he did. She was just so . . . perfect.

"But, you know," she said—only now the sheet twisting was getting more aggressive. "Other people's energy will be there, too."

Ding, ding, ding! *And there we have it,* he chuckled silently. His Feng-Shui believing, yoga doing, meditating, nature loving bride was having none of anybody else's shit on her big day.

Was he thrilled that she took their marriage so seriously? *Hell, yeah.* Was he fucking ecstatic that she pretty much just told him that she regarded submitting to him in their relationship as a sacred vow? *Oh, fuck.* Knowing she gave him her total trust and faith to always put her first and see to her well-being struck a chord deep inside him. They were made for each other.

"I hate the idea that half of the people in the church will be judging everything we do. My dress. Your hair. The flowers. The babies will cry. Maybe it'll rain and be a shitty day. Who knows? My point is . . ." She drifted off for a second like she wasn't sure where her thoughts were leading.

"Well, I don't know what my point is." She half-shrugged. "I just don't want any negativity, you know? I hate that shit. Negativity, I mean. I don't want to be standing there, having this huge moment, but feeling like flypaper for everyone else's twaddle. Does that sound crazy? It does! Doesn't it? Oh, my god, I'm losing it," she groaned as her head dropped into her hands.

After a minute, she looked at him with wide eyes. "I mean, some part of me thinks we should elope. Have it be just the two of us. And then I think about our families. They'd be crushed if we did that."

"Okay. So let's review here for a minute. Make sure I understand," he told her as he playfully tapped the end of her nose.

"So all this hemming and hawing—the heavy sighs—the worried frowns—the sleepless nights and the running away . . . all that is because you think other people's energy is going to pollute our vows? I got that right, yes?" He recalled an earlier conversation when she'd spoken wistfully of energy.

She nodded, and unless his eyes were betraying him, she actually blushed.

Alex reached, took her face in his hands, and drew it toward him.

"I fucking love you, lady. Fucking love that you see things that way."

And then he kissed her. Meghan's lips were the sweetest, most seductive treasure. When he finished devouring her mouth, she sat back and did this cute little smirk-pouty thing that made his dick turn to stone.

"I know there's nothing we can do about it," she said, but he cut her off.

"Well, I wouldn't be so sure about that. Let me think about it, okay?"

"Thank you for not over-reacting."

He speared her with a no-nonsense look. "You talk to me in the future and don't worry about me freaking out. You are my one and only priority, Meghan. Nothing else even comes close. I'd walk away from Justice tomorrow if a choice had to be made."

Nodding, she reached out and ran her fingers through his hair, laughing. "You've got after-sex hair."

"And whose fault would that be?"

"Oh, shut . . ."

He yanked her hard when he heard the words *shut up* about to come out of her mouth, and she tumbled on top of him. With the sheet trapped between them now, her ass was beautifully bare so he pulled his hand back and brought it down with a wicked smack.

"Will you never learn, woman?" he *tsked.*

She gave him a naughty leer and then propped herself up on his chest.

"So, about these points. The scoreboard is sorta stacked against me, don't you think? I'm not sure my poor bum can handle so much spanking."

Alex chuckled and kneaded her ass for emphasis. "Oh, this oughta be rich."

She ran her finger down his chest and toyed with a nipple. Witch. She was asking for trouble.

"I was thinking maybe we could work some of those points off another way."

"Is that so?"

"Mmm hmm . . ."

"What did you have in mind?" This was fun! He hadn't considered their playful game had other possibilities. Hot damn!

"Well, short of calling you daddy, master, or sir—because you know that shit's not ever going to happen—I believe the choice is yours."

He laughed. They both knew she'd call him *Your Highness* if he asked her to.

His overactive, over-sexed, mind hit on the perfect solution. Something they'd both enjoy.

"Okay," he told her as he grabbed a good handful of her ass. "Here it is. I'll take back ten points if next Friday, you let me kidnap you from our bed, take you out into the desert, and fuck you without mercy."

She squirmed on top of him and he smiled. Her desires were so easy to read sometimes. "Oh wait, darlin'—there's more."

He rolled them until Alex had the advantage, wedged perfectly between her spread legs with the sheet pushed aside.

"When *I'm* satisfied and finished coming inside you, I'll dress you and then will personally deliver you to Ben."

She arched a surprised eyebrow at him. Bah! As though Ben would somehow be involved in their fuckery. Shaking his head at her foolishness, he gave her a wry grin. "Who will then drive you and Angie into Sedona for a long weekend at L'Auberge."

She smiled. No, actually she beamed at him.

"And just to be clear, you'll be making that drive and checking into the hotel with our cum in your panties."

"Deal," she groaned, her eyes smoky with desire after his wicked description.

There wasn't anything left to do except shift his hips and slide into Meghan's welcoming heat.

"Thanks, Unc. I'll tell Meghan you say hi. She'd want to get in on the conversation, but she's in the shower," Alex said with a grin, cell phone pressed to his ear. "Let me know right away what you find out. And Calder?" he drawled. "About Stephanie—don't fuck this up, dude. I agree that going to Atlanta is the thing to do. If she's yours, man . . . go get her."

Alex's attention was drawn away when he heard Meghan moving around in the dressing room. He was curious to see what kind of mood she was in. It had turned out to be an emotional day, and he knew she was particularly fragile now that she'd shared her fears with him. He hoped she'd be happy with his solution to their unusual predicament. What he'd come up with was definitely unconventional, but fuck, so was their entire relationship.

"Uh, listen Calder. I gotta go. Stay in touch," he absently muttered, ending the call and tossing the phone aside.

Not able to wait for her to make an entrance, Alex strode into their dressing room and stopped short when he saw her. How the fuck had his sorry ass been fortunate enough to find this magnificent woman and make her his? When he saw her like this—subdued, relaxed, and completely natural—he couldn't believe how damn lucky he was.

"You look ravishing," he murmured—his eyes devouring every detail. The white silk of her robe. Her sexy auburn curls piled atop her head and the delicate tendrils that escaped and lay against her lovely neck. Her face, fresh from the shower, was flushed from the heat and looked like something he wanted to lick.

She watched his reflection in the mirror, a shy quirky smile on her lips.

"Do you remember when you took me to L'Auberge?" she asked softly. Her eyes were shining as he watched her reflection.

Of course, he remembered. Their stay there in a private cottage had been magical. He smiled warmly. "We spent so much time by the fireplace that you smelled of wood smoke and cashmere. Very sexy, actually."

Alex moved closer and stood directly behind her, his hands first on her shoulders, then one encircling her neck as they stared at each other in the mirror. She relaxed in his grip and leaned into him.

"Were you trying to tell me something with this weekend getaway?"

He smiled and softly caressed her neck. "Perhaps. It's a warm memory for me—our time there was very special. You were," he explained, "so happy. Relaxed. You've been anxious lately, and I thought it would do you good to have some girl time."

"Girl time?" she smirked.

"You know what I mean," he chided her gently with a quick squeeze of her neck. "It's not like we're set up for mani-pedis way out here."

"True."

He could see her thinking about their memorable L'Auberge interlude and could practically pinpoint the second she bought into the indulgence of a spa weekend with Angie. Women! So predictable sometimes.

"And while you're there getting pampered, I give you permission to let go and just have fun with the wedding. Get silly. Indulge every whim, no matter how absurd."

She rolled her eyes and mocked him with a grunt. "You give permission, huh?"

"Yep!" He shot her his best cocky grin. "Trust me. I've got this, babe. You are to have nothing but fun from here on out. Got it?"

"What are you up to Major Marquez?"

The adorable look of suspicion reflected in the mirror made him laugh.

"Why, I'm giving you your happily ever after, of course! And, by the way, I have it on good authority that a certain relative of mine, the aging surfer who needs his ass kicked, to be exact, has finally come to his senses. I do believe a trip to Georgia is now on his mind."

Meghan gasped and a bright, happy smile lit up her face. "You spoke to Calder?"

"Yes. Yes, I did."

"And?" she grumbled.

"And for the rest, you'll just have to wait and see," he teased.

Okay. So Parker had until tomorrow night to come up with some kind of plan. Being thrown together with Angie in a group outing and seeing her out in public was the easy part. It was what he was going to say and coming up with a way to get her alone. So they could talk. Maybe clear the air.

But it wasn't all that easy to make all the fractured pieces of their story fit neatly together, due to the fact that it wasn't just him and Angie anymore. Alex was involved. So was Meghan. Both their families had to be considered. It was fucking a lot and the outcome was mostly on him.

He was too old for this shit. It was embarrassing on some level. Here he was, watching forty round up the bend, and for all his success, good looks, and rock 'n' roll badass charisma, his personal life was a tired joke.

And why was it a tired joke? Because the fucking truth was that he'd given his heart away a long, long time ago to a scrap of a girl who loved to laugh, never met a taunt or challenge she wouldn't try to defeat, and looked at him with the most adoring sapphire colored eyes.

He'd wanted Angel, and when he had her, he hadn't been careful. Hadn't been honest. It seemed the cruelest irony of them all that she still believed he'd regretted their involvement.

How could he tell her now that he'd loved her every day of her life? How, since she was a teenager, he'd lusted after her in ways that still haunted him? Could he make her believe?

Maybe all he should hope for was a foot in the door. A chance to control the inevitable firestorm that would erupt when Alex figured out what had gone down. His friend getting all bent out of shape about upsetting Meghan was a sign that the shit was already approaching the fan.

Angie's drunken performance the night she came back only made matters worse. He was pretty damn sure all that bullshit about Ronald McDonald, or whatever the fuck that Spanish asshole's name was, was meant to piss him off. And it worked. The more she'd taunted about this great love of hers that crashed and burned because of timing, the more he'd wanted to break something.

And *timing* as an explanation for calling off a wedding? Who the fuck was she kidding? Her breakup had nothing to do with timing. He knew her too well—even after years of silence. There was something completely disingenuous about the way she'd talked about her life in Spain and this so-called love of hers.

Them yelling at each other at the foot of the big staircase in the hacienda was not a proud moment, either. *Still not sure how I kept it together,* he thought. At one point when she was hopping up and down on the bottom stairs and snarling two inches away from his face, he'd been sorely tempted to haul her over his knee and blister her ass for acting like such a brat.

Actually, that might still be an option. This was Angelina, after all, and few knew better than him what an indulged princess she'd been as a child. The grown-up version exuded an energy that was electrifying, but her spoiled inner bitch-child was a right royal pain in the ass. As far as Parker was concerned, what the girl needed was a firm hand. Someone to temper the fire. And that someone was him.

Chapter Fourteen

"SO, WHEN DO YOU GUYS leave?"

Wiping away a glob of hot sauce that had clung to her mouth, Lacey smiled at Victoria with a conspiratorial grin. "Tomorrow afternoon. Sawyer's all jazzed. Said the last time he flew anyone from Justice into Vegas, well . . . you know the outcome."

"Oh, I know that outcome well!" Tori trilled with a giggle. "Fuck the souvenirs. Try a baby on board and an arrogant playboy in denial. Now, there are two things that did *not* stay in Vegas."

Everyone cracked up laughing. They were crowded around a high-top table in the back of the bar, annihilating a platter of buffalo wings while Meghan, who was wandering around at the moment, scoped out the dirty on their supposed karaoke competitors.

Enjoying their comical interplay, Angie nodded in Meghan's direction. "By the way, you guys have nothing to worry about. Those good ol' boys at the mic before did a passable harmony, but they lack the tits and ass to bring the crowd to their side!"

Lacey snorted. "T and A. I think we're better than that."

Angie agreed. When the girls had told her about the karaoke fever they had going on, she figured it was just a bit of housewifey fun. Boy, was she ever wrong. Earlier, when they were waiting for the men to get their rides sorted out, she'd listened in delighted disbelief as the three women gathered around the grand piano in the Villa's magnificent open foyer and picked apart a harmony for a song they wanted to perform.

Why . . . Boots, Ass, and Sass needed a record contract! These ladies rocked out with their tits out as Tori so succinctly put it.

Besides the fact that it was completely, awesomely hilarious that the Justice wives got their giggles through sing-along performances in a dusty old honky tonk bar, there was something touching and sweet about their intense camaraderie. A year ago these women didn't even know each other. Today—they were a family.

"Hey, guess what?" Meghan blurted breathlessly as she dashed into their midst. She had the look of someone with gossip to share.

"Oooh, wings! Yum," she murmured, reaching between them to snag one. "Please tell me these aren't nuclear before I shove it in my mouth."

Tori smirked. "You've had hotter things in your mouth, Red."

Meghan smirked right back, earning a hearty snicker-snort from Lacey, who clapped her hands with praise when Meghan arched an eyebrow at Tori, opened her mouth, inserted the entire little drumstick covered in sticky red sauce, and in one nibble, stripped it to the bone all while glaring comically at Victoria.

"Well done, Lady Mama," Lacey hooted. "That's showing us!"

Angie cracked up when Tori pushed her Kahlua and cream toward Meghan, who now had the look of someone with the hot sauce sweats. "Here, take a sip. It will cut the fire better than water."

She took a healthy swig of the creamy drink and smacked her lips. "Mmmm. Thanks. That was like breathing fire. Shit! Is Pete insane? Those wings will kill someone."

Angie nudged Meghan playfully. "Um, they're on the menu as *insane wings*."

"Seriously?" Meghan scoffed.

She polished off the rest of Tori's drink and looked around the table. "So anyway, as I was saying before swallowing a mouth full of molten lava—some chick at the bar told me that Wally, the little guy who sings with those old-timers? He's off on an oil rig for the next couple of months so they're like mad scrambling trying to find a lead."

"Well, if that duo earlier are in the competition, y'all don't even have to bother swinging for the fence. A nice double up the middle will do fine 'cause those guys sucked."

"Agreed, Angie," Lacey said as they fist bumped. "And now that we have another musician," she added with an exaggerated air-kiss in her direction, "we've totes got this."

"I wish my mom was here," Tori sighed with her mouth full of food. "She could help us with some choreography."

Oh, right! Tori's mom was a pageant consultant. She must know all sorts of cool moves. "I can't wait to meet her," Angie gushed. "Stephanie Bennett sounds like my kind of lady. Anyone who could stop my Uncle Calder in his tracks has to be the bomb."

"Any news on that front?" Lacey asked.

It was definitely funny how all eyes swung to Meghan at the asking—as if she had all the answers.

"Okay, look," Red snapped. "All that Lady Mama stuff and expecting me to be an extension of Alex . . . I really don't know as much as you think I do. Marrying Big Daddy doesn't come with any special privileges."

They all exploded in shrieks of laughter at the exact same time. Who the fuck was she kidding? Angie couldn't remember laughing this hard in forever.

After a round of good-natured teasing at Meghan's expense, the mood around the table changed in a nanosecond when Lacey returned after a beer run and mock whispered as she bent to put her burden down, "Something seems to have crawled up the good counselor's shorts because he's corner lurking with an expression suggesting he's about to poop out an egg roll."

Everyone turned in unison, like a damn synchronized routine, and fixed their gazes on Parker who, indeed, was skulking in the shadows across the room.

A tiny smile fought to overtake her lips. The energy coming from the dark corner was focused on her—she could sense it. Shivering, she turned away and groaned when her companions continued to stare at him like he was on display in a zoo.

"Anyone got some chocolate? Maybe a marshmallow or two, 'cause we could melt some yummy s'mores from the heat coming off that man."

Tori. *Of course.* She was the resident wiseass. Always ready with a quip or a zinger. Only, in this case, Angie had to hand it to her. She was spot on because right now? Parker had clearly let his fire-breathing dragon off the leash.

With all eyes now on her, she squirmed and looked around at the frank, assessing expressions coming her way. Oh, boy.

"Angelina Marquez," Meghan drawled. "Enough with the zipped lip, enigmatic bullshit. I've never seen Parker so fired up. Have either of you?" she asked Tori and Lacey who smirked and shook their heads. A chorus of "*Nope*" and "*Hardly*" followed.

Uh, neither had she, and Angie had certainly known him longer, better, and more intimately than any of them. *Good heavens.* Even she was surprised by the intensity he'd been putting off from the moment they all met up out in the parking lot.

She saw the three women exchange glances. Meghan cleared her throat. Lacey sat there and sipped her beer, watching. Finally, Victoria spoke up.

"I think all of us here know that look," she said as Meghan and Lacey chuckled. "That man's been inside more than your head, senõrita. And the fact that he's still got two working legs means your brother is unaware that his oldest friend has," she smirked and took a pull from her beer, "known you in a . . . uh, biblical sense."

"Mmmm," Lacey murmured on a sip. "Well put, Mrs. St. John! Well put."

For the first time, Angie really considered that whole alpha male thing and realized she was hip deep in them at the moment. Christ. Alex and his band of merry men were the Alpha poster boys.

Dominoes began falling fast and furious in her head. How had she never seen this before? Her entire world was made up of strong men. Her distinguished, patrician grandfather and her forward-thinking father. Both alphas in their own right. Calder. *Uh, duh.* Even Uncle Eduardo. Being a priest hadn't diminished any of his natural alpha tendencies. And Parker, well, he'd always had the intensity and strength she'd associated with Alex only more so. He might very well be the most powerfully alpha of them all.

That was what she knew. Men who tended to be bigger than life. No wonder people were mystified by her engagement to Ronaldo. He was so polished, and yes, she meant that in a slightly derogatory way. That whole suave, continental, shtick bored the ever-loving shit out of her.

No. She dreamed about a man whose jeans dropped to the floor with a thud from the weight of his belt buckle, who had eyes that saw through her, and had the broad chest and strong arms that could make her feel safe.

But she'd been foolish before. Believed sex meant the same thing as love. Having her nose rubbed in that fact had been a misery she'd never quite overcome. Judging by the way he was looking at her—as if she was about to be devoured—she could have the sex if she wanted. He was a guy, after all. But what did she want beyond that? Anything? Everything?

Remembering that the ladies were still waiting for her to say something, she quirked a half-grin and hung her head for a second. Looking around at their amused faces, she choked off a giggle and rolled her eyes.

"Suddenly, this Family Justice thing is starting to make sense. I mean, is there something in the water here?" she snickered.

Red laughed. "It's like the damn love boat, only in the desert, of all places!"

Angie laughed at Meghan's description. *Indeed.*

"Okay," she sighed. "I suppose it was insane to think this wasn't going to come out at some point, but yes. Guilty of that biblical thing," she said solemnly while nodding at Tori.

Turning to Meghan, she said, "And no. Alex has no idea. It was a long time ago when we were all in different head spaces."

Meghan snorted and laughed at the same time. "You've met your brother, right? Do you actually imagine for a second that he knows nothing? Tell me you don't feel his fingerprints all over what's going on now!" she squawked, incredulous that Angie was so out of touch.

Finishing her beer, Meghan pushed the bottle to the center of the table and looked at her thoughtfully.

"I'll say it again; he may not know the details, but he knows *something.*"

Lacey, who seemed to have a unique way of not letting anything get by, said, "And for extra giggles, ladies, check out the menacing glare the pretty boy at the bar is getting. He's been eye-balling the señorita here and somebody doesn't seem to be liking that!"

Tori pretended to cross herself then muttered, "Heaven help us.

Another Justice top dog has come into our midst!"

This time, their raucous laughter bounced off the walls.

Parker ground his teeth as his jaw locked down tight and his mouth grew grim and taut. Peals of laughter from the table he was watching ricocheted off the walls and slammed into his chest. At least the ladies were having a great time.

Him? He was in hell. Left on his own at the corner table they'd commandeered while Alex and the guys wandered off to show a couple of guys from the construction crew the ropes. When the girls scooted away to eat bad things and gossip; he was nursed a drink and a bad attitude.

Goddammit, if Angie wasn't being an absolute bitch. And by bitch he meant her regular adorable self, charming everyone who came near, only with a fine veneer of *bite me* directed solely at him.

Women. *Fuck*. Anyone who thought they had them figured out was so full of shit.

And to make matters a million times worse? Dammit. If there wasn't a dumb fucking cowboy wannabe at the bar checking out his Angel with a look that had Parker seething with anger.

The second their noisy boisterous group had burst into the place, every single, on-the-prowl guy in the joint started sizing her up. Yeah—there were other unattached females in the club but none who came close to Angie's unique beauty. And it did not help in the fucking least that she was wearing the sort of outfit that screamed *innocent* and *available* . . . even though as far as he was concerned, she was neither of those things.

Abandoning the table after moving some shit around so it was clear the spot was occupied, Parker stomped toward the far end of the long bar where he could keep an eye on the whole room.

"Dude!" a barrel chested bartender covered in tats bellowed at him over the sound of the music. "What are you drinking?"

Leaning over the rough-hewn bar, he barked a response. "Corona and lime."

Glancing down the bar at the urban cowboy-type with his shiny new boots and jeans that had a fucking ironed-in crease running from knee to the hem, Parker contemplated dragging the douchebag outside and dropping him with one punch. When he saw the fucker trying to get the bartender's attention, Parker made an impulsive decision and acted on it without any consideration.

When the bartender returned with the beer, he asked, "You're Barry, right? Pete's new barkeep."

"Yep. That's me. Barkeep Barry!" the guy chuckled.

Extending his hand for a hearty shake, Parker smirked at the jest. "I'm Parker. My band takes the stage every couple of weeks. Me and Pete go w*aaaa*y back."

Barry grinned. "I know who you are, man. Desert Thunder. Me and my girlfriend have been to a couple of your shows. She loves that old-school rock shit."

"Old-school *shit?*" Parker drawled. "Fuck, Barry. Bit harsh, don't you think?"

They each chuckled and smirked at the same time.

The barkeep came back with a crooked grin and half a shrug. "I'm more a Metallica -kick-your-ass kind of guy but my lady? She's all about the rock 'n' roll and you know how that shit goes," he quipped with a good-natured conspiratorial wink. "Whatever keeps her happy, right?"

Uh-huh. He and Barry were going to get along just fine. Shooting a malevolent glare down the bar, he nodded to the barkeep.

"See that city boy pussy?"

Barry absently swiped the bar rag at some imaginary mess and sneered at the object of Parker's attention. "You mean the pretend Keith Urban? What an asshole."

"Yeah. My thought exactly. Look, he's gonna call you over and try to send a drink to that lady standing over there." He nodded at Angie. Reaching into his back pocket, Parker pulled out his billfold and removed a crisp hundred-dollar note that he slid across the bar to Barry. "Make sure any drinks he sends don't make it there or better yet, are of the non-alcoholic kind."

The barkeep studied Angie a minute. "She your gal?"

And there was the million-dollar question.

"Will be when she stops running," he murmured.

Barry snorted a laugh. "Women! Right?"

For good measure Parker threw down a bit more information.

"See that big guy across the room? The one standing with a bunch of other big guys?"

"You talking about the Justice crew? Good men, all of 'em. Do a lot for the vets around here."

Bingo. "Yeah. Justice. The lady is one of them, and I don't need to tell you what sort of shitstorm will blow through here if anyone fucks with her."

The other man's eyebrows bumped together. "Understood and duly noted." Then he pushed the hundred-dollar bill away from him. "Don't need to do that, Parker. I got your back, man."

Taking a draw of his beer, Parker nodded but told him, "Thanks, Barry. I appreciate it. And you take that hondo and treat your lady to a night out. On me. Okay?"

"*Hehehe*," Barry chuckled. "Tell you what—next time your band plays, can I bring Shelly round? She'd totally get off on a meet and greet with y'all."

"Deal. Now make sure pretty boy Keith strikes out, okay?"

"Leave it to me, man."

They did one of those bro-handshake fist bump things and then Parker turned and put Angel squarely in the crosshairs. Fuck this run and pretend bullshit. The girl was his. And it was time that she understood that.

Chapter Fifteen

WITH KARAOKE OVER FOR THE night, the house band was on stage playing that damn song. Angie was in shock but did an amazing job of looking like she was a little bit bored, while inside, she was running in a circle, screaming at the universe to stop the avalanche of memories those lyrics and that tune unleashed inside her.

The minute the music started up, everyone followed the Noah Protocol and paired up two-by-two around the dance floor, effectively leaving her to her lonesome, single self. She was content to hover near the back, enjoying the set of old and new rock 'n' roll tunes that the band played.

They pounded out a couple of country songs, an old-school rock anthem, and a send-up of a Katie Perry song that was pure YouTube platinum on the hilarity scale. The lead singer, a goofy guy who looked like he'd be more comfortable in a Secret Service contingent than with a band on stage, yapped on about eighties rock and how that shit ruled the world and then announced they had a request. Next thing she knew, her feet were glued to the floor, and every nerve ending in her body short-circuited at the same time.

She could name that tune in three notes.

Oh. My. God. This wasn't happening. Not that damn song! Had Parker done this? She'd been going out of her way all night to act like he was invisible. Was this his way of taunting her?

And then he was there. Right behind her. She could feel him. Lord knows how long she held her breath until she let out a huff of air as a tingling danced along her spine from neck to tailbone. She was in trouble.

He closed in, crowding her until she felt his body heat. Swallowing a lump of unwanted emotion that lodged in her throat, her eyes drifted closed before she dropped her head into her free hand—keeping a half-assed grip on the bottle of beer in the other. She didn't want to be here with him. In the dark. While that song filled the air.

His hand reached around and snagged the beer before fingers that no longer seemed steady let it drop to the floor. Angie didn't care that he stole her drink and was barely aware of what he did with the bottle. Didn't matter. All she cared about at that moment was keeping a hold on her dignity.

Parker stepped even closer. She felt his breath on her exposed neck. Damn. Regretting having worn her hair up, she reached for the clip on top of her head and yanked it free. As the waves of brown tumbled across her shoulders, he reached for the clip and took it from her hand as well.

The song played on, inciting a growing need to take flight and run as far as her feet would carry her. "Do you remember, Angel? This song reminds me of you, *little sister.*"

An arm, big and heavy, snaked around her waist, pulling her against him. Though she tried not to, a soft whimper escaped her lips when she felt the unmistakable evidence of a serious erection pressed into the seam of her ass.

Next thing she knew, Parker walked them several steps backward into the shadows. From the corner of her eye, she saw Alex watching them. His arm was slung across Meghan's shoulders, and a look of concern was spreading across his face. He whispered something to his fiancée who looked over her shoulder directly at Angie and Parker. Whatever Meghan did kept Alex from interfering. So much for the protective older brother.

Held firmly against his warm body, Parker gently swayed them back and forth in time to the music. She didn't realize she was doing it at first, but Angie's fingers were attempting to pry his hand from about her waist.

"Stop trying to run," he growled with his nose buried in her hair.

Shit. The sensory overload she experienced as his warm breath landed close to her ear was too much. Just too damn much.

"Let me go, Parker."

He stiffened slightly but didn't release her.

"Turn around, Angel," he demanded in a rough voice.

"No." Her voice sounded braver than she felt.

He spun her around so fast that she squeaked and collided with his hard body. Immediately struggling to free herself, Angie pushed against his chest, but he just laughed with a deep grunt and held her tighter.

When he began singing along with his hand quite audaciously mapping out her ass, she knew she was lost.

Her brows furrowed with an inner sadness she couldn't speak out loud. Her heart cried, *Why can't this be real?*

Through the shadowed darkness, she felt his heated gaze on her face.

"If I thought you really wanted me to let you go, I would."

She stopped squirming and clutched at his shirt instead. "I can't do this with you," she muttered quietly. Searching his face in the murky shadows, she didn't know what she expected to see. "Don't make me remember." Her words were more plea than demand. Where had her spine gone?

"But you do. *Remember.* I can see it in your eyes, Angel."

Oh, crap. Why did he have to call her that? Hearing it in his deep, sexy voice did things to her. Things she tried to forget.

The swaying continued. So did his soft singing—close to her ear. Words that once upon a time had made her laugh and explode with happiness.

Maybe the memories were a distraction or perhaps she was just a damn fool. It didn't matter which because, in the end, she stood there, hidden in the shadows, his arms holding her tight with one banded about her torso while the other slowly pulled the hem of her dress up as she did nothing.

He went straight for her mound, cupping with a firmness that threatened her sanity. Worst part? She involuntarily pressed against his touch, her body reacting on instinct.

"What color are your panties?" he husked so quietly she wasn't sure he'd actually asked.

"P-Parker," she stammered as his hand ground against her.

"What color, Angel?"

Still clutching his shirt, she whimpered quietly into his chest. "White. They're white."

His response was a sexy grunt that tore through her.

"White for my Angel."

Angie laid her forehead on his wide chest and shuddered.

"I can feel your need, baby girl," he groaned.

She feared what was coming next as much as she yearned for it. There was no stopping him when his long, clever fingers slid into her panties and went straight for her femininity.

Finding her wet and willing, he pushed two fingers inside and went deep. An earthy growl rumbled in his throat that she felt on the cheek still pressed to his chest.

"Every man in this place has his eyes on you."

Why did he sound so angry? *Unf.* She couldn't process what was happening. In seconds, she was trembling all over as he massaged her aching depths with those damn, wicked fingers.

"Don't even try to pretend this is for anyone else but me."

Pretend what exactly, she wondered. That ship sailed the minute she saw him again and her body was rather recklessly proving the point.

Knowing exactly how to touch her in a way that wiped out any resistance, Angie moaned huskily as his fingers demanded and she not only yielded but drenched his hand with a release of wet heat. *Oh, god.* She was going to lose control if he kept it up and what exactly would that say about her?

"P-parker, nooo," she stammered desperately, fighting to hold it together, but her plea came too late. She however, did not. Come too late, that is.

A climax burst to life so swiftly and so violently that she nearly collapsed as shock waves ripped through her. Every muscle in her quaking body contracted in a savage release. The arm around her waist tightened until it became hard to take a complete breath. How she didn't scream when she came was a mystery for the ages.

As the fierce pulses eased, he stayed absolutely still but didn't take his fingers from inside her, the devil. Then, sinking deep and rotating, he slowly pulled them out, groaning as the proof of her passion covered his hand.

Shocked by how quickly she'd fallen apart, Angie struggled to recover and wasn't thinking when he roughly demanded, "Open your mouth."

Reacting on instinct to his command, she did, belatedly realizing what a mistake that was when he put those same fingers, the ones that had been inside her, into her mouth.

He was breathing heavily. So was she. Tasting her desire coating his fingers was her undoing and without thinking or picking apart why, she eagerly sucked, swirling her tongue and swallowing with a low moan.

When she had nearly scraped the skin from his fingers, he pulled them out and grabbed her chin.

She had less than a heartbeat to prepare for the ferocious way he kissed her. There was absolutely nothing gentle about his ravishment of her mouth. It was blatant, possessive, demanding, and terrifyingly primitive.

He pulled back slightly, her chin still in his grip and growled, "I taste how much you want me so don't fucking pretend otherwise."

She started to say something, but he cut her off. "What? What bullshit are you going to throw out?"

Angie pounded on his chest but no words came.

"You can't run from me, Angel. I remember how that virgin pussy tasted. You didn't just come for some fucking dweeb at the bar. What you sucked off my fingers was for me."

Okay. What the hell was going on here? First, he was mad because guys were looking at her. What was she supposed to do? Wear a bag over her head? Now he seemed pissed because she got off. And not only that, she didn't really think coming as he fingered her in a public place supported his running away argument. There was no pleasing him.

"All that's missing is you coming on my tongue and all over my cock. Stop running, Angel. This is going to happen. Your body just proved my point."

Angie knew she was being an ass, especially since she'd just behaved like . . . well, she didn't want to think what her behavior suggested and that might all be true, but there was no way she was giving him the satisfaction of thinking she'd be that easy. Or that gullible. *Ever again.*

Hauling off with a mighty swing, she slapped him across the face and snarled, "*Are you fucking kidding?* Been there, done that, asshole."

The blow shocked him and when he reeled, his grip loosened as she spun on her cowgirl boots and fled.

Chapter Sixteen

WELL, HE'D CERTAINLY FUCKED THAT *up,* Parker thought as he ran his hand across what he knew damn well was going to be a handprint on his cheek.

Watching with a doleful expression as Angie's tight little ass ran away from him yet again, he ignored as best he could the dark scowl directed his way from Alex who must have witnessed or at the very least heard the impressive slap.

He. Was. An . . . *idiot.* What had made him say what he did? The virgin pussy comment wasn't going to score him any points yet stupidly, though he argued and talked circles around people for a living, that was precisely what he'd said.

Picking up the beer he'd taken from her, Parker downed the lukewarm brew in one, long slug. Would he never learn? Saying the wrong goddamn thing to that woman was something he excelled at.

And then it all came crashing into his memory like it was yesterday.

Washington. He was at the Department of Justice and Angie? She was a sophomore at George Washington earning a degree in International Business. Without friends and family around to muddy the waters, they'd been hanging out with Parker playing the family connection card to ensure it was a regular thing.

That night, the one when they'd gotten shitfaced together, even though she was barely twenty and still under the legal drinking age—

he'd thrown caution to the wind after an outing to a club to celebrate a big courtroom win. This damn song, the one he and Alex used to play to just fuck with her, had set the mood for everything that came after.

They'd been their usual flirty selves—dancing, messing around playfully, with Parker singing along while Angie beamed. It was just what they did. What they'd always done.

And as always, he had his arm around her. Sometimes the arm signaled protective older brother mode. And sometimes the arm was a blatantly possessive move intended to stake a claim. One he wasn't entitled to but that never stopped him from doing it anyway. At the club, he'd kept an arm around her waist or across her shoulders that clearly said *back the fuck off* to anyone thinking they might approach her.

Finding their way to his apartment, the flirting turned very real. He couldn't remember how or why their conversation turned intimate, but it most certainly had. He'd been teasing her because he liked the shy blushes and the way she fidgeted whenever things got personal. Every time she squirmed, he got harder.

By the time that night rolled around, he'd been lusting after Angelina Marquez for years—something he only managed to keep in check because of who she was. Who Alex was. And who their families were to each other.

None of that however had played a part in what had happened. They were engaged in some half-assed truth or dare game when he'd gotten her to admit she'd never sucked a dick. He'd been ferociously pleased to learn that and turned on by her charmingly hesitant use of vulgarity. Taking things a few steps further, he'd found his opening and balls out asked her if she'd ever had her pussy licked. *Shit.* He could still see her squirming on his sofa, her face a deep red as he'd smirked at her discomfiture.

"Um, no," she'd admitted with an adorable shyness that got his dick so hard it could have cut diamonds. "Never."

Instead of paying attention to her body language and the way she looked away, he'd barely heard the words. "If only, *if only,*" he muttered silently at the memory. Jesus, he'd been stupid. For someone who was trained to study nuance from clients, witnesses, and juries—he'd completely missed what was happening right in front of him.

He'd teased her, barking with laughter, "Are you fucking serious?

What's wrong with today's college boys? They insane or something?" he'd scoffed.

"Screw you, Parker." She giggled. "Don't embarrass me."

"Oh, no fucking way," he drawled. "There's virgin pussy in the house and I can't let that challenge go unanswered!"

"Stop!" she laughed as he launched himself at her, tickling until she pleaded for him to cut it out before she peed her pants.

"Oh, Angel baby," he growled. "On your back, honey. Let me show you how the big boys do it."

Her shocked reaction didn't hide the spark of heat he saw reflected in her eyes. When whatever was left of rational thought had deserted him, Parker had been well pleased when she didn't exactly try to slow down or stop the dangerous but oh, so sexy path they were on.

Remembering how he'd pushed her dress up and pulled down her panties to reveal the most delicious looking mound he'd ever lay eyes on with its soft tufts of brown hair and a scent that drove him wild, he groaned aloud in the present.

Getting her to surrender, to let him part her legs and go to town, had been quite the ordeal. But he wore her down with his fingers and his words, telling her how beautiful her pussy was and how he couldn't wait to taste her.

And holy shit, had he ever tasted. Actually, thinking back, a more apt word would be feast. He'd feasted on her untouched flesh—licking, sucking, and nibbling till she shook and whimpered. He'd never forget what that first orgasm tasted like.

After breaking her down completely that night, it hadn't taken long to get Angelina Marquez naked and in his bed. Where he'd always wanted her. Where he'd dreamed of being with her.

But he'd been an ass when it finally happened. Wanting Angel under him while he lost himself in her body had become a way of life. One he'd been living from the moment he realized she'd gone from annoying kid to voluptuous young woman. When the time came to make her his, he'd fucked up royally.

It wasn't just orally where she'd been a virgin only he hadn't been smart enough to figure that out beforehand. Her fist time had been a disaster, plain and simple. Instead of making love to her—as he'd fantasized about doing for so long it was in his damn DNA—he'd fucked her mercilessly, ramming past her maidenhead and losing himself. Totally.

She hadn't come. How could she? It was her first time and even after discovering she was completely naïve, he'd been too overcome with arousal to dial back his response.

It was one of the most horrendous experiences of his life, having at long last gotten her into his bed only to behave like a dickhead college boy with no control over his cock.

And then he'd made things worse. Instead of talking to her, telling her anything at all about how he felt, how much he'd always wanted her, and how special she was—he'd lost his fucking mind and said nothing. Never even acknowledged that he'd taken her virginity.

Later, he'd been determined to make up for his brutish lovemaking but hadn't bothered to tell her that, either. Instead, he'd set about instructing his young lover in the bedroom arts. What a fucking shithead he'd been. So much hurt and misunderstanding might have been avoided if he'd simply told her the truth. That he was probably more than a little in love with her and had been for a very long time.

No. That would have been the sane and reasonable thing to do— but for some inexplicable reason, he'd adopted this weirdly disjointed Professor Orgasm way of dealing with things. Without ever speaking of their feelings, he set about teaching his sweet Angel how to do and most certainly enjoy things that fired up the imagination and lowered the inhibitions.

They'd fucked like maniacs for six or seven weeks. He'd even taken her on a no-holds-barred erotic adventure when she'd had her period, filling her head with all that *your body is a wonderland* crap. In short—he'd been an epic tool. Looking back because, after all, hindsight was generally a perfect twenty-twenty, he could see where giving her an endless parade of orgasms meant absolutely nothing because he'd overlooked the part where he also gave her his heart. She'd had no idea and that was his damn fault.

And then . . . well, and then the shit hit the fan in a really big way. On a break from school, she'd gone home to Arizona for some family time while Parker was embroiled in a sensitive case that required him to make a trip to Guantanamo. He was distracted, on edge, and overworked. The terrorism cases were a big fucking deal and being singled out for the prestigious assignment had made him more irritable than usual.

Angie had been gone for about ten days and he'd been missing her like hell. As far as he was concerned, she couldn't get back to Washington soon enough. He needed her in the worst way and not just for sex. He craved her adorable charm and that old-school ladylike way she had. She was a breath of fresh air amidst the stale, stagnant atmosphere in Washington. She was like the warm desert winds he missed—the ones that calmed the endless racket in his head.

Unaware that she'd returned to the city early to surprise him, he'd been having a brain fart moment with one of his colleagues—a very nosy co-worker who Parker didn't particularly like or trust.

"Counselor, you are a dog! Who's the fresh-faced coed we see you traipsing around town with? Jailbait, much? Hmmm?"

He'd been pissed right away. Knowing that people were talking about her—he couldn't give a shit what anyone thought about him—infuriated Parker. Thinking he was protecting Angie, he'd said a bunch of dumb shit to throw the colleague off. Words that blew his relationship with Angelina Marquez into a million pieces and that stood between them to this day.

"Watch your mouth, Anderson. She's family. Sister of my best friend who happens to be Special Forces in Afghanistan. She's in D.C. for school and it's my job to keep an eye out for her."

And then he said the words that damned him for all time.

"Bit of a nuisance, really. Had a crush on me since she was like ten years old. But bro code, you know? While her brother is fighting Al-Qaeda, she's my responsibility. It's like having a baby sister."

As soon as the words left his fucking mouth, he heard a gasp and looked up to see his Angel standing right outside his office door. She looked—*stricken*. Her face was ashen and her expression felt like a painful brand being pressed on his soul.

Muttering a horrified, "Fuck," he'd jumped to his feet and made for the door as she turned around and hauled ass to the elevator. He had caught up with her seconds before the doors slid open.

"Angie . . . I can explain."

"Fuck you, Parker! Baby sister? A bit of a nuisance? What was I? A pity fuck?"

And then she threw something at him. He'd asked her to bring him back a jug of his favorite saguaro syrup. When it hit his chest with a thud, he'd been jolted back a step. The girl had an arm on her that rivaled any minor league ballplayer.

She bolted into the elevator in a mass of shaking limbs, wide, teary eyes, and a trembling mouth. He'd stood there slack-jawed as the horror of what just happened exploded in his head. When the doors slid shut, the last thing he saw was his Angel's wounded expression as she flipped him off.

Afterward, she'd cut him out of her life so completely that he'd had no choice but to let her go. He hadn't seen her alone or spoken to her since that day. Not even when she came home with her folks two years ago after his father had his heart attack. He'd been in shock and out of his head dealing with his hysterical mother and ailing father and a never-ending slew of practical details—the type that ended up forcing him to leave the DOJ and return to Arizona to take over the family firm.

After that, with Angie on another continent and engaged for the past year to a pansy ass looking Spaniard, he'd never expected to see her again. Maybe that was why he was a fucking mess and acting on impulse. She wasn't engaged anymore. They were back on home turf. And he wanted her as much today as he had for more years than he could count.

"Do I have to kick your fucking ass?" he heard a familiar voice snarl that snapped him back to the present.

Alex. Oh, great.

He looked at his old friend and did nothing to hide the regret he was feeling.

"Probably."

He looked at Angie. Meghan was by her side, and except for a brief sympathetic look in his direction, she kept her attention on her soon-to-be sister-in-law.

"Dude—I'm not blind. Or stupid." Alex was shaking his head at his sister's back and frowning at Parker.

The band told the cheering crowd they were taking a break between sets. Thankfully, when the music stopped, his head started to quiet down. Not that it helped much—Alex's frown was right on the edge of a menacing scowl. Shit was about to get real.

"I need another beer," Parker grumbled.

Alex's stone-faced response scared the piss out of him. Elbowing him toward the end of the bar, they walked in silence. As soon as they settled on a couple of empty barstools which magically got vacated when his friend's angry scowl preceded them, Barry appeared with two cold ones and a bowl of peanuts.

They sat there—more silence—both of them nursing their drinks while he searched for what the hell to say. Alex Marquez was family. More a brother to him than if they'd been blood-related. The man wasn't going to like what Parker had to say.

"In the interest of cutting through the bullshit, what do you know? What has Angie said?"

Parker had argued cases before the Supreme Court, and those black-robed justices weren't nearly as scary as Alex and his dark scowl.

"Don't cross-examine me, counselor. You're on the witness stand, not me, you asshole," his friend bit out.

Shit. He winced. This wasn't getting off to a good start.

Alex slammed his beer down and growled. "Why don't you start with why my sister just left a handprint on your ugly face. You said you wanted to talk to her. Not start up a fight club."

Parker zeroed in on Angie where she stood with the gaggle of women as they laughed and looked like they were having the time of their lives.

Alex's warning growl, the second in less than a minute, cut through the noise at the bar.

"Look at her again, dude, and I'm going to stick a fork in your eye. You have like ten seconds to start talking or I'm calling for backup and you can find out what a Justice smack down feels like. Hope your health insurance is paid up."

Crap. What choice did he have at this point? He had to tell Alex the truth and just hope he survived the confession with all his body parts still intact.

Downing most of his beer, hoping for a bit of drinkspiration, he put the bottle down, lowered his elbows on the bar, clasped his hands together, and rested his chin on them for a moment while gathering his thoughts.

"Your sister," he began rather apprehensively as Alex speared him with a hostile look, "um, I mean . . . oh, shit. Let me start over."

To Parker's astonishment, Alex held up five fingers, then lowered them one at a time, muttering, "Five, four, three, two, one," until a beefy fist was formed. "I said ten seconds."

The gulp was a reflex. The sigh was a silent prayer that he was doing the right thing.

"I'm in love with Angie."

Alex's eyes widened but the clenched fist still hung in the air between them.

"Excuse me?"

He knew exactly how his friend felt. Parker was also astonished at the words that just came out of his mouth. Until that second, he'd never said them aloud.

"You heard me," he muttered.

This time it was Alex who looked toward the group of women with an expression that seemed a bit . . . incredulous. Thankfully, the fist dropped away leaving only his friend's flabergasted face.

They sat there quietly, absently twirling their bottles in unison.

"What the fuck, Parker," Alex finally muttered. "I always thought there was something going on with you two, but shit, man. Hearing you admit to being in love with her—well, seriously. A bit of a game changer."

This was news, Parker admitted silently. Here, he'd thought all these years that he'd covered his love-struck tracks pretty well.

"For me, too." He sighed deeply and shook his head. "I think she hates me."

"H*mmph,* well, what the fuck did you do?"

"You're not going to like the answer."

Alex was quick to respond. "Maybe you better not tell me then." He thought for a moment with an unhappy frown on his face and added, "How 'bout you just nod or shake your head?"

"Uh, okay. I suppose. But I reserve the right to plead the fifth if necessary."

"*Pfft.* Fucking lawyers."

Parker shrugged. Occupational reflex.

"The *she hates me* thing. Is this recent?" Typical Alex. Straight to the point.

With a strangled groan, he shook his head, no.

"Okay. Did she, uh . . . hate you when she and my folks were here last? When your dad was in the hospital."

"Fuck." He nodded.

Thinking out loud, Alex murmured, "Guess that explains why you and she managed to never cross paths even once that trip. I thought it odd at the time."

Parker grimaced at the reminder and groaned, "Fuck," again.

"Did you have anything to do with her breaking off her engagement?"

Parker clenched his fists and his mouth formed a thin, unhappy line. He shook his head, no.

"Whoa. Little too close for comfort?"

"Sidebar," he mumbled.

"Go ahead but keep it short."

"That little prick wasn't good enough for her."

Alex snorted, obviously amused. "Off the record? My folks did a happy dance when she broke things off. Something wasn't right with those two." Raising his eyebrows, he added, "Think I'm starting to understand. She didn't agree to the engagement until after she'd seen you. Smacks of desperation or surrender."

"My fucking life passed before my eyes when I heard she was getting married."

That seemed to strike a chord with his friend.

"Understood. That's how I felt when Meghan kicked my ass to the curb and left. Worst feeling ever. Didn't think I'd recover."

The band was making its way back to the stage and people began shifting to the dance floor. A couple of guys called out to them, motioning for him and Alex to come join the fun, but they both stayed seated and basically ignored everything going on around them.

"Okay. Two more questions and don't even think about not answering."

Parker sighed and waited like a man condemned—pretty sure he knew the question that was coming.

"Did you sleep with her while I was in Afghanistan?"

Shit, shit, shit. He covered his face with his hands, leaned on his elbows, and hung miserably over the bar. Turning just enough to peek out between his fingers, he gave his friend the respect he deserved by looking him in the eye and nodding, yes.

The punch Alex threw knocked him off his barstool and sent him flying to the floor. If anyone even noticed, they certainly didn't interfere. This was Whiskey Pete's, after all. Punches thrown at the bar were commonplace, and unless a holy hell scuffle broke out and the bouncer had to get involved, people tended to mind their own damn business.

While his friend calmly went back to nursing his beer, Parker hauled himself from the floor, knocking peanut shells off his clothes. *Fucking, eh.* First, a ferocious slap, and then, a heavy punch. On both sides of his face, too. Looking in the mirror tomorrow morning was going to be fun.

Resuming his spot on the barstool, he swallowed what was left of the beer and cleared his throat. Massaging his jaw, Parker growled at his friend. "Thank you, sir. May I have another?" he sarcastically bit out.

Alex scrubbed his hands back and forth against his skull and snickered. "I'd count on it if I were you."

A few seconds ticked by. "Last question," Alex grumbled.

Jesus Christ. What the hell was left to ask?

"Got a plan for how to fix the mess you made, shithead?"

Parker shook his head. "Not a fucking clue, man."

Chapter Seventeen

"Okay then," Meghan chuckled after looking over her shoulder in time to see Parker go flying off a stool and onto the floor.

Lacey gasped with Tori hanging onto her arm as she doubled over giggling.

"Holy crap!" Typical for Lacey Cameron. That was about as pithy as the woman ever got. Someday, Meghan was sure her friend was going to let rip with an epic tirade of vulgarity that would make the *Guinness Book of World Records*. She hoped so, anyway.

"That was fucking awesome!" Tori choked out between giggles.

Cam and Draegyn, their ever-present protectors who were just a few feet away, stood staring in bemused silence at whatever had just taken place at the bar.

She loved it when her sexy Major got all alpha and went into beast mode. Meghan should probably thank Angie now because she was pretty damn sure that once she and Alex were alone . . . well, after they laughed about whatever was going on, he'd be finishing out the night on top. The sound she made fell somewhere between a giggle, a sigh, and a moan.

Tori's knowing snicker forced a rush of embarrassed heat up her neck and onto her face. Wrinkling her nose, she stuck her tongue out playfully at her friend and rolled her eyes.

"Shut up."

"Didn't say a word, Irish," the naughty imp chuckled.

Watching their exchange, Drae walked over and jokingly smacked his wife on the butt. "Behave, woman!"

Tori snickered some more and whispered something in her husband's ear that got the man laughing gleefully. Those two were always the life of the party.

Cam motioned to Drae, caught up with him, mumbled a couple of words that she couldn't hear, then headed in the direction of the bar.

She stuck her free hand out to stop them. "Hold up, guys. I think we should just let the Major handle that by himself."

Angie, who had run to the ladies' room, was weaving through the crowd on her way back to join them when she noticed where everyone was looking. Meghan quickly got to her side and nudged her playfully.

Angie looked up, a curious expression on her face. "What?" she asked.

"Well, your brother—my hunky fiancé, just put Parker's ass on the floor with one punch. Any idea what that was about?"

"How'd you know?" Parker asked.

His friend chuckled as he scooped up a handful of peanuts and put them down in a pile next to his beer. "The signs were all there. Just took me a while to put all the clues in the right order."

Shelling a couple of nuts, Alex dropped the dusty hulls on the floor and popped the small nuggets into his mouth with a shrug.

"My sisters were pen pal fanatics when I was overseas. They used a team tag approach. Got a letter every week. Sophia would write about her exploits and give long, detailed updates on what our folks were doing . . . but Angie. *Shit.* All Angie ever talked about was Parker this and Parker that."

More evidence for Parker that he'd had his head up his own damn ass. It'd never even occurred to him that anyone in their two families, let alone Alex who was halfway across the globe, saw anything unusual about his closeness to Angie. Had he really been that stupid?

"I might have had a shit ton of other things on my mind at the time, but it didn't escape my notice that at some point, you more or less fell off the face of the earth as far as Angie was concerned." Alex shrugged and continued to feed peanuts into his mouth. "If she'd had a boyfriend, it would have made sense. She'd always had a crush on you. Just figured that shit would stop when someone caught her eye."

Parker made a strangled sound somewhere between a groan and a gasp. "I fucked up and she, well . . . she got hurt. I didn't mean to. It just happened and . . ."

"I will fucking kill you if the word *cheat* comes out of your mouth," Alex growled in a not-at-all-friendly tone.

Parker jumped and almost toppled off his stool. "Fuck, no! Shit, Alex. It wasn't like that. Nobody cheated. *Fuck,*" he ground out.

Suddenly, Alex grew menacing. "You're too fucking old for her, man." The barely concealed displeasure radiating off his oldest friend cut like a knife.

With all the sincerity he could muster, Parker met his friend's gaze. "That was true then—but it's not true now. She's grown up and I've stopped pretending. Has to count for something," he mumbled.

Alex sat quietly and worked on his drink. Finally, Parker said, "I can fix this," without actually knowing how.

"In case you hadn't noticed, so far you're zero for two. Each time you two occupy the same space, UN Peacekeepers are needed. And tomorrow your face is gonna be a sight, so . . ."

"Let me ask you something," he murmured. "If Meghan had refused to come back after you came to your senses, would you have given up and gone away?"

"Fuck to the no," Alex growled. "I would have bought the house next door and driven her up a wall until she gave in. The woman belongs to me. Plain and simple."

Parker sighed heavily. "I've made my share of mistakes with Angelina. Coming on too strong earlier was one of them. It's just that when that damn song started up . . ."

Parker noted the way Alex tightened up and cleared his throat when he mentioned the song the band played. They'd said it was a request.

"You motherfucker," Parker ground out. "That was you, wasn't it?"

Alex didn't exactly say anything—just sat there with an amused smirk on his ugly face.

"Why, I oughta kick your sorry ass for a stunt like that. You knew that fucking song would stir the pot!"

"Settle down." Alex chuckled. "I figured it would lighten things up—never expected you to drag my little sister into the shadows and accost her."

The whole thing became funny. Laugh out loud, write a screenplay about it, never gonna get old funny. They had laughed together for a minute before Parker smacked Alex hard on the back.

"Help me, Major Obi-Wan. You're my only hope."

"Stupid, you are," Alex smirked. "Women" he snorted. "Strange and mysterious creatures. Surprise them you must! Upper hand you must take if hope you have of winning."

"Well, fuck, dude! The surprise dinner worked out so damn well, right? So did tonight's little unplanned get-together. I think the surprise factor is a bust. Got anything else?"

Alex thought for a moment then told him, "I'm sending Meghan and Angie to Sedona for the weekend. They'll be at the L'Auberge. You'll look in on them for me while they're away from the Villa, right?"

Chapter Eighteen

"Guys . . . gotta tell you. Digging these morning meetings. Including Brody and adjusting for the time difference totally works for me."

Drae looked over at Cam, who was gathering a bunch of blueprints into a pile, and jeered, "How 'bout you take your mouth off his cock and stop with the goody-two-shoes act? It's too fucking early for words. Admit it, you asshole."

Alex laughed when Cam grabbed hold of his crotch growling, "Suck me, St. John, you pussy."

Drae hurled a wadded ball of paper at Cam's head, snarling, "Lube up your asshole, more like it!"

Ah, the boys! He sure did love it when they were around.

Flexing his dad muscles, he told them, "Settle down, kids. Class is still in session."

It was like watching a meerkat comedy routine when his two closest Justice brothers pushed and shoved each other to get to the head of the line then stood at attention like it was troop inspection time . . . waiting on his next words. Sometimes, like now, he couldn't tell if they were just fucking with him or if their reaction was a result of their brotherhood.

"So, while Brody's the subject . . . any news on locating his kid yet? Was a fucking stroke of luck that he pinned down the birth certificate. Did it help any?" he asked Cam.

Cameron Justice was their official tracker. The guy turned finding Waldo into an art form. Alex had heard it said about Cam that if they'd really wanted to find Bin Laden in a hurry, they should have just let him have at it. He coulda located that motherfucker and been done with it. In that respect at least, he was practically a legend so if anyone could figure out what happened to Brody's kid, he could.

"I wish," Cam snorted. "Turns out this isn't going to be so easy. The kid's too young to be in the system as far as the department of education goes and Pole Dancing Tracey embraced that whole off-the-grid mentality. Poked around a bit in her parents' business, but that's essentially a dead lead. They've been estranged for years."

Drae cut in. "What about the boyfriend? Simon. Find anything on him?"

Alex looked expectantly at Cam, who was shaking his head with a grim look on his face.

"No. And I'm not sure he's worth focusing on. Not even sure that's his real name. What I have found out is that Tracey made buck working the pole. Fucking San Diego, man. Service town, you know? Tons of horny guys all eager for pussy."

They each shuddered or shifted uncomfortably remembering when they were the horny soldiers looking for some strange.

"Anyway—she was doing all right for herself and with Brody, *that stupid fuck,* paying all her bills, she started betting on the horses. Strippers and racetrack folks—not all that interested in talking, if you catch my drift, but I'm checking out a new angle. She had to deal with a bookie. Let's see where that takes us. One thing's for sure though, she isn't in San Diego. That trail went cold right around the time Brody said."

"He's going to Boston for the wedding, right?" Drae asked.

Alex snorted out a harsh laugh. "Did you imagine for even a second that Meghan would let him decline the invitation?"

Both men chuckled. Everyone knew his Irish beauty had a soft spot for the agency's dog guru. The two bonded over their backgrounds as teachers, and while Alex pretended to be okay with their friendship, he knew damn well that Cam and Drae were aware that the handsome veteran's innocent interest in Alex's woman made him see red. And not in a good way. On more than one occasion, he'd come close to ripping the man's head off.

"He's bringing someone."

"What?" Alex and Drae asked in unison, looking at Cam who was openly snickering at them. Leave it to him to drop a grenade in the middle of the conversation and then laugh about it.

"Yep. Bringing a plus one." To Alex he jeered, "Dude—maybe you better step up with all that wedding shit. He and his date are on the seating list for the reception."

"And what the fuck do you know about *my* seating chart?" Alex hollered.

"Lot more than you do, apparently," Cam taunted.

"Totally whipped," Drae sniped, motioning with his head toward Cam. "Spends more time in that sewing circle the girls have going on than with us manly men."

Cam mimicked someone belly laughing then arched an eyebrow at Drae. "Laugh all you want, dickhead, but you'll find out. If you want to see your son, better keep track of the women."

"So . . . wait a minute," Alex interjected with a sharp snap of his head. "Let me get this straight. Jensen is bringing a date to my wedding and you know this because Dylan is held captive by the women?"

"Pretty much," Cam shrugged. Nudging Drae, he added, "By the way. Remind me later to go over your part of the flash dance the groomsmen are doing."

His two brothers looked over at him and openly laughed. *Shitheads.*

"Nice try," Alex smirked. "Maybe I'm not plugged in when it comes to seating charts, but I know a whole hell of a lot more than you two dicks about my own goddamn wedding. Turned into a high holy day. More likely that the Pope would make a guest appearance than a YouTube stunt."

Cam grinned broadly. "Meghan's a lucky girl."

"Yeah. And so is Lacey," Alex agreed. "Tori—I'm not so sure about."

"Oh, bite me, you two!"

Not for the first, hundredth, or last time, Alex marveled at the twists of fate that saw the three of them to this extraordinary moment in their shared history. Cam. Blissfully married and a new dad to boot.

Draegyn, likewise, although he might be the biggest surprise of them all when it came to being a married man with a family. He'd grown up when things got tough with Tori's pregnancy. Being a husband and father suited the man.

"Listen," Cam said in a deceptively offhanded way.

Alex and Drae became very still. They recognized that tone and knew a change of subjected when it happened.

"Um, when the wife and I go to Las Vegas for our anniversary . . ."

He drifted off after that and looked sort of bemused. *Yeah? What? Finish the fucking sentence!* Alex wanted to grab Cam by the throat and shake him. Sometimes he took being laid-back too damn far.

Draegyn cut in. "Jesus, Cam. Learn how to tell a story, would you? Don't fucking stop a reveal."

Cam stood there, arms crossed, with a brooding expression. The usual. Except for the wedding ring and occasional smile, the man hadn't changed from the serious hardcore, kickass beast he'd always been.

"I'm going to tell my wife that I've located her father."

Was that an actual pin Alex heard dropping? Holy fuck! Lacey's old man? This was *huuuge*.

"I didn't know we were looking for him," Drae sarcastically bit out.

Alex understood the anger he heard in Drae's voice. Lacey's dad was a bastard. The man wouldn't find any friends among Family Justice.

"Well, we weren't. But Lacey was doing one of those ancestry things online for Dylan. She left the browser open one day and I saw the full names and birth dates of her parents. Just got me thinking . . ."

"Does she know?" Alex asked. Good lord. He couldn't imagine she'd be all right with her husband bringing that man back into her life. Grandparent or not. He'd fucking abandoned her. Plain and simple. The man was dirt.

"Nooo," Cam droned. "I was curious—not insane."

"What did you find out?" *Hmmph.* Drae. Always sticking to the facts.

Cameron shrugged and relaxed; he unfolded his arms and casually checked to make sure his shirt was tucked in.

"I think it's Lacey's right to hear the details first. I can tell you that he's not a threat in any way except, of course, by his mere existence. And, uh . . . he's got other kids."

Alex and Drae groaned at that news. Poor Lacey. All she ever needed was a family to love and support her. She'd found that here in Arizona. Cameron worshipped the ground she walked on. All of Family Justice adored her. She had a son now to carry on the family she and Cam had created. From nothing. Learning she had siblings was going to kill her.

As if that wasn't enough, Drae cleared his throat abruptly and kind of choked out the words, "Uh . . . my parents want to come for a visit. Meet Daniel. And Victoria."

Was he being punked? Seriously, Alex wondered. What the fuck planet was he on?

Meghan wanted to elope and make babies.

Angie and Parker were keeping secrets.

Brody had a female friend.

Cam went searching for Lacey's M.I.A. father and now the St. Johns came out of the woodwork?

Jesus Christ. In all these years that the three of them lived side-by-side in the compound, not once had those people ever expressed any interest whatsoever in Draegyn or his life.

Cam seemed stunned to hear this, too. Thank god. Alex didn't want to be the only one standing there with his mouth hanging open.

When neither of them recovered sufficiently to say anything, Drae rolled a shoulder and jammed both hands into his pockets. "I know, right?"

Alex managed to rumble a confused sounding, "Uhhh . . ." but that was it.

"Dude!" Cam groaned. "What did you say?"

"Said no, of course!" he growled. "I've got enough on my plate right now. I don't want their toxic bullshit anywhere near Victoria. Or my son."

"Maybe if Stephanie comes back it'd be easier for Victoria. She'd have her mother as a buffer." Alex chuckled. "Stephanie Bennett can be a scary monster. That genteel Southern drawl is one hundred percent bullshit!"

"Stephanie's coming back?" Drae barked. "When were you going to tell me this, you dick? Do you have any idea what dealing with my wife has been like since her mother hightailed it back to Atlanta?"

"At ease, man," Alex cautioned with a meaningful look. "Don't have anything definite, but when I do, you know damn fucking well that I'll let you know. But . . . I did talk to my uncle recently and I'm pretty sure he's going to man up and go to Georgia."

Drae picked up a leather jacket and slid his arms into the sleeves. "Oh, thank god. I've wanted to fucking murder Calder in his sleep for weeks, man. I mean, shit! Do you have any idea how weird this is for me?"

Alex shook his head and snickered, too. "I'm totally with you on this, Drae."

"Oh, hey," Cam horned in. "I hear Irish and your sis are headed out for a spa weekend in Sedona."

Alex checked his watch and noted the time. *Yeah.* These ass crack of dawn meetings worked for him, too. He got business out of the way, sometimes before Meghan had done much more than open her eyes and stretch. Gave him a chance to circle back when he was through and get the day started off right. And today was going to be fucking awesome. He had plans, man. Plans to rock Meghan's world. *Big time.*

Angie was puttering aimlessly around her room. It was still early. Way too early to go wandering, so she took advantage of the massive suite, one of several that made up the family quarters in the old hacienda, and simply enjoyed being home again.

Pushing open the arched double doors leading to a small balcony hung with creeper vines and a smattering of flowers, she eased onto a comfy lounger and propped her bare feet up.

Excited about the spa trip, she found herself envying Meghan. Alex was being such a sweetie. Seeing up close and personal how he doted on her was freakin' adorable and then some.

Remembering the wedding stuff she had in a file on her computer, she thought about how perfect it was that they'd have a long weekend—just the two of them. And! She'd finally get a chance to see Red in her wedding gown. The exclusive shop Meghan was using was eager to run through the alterations again so they'd arranged a fitting for first thing Saturday morning. Angie couldn't wait.

Sighing, she rested her head on the back of the lounger and stared at the sky. Soft, billowy clouds moved slowly against the vibrant blue of a newborn day. Sedona made her smile. So many memories here.

Right now, surrounded by the things that spoke to her soul, it was hard to miss her life in Spain. Although the Villa kind of reminded her of the Valleja-Marquez casa grande, the similarity stopped with the architecture. Instead of an Arizona landscape outside the front door, it was their birthright—the rolling hills covered in ancient vines and the winery that bore the family crest.

She loved her life there. For a million different reasons. But she *needed* this life here. Drifting as she cloud-watched, Angie's thoughts swung from one unconnected thought to another.

Did I pack enough sunscreen? Gosh. I better check.

Mmmm. I like my toe polish. S'pretty.

Sigh . . .

Should I get my hair cut now? I'll just have to do it again before the wedding. Eh, what the hell. Big brother is paying for it. Might as well let the stylists have at it.

It smells so good when the sun first comes up.

Better call Mom later.

Sedona. I love Sedona.

Sigh . . .

Parker lives in Sedona.

Angie sat up so fast, her hair snagged in the tight wicker. "Ouch!" she yelped. Her hand flew to her head when her movement was restricted.

Carefully pulling her hair from its tangled snag, she muttered darkly, "Is that like some kind of a sign? Think about Parker and what? Zap?"

Growling, she righted herself and kicked the lounger for the hell of it. Angie wasn't totally dense. She knew Parker would have to make an appearance while they were in Sedona. No way around it.

Thinking about what happened between them at Whiskey Pete's didn't help.

Stomping back inside, her early morning reverie shattered, she headed for the shower. Hopefully, a nice long, steamy bath would be a better way to start the day.

She was about to spend a couple of days being pampered, massaged, and waited on at one of her favorite spots, and she was going to enjoy herself, dammit!

Chapter Nineteen

"You really have upped my brother's style score," Angie quipped. "A limo? I mean, really! Alex has always been more of a beater truck kind of a guy."

Meghan blushed at Angie's observation and smiled. Oh, he had the old truck all right and it had been the backdrop of some memorable fuckery. Shifting in her seat, she silently admitted, *And so has this limousine.*

"Well, if I can learn to sit a horse, the Major can adapt to a fancy car!"

"He's really happy, Meghan. I've never seen him so full. Of life. Of love. Of the future. You know we almost lost him," she ended on an emotional croak.

Meghan instantly reached for Angie's hand.

"And afterward, for a long time, he just seemed really serious. Like he was always on a slow burn. Our folks were so worried. Especially Mom. He scared the shit out of her with the way he closed off. But now? Oh my god, Red. He's Alex again. You just have no idea . . . thank you so much."

Emotion clawed at Meghan's throat. No one should be thanking her. It was Alex who made the journey from doubt and remorse to happiness and hope. That was all him, and she'd never been prouder than at that moment when he left the past behind and turned toward the future.

Had she been forced to leave his sorry ass and put thousands of miles between them in order to push him to that point? Yes. And it had almost killed her because until the moment when he laid it all on the line, the outcome had been uncertain. But he got there on his own—surrounded by good people who loved him. If he was Alex again, as Angie said, it was because he'd done the work to get himself there.

"Angie," Meghan murmured, still holding the other woman's hand. "I swear to you that nothing matters more to me than your brother's happiness. I think if I had to go away in order for him to be truly happy, I would. Even though it would kill me to lose him, I'd have no choice. I love him that much."

"Wow," Angie whispered. "I guess that's what unconditional looks like in actual practice."

She half-shrugged. "It's not about me. I can't live unless he's happy."

"That's what he would say too, you know. All he cares about is you, Red."

Indeed. Meghan smiled and settled back in her seat. Angie prattled on for a bit until her phone buzzed. Looking to see who was calling, she waved it and winced.

"Eek! Mi madre."

Ah haha. Meghan understood. "Go on." She chuckled. "I'm just going to sit over here and daydream for a bit."

While Angie launched into a spirited conversation with her mother, Meghan stared at the scenery going by. It was a nightmare sitting there like nothing was amiss when each time she moved or squirmed, she became super aware of what she was wearing and the unavoidable fact that her panties were definitely a tad on the icky side.

Alex. Their playful bargain where he wiped points off the slate if she let him assert his bad-boy charms had ended up being quite memorable. Damn him for it too because there was little possibility Meghan would be able to do anything now except replay the sexy scene he put her through earlier, over and over.

Earlier that morning . . .

They had breakfast together and, though he looked at her with a covetous hunger, no mention was made of what she should expect.

He'd told her all she needed to know when they struck their deal. To lose the points, she was to let him kidnap and take her to the desert to be mercilessly fucked. His expression, not hers. What he wanted to do sounded so hot that she'd agreed so fast, she almost left skid marks.

A couple of hours after breakfast, he called her into their bedroom and started barking orders about overnight bags. Bemused, she pointed out what she was taking, watching silently as he gathered her things and headed for the door.

"I'm taking these downstairs for Ben. We leave the house in forty minutes. Get ready."

"Okay," she murmured, completely turned on by his aggressive voice and body language.

"And bathe yourself. I want to find you in the tub when I get back."

"But I already showered this morning," she assured him.

"Don't care. Bathe again."

He stomped away after that, and she shivered with a smile. This was new to their playtimes. The role-playing. She'd gotten very good at understanding Alex's signals. She knew when he wanted soft and when he needed hard. With just a few clipped words, he'd spelled out where this was going.

Kidnap.

Oh, now see, she thought shivering slightly. *There was that pussy-clenching thing again.* Just thinking about how her Major intended to play out an abduction scenario made Meghan bit her lip against the moan that wanted out

Even though she was dutifully in the tub as commanded and was expecting him to take possession the moment he returned, she was surprised when he didn't. He was so good at this. The whole time she bathed, Meghan was super conscious that he was preparing her to be consumed. By making her wait, and wonder—he was stretching out the anticipation.

Sounding gruff and impatient, he called from the bedroom, grunting, "Get dressed." She hurried to towel off before tiptoeing from the dressing room.

Alex was waiting for her by the bed. A jolt of pure animal lust shot into her center when she looked at him. He was big and rather fierce looking, dressed in black jeans and a dark button-down shirt with the sleeves rolled back. His expression was hard, but Meghan caught the gleam of excitement in his eyes that let her know he was already enjoying himself.

"Put that on." He pointed to a pile of clothing on the bed.

The menacing growl in his tone made her bones melt. Oh, my. This was her demanding Major, and he was just getting started. She hoped to survive and giggled lustfully before gasping in horror when she realized what she'd done.

He smacked her on the ass so hard, she yelped and did a little jig to escape. "Think this is funny?" he snarled.

Funny? No. Hot? *Yes.*

Lowering her eyes in surrender, she reached for the clothes he'd put out and nearly shit when she saw a roll of masking tape and a wrapped up length of rope laying alongside.

Crowding her personal space, he stood right on top of her as she dressed, touching each section of her body as she pulled on the clothing like he was inspecting his prey. First, he handed her a bra. As she straightened the garment and prepared to slide it on, he'd grabbed at her breasts and pulled her nipples. Even after she was covered and had hooked the two sides together, he'd tweaked her lace-covered nipples—*hard.*

It just got worse from there. He slid her panties on, stroking every inch of her flesh from ankle to belly button. When the teal satin was in place, he'd calmly pulled the crotch aside and put a finger inside her.

"Not wet enough," he grunted after a minute of teasing and pulled his hand away.

After that, she shook as he dropped a plain cotton dress over her head and yanked it down like he was mad at her for being undressed in front of him.

Pulling the clip from her hair, he let the auburn curls tumble free then grabbed a handful and jerked her head back.

"When we leave this room, walk straight to the driveway. Do as you're told and maybe I'll be gentle."

He retrieved the tape and rope from the bed, giving her a meaningful leer when he did, and motioned toward the door.

The moment they left the bedroom, he put his hand on her neck, like he owned her and marched Meghan down the long hallway to the winding staircase. He grabbed her forcefully by the arm as he moved them swiftly down the steps then took her neck again as they left through the front door.

To be honest, she was practically skipping along with glee. The possessive grip on her neck, his gruff manner, and the rapacious vibe he was putting off . . . well, it all was incredibly erotic. She *loved* this shit and knowing he did too allowed Meghan to immerse herself in his desires.

There was absolutely nobody around. She had no idea where Angie was. Drae and Tori had driven into town with Daniel for a well-baby visit. Cam and Lacey were busy at home, loving each other up after having been apart. It was the perfect moment to be kidnapped. No hope of rescue. Her fate was sealed. It was the wrong time to smile so she chewed on her lip and whimpered instead.

He marched her to the driveway, snarling when she stumbled, but careful to make sure she was all right at the same time.

At the truck, a grim looking Alex forced her into the front seat, immediately wrapping her wrists with the tape before doing the same to her ankles. Opening the glove box, he withdrew a red bandana, rolled it up, and used it to gag her. The tying up she expected. The gag she had not.

When she was restrained and gagged, he leaned back and surveyed his handiwork. Meghan saw the smoldering look in his eyes and moaned.

He ran a hand up her leg from knee to the inner thigh, pushed aside the panties again, and thrust two fingers deep inside her. She'd gasped into the gag and quivered. *Holy fuck.*

This time when he withdrew, his fingers glistened with her arousal.

"Much better," he grunted, then got an inch of her face and made a show of licking his fingers clean. "I taste your excitement," he murmured quietly. "And your fear."

He drove them out into the desert after making her lay on her side in the front seat. With her hands and feet tied, all she could do was flop over, exposing her backside in the process. Alex chuckled and lifted her dress even further so basically her ass was lying there on the seat right next to his thigh. Something he took advantage of during the bumpy drive.

She wasn't all that surprised to see where they ended up. It was their special place updated with a wooden bench and a beautiful pergola—both handcrafted by Draegyn. They were out in the open—yes. But had total control. No one could come upon them without them knowing it and having plenty of warning. The perfect place to ravish someone who'd been kidnapped. Lord. It couldn't get any better than this. Could it?

Oh, hell yeah, it could!

With the kidnap accomplished, it was time to move on to the fucked mercilessly part of Alex's bargain.

Hauling Meghan from the cab of the truck like a sack of potatoes, she grunted when he tossed her over his shoulder, walked her to a pile of spread out blankets, and dropped her on unsteady feet. He ripped the tape off her ankles and hands but left the gag in place.

Like a champion rodeo roper, he stripped the dress off her in one smooth motion then spun her around and pulled her wrists together in the small of her back. Leaning close, she felt his breath and trembled at his menacing growl.

"It excites me when you're helpless."

Oh shit. The trembling became a full-body quiver. He meant business by wanting her hands behind her back. It always frightened her a little. The total surrender. He knew it challenged Meghan and would back off in an instant if she hesitated, but she wanted to let this scene play out the way he saw it in his head. She trusted him to take care of her, and he'd never once orchestrated anything that came even remotely close to making her truly afraid.

He gave her a chance to deny him, but when she didn't move, he quickly bound her wrists together.

Leaving her standing half-naked in just a bra and panties, her hands bound behind her back, a gag in place, her hair all over the place—he casually went and sat on the bench, arms spread wide across the back and enjoyed the view she made.

And while he watched her, she watched him just as intently. He was, simply put, the most magnificent specimen of masculinity she'd ever seen. The shadows from the pergola danced on his skin, his massive muscular chest rising and falling with each breath. Was bad enough that the gag made her drool, but looking at him sitting there eyeing her up, deciding how he planned to fuck her, well, it made her mouth water even more.

She glanced down to his lap and froze. An ominous bulge was forming and growing right before her eyes.

"That's right," he snickered when he saw where she was looking. "All of that's going to be inside you. Every hard, thick inch."

The whimper she let out wasn't play-acting.

"Come here," he demanded. She took several hesitant steps forward and stopped at his knees. Reaching for her bra, he yanked the stretchy lace cups down and exposed her breasts. He'd even chosen her underwear well. With the fabric shoved beneath her mounds, it acted as a sort of naughty truss for her tits, framing and cradling them perfectly for his pleasure. Her nipples puckered as excitement rushed through her. He noticed and immediately latched onto one and sucked hard. Until her knees trembled. Repeating the greedy suckle on the other side, Meghan struggled to stay on her feet.

Releasing her nipples, he swept the panties down her legs and hung them on the corner of the bench. A stark reminder about the rest of Alex's plan. How after he was finished with her, she would put those pitiful panties on and go about the rest of her day as their shared arousal leaked from her body.

He looked at her mound and smirked. Putting a hand on her hip, he drew her further forward until her legs opened on either side of a knee. Holding her firmly with one hand, he looked her straight in the eye and began fingering her.

"Priming the pussy," he leered as his fingers went deep. "Getting you ready to come all over my cock."

He knew just how to arouse her and used that knowledge with ruthless efficiency. When an orgasm began building, he calmly withdrew and snickered.

"Let me up," he demanded. Meghan stepped back as her sexy giant rose from the bench and started to undress. When he was completely naked, he grabbed hold of his proud cock and stroked it. The gag in her mouth barely absorbed the groan she couldn't help. *Fuck.* She never failed to be completely and utterly mesmerized whenever she watched him handle his impressive sex.

"This won't be pretty, my love. I've had days to think about fucking you and for what I have planned you need to keep up."

He moved in closer and aggressively thrust his fingers inside her again. "But you won't last if I don't let that greedy pussy come," he told her, his eyes locked on hers.

He grabbed her arm and let go of her mound, yanking her toward the bench. Sitting, he adjusted his body then pulled her into position with her back to his chest. Keeping a hand wrapped around her bound wrists, he pulled her down until she felt the fat head of his cock at her opening.

"You will fuck. *Now,*" he demanded and forcefully impaled her with his entire length.

She screamed into the gag and squeezed her eyes shut. Holy shit. In this position, he had her at an angle that made her toes curl. The exquisite sensation of being filled completely made wet heat gush along his staff.

He lunged upward, and she saw actual stars as indescribable pleasure ripped through her.

"I said—*fuck.* Do it now! And fuck hard. I want your pussy to explode when you come. Drench me, woman. Now!"

If it weren't for his strong grip on her wrists and the way he'd banded his arm about her middle, Meghan wouldn't have been able to go as wild as she did. Pounding on him, her legs spread on either side of his, she rode his cock, writhing and undulating in a frenzy of need.

He laughed and bit her shoulder when her pussy tightened. "You fuck good, woman."

It didn't take long. *Oh, god.* She'd needed to come. Senses on overload, she grunted into the gag and shook from head to toe when her inner muscles starting contracting wildly. This wild release felt like no other.

"Good girl," he cried huskily as her pussy throbbed. "You come so hard. I'm going to enjoy fucking you until my balls are drained."

Before the last pulses from her orgasm died away, he lifted her off and grunted, forcefully pushing her to her knees with her ass in the air.

"Again," he commanded and entered her with a ferocious lunge.

In their special spot, alone in the desert, her sexy, alpha Major was imbued with lust-fueled superpowers—subjecting her to every imaginable ravishment, pounding her till she actually cried for mercy. Licking her until, overcome with emotion, she cried.

He'd taken her from behind. She'd ridden him with abandon as he growled and played with her bouncing tits. When he'd pounded into her while standing with one of her feet up on the bench seat for leverage, she'd screamed in ecstasy. Finally, when she was barely able to function, they'd been chest-to-chest on the soft blanket, her legs resting on his shoulders, gag discarded and ropes undone, as he literally fucked her into complete submission. Sure, there was nothing left, but her alpha Major had one last surprise. Something she still needed time to process. When he was finally finished, she'd come so many times—had been pleasured and given so much pleasure—that she was completely spent.

With her in a post-orgasmic trance, he dressed her afterward, like he'd said he would. Pulling the teal panties into place, Alex gently cupped her mound and kissed that spot low on her belly just where the auburn curls of her womanhood began.

"You smell so good after we make love," he told her with shining eyes.

That right there was why she adored him. He'd done just as he promised. Kidnapped her. Fucked her without mercy and then palmed her aching mound at the last making sure her panties got soaked. Calling what they did making love was a reminder that everything they did, no matter how free-spirited or wicked, began and ended with love. All that for just ten points? She wasn't entirely sure, but Meghan certainly believed she'd gotten the best part of that bargain.

Chapter Twenty

They'd checked in at L'Auberge and were settling in when Meghan texted.

Can you come to my cottage in 10 min?

Sure. What's up? she replied.

Making dinner plans and confirming appts for tomorrow

Understood. I'll bring my computer.

Tossing her phone aside, Angie twirled in a circle like a kid, and took in the spinning room. My goodness! This place was seriously awesome. From the humongous wood framed bed to the crackling of the fire in the stone hearth. And the splendid creekside view made her feel like she was in her own little corner of nature.

Thirty seconds after coming through the door, she'd been perusing the list of treatments available and all but salivating at what was offered. In all honesty, there was so much going on at the spa that she didn't know where to start.

But it wasn't all about her—this was really Meghan's weekend. When Alex had told her about the surprise getaway, she'd gotten the distinct impression that Red was having a hard time and her brother wasn't the type to sit back and do nothing if she was out of sorts.

Gathering her laptop and a binder full of notes, swatches, and scraps of paper, Angie set them by the door and went to freshen up. She had a ton of wedding things to show Meghan and one particular surprise she couldn't wait to share. Hopefully, the relaxed atmosphere and some serious pampering would help bring the bride back from the edge.

The walk between their cottages was short—too short. She would have liked to keep on walking, listening to the nearby creek, and breathing in the beauty. *Mental note to self,* she thought. *Early morning stroll.*

Tapping on the cottage door, she nudged it open with her hip and called out, "Hey, Red! Here I am—wearing my wedding planner hat. Get out here!"

Meghan came around a corner looking completely flustered. "Shit, Angie. Parker's coming and I can't see him like this!" She was waving her hands indicating something, but Ang didn't have a clue what. "I have to take a shower. Right now. You'll have to deal with him, okay?"

"Meghan, hon. You look fine. Settle down. What's really going on?"

The frazzled redhead looked at Angie wildly for a moment and then burst out laughing. She covered her face for a second as loud snorting giggles ripped from her mouth.

"Oh, my god!" she choked out between wheezing laughs. "I can't even!"

Angie started to laugh, too. Uncontrollable giggle fits had a way of becoming contagious.

"Blame your damn brother," Meghan hooted.

"Does this have anything to do with the rather fresh set of bite marks on your neck?"

"What?" Meghan screeched, her hand quickly covering her neck. "Oh please, tell me he didn't!"

Angie bent over and grabbed at her stomach as great guffaws of hilarity filled the air.

"Go clean up, Irish," she finally managed to get out between hiccupping giggles and wiping the tears from her eyes. "I'll handle the lawyer with the shitty timing."

"You sure you don't mind? I'm sorry Angie, but there was no way we were going to be able to sashay in and out of Sedona without Parker making an appearance. Alex would murder the guy if he didn't step up while we're away from the Villa!"

"I know, I know, and don't worry. Go take a bath and relax. I've got this."

Ten minutes later, she regretted the pretense of acting like she was in control. She also regretted her wardrobe choice. Looking more like the clothing of a teenager than a grown woman, her black skirt was too short and the oversized sweater with a long scarf wrapped several times around her neck, made her look dumpy. She'd been dressed for a car trip, not a date. The black tights and comfy ankle boots she wore completed an outfit that made her look like she should be carded at the bar.

Angie paced back and forth, waiting for their guest to show up, wishing Meghan would somehow take the shortest shower in history and get the hell out here. Counting on Parker's impromptu visit being a quick courtesy call, she decided to play it cool when he arrived—like him being there was no big deal. She'd be pleasant and civil. Say all the right things and play the hostess till Meghan reappeared.

Simple was always best. No need to overreact just because there was that little matter of his fingers in her pussy the last time he'd seen her.

Uh, yeah right.

"Knock, knock," a deep voice called out. "Stressed out bride in da house?" The screen door opened and the cottage door flung wider as Parker stepped into the bungalow. Damn, but he really was big. Like *big,* big. And it wasn't an optical illusion. He took up the entire doorway.

The awareness his arrival triggered freaked her out. Nervously pulling on the sleeves of the sweater, she twisted her fingers together as playing it cool was no longer an option.

A devastating smile appeared beneath a pair of dark sunglasses that obscured his eyes from view. *Er, crap.* When he smiled like that she forgot her name.

"Oh, hey Angel." He chuckled with mild surprise as he removed the glasses. "Didn't expect to find you here."

"Um . . . Meghan's taking a shower," she mumbled. Oh, my god! What the hell was wrong with her? No hello? No calm, cool disinterest that he was there?

Turning away as if she wasn't even there, he headed for the welcome basket and dug through it. "Any chocolate lurking in there or did you already snag it?"

"What?" she barked. "No! Of course, not. That's Meghan's basket."

Seriously. What the fuck was wrong with her? He was just being Parker. Teasing her about stealing sweets. She should have laughed off the comment instead of reacting like he'd accused her grand theft.

"Whatever," he replied with a dismissive shrug. Tuning her out, he dropped into an easy chair, reached for the remote control to the TV, and started channel surfing while Angie stood there gaping at him. He was acting like she was of no more interest to him than a commercial about Pampers.

With a news program set to mute, he glanced nonchalantly around the cottage. "What's all that shit?" he asked, nodding to her overflowing binder. "You still carry a slam book?" The snicker accompanying the sarcastic jest was like fingernails on a chalkboard.

A slam book? Really? Was there some reason why he was treating her like she was ten?

Maybe because that's how you're acting, you stupid shit, her inner voice scolded.

Glancing down, she saw her fingers clutching the ends of her sleeves until the fabric almost covered her hands. Standing there in the huge sweater and short skirt, Angie felt like someone playing dress-up with the wrong clothes.

Feeling completely put off and awkward as hell, she unwound the scarf from around her neck and pointed at the notebook with the wide Velcro flap stammering, "Um, wedding stuff."

"Oh?" He considered the sloppy binder for a moment and said, "Let's see then. Show me what you got, Angel."

His devilish smirk cut through her nervousness. Say wha*aat?* Arching an eyebrow, she crossed her arms and cocked a hip, trying very hard to make it seem like she was looking down her nose at him.

"Fat chance of that, counselor. I *could* show you, but then I'd have to, uh . . . hurt you. Very top secret stuff."

He grinned and tossed the remote aside. When she shifted away, he reached behind her and grabbed the binder with a theatrical laugh.

He chuckled. "Better luck next time." When she tried to grab it back, he swatted her hands away and said, "*Uh-uh-uh.* Best man's prerogative!"

"There's no such thing!" she shrieked, the arms of her baggy sweater flapping like batwings.

He ripped at the Velcro and the book fell open to a section loaded with pictures and clippings. He looked at the unorganized mess for a minute then gave an appreciative whistle and drawled, "Whoa." Looking at her with wide, surprised eyes, he added, "Is that what I think it is?"

"Shh! It's still a surprise," Angie squawked in alarm, looking over her shoulder to make sure Meghan wasn't around.

Parker nodded briefly, watching impassively as she snatched the binder away from him and rather dramatically shut it.

"Hell of a surprise."

His voice gave nothing away, but she had the distinct feeling he was impressed with the tiny view he stole of Alex's upcoming wedding.

"Meghan will love it," she defended.

He chuckled. "Hell, baby girl, I love it."

Oh. He loves it? Sweet tingles of excitement took hold of her. "Really?"

"Yeah. And you're right. Irish will, too."

Hiding her flustered expression, Angie lowered her head and let some hair fall around her face. She didn't want him to know how pleased she was by his reaction.

From the moment she'd taken over the wedding plans, Meghan easily approved every suggestion and had actually brought very little to the table beyond her insistence that the event be dignified. The spiritual aspect held more significance than the romance, and despite the fact that she could afford to have Elton John sing at the reception if that was what she wanted, she was far more interested in the actual ceremony than the party afterward. Made being the planner a walk in the park.

So, with the help of Meghan's hilariously kickass mother, Angie had come up with a wow factor that was going to blow the former teacher's mind, which in turn would make Alex a very happy man. Win-win.

After a long minute of silence, he looked at her sideways and winked with a grin. "Fuck me, Angel! That's some impressive shit. Hell, honey—you can plan my wedding if that's the kind of ideas you have."

You know what? She wasn't a kid anymore and she wasn't stupid. He was totally fucking with her and having a good time doing it. Ignoring her? And then saying, *Fuck me? Plan my wedding?* Unbelievable, this guy. Would kicking him in the shins be overkill?

Angie couldn't help herself. She glared at him. The other night he was all like, *can't we be friends* and then the embarrassing make-out in public catastrophe at Pete's only to turn up here wearing a general air of dismissal. And now he was going to dive-bomb her with a precision attack of very specific innuendos intended to get a reaction. Was he kidding?

Meghan chose that moment to awkwardly bustle into the room after flinging open the bedroom door like she was leading a SWAT team attack and then kind of stumbled to a halt.

"Oh my god, Parker! Thanks for hanging out while I freshened up."

Parker jumped to his feet the moment Meghan appeared and went straight to her for a big hug.

"Dammit, Irish." He chuckled. "You get more beautiful every day. Are you sure I can't steal you away from the Major's moldy ass? Y'know . . . it's not too late . . ."

"Shut up, counselor." Meghan giggled as she pushed him away.

Angie was not at all happy to hear Parker tease the other woman about running off with him. It was a jest, of course, but the minute she heard the words, a reflex of possessiveness shot through her. *Excuse me, universe,* she griped. *Was that really necessary?*

Parker suddenly groaned like he'd been shot and clutched at his chest with a great deal of dramatic flair.

"Fuck," he ground out. "You're killing me here, Irish. You know the bro code requires me to report that you used the prohibited *shut up* expression."

Meghan straightened, her expression stern. "Oh. My. *GOD!*" she growled. "And what would you know about that, Mr. Sullivan? Was it in that damn prenup?"

"Uh . . . hang on," Angie croaked, one hand bouncing atop the fingers of her other hand as she made the timeout motion. "Prenup? Bro code?" she asked, her eyes darting toward Parker who was standing there with an amused expression. "What am I missing?"

After a barely disguised humorous wink, Meghan raised one eyebrow at her and grumbled, "Your brother has control issues."

Control issues? She almost snorted out loud. Damn straight, he had control issues. Alex didn't have what you would call a laid-back attitude.

"Mmmm," she wondered out loud. "Would this have anything to do with what we were talking about? Y'know," she half-shrugged, "all that nonsense about demerits."

Meghan didn't laugh, but she did crinkle her nose and slightly nod. Really? Well, shit! This could be fun.

Giving Red a heavy look, she playfully pushed Parker into an easy chair and hovered over him. Meghan also closed in and stood there, arms crossed, with a barely contained smile.

Chapter Twenty-One

CHUCKLING WHEN ANGIE GAVE HIM a good shove, Parker sank into an overstuffed chair and took in the women bearing down on him like two detectives choreographing an interrogation. He wondered briefly which one would play good cop and who would be the bad one.

Both women crowded close, pinning him in place. He put his arms along the sides of the chair and dug in. Whoa. Tag teamed. Fucking awesome.

"Now you know," Angie simpered with an outrageously flirty growl, "bro code notwithstanding . . ." The look of smug triumph she flashed turned his sex to stone. Heavy stone. "There's another code that trumps the bro."

He arched an eyebrow and totally got off on watching her flawless performance. Little witch! He loved that she openly taunted him. *Hey, what the fuck,* he figured. She'd earned the right after how he'd mishandled her the last time they were in the same room. And besides, how bad could a penance be that gave a guy a hard-on in record time?

Angie looked at Meghan as the two women bobbed their heads in sisterly unison. Slamming her hands upon her hips, she moved in for the verbal kill. God. He loved being a lawyer. Knowing how to read body language and lay out a case gave him an advantage, but with Angie, it helped him to stay on his toes because she was a full serving and then some, even when she was being quiet.

"Nothing comes before a little sister's right to snitch. I believe that's called . . . um, what's it called, Meghan? You've got brothers. You know what I'm talking about."

Irish smirked and gave him some minor stink eye. "I believe it's called the Nanny Nanny Boo Boo Clause."

Oh fuck! Parker started hooting with laughter. He wasn't quite sure where they were headed with this, but it was amusing as all hell.

Angie got right up in his face so fast that he flinched and quickly sat back.

"You won't be laughing, counselor, after I tell my big, bad, overprotective brother that you were taking liberties with his woman. Suggesting she ditch him for you, Parker?" She made some disgruntled sounds and rolled her eyes at him.

Uhhhhh . . . what the fuck?

He looked away from Angie's self-satisfied smirk and found Meghan quietly snickering. Why the hell didn't women run the world? Someone needed to explain that to him because in record time they had shut him down. It was pretty goddamn funny as far as Parker was concerned.

Irish muttered, "No one knows better than you do what a fuddy duddy the Major can be."

Not laughing was really, really, REALLY hard. Did she just call her fiancé a fuddy duddy? Absolutely fucking priceless.

"*Ohhh,* you ladies are good!" He chuckled.

"Thought you'd see it our way." Angie snickered, turning for an enthusiastic high five with Meghan.

"Now, wait a minute, wait a minute, wait a minute," he drawled. "Not so fast. I have a counter closing argument."

"So?" Meghan wisecracked. "Is a rebuttal more important than your balls?"

Goddammit, Alex Marquez was one lucky fucking bastard! She could throw down with the best of them!

It was Angie though, who brought the house down with one pithy and very suggestive remark.

"Hold on, hold on. His balls?" she squeaked at Meghan. "I'm afraid I'm going to have to plead for his balls. They may still prove useful."

Apparently, that was the funniest comment *ever* because the two women laughed loudly and ogled him as if he was a designer handbag marked fifty percent off.

"You two are scaring the shit out of me," he mumbled.

Meghan laughed and swatted him on the arm. "Relax, Parker. We're just fucking with you. Go ahead and rat me out to your butt buddy." She snickered. "But then don't be surprised when I get a headache every time the band plays."

Looking at him like she'd just announced he had detention every Friday for the next six weeks, he had to hand it to her. She was in every way that mattered a female version of his best friend. Quick. An edge of sarcasm dripping from every statement. Vulgar as fuck and funnier than a comedy marathon.

He came back with a pithily stated, "Not so fast, Irish. This is where we negotiate. A plea bargain."

She rolled her eyes and snorted. "Did you hear that, Ang? He wants to bargain!"

Angie had taken up a spot near the open doorway. In the soft light of early evening, she looked positively angelic. She was still mostly avoiding his eyes, but he was okay with that. Pretty soon he'd have her undivided attention.

"Sheesh," she muttered with a brisk shake of her head. Fiddling with her long braid, she half-smiled at Meghan. "What is it with the demerits and the bargaining? Guess Victoria is on to something, huh?"

Uh, yeah. Whatever. Girl speak. Women talk. He didn't stop to try and decipher what they were jabbering about. He was already on to other things. Shit. He had a plan to put into action!

With a heavy dose of lawyerly gravitas he spelled it out. "I will meet your forbidden *shut up* plus ignore the imaginary groping you made up in your mind in exchange for . . ."

He crooked his finger to draw Meghan near enough for a whisper. Ever game to play along, she grinned and dutifully leaned in close.

"This better be good," she whispered with a soft giggle.

Swiftly assessing that Angie was out of earshot, he whispered back, "Thunder Foot gave me permission. I want to take Angie out so we can talk. *Alone.*"

She nodded imperceptibly then straightened with a shocked gasp and smacked him on the shoulder. "No, I will not give you a pair of my panties!" she screeched. Looking at him with theatrical horror, Meghan clutched at her throat like an outraged innocent being propositioned for the first time.

Next, she whirled to Angie and let loose. "He wants to play with my underwear! Can you believe it? That makes him a pervert, right?"

Parker was stunned by Meghan's insane outburst. Frozen with shock, he couldn't move or react. This was surreal.

Upon hearing Meghan's screech, Angie bolted from the doorway with a look of utter horror on her face. White as a sheet, she moved her mouth but no words came out.

Dead silence could be really, painfully loud. After a long minute, Meghan sighed heavily and looked back and forth between him and an open mouthed, gaping Angie.

"Okay," she snapped. "What the hell is wrong with you two? C'mon, guys. That was funny as shit. Tori and Lacey would be peeing themselves if they were here. But you two?"

She turned to Angie and said, "You look like someone just ran over your dog."

To Parker, she said, "And you? You're the biggest surprise of all. If you start crying, big guy, I'm throwing you out."

"Oh, my god," Angie mumbled in a choked voice. "You were kidding?"

"Of course, I was kidding," Meghan jeered. "Well, not about the pervert part. I don't know for sure, but I'm pretty certain he's a complete perved-out freak."

Parker glared at Meghan. *Oooh.* He was *sooo* getting her back for whatever she was up to.

"But I thought you'd laugh at the underwear thing. I mean, I thought you both would. But instead you each reacted so . . . strangely."

More silence. Fuck. Parker wasn't capable of anything right then except remembering to breathe. Yeah—that he was doing.

Meghan went and put an arm around Angie for a brief hug, before rubbing between her shoulder blades. "Honey, I know we're not sisters yet, but I feel like we already are. I'm not blind. There's something going on here with you two. I care about both of you," she said as she looked at him.

"Meghan," Angie whispered.

"Nope. Sorry. Alex wants you two to settle up. Can't make it any plainer than that. Whatever this is, you guys have to figure it the hell out."

Parker wanted to hug Meghan for what she was doing. He envied his old friend, for Alex had found someone who was truly his equal and so eerily compatible that it made him pause. Big Daddy really had found his Lady Mama. As a team, they would be invincible.

He stood up slowly and gathered his thoughts along with his voice. Angie was looking everywhere but in his direction while Meghan was encouraging him with her expressive eyes.

At Angie's homecoming, he'd been so overwhelmed and desperate that he was willing and had even tried to take full measure of the blame for what happened and goddamn beg for her forgiveness. She'd thrown it back in his face so he was done with that shit.

Yeah, so maybe he was still overwhelmed and desperate, but he was done playing the wimp. Screw that. They moved forward on his terms. Taking the initiative, he rather gruffly spoke while sliding his hands into his pants pockets.

"It's well past time we talked, don't you agree, Angelina?"

Challenge served.

Her sapphire hued gaze swung his way slowly.

"It's how you make your living, after all," she commented in a flat voice.

Challenge accepted.

He was going to let her have that one. Was easier than the exhausting back and forth that would fire up if he played her game where every question was met with snark. She was trapped. They both knew it. No need to beat it to death. Nobody ever won in those cases.

"Meghan," he said. "What's your dinner plan?" Parker didn't doubt for a nanosecond that she'd have an answer—and a good one—at the ready.

"Well, the Major is having dinner at the cabin so I'll be video chatting with Cam, Lacey, and Dylan, too. They're taking care of Alex for me while I'm occupado. I was going to do room service for something light and then spend the evening with my family through the wonder of technology!"

He hoped that she understood the light of thanks shining in his eyes.

No flowery words. No hemming and hawing. No jumping through any hoops. Just put it out there. *This is who you are,* he thought. *Don't even bother to fuck around.*

"That makes it simple then," he said. "So, dinner it is, Miss Marquez. Grab your purse and let's go. I know the perfect place."

She frowned, sputtered, squeaked, and twisted her fingers. Angelina Marquez at a complete loss for words. *Wow.* Under different circumstances, her reaction would have been amusing.

Before he knew it, Meghan had shoved Angie's purse into her hands and pushed them out the door. During the walk to his car, they'd been silent. Him—on purpose. Her—he wasn't sure why. The only sound was the low thud of her boots on the pavement and an occasional heavy breath.

At the car, she hesitated when he opened the passenger door to his kickass Porsche. Since it wasn't suited for off-road desert adventures, the only time he drove the high-end luxury car was when he was in town. He'd deliberately brought it tonight.

Was he being an arrogant shithead by showing off his shiny toy? Yes. Yes, he was. He was a guy, after all. A guy who worked fucking hard and earned himself a motherfucking Porsche. And right now, he wanted Angie's hot little Spanish ass in his sexy car.

Ignoring the hesitation, he instructed her, "Get in," as he held the door open and motioned for her to get moving.

It was funny on some level—the way she obediently responded—because it was so unlike her. Then again, it was also kind of hot as hell, too. Was it just him that affected her that way? Just by not taking any more of her crap and reasserting that he actually did wear the fucking pants, she'd stopped being a petulant child. Conscious of the signals he was getting, he was making quick, on his feet, tactical decisions.

When she was seated and had dropped her purse between her feet, he took hold of the seat belt before she could and set about buckling her in. It was a simple power play. One that he rather enjoyed as he pulled the strap across her chest and adjusted it accordingly. Snapping the buckle, he ran his fingers beneath the strap to ensure her comfort and managed to stroke his fingers across her breasts along the way.

She was panting slightly when he'd finished. Satisfied with the way the harness crossed her body, he took a second to enjoy that he was finally able to discern her shape beneath the butt-fugly sweater. Thank god for seatbelts.

Chapter Twenty-Two

SOMEHOW, AND SHE REALLY WASN'T sure how, Angie had been railroaded into having dinner with Parker. And going out with him meant she was currently hyperventilating inside his very flashy Porsche as he drove them to god knows where.

What was it that was so scintillating about watching a man handle a fast car? Was it the visual of his hands gripping the steering wheel and manipulating the gear shift? Maybe watching his thighs tense as his feet moved on the pedals. Perhaps the intense focus and concentration. Parker hit all those notes.

Big hands. Rugged thighs. Steely focus. Angie shivered and just barely cut off a telltale moan before she gave herself away.

Say something, you dolt! her inner voice snapped. *Don't just sit there. You're a grown woman. Act like one!*

"Um . . ." She had to clear her throat to continue. "I'm not really dressed for anything too nice."

When the car idled at a stoplight, he looked over at her. It had grown dark so all she had to help her see his face was the light from the dashboard. He had a pensive frown on his face. What was he thinking?

"You look fine," he grunted.

The light turned green, and he accelerated the car; his attention back on driving. So much for dazzling him with her wit, beauty, and charm.

Oh, for heaven's sake! Really? Dazzle him? When in bloody hell had she gone from wanting to rip him a new one to wanting to captivate his attention?

They drove for a few more minutes in uncomfortable silence. Ready to leap from the car at the first opportunity, she was relieved when a valet approached her door as the car slowed in front of a restaurant with a candy apple red awning. Not waiting for her companion, she struggled awkwardly to climb from the low car in her tiny skirt, silently cursing at the indignity.

Parker came around the car and tossed his keys to the valet. "Park it in the owner's section," he instructed the bow-tied young man. "The name is Sullivan. Gus will give the okay."

"What is this place?" she asked while straining to see the name above the awning as he bustled her toward the door. "You know the owner?"

"Yeah. A neighbor of mine, actually. Gus Foster. Great guy."

Ushering her through the door, he walked them straight to the hostess stand where a young woman met them with a broad smile.

"Welcome to Fon Do Me," she said. "Do you have a reservation?"

The Sullivan charm oozed so thick when he answered, Angie practically picked her feet up to avoid getting stuck in the goo.

"No reservation needed, darlin'," he drawled. "Permanent guest list. Family table. The name is Sullivan."

She tapped on a screen a few times then smiled and nodded. "Here you are, Mr. Sullivan," she observed, as she swiped and scrolled a few more times.

"You're in luck tonight," she told them. "The alcove table is empty this evening, sir, and you've come at the perfect time. The chef has a fabulous new hot pot in tonight's specials."

Nodding his approval, Parker motioned to the hostess. "Lead the way," he said as she picked up two leather bound menus and showed them to their table.

Parker held her arm and whispered close to her ear. "You'll like this, Angel. Get ready to be amazed."

Did he realize that dealing with him was like skipping puddles in the rain? One second, he was dismissive and she wanted to step around him and hide. The next, he was Mr. Friendly, making her long for a chance to jump wildly into the center of the deepest puddle just for the sheer hell of it.

The hostess placed them in what ended up being a very private, very cozy alcove with plush, curved seating and low lighting. Behind the banquette, arranged in an art niche, were a collection of ornate empty frames and a deep hurricane illuminated with a flickering candle.

It was all so charming and romantic. Angie sighed, wishing she were there in a killer outfit wearing fuck-me-till-I-scream shoes and under completely different circumstances.

After leaving them with their menus, which she noted Parker took control of, the hostess scurried away and Angie finally found her voice.

"Is this place seriously called Fon *Do Me?*"

He laughed and shot her a good-humored smirk. "Yeah. Clever play on words, huh?"

She had to admit that yeah, it really was! Boy. Would she ever love to do a PR event for a unique business like this. A cascade of random ideas sprang to mind. Do Wop sing-along nights. Do and Brew featuring local craft beers. Little Dipper tastings for kids. The possibilities were endless.

He tapped her lightly on the nose and chuckled. "Your face just lit up and you got this faraway look in your eyes."

"Sorry. Occupational hazard," she quipped. Angie shrugged her shoulders and smiled as she dropped a cloth napkin in her lap.

"You as an event coordinator. Didn't see that one coming, Angel." Parker smiled warmly at her. "My folks still rave about the celebratory event when your label topped several wine festival rankings. You did the family proud."

She felt herself warming as his approval seeped into her bones. Angie was damn proud of the work she did. No, it wasn't exactly what she'd gone to school and trained for, but over time, the idea of pursuing something diplomatic in the Foreign Service died a slow, agonizing death. Her decision to follow Sophie and their parents to Spain altered her career path, and instead of international relations for the government, she did it for the vineyard.

Having a hand in continuing her family's legacy was deeply personal to Angie. It wasn't easy; there were hundreds of vineyards and wineries competing with them. Each success wasn't a stopping place—only a stopover to the next challenge. Hearing him say that he was aware of her accomplishments was an emotional watershed moment for her.

A waiter discreetly approached and introduced himself. Parker took immediate control of the situation as he issued orders, asked questions, and never once requested her input. Who the hell made him king?

"I ordered a bit of everything," he told her when they were alone again. "The chef will go all out because I played the owner's privilege card."

He seemed amused by the situation and winked at her. "Friends in high places, you know?"

So much was going on inside Angie that she honestly wondered if she was about to jump out of her skin. His lighthearted wink was almost the end of her control. The whole vibe he was putting off had her tied up in knots.

While in his very impressive car, she had to fight back the urge to explode like a hyperactive toddler—touching everything, pushing buttons, and adjusting dials. She'd squirmed in the contoured seat, dug her fingers into the decadent soft leather, and purred. This guy played with the big kids now.

Apologetic and on-his-knees Parker was gone and in his place was a serious grown-up who was challenging her on her shit. Ballsy move but, rather like Meghan playing the big brother Alex frowny card, also probably unavoidable.

But acting like an adult around him wasn't easy, due entirely to Parker's smoking hot body and that *oh-so-familiar* suck-my-dick attitude. She was at a disadvantage—didn't have any clue what to expect next, was dressed like a slob, and had given up on trying to get out ahead of whatever was going on.

He was staring at her quite intently. Instead of sliding into the deep curve of the plush banquette to sit closer, Angie had stayed across from him. She could feel the heat radiating off his big body beneath the small cloth-covered table between them. Afraid to move in case she accidentally bumped or nudged him, she actually slid her fingers under her thighs to keep them still.

Parker leaned slightly and put his forearm out on the table, his hand loosely fisted. She stared at his hefty, masculine hand with less than a foot separating her from his touch. His hand rolled palm up, fingers extended as he captured her eyes with his. Expectation hung in the air as he waited. The invitation was clear. He wanted her to give him her hand. Even set it up so it looked like her decision, but make no mistake about it, his expression told her that he fully expected her surrender.

Eyes narrowed, she hissed at him and ungraciously put her hand quite reluctantly into his grasp. "Dammit," she mumbled.

He sat forward, both elbows on the table now as he scooted close and took her hand in both of his. Turning it over, he slowly swept their palms together, then with one hand holding hers, used the forefinger of his free hand to brush her open palm.

Angie shivered—it was an unexpected, full-body shiver—and it wasn't because she was sitting too close to the air conditioning vent.

His light touch against her palm and across the sensitive skin on her exposed wrist made her squirm. Damn. She wished she were wearing something sleeveless instead of a granny sweater because his teasing caresses feathering up her arm would have melted her completely, making her the fondue on the menu.

When his fingers slid against her wrist, she was sure he could tell how quickly her heart was pounding.

"I'm a lawyer," he drawled in his sexiest, growly voice. "I don't do 'he said, she said' cases. They're counterproductive and waste a lot of energy."

He was talking about them. Angie held her breath. She wasn't aware that she had until he squeezed her hand and murmured, "Breathe, Angel." Her chest heaved with the effort.

"Look at me," he demanded.

What? Look at him? Okay. He was beautiful, after all.

He lifted her hand briefly to his lips for a gentle kiss upon her knuckles and said, "I don't think you're a nuisance, and I never did. The crush you had barely equaled the fantasies I had for you and believe me when I tell you, no one is more thankful than I am that you aren't my sister."

Angie gasped. Twice. What the hell? He'd unexpectedly just owned, in his own unique way, every single awful reason their relationship imploded. Having all the wind taken out of her sails meant continuing to be pissed off just became a moot point.

"We used to be friends once. Good friends," he teased with a sly smile. "There's no reason why we can't try again. To be friends, I mean."

He seemed so sincere. His warm brown eyes and unwavering gaze as he held her hand were making butterflies do an aerial show in her stomach.

Here, at last, was her opportunity to have her say. Spout something grown-up sounding and profound. Maybe recover a smidge of her dignity. It would be helpful if they could, at the very least, level the field and stow the past. Move forward. As friends.

Gathering what she wanted to say, Angie sat back in awkward silence when Parker suddenly released her hand and quipped, "Well, good. That's settled then. And just in time, too. Here comes our dinner."

Her mouth fell open. No, seriously. Completely slack-jawed. Was this guy kidding? Angie's brows bumped together in a telling scowl. That was it? He got to play the mea culpa card and boom! What? All better now? Was she invisible or something?

She sat there and stewed as the wait staff piled food and fondue equipment on their table while Parker kept up a running conversation about what was on the menu. Judging by the endless plates and dipping options, the only thing missing was the actual kitchen sink.

It took so long to get everything laid out and explained that she was positively squirmy and sputtering by the time they were alone again.

Holding up her hand in the customary *talk to it* gesture, she snapped, "Was that some kind of lawyer speak 'cause that shit may fly in the courtroom, but it most certainly won't move me."

He arched an eyebrow at her outburst and sat back heavily. Staring at her. Damn him. Was that a flash of amusement she just saw flit across his face?

She was on a roll and couldn't very well back down now that she'd started.

"Didn't you tell me once that *Say Sorry and Move On* was the first thing you learned in Jury 101?"

His amusement was a full-on grin now.

She kept going. "You're sorry? Let's be friends? Time to eat?"

"No?" he sniggered on a strained cough. He shrugged and crossed his arms. "Okay. What's it going to be then? A lecture or an inquisition?"

Angie was startled by how quickly she answered. And her answer? Pure reflex.

"Just tell me why. Why did you hang out with me? Let me think that we . . . um, I mean . . . let me think I was special? Why'd you do it Parker?"

"Fair enough, Angel," he responded soberly.

She nodded but said nothing and waited.

"What you heard that day was me being an idiot. I spoke before thinking my words through. One of my co-workers was giving me shit about seeing us together all the time. His head was in the fucking gutter, and I couldn't let him think like that about you. So, I said the first thing that came to mind. Something that would instantly squash whatever rumors were going around and also make the guy feel like a perverted piece of shit for having dirty thoughts about a kid. Did I handle things badly?" He grunted. "Yes, yes, and yes."

If silence was precious, they needed an armored truck to accommodate the priceless quiet that hung around them.

His explanation made sense. Dammit. But she noticed that while he gave a straightforward accounting of what had gone down to start all this, he did not elaborate on the finer points of her question. The part about hanging out with her and letting Angie believe that she was special.

Had it just been sex after all? Older man. Younger, innocent girl. Was that all it was ever meant to be?

Chapter Twenty-Three

PARKER KNEW WHEN HIS INSTINCTS were right. It was something he could feel; a useful ability for anyone who had to think quickly on his feet. But he wasn't going to get involved in a postmortem that would get them nowhere. He was all about moving the ball downfield. The *I'm Sorry* portion of the campaign was in the can. Now he wanted to start advancing on the future instead of replaying the past.

She wasn't the twenty-year-old he remembered, and she'd certainly matured into a savvy businesswoman, but none of that changed the fact that what he told Alex was true. He was in love with her. Probably always had been. He'd been thinking about it in the shower this morning. Shit, he was always thinking about it, but earlier, it occurred to him that there were so many different kinds of love.

There was love at first sight, which perfectly described Alex and Meghan.

Not to be outdone was second-chance love and lost love.

And then there was the kind of love that was pure destiny. That written in the stars crap. Two souls who are part of the other. Infinite. He figured his fate had probably been sealed the first time he'd ever laid eyes on the chubby bundle of pink and put a grubby little boy's finger into the tiny fist of the baby girl with the shocking sapphire eyes.

He'd been a dumbass. So much time wasted, but he was done with that now. The girl was his. Belonged to him. He was through sweating bullets over past mistakes. Fuck that crap. This was how he rolled.

Once Parker made up his mind about something—that was it. He didn't vacillate or go back and forth. It was part of what had made him a successful attorney. He wasn't swayed by extraneous crap.

The universe had given him another shot at getting this right. Dropping Angie into his lap in a situation that forced them to deal with one another was an opportunity he didn't plan to fuck up. She needed a real man, not that fruit loop she'd been engaged to.

"You're my best friend's sister. I've known you for your whole life, Angel. Our families couldn't be closer if they tried. Were we stupid? Yes," he assured her with a dark look. "But seeing you again, after all this time. . . . well, it made me realize that I've missed you, baby girl."

She stared at him, occasionally blinking but with an otherwise blank expression. He wasn't doing what she expected and knowing that gave him the upper hand. By the time the wedding rolled around, he had planned to have her wrapped up tight. There was no way he was letting Angelina Marquez go back to Spain when her time in the States came to an end.

"And that's it?" she drawled after a tense hesitation.

He almost laughed. She kept trying to flat foot him by acting all bent out of shape that he wasn't taking any of her shit.

"Give it up, Angel baby," he chortled. Reaching for her wrist, he grabbed hold and started pulling her across the banquette, sliding her closer. "Now get that cute ass over here and let's dig in. If you want to keep bitching at me while we eat—then, fine. But you'll be doing it with a full mouth."

He saw her gasp at the intended innuendo and plowed ahead. Keeping her off balance was amusing as shit.

"Have you ever shared a hot pot before?" he asked as he picked up a set of chopsticks and began dropping things into the double-sided pot. "One side is broth and it's hot as balls so be careful and the other side is oil."

She was so predictable, just like the Angie he remembered. Put something new or unique under her nose and she was hooked. He chortled softly when she leaned closer and watched what he dropped into the scalding hot broth.

One time he and Alex had terrorized a very young Angie and her older sister, Sophia, during a Dia de los Muertos charade. Soph had completely lost her shit while he and Alex laughed their asses off. Angie though, young as she was, got over her fright quickly and immediately became all-curious. How had they made those scary noises? Where did the masks come from? Parker was watching her play those emotions out again right in front of him. This was the real girl he knew so well. By putting something unexpected in her way, he'd sidetracked her outrage by stoking her natural curiosity.

"Oooh, can I do that?" she asked nodding at the chopsticks and plate of tantalizing tidbits. "What do you do? Just drop it in?"

He couldn't help the smirk. Damn woman was practically shoving him out of the way. Using a long handled basket utensil, he scooped the lobster chunks from the flavored broth and put them on a plate. When she reached to snatch a bite, he was ready for her, swatting her hand away with a laugh.

"Chill your tits, woman," he drawled.

She sputtered and sat back with an astonished look on her flawlessly beautiful face. "Er, uh . . . excuse me?"

"You heard me," Parker said on the edge of a growl. "This is your first time. Chill."

He paused for good measure and gauged her reaction so far.

"Let me show you how we do it."

Using the chopsticks, he picked up one of the lobster chunks and held it up to her mouth.

The expression on her face was really, really funny. He'd chosen his words carefully to see if she remembered. Well, he chuckled silently. I have an answer to that question! Not only did she remember, her eyes told him that he was on thin ice. *Fuck yeah, this was fun.*

"C'mon," he urged with a cheeky grin that he just couldn't stop. Motioning with the chopsticks to encourage her to take a bite, he said, "Trust me."

He couldn't wait to see what she did. Challenging her so outlandishly was either going to pay off handsomely or get his ass handed back to him. Depended on what she really wanted. If all that was left was anger, she'd push back. And he'd know. But if she let him play this out, well. . . .

She didn't hesitate. Not really. Nor did she surrender. Typical Angie. But she did open her mouth and let him slide the lobster tidbit onto her tongue while staring him down with a mocking glare.

When she bit into the seafood, he quickly snagged the other piece and popped it into his mouth.

"Oh, my god," she groaned. "That is so good." *Unf.*

Hehehe. Score one for the lobster. That shit was so good, it'd make you forget your name. He had her fucking attention now.

Next, he took a few chunks of marinated beef and lowered them into the hot oil using long skewers. She watched everything he did.

And so it went on for the next hour as curiosity kept her entranced and Parker pressed his advantage. In the end, she'd allowed him to feed her. He'd orchestrated every mouthful. Chose each morsel. It was a powerful statement he was making.

Fuck it, he thought. This was who he was. If she couldn't handle it, better they figured that out now because if she was game, he was going to move heaven and fucking Earth to make this work.

By the end of the evening, they'd consumed a surprising amount of food, ending the fondue feast with an assortment of dessert and fruit items, pots of melted chocolate, and thick gooey caramel, as they indulged their mutual affinity for all things sweet.

But the best part? They'd done it as friends. Yeah, he'd pulled a power play by taking control, but they'd talked, a lot. Laughed a little, too. Glimpses of their previous friendship shone through. It was good stuff and had been worth the challenge. Finally, real hope.

As they walked out of the restaurant, Parker thoroughly enjoyed watching her as he brought up the rear, enthralled by her incredibly long legs in the very skimpy skirt. Even dressed down as she was, the woman was hot as shit.

Waiting at the valet stand for his car, he kept a proprietary arm around her waist and balls out stared down another person waiting nearby for a cab who was checking Angie out with a rather obvious leer. The venomous look Parker shot him duly chastened the man who quickly ducked his head and looked away.

Just as he spied his car coming round the bend, Angie flinched at his side and let out an enormous belch that made every eye in the vicinity turn. He couldn't believe a sound that big had come out of such a little thing.

Parker was flabbergasted and watched with barely controlled hilarity as her hands flew to her mouth in embarrassment. All he could see were two startled eyes, wide and mortified, looking at him over her fingers.

Dramatically rolling his eyes as the Porsche pulled alongside them, Parker murmured in a low, mockingly long-suffering voice low that only she would hear, "Can't take you anywhere . . . sheesh!"

Angie was giggling uncontrollably as she flopped like a true klutz onto the passenger seat when he held her door open. She was still giggling as he leaned across her to buckle the seatbelt in place. Taking full advantage, he slid two fingers underneath the belt from shoulder to hip caressing her the whole way. She wasn't laughing by the time he pulled back.

After handsomely tipping the valet, Parker slid behind the wheel of the powerful car and pulled out into traffic only instead of immediately heading back to L'Auberge where Meghan was no doubt waiting to see how they'd fared, he made for an area nearby. Pulling into a parking spot that offered some privacy, he put the car in park and reached for her. Sliding his big hand to the nape of her neck, he tugged her toward him and growled, "If you're wondering if I'm going to kiss you, the answer is yes. So why wait?"

And he kissed her. Gently at first. Sweet sighs mingled with the sound of their smacking lips until her sighs became muted whimpers. And then the kiss turned hot and carnal. His tongue demanded everything, and she answered, shyly. Her bashful response thickened his blood. Before long, she was demanding as much as she was giving. The whole thing was a delicious, intense tasting that was wet, deep, and intoxicating.

Back on the road, Parker was wildly satisfied with the knowledge that regardless of whatever conflict remained in her heart and mind, Angie couldn't subdue her need for him. It was there for him to taste. Yep. This was more than worth fighting for.

After parking in the visitor's section at the hotel, he kissed her again. I mean, what the hell, right? He had a well-known sweet tooth, after all, and nothing was sweeter or more satisfying than the taste of his Spanish Angel. And she melted each time his lips touched hers, so how the hell was he supposed to resist such overwhelming temptation?

When he helped her from the car with a gentle tug, she propelled straight into his chest with a slight thud. Looking down and seeing her dainty hands splayed across his broad chest as she struggled for balance nearly brought Parker to his knees.

He couldn't help himself. Shutting the car door, he trapped her against the Porsche with his body. Panting slightly, she stared up into his face.

"No more running, baby girl. Understand?"

Angie bit her lip and looked away.

"No," he growled. "You will look at me, Angelina. Whatever happens—you don't hide your eyes from me."

He had to give her credit. The fearless girl he knew looked back at him with eyes that never wavered.

"I'm confused, Parker. By everything. You. Me. Being back here again. The way that makes me feel." She shook her head and grimaced. "I'm not running, but that doesn't mean I know what I'm doing."

"Understood."

They walked in silence, holding hands the whole way until they made it to the cottage where he kissed her yet again. Ever the gentleman, he escorted her to the door but declined the invitation to come in and say good night to Meghan. He wanted the last moment they had together to just be the two of them.

"Enjoy tomorrow and make sure you set your brother's credit card on fire, okay?" he snickered.

She smiled sweetly and told him, "I hear they have an awesome mani-pedi for guys. Wanna slide by and get your nails done?"

He laughed and gave her a hearty smack on the behind. "Fuck, no."

Chapter Twenty-Four

"Sooo...?"

Angie chuckled. The door wasn't even completely shut and already the third degree had begun.

"We smoked the peace pipe. There won't be any need for pistols at dawn," she smirked. "What are you watching? Is that John Wayne?"

"Yes, yes, yes." Meghan laughed. She was sitting cross-legged on the floor in front of the fireplace, her back against the sofa, a pillow in her lap, and a bowl of ice cream balanced precariously on the pillow.

"Found it on Netflix. John Wayne and Maureen O'Hara. A favorite of my mom's. Filmed in Ireland, of course! It's called the *Quiet Man*. The lead character reminds me of the Major."

"Is that a blush I see?" Angie quipped.

Meghan snatched up the remote and muted the TV. "All right, lady. Enough about some old movie and me. Spill the beans, Angie. Is Parker still on the naughty list?"

"I guess everyone knows now, huh? About me and Parker."

"Did you really think you were going to keep something like that a secret? C'mon! We knew after ten seconds with both of you in the same room that something was up. What the hell did you think would happen?"

"Alexander hasn't said anything," Angie mumbled.

"Nor will he," Meghan was quick to assure her. "Unless, of course, you two make a mess of things. Or if a certain lawyer needs an ass kicking."

"Does Alex know . . . I mean, did Parker tell him what actually happened or are we talking about a non-specific blanket admission with no detail?"

"Honey," Meghan jeered as she patted Angie's hand. "Men don't generally do detail—not even with each other, unless there's a crisis. I can tell you that the confession was rather broad but time date stamped. Alex knows whatever happened, took place while he was playing war."

"Is he mad?"

Meghan shook her head as she finished off the last of her ice cream. "Mad? No. I wouldn't call it that. I think the timing got to him. If I understand correctly, you were still a teenager and Parker should have known better."

"It was all a misunderstanding," Angie began, but Irish cut her off with a deep laugh.

"Misunderstanding? How do you figure? Did his penis fall into your vagina by accident?" she jeered.

Angie screeched. "Oh, for god's sake, Meghan. What the hell?"

"What? Too blunt or not blunt enough?" Irish blurted. "Sometimes it's hard for me to tell where to draw the line. Tori, on the other hand," she giggled, "would have gone full on cock and pussy."

"Yeah, while Lacey would be covering her ears and muttering about Mr. Stiffy and Miss Wetagain."

They hiccupped and wiped away tears after having a good old-fashioned giggle fest.

"If you want to tell me, Angie, I'm all ears. I won't lie to the Major, but I do know how to explain things to him in a way that won't send him off half-cocked. It might help if I knew a little bit of background."

They sat together on the floor beside the fireplace and talked. Meghan was a smart lady. Telling someone she trusted her side of what happened was long overdue.

"So, let me see if I have this straight. It was just sex, you overheard him being a guy, and what? No big deal even though you haven't spoken in years?"

"Sounds ridiculous when you put it like that," Angie muttered.

"Aw hell, Angie. You were what? Nineteen? Just barely twenty? I was a fucking idiot at that age. College keg parties in the woods. Beer pong. Whatever happened with you guys back then was far from ridiculous. And, for the record . . . if it had been me, I would have caused a huge scene and probably ended up having one of my brothers neuter the bastard. Of course, that would have proved a little embarrassing after hearing his explanation, but at the time? He would have been toast."

"I think I always knew I was overreacting, but honestly, if it hadn't been that, it would have been something else. You're right about one thing. I was too young. Wa*aaay* too damn young to be playing those sorts of games with a man so much older. And more experienced."

"Hmmm, that part surprises me," she admitted to Angie. "Makes me question what was really going on in Parker's mind."

"What do you mean?" she asked.

"Well," Meghan began thoughtfully, "Parker and Alex are a lot alike and while they both have a dominant streak a mile wide, they're also two of the most decent, honorable men alive. All the Family Justice guys are. It kind of baffles me how he acted so out of character, considering your age, if all he was doing was fucking around. If it was, as you say, *just sex*. That doesn't sound at all like the man I know. I mean, if you think about it, he was jeopardizing his relationship with Alex and for what? To get laid? And destroy two friendships? Are you so sure it wasn't more than that?"

"Oh god, Meghan," she groaned. "How the hell should I know? It was all so fast. Not our friendship, of course. The intimate thing. One minute, we were the best of friends, and the next, I was so far out of my league it wasn't funny. The man overwhelmed me sexually, and in a lot of ways, that experience still affects my life and the decisions I make."

"You're talking about your engagement?"

She nodded but Aldo wasn't the only example of her poor decision making. Right after she'd relocated to Spain, some three years after the blow-up with Parker, she'd had a brief fling with an English wine merchant. But he, like Aldo, was a paler version of her ideal man. And Parker had everything to do with that. She'd begun to worry that what was best for her didn't seem to peacefully co-exist with what her heart wanted.

A marriage between the Esperanza and the Valleja-Marquez families wouldn't have been a bad thing. Two old world patrician Spanish families? *Shit.* Magazine articles were written about stories like that.

But while she respected Ronaldo Senior and his long career as a financial expert, she despised what Aldo did.

He was what was called a celebrity handler, managing a stable of so-called VIPs with a heavy emphasis on one peculiar category—that of the celebrity DJ. Angie always wondered what the hell that even meant. She hated having to go to events that normally would have fascinated her on a professional level purely because she despised the fake kissy face nonsense and unctuous entitlement that came along with the whole celebrity thing.

But Ronaldo? He loved that crap. Thought they'd make an awesome team—he with his management credentials and business skills and her with her extensive experience planning everything from product launches to award celebrations.

On the surface, it would have been the smart thing to do. Marry into an old family and get a suave European husband with a career in sync with hers. Hobnobbing with the rich and famous. Vacations on the Riviera. Sailing in Greece. Weekends in Tuscany. Whoop-de-fucking-do. Only thing was, Aldo brought out the wanton in her exactly never. As in *ever*.

While he was pursuing her and even after their engagement, he'd behaved himself appropriately but Angie wasn't stupid. She had no passion for the man whatsoever, and he wouldn't have put up with that shit after they were married. Eventually, she was sure, being surrounded as he was by too much goddamn privilege, he would have ended up cheating. So what seemed like perfection on the outside had a nightmare inner core.

It would have been different—maybe, if she'd been able to work up any sort of desire for Aldo. He was good looking in that haute couture kind of way but he wasn't what you'd describe as being a manly man. Everything about him left her cold.

She wanted a man who would take her in hand and make her feel like a woman. Someone who challenged her on every level. He had to be firm and commanding with a strong protective streak that would make keeping his family safe from harm a priority. And he must have a sense of who he was as a man. She wasn't interested in a poser or a wannabe. No boys need apply.

Gee, she snickered. *I wonder who I just described.*

"Aldo was the least of it," she finally admitted to Meghan. "I cut myself off from the things that makes me happiest because I couldn't face what we did. Staying away only hurt me. I'd say that qualifies for questionable decision making."

The fire crackled quietly as the two sat there deep in thought.

"Is that why you wanted to come here now? To re-visit some of the decisions you think were bad?"

Pfft. "I knew the minute I ended my engagement that returning to Arizona was inevitable. Even then, everything was already leading me here. When you asked me to help with the wedding, I figured waiting for any more signs would be kind of ridiculous."

"*Hmmm.*" Meghan fiddled with her engagement ring and settled back against the sofa, stretching her legs out toward the fire. "And what about Parker? How did you see this playing out?"

An excellent question. How *did* she see it all play out?

"God, Meghan. I've loved him since I was old enough to know what love was. There isn't a second of my earliest memories that don't include him. He's my touchstone in some strange way. When I made the honor roll, it was Parker's praise that meant the most. If something made me unhappy, three words from him and I'd be smiling again. Does that make sense?"

Meghan snickered and rolled her eyes. "You're making a funny, right? My whole life changed the second your brother came into it. From that moment on, everything got filtered through him. Every thought, feeling, taste, desire, *everything.* Does Parker being your touchstone make sense? Honey . . . nine months ago, if you'd said that, I would have thought you daft or a hopeless romantic. Today, I say, welcome to my world."

Angie smiled. Red was so easy to love. Alex better realize how fucking lucky he was to have such a strong, spirited woman.

"Can I ask you a question?"

"Aww . . ." Meghan smiled warmly. "You can ask me anything. You know that."

"Okay, well . . . you and Alexander seem so well matched but that's now. When did you know? For sure."

Meghan smiled sort of wistfully. "I felt something immediately, but I knew for sure when I left him. I loved him and walking away nearly killed me, but he had to decide what was more important. The future or the past. Until he did, we had nothing."

Sounded like the narrative swirling in her brain. It was funny how she and her brother both came to that moment when letting go of the past became the key to having a future. Could she do it? Just move past one awful moment in time and rethink the future?

"Of course," Meghan drawled mockingly, "once that control freak brother of yours decided . . . well, my life has been completely taken over. So there's that."

They laughed. Angie knew it was true. Alex was seriously overprotective of Meghan.

"You know what would be funny?" she chirped.

Meghan quirked an eyebrow.

"A tattoo. Why don't you get a tattoo? Maybe have *Alex* put on your butt."

Instead of laughing off the suggestion, Meghan actually seemed to think it over. "A tattoo has possibilities."

"Really?" Angie squeaked. "This is epic! I want to get some ink before I turn thirty. Now, I know it's still a ways off," she smirked, "but I've been thinking about it a lot."

"What would you get?" Meghan asked.

"Wanna see? I have some drawings in my binder." Reaching for the overflowing notebook, she opened it carefully and flipped a couple of pages. Pointing, she said, "Like this. Really small, though."

"Are those angel wings?"

"Yeah," Angie replied. "They're cool, huh?"

"Wow," Red murmured as she checked out the page of drawings. "They're really pretty. I like these," she said with a finger on a particularly beautiful pair of delicate, feminine looking wings.

"Have you ever considered getting something inked?" she asked.

Meghan grunted out a deep chuckle. "I'm considering it now."

She flipped through a few more pages and stopped. "What this?" she asked. "It looks familiar."

Angie peered at the notebook to see what she was referring to.

"Ah. That. Those are mock-ups of the family crest. For the new label design Sophie is working on. She took the original emblem and had it cleaned up to be more modern and easier to see. It's cool, don't you think?"

Meghan bent over the page and studied the drawings intently. "Which one did you go with?"

"The one with the black griffin and the vines."

"Hmmm."

"What are you thinking, Meghan?"

Red looked at her with a huge grin. "I'm thinking you and I are getting tattoos."

Angie fell over onto her side laughing. "Alex said our mom would kill me if I got a tattoo. I can't wait to see his face when it's *you* with the ink!"

Chapter Twenty-Five

"It's been a whole year since we met," Victoria purred. "Do you remember? I do. Every single detail."

Her wet tongue swirled in and around his ear, making Drae shudder. When he heard her soft, "*Mmmm,*" she sounded like she'd just tasted the food of the gods when all she'd really done was suck on his earlobe.

Excitement had him by the balls. His heart was thumping heavily, and his chest was rising and falling with each heavy breath. She smelled like coconut and warm vanilla and those devastating brown chocolate eyes of hers were lit with a wicked gleam.

Straddling his middle, Victoria met his gaze with unblinking focus.

"You were sitting under some twinkle lights in your tuxedo." Two hands reached for his head and massaged his scalp. "In the soft light, your hair looked golden, and I thought maybe you were some sort of fallen angel." She snickered softly, adding, "Or a sexy Viking."

She ran her fingers from his chin down his throat to the top of his chest. "Your tie was undone and the top buttons of your shirt open. I thought you were the most beautiful man I'd ever seen."

When she leaned in and licked his Adam's apple, then moved lower and pressed a soft kiss in the center of his chest, Drae groaned.

"Victoria," he warned her gruffly—to no avail. All he had were words because his precocious wife had tied his hands to their bed. She was totally in charge and fuck almighty was he ferociously turned on.

The little witch laughed at his distress. Planting her hands on either side of his head, she rose up on her knees to hover over him, close enough that her long mess of curls brushed his skin. She was looking at him like he was a ten-pound box of chocolates and she was deciding which one to devour first. Not sure, but Drae was pretty certain his toes curled.

"Yes," she cooed seductively. "You growled just like that—trying to scare me."

His chest surged when he grunted, remembering well their first encounter. Nothing in his life had been the same from that moment on. *Thank fucking god.*

She lifted away and reached out to touch the ropes binding him to the bed. They both knew he could extricate himself from her girly knots in seconds, but he was always eager to play with his sexy wife. She restrained him just enough that he was able to tense against the ropes, and Drae found that he rather liked the loss of control even though it was more a suggestion than a fact.

Gracefully climbing off him while he groaned his disappointment, she drifted her fingers one last time from his throat straight down to the top of his low briefs. *Goddammit.*

Drae watched her with excited intensity. Everything she did was for effect. Leaving him lying there, arms wide and tied, naked and vulnerable except for his underwear—she drifted away and left him alone with his anticipation.

Looking delicious and seductive in the low lighting, he drank her in with hungry eyes. His little wife had positively bloomed since giving birth. It was unreal how natural motherhood came to her. She was rounder now. Softer. Every inch the sexy Madonna with her ripe breasts and gentle curves.

And the best part? She apparently loved the way she looked because, oh my fucking god, had she ever turned into a twenty-four seven tease. Shit, man, he had a new item in the budget besides the baby stuff. Keeping her hot ass in lingerie and those sexy costumes she tormented him with was costing him an assload. Not that he was complaining any.

Wearing something that looked like it came out of the Fuck Me catalog, she was dressed to thrill. The killer shoes she slid her feet into were a walking advertisement for a style that had to be called the

Screaming O. He very much liked how heels made Victoria's naughty hips sway and when a pair of sheer black thigh-high stockings with sexy lace tops were added, well . . . c'mon.

Tonight though, the pièce de résistance of her risqué outfit was a pair of black panties that nearly stole his sanity. Made up entirely of lace and ribbon, they, along with the matching bra, were a triumph of sensual engineering. With her ass cheeks barely covered, a series of criss-cross ribbons with a dainty little bow framed her beautiful bottom. Same for her tits. Beautifully presented for his pleasure.

She approached the bed from the bottom. Drae strained to lift his head enough to see what she was doing. He nearly jumped out of his skin when she put a hand on his ankle and casually caressed.

"You'll need to stay still, okay?"

He nodded his head and grunted. Fuck. He'd try to but her touch, no matter how brief or innocent was driving him wild.

Drae felt her put something on the bed near his feet a second before she climbed onto the mattress. He heard the shoes thunk on the floor as she slipped them off.

She chuckled. "I like it when you growl at me."

Really? Okay. He growled low and deep, which only made her laugh more. It was her dainty hand sweeping up a leg that stopped any more sound from coming out of him.

"Let's see if we can release the beast, hmmm?"

He sucked in a breath. *Oh, my god.*

"This might get messy," she murmured as if to herself. "The briefs have to go."

Well, shit. Drae had to admit that tending to their son's butt gave her a certain flair when it came time to whip the cotton molded to his bulging erection off his body. But instead of tossing the unnecessary clothing aside, she smirked and with a saucy wink, wadded up the fabric and placed it directly on his throbbing dick.

Not content to simply cover him, she took advantage of the situation and explored him through the cotton. When her fingers made contact with his balls, he moaned loudly. Victoria's hands fondling him that way never failed to reduce Drae to a mass of quivering flesh.

"You know I get distracted by, um . . . *visuals,*" she purred.

Yeah? Him, too. He closed his eyes and tried to rein in the thundering desire running rampant inside him.

Next thing he knew, she was kneeling between his legs and pushing them further apart as if she needed more room. *Now,* he felt vulnerable. Hands tied—legs spread wide.

And then she giggled—which made his cock surge—which got his heart thumping—which made his breathing ragged.

A sound, something he couldn't immediately make out, snagged his senses. There was an odd sensation on his ankle and then the sound again.

"When you growled at me that first time, I wondered if that was something you always did. Or if I could make you. Now that I know a little more about what turns the notorious Draegyn St. John to mush, I intend to harness that beastly grunt and make it my own."

And then he felt something cold and soft drift up his leg.

"The ankle bone's connected to the shin bone," she murmured. "And the shin bone connects to the knee."

Whipped cream. *Jesus fucking Christ.* She was squirting whipped cream from his ankle to his knee.

When she began licking the ribbons of goo off his flesh, Draegyn twitched in his restraints and grunted.

"Fu*uu*ck."

Playing him perfectly, she took her goddamn good time, doing the same to his other leg until her insatiable lips and tongue had lapped up the mounds of sweet cream.

Sitting back on her feet, she looked at him as she swiped her tongue across her lips to catch any leftover dribbles.

"Have anything to say?" she asked huskily.

He wasn't dumb. Drae growled at her, and in doing so, pretty much let his inner barbarian loose. She wanted him pumped up and at her mercy. No fucking problem.

Satisfied with his response, she settled and reached for the spray can again.

"Fuck, I love whipped cream." Taunting him, she dropped her head back and opened her mouth wide. Holding the can a few inches away, she pressed the nozzle and a blast of white oozed onto her waiting tongue. The move was so provocative and carnal, he couldn't help but moan.

Her smug leer told him that she was pleased by his reaction.

"Now, where was I?" She looked around with a hilariously adorable expression then chirped, "Oh, right!" and shook the can still held in her hand.

"So . . . the knee bone's connected to the thigh bone."

With all the focus and intensity of a civil engineer, she made a circle around his knee then drew a line straight up his thigh where it connected with his torso.

He could see her now when he tilted his head. She was holding her hair out of the way as she bent over him and licked the whipped cream, making quiet sounds of satisfaction as she moved up his hairy thigh. He felt his leg quiver and sex swell with need.

Before she moved to the other leg, she sat up quickly, her hand holding her hair, and grinned at him. White globs of cream stuck to her nose and chin.

"Messy business." She chuckled. "Clean me up."

She rose up and put her face near his mouth, a signal he willingly answered. Sticking his tongue out, Drae lapped at the white globs, removing them from her nose, chin, and around her lips. No kissing. Just lots of licking accompanied by a symphony of growls.

Then she replayed the knee to thigh bone tease on the other side. He was so close to being out of his mind with arousal that Drae was fighting to stay still and do as he was told.

From there, she tested his control in every way possible. With his entire torso as a canvas, she became a master artist, drawing naughty objects and writing vulgar terms all over his skin before using her tongue and lips to erase her handiwork.

Thinking that was it, he steadied himself, hoping she'd teased him enough and would get down to business. He was wrong.

What was a can or two of whipped cream without some fresh strawberries to go along with it?

From someplace just beyond his periphery, she produced a beautiful big strawberry that she bit into with a sexy moan. With half the juicy fruit gone, she was left holding the green leafy stem as she chewed and licked her lips.

Unf. Why the fuck were his hands tied? He wanted to kiss her. Wanted to taste the ripe fruit on her tongue. He pulled restlessly against his bindings and squirmed.

With a wicked gleam in her eyes, she used the half-eaten berry as a paintbrush on his chest, swirling it around one of his nipples until his flesh was wearing bits of the fruit.

"Oh fuck, Victoria," he groaned helplessly as she set about licking and sucking the fragrant strawberry from his body.

They went through half a dozen big juicy berries as she went to town all over him, switching back and forth between the strawberries and the whipped cream. By the end of what she planned, his cock was visibly twitching beneath the wadded up briefs and he was seriously contemplating hulking out on the ropes and either sliding from the knots or simply snapping the wooden bed frame into pieces so he could throw her wicked ass onto the mattress and fuck the shit out of her.

"Open your mouth," she demanded. When he did, she squirted a bubble of cream into his mouth then fell on him for a kiss that set him on fire.

He tried to follow her lips when she pulled away and roared with frustration when the ropes stopped him.

"Untie me, wife," he ordered. Ha! Who was he trying to kid?

She smiled wickedly. "Oh, baby. I don't think that's going to happen."

Reaching behind her back, she unhooked the bra, and turned taking it off into a five-minute performance worthy of Dita Von Teese.

Using an arm to conceal her breasts from his eager gaze, she peeled the bra off and tossed it aside, shrieking with laughter when it landed atop a bedside light.

"That would be why we can't have a housekeeper," she jested, overcome by giggles. "Our clothes draped over the railings and leaving a trail, one floor to another, would be hard to explain."

Drae glanced at the black scrap of lace lingerie and smiled. Somehow, it looked so right flung upon the lampshade, one end hanging down to the nightstand and a lacy cup pointing toward the ceiling.

But what really looked right, and fucking awesome, and hotter than hell was the sight of Victoria's dainty hands, cupping and massaging her drool-worthy breasts. Currently in competition with his greedy son for who got more nipple time, Drae was more than happy to share. There was something downright mind-boggling about his wife nursing their son. If ever he was M.I.A. from the compound, it was probably because he was helplessly fascinated with watching Victoria take Daniel to her breast. He'd spent hours drinking in the sight of his two loves, curled up in her favorite chair, while their son latched onto a nipple and went to town.

As if reading his one-track mind, she crawled up his torso and dangled a very pouty looking nipple close to his lips. With Victoria still actively nursing, he had to go easy on her, but she loved having her tits take center stage and he was eager to feel the puckered nub on his tongue.

"Easy," she purred softly as Drae started flicking his tongue against her swollen flesh.

Within seconds, he felt goosebumps break out on her skin as she sighed and quivered so sweetly.

She let him gently suckle, shivered when he nipped and bit, and moaned along with Drae as he licked the plump rounds.

And then . . . well, without much warning, she got big time aggressive. What she did to his body and his psyche with her teeth, lips, and tongue took him to the outer reaches of sensual oblivion. When she bit him, she actually really fucking bit him. With his hands tied, her marking him with her teeth as he lay there helplessly was about the hottest thing ever. He liked being at her mercy.

Right about the time she left a burning love bite below his navel, he lost what was left of his control.

"Victoria," he growled low, deep and menacing. "Untie me . . ."

Her answer to his harshly barked demand? She just shimmied into a better position wedged between his spread thighs, tore the wadded up briefs from his groin, and used both hands to wrestle his throbbing hard-on into submission.

"Ahhhh," he moaned, thrashing on the bed as she worked his manly flesh with heart-pounding sensuality.

Pumping his cock with slow, firm strokes, he literally lost his shit when she added a twist near the super sensitive head, punctuating the whole movement with a sexy sounding, *"Mmmmm."*

Drae pulled against the restraints and grunted. She did it again. And again. And again. The fingers of one hand slid under his balls and began fondling as the other continued to stroke. Yeah. He wasn't going to last much longer if she kept that up.

Yanking forcefully on the ropes, careful not to accidentally ruin her fun by freeing himself, Drae dug his heels into the mattress and began thrusting his hips.

Growling like an animal in heat, he demanded gruffly, "Fuck me or suck me, woman."

She smiled sweetly, openly amused by his loss of control.

"Suck and fuck sounds good to me."

So she did.

Chapter Twenty-Six

"A<small>LEX WENT AHEAD</small>," M<small>EGHAN TOLD</small> Angie as they bumped along an old dirt road in one the Villa's fancy electric carts on their way to this special spot everyone kept rhapsodizing about.

"Wait till you see what Draegyn did out here! He built a pergola and a couple of benches, and next, we're building a hearth."

"This is that place from the framed picture in the den, huh?"

Angie noticed that Meghan colored slightly as she nodded. "Yeah. A lot of history."

It was too hard not to laugh so she did. It hadn't taken long in Alex and Meghan's company to understand that the happily engaged couple pretty much banged morning, noon, and night.

Grinning stupidly, she pithily asked, "Is there any place you two haven't done it?"

Meghan didn't bother pretending not to understand what she was implying.

"Well, your room for one," she answered smugly. "And, apparently, we've missed a couple of feet in the family room."

Their raucous laughter filled the desert air.

"*Mmmm hmmm,*" Angie chuckled. "Draegyn specifically told me not to wander into any room with an unlocked door. Something about traumatic visions and going blind. Or limp. One of the two."

Meghan's head whipped around and even through the dark shades she wore, Angie could see her shocked expression.

"That asshole!" she gasped. "Why in the world would he tell you that?"

"I suppose because the story is funny as shit, Red."

"Oh, dear lord," Meghan groaned. "He told you? What the fucking fuck?" she shrieked with a choked laugh. "Is nothing private with these Justice men?"

Angie snickered quietly as Meghan drove along muttering darkly about paybacks and men with big mouths.

Taking pity on the other woman's discomfiture, she changed the subject. "So what's up with the Cameron's? They've both been off the radar since Las Vegas. What gives?"

"*Hmph*," Meghan uttered huskily. "Dunno. Something's up, though. The Major is saying nothing, but I'm not blind. He and Drae are sending smoke signals with their eyes."

"Have you tried to get it out of him?"

Laughing as though what she'd asked was the funniest goddamn question ever, Meghan looked over at her with an eye roll.

"Oh, darlin'," she drawled comically. "That's not how this shit works."

"Do tell," Angie quipped with a short laugh.

"Take notes, sis. This is how you handle a Justice alpha."

"Knowing about these so-called control issues you say my brother suffers from, I cannot wait to hear your next words of wisdom, oh wise one!"

"Okay, well, first of all . . . alphas like to think they're in charge."

Once again, they both cracked the fuck up hooting with laughter.

"Yeah, I got that," Angie agreed with a snorting grin. "Did I tell you that at the fondue restaurant, Parker didn't even let me glance at the damn menu? Honestly! There's *in charge* and then there's *over-charge*."

Meghan roared. "Overcharge! That's a good one."

"Whatever," Angie groused. "Pissed me off, actually. I kept thinking . . . who died and made him king?"

"Get used to it," Meghan wisecracked. "I'm thinking since Parker basically showed Alex the ropes as they were growing up, all that bad-boy fuckery your brother does so well had to start somewhere, and I blame Parker Sullivan."

Wow. She really thought about that comment long and hard. Great observation on Red's part. A small shiver of excitement skated along her nerves. She'd have to be a mindless idiot not to have noticed the relationship dance Meghan did with her brother. He was and always had been what she and Soph called the top dog. With just one look, he had the gravitas to cower both his younger sisters. And while Meghan most certainly did not cower, she did pay extra attention to his alpha tendencies—something that Angie viewed as brilliant.

"Lesson one. Never but never assume that you can manipulate a dominant male. It can't be done."

Angie made a face and groaned. "Great."

Laughing, Meghan kept on. "But that doesn't mean he has the upper hand. Far from it. Just by admitting that you can't manipulate him, you've already won."

"Missing the point, I'm afraid."

"It's simple, really. If he knows you've already thrown in the towel on trying to get the upper hand, he'll be easier to handle. Mostly, I just wait Alex out. Sometimes," she giggled, "I know he's dying for me to ask about something, and I say nothing. Eventually, he'll spill the beans because he has to!"

"I would have thought with how close you two are, that if something was going on with Lacey and Cam, he'd share it with you."

"Oh, he will," Meghan assured her, "when he's ready. The bond between Draegyn, Cam, and the Major is a force of nature. They're hardwired into each other. Whatever it is, the Justice men are handling it and that's enough for me, right now."

"Aren't you worried, though? About Lacey?"

Something appeared off in the distance, making Angie sit up and take notice. She could just barely make out Alex's old truck parked in a spot surrounded by some of the most beautiful scenery she'd ever seen.

"Of course, I'm concerned, but Cameron worships Lacey. He'd never let anything happen to her. She's in excellent hands and I trust him, and Alex and Drae, to keep her safe."

"Will she be okay with singing at Pete's this weekend?"

Meghan didn't answer right away. Obviously, she was worried about the state of affairs down at the cabin.

As the buggy bumped along, getting closer and closer to this special spot, she got a clearer view of the setup. Eventually, a wide distinctive pergola took shape with a curved top that gave it an oddly Asian flair.

"Oh my," she muttered.

"Just wait," Red sniggered with a half-laugh. "Sedona has its vortexes and Villa de Valleja-Marquez does, too."

Angie shivered from head to toe. An energy vortex. Damn, she loved that kind of shit. Was sort of why she felt so drawn to this locale. She grew up thinking people who were skeptical of such things were really missing out. She friggin' lived for that feeling—out in nature and swept away by a beneficial source of energy.

All of a sudden, she was that eleven-year-old girl again—adventuring on her own out into the desert and stumbling upon such a spot. The very idea that this place they were headed to was infused with the energy of her ancestors made Angie giddy.

As the pergola came into better view the closer they got, her eager eyes took in a thousand little details since this was definitely something she wanted to remember later.

Cataloging every little thing that hit her eyes, she was startled when Meghan informed her, "Parker seems to be here as well."

"What?"

"*Mmmm hmmm,*" Meghan drawled. "He's kind of hard to miss. The guitar is a nice touch though, don't you think?" she simpered mockingly.

Oh, for the love of all that's holy, Angie groaned inwardly. Really?

She hadn't noticed him at first because he was standing against one of the massive wood posts supporting the wide arched top of the structure so he kind of blended in.

"Fuck my horny life," she muttered under her breath, earning a loud giggle-snort from her companion.

Did he have to look so hot? *Goddammit.*

Casually leaning, he had one foot up to mid-calf on the post behind him and a guitar in his hands looking every bit the rebel rocker sporting rumpled looking hair, a pair of dark Ray-Bans, and flashing a toothy grin at them as they approached.

They pulled up next to Alex's truck and switched off the ignition.

Half a second later, Angie jumped when she heard Meghan squeal as Alex came out of nowhere and hauled her from the cart.

"About time," he barked in that funny He-Man way her brother excelled at. "We're starving. What did Ria send?" Alex the barbarian inquired as he started pawing through the enormous cooler packed with all sorts of goodies for their afternoon delight.

"Brought that asshole with me," he grumbled jokingly. "Hey! Dumbass. Come lend a hand." He hollered at Parker who sauntered toward them, stopping to drop his guitar onto a bench.

"Thank god you've arrived, ladies," he drawled. Making a clownish face, he whooped it up and pointed at Alex. "He's worse than a three-year-old being told no in a candy store when he's hungry. How do you put up with his shit, Irish?"

Meghan stepped up and let Parker throw his arm around her shoulders while she wrapped one of hers around his waist. They both stood there with sad expressions as they considered poor Alex.

"I've got him on a feeding schedule," Meghan teased. "No! I shit you not," she insisted when Parker broke out with a laugh. "Seriously. It's the only way to manage him! He's like Dylan. Or Daniel. Or hell, all of you boys," Meghan jested as she turned and socked Parker on the arm. "Don't try and pretend you don't tie the feed bag on every couple of hours," she taunted.

Alex snickered, held up a roast beef slider, and said, "Word," then went back to stuffing his face. Angie had to laugh. These people were a living, breathing comedy act. Their dynamic was something to see. She wondered where she fit in.

Parker chuckled and turned all of his attention to Angie. She could feel his sexy x-ray vision through the dark glasses covering his eyes. His lip curled. She liked to think of it as his Elvis move.

"Don't suppose you brought an instrument with you?" he asked.

Now . . . why the hell did it seem like everything he said made her sizzle? He was asking if she had a guitar. He knew she played. It was a normal question seeing as how he had his. But it was the way he asked and the suggestive emphasis on the word *instrument* that rendered her half-a-moron.

Meghan heard the inquiry and jumped in.

"Oh, that's right. You told us you could play. Guitar, right?"

"She plays beautifully," Parker declared with a warmth that surprised her.

Alex walked past them carrying the enormous cooler by himself and sneered at Parker as he went by. "I thought you were here to be helpful, dude. Not drool like a twelve-year-old over my sister."

As if on cue, Meghan dissolved into giggles as Parker opened and closed his mouth like he might say something but no sound ever came out.

"C'mon," Meghan said as she twined her arm around Angie's. "Let me show you around. We call this place Amor Vórtice. Our very own power place."

The minute Meghan led her into the shade of the pergola, Angie was in heaven. Oh, my god. This was amazing!

A big circular area, quite large in fact, had been laid with muted earth tone pavers that bore the shadow created by the lattice worked over the arched top of the pergola. Small wind chimes hung at opposite ends of the structure from the top of the vertical posts. Two heavy wood benches were at one end and a couple of Adirondack style chairs and a small table sat nearby.

Next to a large storage chest was a pile of brick and stone that Meghan told her was there for the hearth they wanted to add. It was a unique, in-the-middle-of-nowhere oasis.

"The chairs are new," Red chimed happily as Alex plopped down in one.

"Yep. Lugged 'em out here in the truck. And Tori sent along some chick thing. A couple of hand-blown hanging candleholders. Very cool. They're boxed in bubble wrap and in the truck bed."

"This is amazing," Angie murmured. And it was. Big enough to handle at least a dozen people comfortably, the space was blooming with potential.

"Place needs a grill," Parker declared rather decisively.

Angie ducked her head and smiled. Meat and fire? Yep. Seemed about right.

They dragged the benches and rearranged what furniture they had until everyone was comfortable. Settled, an hour flew by as the four of them lounged, ate, drank a little bit, laughed, teased, and told stories.

It was, as far as Angie was concerned, a little slice of Southwest heaven.

After a bit, while she and Meghan cleared away their trash and secured the leftovers, the guys sat across from each other on the big benches and started doing what was essentially a form of dueling banjos. *So competitive, these two!* she thought. Just as it had always been

She sighed, looked with loving eyes on her brother, and sighed again. By putting so much distance between them, she'd deprived Alex of this. The three of them hanging out; only now, the numbers weren't so lopsided with Meghan along. Now it really was boy-girl, boy-girl.

Enjoying their bawdy repartee—something that would never get old—she sprawled in one of the chairs and quite simply, drank it all in. The beautiful setting, the clear blue sky overhead, the distinctive red-hued rock formations, all second to the two men who had settled into a strikingly beautiful acoustic version of an old Bon Jovi standard.

Meghan slid a chair next to hers and gave Angie a knowing look before she settled in for a listen.

As if the two guitars weren't enough to fill the air with rich and vibrant sounds, when Alex and Parker started singing, they harmonized effortlessly, just like they'd been doing for decades and the result was staggering.

She felt unusually honored to witness the two powerful men, completely relaxed and in sync with each other and the music they were making. The moment felt magical.

They sang about cowboys and being wanted, and without glancing her way, Meghan's hand shot out with the neck of her beer bottle tilted in Angie's direction.

Indeed.

Responding by firmly clinking their two bottles, Angie and Meghan drank deeply and sat back as they enjoyed the desert alpha show.

Chapter Twenty-Seven

"They're so fucking cute I can barely stand to be around them," Angie joked when Alex and Meghan wandered away hand-in-hand for a short walk.

Parker watched his friend and Irish cling to each other as they strolled beyond a cluster of shrubs next to the big wood structure that Drae had magically built. They really were cute, those two. He'd never seen his old friend happier. Shit. He didn't even realize Alex could actually *be* that happy. If that dumb fuck could get his happily ever after, maybe there was still hope for him as well.

Eyeing Angie as she watched the couple with a sweetly wistful expression, he tried to control his crazy hope that one day soon he and his beautiful Spanish Angel could be like that, too.

She sighed and turned away, leaving them to their private moment. "Red's one in a zillion, huh?"

He snickered and nudged her playfully. "Puts up with his tired-ass shit so yeah, she's something."

"I'm serious, Parker," she mumbled. "You know what I'm talking about. I mean, you saw my brother a hell of a lot more than I have these past couple of years. He's been so . . . empty. It was awful."

She was right, and he shouldn't make light of what she was trying to get across. He'd been freaking out for years—even well after Justice had been firmly established and started churning and burning some serious bucks—because, despite the success and the stability afforded by the business he built, Alex remained but a shadow of his former self for much longer than just while he was convalescing from his injuries. That damn war had nearly sucked his soul dry.

Meghan coming to the Villa had changed everything. Angie was so right. One in a zillion.

"It's this place," she added solemnly with a half-shrug. "It changes people, or it brings out their best . . . best qualities, best hopes, best efforts."

She smirked shyly and dipped her head just as he spied a rosy blush creeping up her neck.

"Sorry. Sometimes my hippy dippy side takes over! Blame my mother."

Aunt Ashleigh. Parker grinned broadly. The woman was a force of nature and he loved her to death. She was always the first one to crack everyone up with an inappropriate comment or observation while her husband rolled his eyes in long-suffering mock-horror. Angie was so much like her mother. A free spirit in every sense of the word—such a far cry from Sophia, who got more from the sober and serious side of the family DNA.

Leaning in, he jostled her with his shoulder. "I blame your mother for a lot of things—that sorry piece of shit you call a brother, for one—but the charming way you put things is all you, Angel. And your mom would be proud."

More shy blushes. So unexpected. He didn't remember her being so . . . *something.* Not shy so much as shocked. Yeah. That was it. She was shocked.

"It's weird."

He looked at her with a questioning gaze. *Weird? Shit.* There wasn't anything about this that *wasn't* weird.

"Not being afraid to be around you. That's what's weird. I almost don't know how to act."

Her quietly spoken admission started a brawl inside him.

The sensible guy, the one who drove a sports car and had a kickass career, tried to listen and think supportive thoughts.

While the man with the cock 'n' balls swagger wanted to pin her to the spot and show her exactly how he wanted her to act.

Talk about a dilemma.

"I've missed you in my life, Angelina," he told her gently.

He was getting so many different signals that were all jumbled and messy. She searched his face. *Dammit.* He could see it in her eyes—she still didn't trust him. Or herself.

Careful not to cross a line because dragging her ass to third base at the club hadn't worked out so well, they were dancing around one another trying overly hard to be friendly, polite, and leave the drama behind.

Shit. Parker was actually a little afraid of what might happen the next time he touched her if he didn't get control.

Okay, he thought. *Maybe this will help ease some of her fears. Remind Angie that they already have a place in each other's life.*

"My folks are asking when you're coming round for dinner. Mom's dying to talk about the wedding. Something about choosing a dress color." He chuckled with a mystified shake of his head.

He hadn't expected her to gasp or reach and grab his arm. Her reaction revealed so much. She knew damn well what would happen two seconds after they had dinner with his folks. The fucking phone lines between Arizona and Spain were going to be on fire.

Wait a minute, wait a minute. *That might be a good thing,* Parker considered as he patted her hand reassuringly. If his mom got it into her head that he and Angie had a chance, she'd move heaven and Earth, with Ashleigh Marquez egging her on the entire time, to get them together. Hm*mm.*

"C'mon, Angel," he chided. "Tell me you weren't thinking about hiding from them because of . . . well, because of me. My dad loves you. Calls you his Desert Angel."

He'd certainly seen some shit and some stuff in his day but seeing Angelina Marquez melt right in front of his eyes was huge.

"Really?" she squeaked, her voice brimming with emotion. "He calls me that?"

Parker slung an arm around her neck and pulled her in for a friendly hug. "Yeah. He does. Stealing my best shit, too."

She looked at him curiously. "What do you mean?"

"I wanted to be the only one calling you Angel," he admitted with a self-conscious snicker. "But lately, I've noticed the name falling out of everyone's mouth. Even my dad."

She laughed and pushed against him, stepping out of his half embrace. "I know, right? Here I thought that was some super cool private thing between you and me . . . and now? That's what the girls call me in their little karaoke dojo. Shit!" she hooted. "I'm thinking about having a t-shirt printed with Desert Angel across my boobs."

Do not look at her boobs. No matter what you do, man—do NOT look at her boobs. Oh, shit. Can't be helped. Angie's boobs were fucking magnificent with or without a t-shirt.

Like right now, they were perfection. A nice, big round handful. And the nipples on those perfect tits? Damn. Also perfect. His teeth ached for a chance to nibble on the naked globes.

He cleared his throat and moved around a little, trying to bring some relief to the hard-on threatening to destroy his vascular system. Was it possible to think clearly when all the blood in your brain detours to your cock?

"Um, so back to dinner at the Sullivan's. What do you want me to tell Mom?"

She paused and let go of a little sigh. "Will we be going together?"

For once, Parker fervently hoped that was a loaded question. He wanted there to be a lot of *togethers* from here on out.

"Abso-fucking-lutely."

He held back a smirk. She wanted so badly to say something. He didn't know what, but frustration was written all over her face.

A few strands of her hair moved as a slight breeze blew by and the chimes on the pergola tinkled sweetly. Brushing the wayward strands away from the face staring so intently at him, Parker twirled the dark curl in his fingers and marveled at how soft her hair was.

Brain farts, when they occurred, tended to either send everyone to the floor with laughter, die a slow, painful, silent death, or shake things up.

Half-consciously, he lifted the smooth, glossy curl to his face and inhaled. She made a soft, sweet sounding gasp that he ignored—he was too busy taking in the delicate scent that was so Angie.

"How do you do that?" he asked, giving her back her body space. "Get your hair to smell like that all the time?"

She gently laughed. "It's called shampoo."

"Don't shake your head at me like I'm a dolt," he sniggered. "The shampoo smell lasts about twenty minutes tops after a shower and you know it!"

Parker arched an eyebrow and smirked into her smiling face.

"It's you. Your smell. Nobody smells like you, baby girl."

Yeah—the smell brain fart shook things up.

Her eyes flared. Next to her sexy-as-fuck lips, or her badass tits, or that please-spank-me ass . . . or, well . . . what was he driveling on about? The throb in his groin scattered his thought process. Oh yeah, right. Her eyes. Or was it her smell? *Shit.*

Anyway, her eyes were a treasure map that he could stare at and try to decipher until the end of fucking time. They changed color. Sapphire with the emphasis on fire, or sometimes a dusky blue–warm and peaceful. He'd seen them flash violet too, and when they did, holy shit, cover your balls and run for cover.

But what he saw was more like the shifting blues of the ocean on a moonlit night. They were both trying so hard to stabilize their friendship. As if that wasn't enough, there were these little telltale heartbeats of intense attraction that kept happening. She looked hungry and cautious at the same time.

"I, um . . ." She gulped and shook her head slightly like she was bringing some sense into the discussion because he was pretty damn sure they had just been about two seconds from jumping on each other. "Can I get back to you about dinner? Ask Aunt Wendy what works for them and we'll go from there, okay?"

Parker was about to answer when he heard Meghan shriek, and not in a happy way, "Are you fucking kidding me?" *Uh-oh. Not good.*

He and Angie turned toward the sound at the same time. Irish was on fire; that much was pretty clear. Her body language suggested his old friend had stepped in it, and judging by the way Meghan's head was wagging as she laid into him, he'd stepped into it pretty good.

Angie mumbled, "*Uhhhh*," and leaned into him seeking protection from the nuclear meltdown happening seventy feet away.

Meghan began stomping angrily toward where the truck and cart were parked with Alex right behind her.

"What is wrong with you? Why the hell would you tell me that? Are you insane?" she screamed, whirling on Alex without warning.

Parker shuddered. *Holy shit.* The trifecta of hollered challenges that were every man's worst nightmare. What the fuck had Alex done?

Alex's hands were hanging in the air in that *whoa, slow down, remain calm* gesture that Parker imagined was going over like kerosene on a bonfire. *Jesus, dude!* He groaned silently to his friend. *Do not ever infer a woman should calm down.*

"Baby," Alex chuckled. "Meghan, come on. Seriously. I thought you'd laugh. This is nothing, hon. We're talking like what? More than twenty years ago."

"Oh! And what?" Meghan screeched. "There's a time limit on being an asshole?"

Her arms were waving all over the place, and Parker was pretty sure if there was anything laying around that she could throw, she would have.

And then she did that Wonder Woman thing that shriveled a man's balls. Jamming her hands on her hips, she adopted a fuck-with-me-at-your-own-peril stance, sucked in her gut, and thrust her boobs out front. *Bombs away.*

"So, just the once then?" she barked sternly.

No, no, no, he groaned silently. Wanting to jump in and holler "Objection! Leading the witness . . ." Parker tried to psychically prevent Alex from making things worse by answering the obvious gotcha in the question.

"Baby, it's not like it sounds . . ."

"I'm a teacher, Major. And I can count. A threesome sounds like what it is. Do not try and change the subject."

Parker groaned and hung his head. *Oh, dude. You dumb fuck. Please do not have told her . . .*

Angie stiffened when he reacted and looked up at him. "Parker Sullivan," she growled softly. "Oh. My. GOD! What the fuck did you two do?"

Shit. She knew him, and them, too well.

"Fuck my life," he gritted with a heavy sigh of resignation. Jumping into the verbal fray was what he did. Didn't stop him from wanting to throttle Alex for opening his damn mouth.

Parker had been worried this might come back to bite them in the ass—admittedly his fault for bringing it up in the first place—but he thought his friend would have at least half a brain cell operating and not spill his guts. Shit. Some stuff wasn't meant for public consumption and generally the more embarrassing or salacious the secret, the more drama down the line; and this one deserved a Tony nomination for best performance by two horny teenage fucknuts.

Whatever Alex was saying to talk his way out of the mess he'd made wasn't working as evidenced by an angry huff coming from Irish a second before she turned her head. Immediately zeroing in on the woman at his side, she barked, "Angelina. We're going. Leave these two perverts to reminisce about old times."

Ohhhh, fuuuuck.

"Oooop, that's my cue to ramble on," she teased, turning toward him with a wicked smile on her face.

That she was openly laughing told Parker that she found her older brother's dust-up with Meghan to be funny as hell. Laughing merrily, she whispered so only he would hear, "A threesome? Really? Is that how the big boys do it?"

He scowled at her. Witch.

Watching her hot ass sway with that sexy jiggle that might one day make him go blind, Parker growled quietly as she sashayed away from him. The afternoon had been going so well. They'd made actual headway and hadn't ended up screaming at each other. He was going to throttle Alex for fucking things up.

As Meghan and Angie zipped away in the electric buggy, Parker boomed with laughter at the comical expression of astonishment on his friend's face.

Seriously? Was the man daft? He'd obviously just foolishly admitted to his stressed out bride-to-be that he'd been a dirty dog and crossed 'threesome' off the bucket list.

"Oh, man . . ." He coughed as laughter wracked him. "You're going to pay for that, you dumb fuck."

Looking thunderstruck, Alex grumbled, "But she asked. I thought it was no big deal . . . was so long ago, y'know?"

"And let me guess," Parker drawled mockingly, "you figured you could tell her anything. Right?"

The *"Pffft"* that answered his question said it all.

Slapping Alex on the back, he chided him, "For a smart man, you are one dumb motherfucker. Telling her anything? *Yeah.* That works for the big stuff—the important stuff. Not past sexual exploits. Irish was right. Are you insane?"

"Parker, come on! That shit's funny no matter how you tell the story. We were high as fuck. That has to count for something."

He chuckled some more. Having been the Grade-A fool who spoke before thinking, he had a bit of an idea how Alex felt right now.

"Major Marquez. Rocky Mountain High is not an explanation for what happened and you know it! Have some dignity, man! I was fifteen years old screwing some hot MILF while she sucked you off. Teenage benchmark! Don't sully the memory with your apologies and crybaby bullshit," he hooted.

Now that got a laugh.

Alex was almost doubled over when he said, "Shit! How did a dinner conversation about campfire cooking lead to me getting my balls ripped off?"

"I don't know," he replied, "but, seriously, man. You're fucking with my chi here. Every time I think I'm making progress with your sister, you come along and fuck things up."

"As if," Alex answered snarkily.

Fixing him with his cockiest courtroom sneer, he spelled it out. "Throwing me and Angie together without warning."

Alex smirked.

"Requesting that fucking song at Pete's knowing we'd react."

The smirk became a shrug.

"Bringing the word *threesome* into the conversation. Smooth move, butthead."

"Okay, come on," Alex replied with a heavy dose of grumpy. "Let's load up the truck and get back. Looks like I've got some damage control to do."

Chapter Twenty-Eight

BY THE TIME THEY WERE halfway back to the hacienda, Red seemed a little less steamed but not by much. Angie kind of understood why a conversation about a kinky escapade might ruffle the bride-to-be's feathers. But for her? As used to Parker and Alex's fuckery as she was, her first instinct had been to laugh.

Peeking sideways at the stern-faced redhead navigating their cart along the sometimes bumpy trail, Angie bit back a giggle. Meghan was having an emotional Bridezilla moment that she was happy to witness. From day one of planning for the wedding, this particular bride had been oddly detached from the details. But seeing her rip into an astonished Alex was nothing short of pre-wedding hilarious.

Angie might not understand Meghan's nonchalant wedding approach, but she had no doubt about the underlying passion that drove her brother and his fiancée. If she had to freak out about something, the suggestion of a decades-old threesome was a good place to start.

Instead of going back to the Villa, when they hit the main road, Meghan turned the cart and continued down the private lane toward the Cameron cabin. Looked like Red needed a distraction.

"Wanna tell me about it?" she asked.

There was a moment of silence before Meghan sighed. "Men are just so fucking. . . . *aarrgghh!*"

She stopped the cart and turned to Angie with an exasperated growl.

"I mean . . . shit! I'm not stupid! But seriously!"

"He loves you," Angie murmured—not knowing what else to say.

"Oh, fuck. I know that," Meghan snapped. "And it's fine. Really. It's not like I believed he was celibate until we met. Everyone has a past. But what the hell was he thinking by telling me that he and Parker doubled up on some slutty campfire mother? I can't have that shit in my head! We're getting married, for fuck's sake."

Angie bit her lip to stop from laughing. Slutty campfire mother. Too funny for words.

"You know, I have like *zero* experience with this stuff."

Really, Angie thought, completely amazed. Wow. She and Red had a lot in common.

"Oh, my god." Meghan yelped in obvious distress. Lowering her face into her heads, she groaned out loud. "You don't think that's something he's into. Do you?"

"Meghan," she drawled. "Think about what you're asking. I'm pretty sure my brother would kill anyone who touches you and I'm not being facetious."

Two worried green eyes stared back at her.

"I'm sure there's plenty of hair-raising debauchery that stretches back ages for those two. Actually, I guarantee it." She shrugged with a half-smirk. "But those experiences are what formed who they became. Alex most definitely does not share. I mean, shit. Weren't we just plotting to put his brand on you?" She laughed. "Property of an arrogant, possessive Marquez."

"I'm sorry," Meghan mumbled. "You must think I'm crazy. Alex is your brother and all."

"Actually, Red," she answered cautiously, "I don't think you're crazy at all. And, um . . . well," she muttered, "I think I know what got your knickers in a twist."

It was funny how Meghan looked at her like she was completely crazy. Hell. She understood way more than poor Red had any notion of.

Turning sideways in her seat, Angie whipped off her sunglasses and pinched the bridge of her nose. "You sometimes worry that your man has, uh . . . needs. Because his . . . um," she fidgeted. "His appetite, I mean, his focus is so . . ."

"Demanding?" Meghan whispered.

"Yeah." She nodded. "Good word."

They sat there surrounded by beautiful stillness.

"We're pretty much the same age, right?"

Angie nodded.

"Do you ever think that men like your brother . . . and Parker, well—they're grown-ups, y'know? Those two are not boys." She snickered.

"I know where you're going with this," she was quick to assure Red. "Aldo was only three years my senior, but in many ways, I was the one who was oldest. In the end, he was easy to chew up and spit out."

Meghan snorted with laughter.

"But Parker? Oh, my god. I've known him my whole life, and by the time I was old enough to really consider who he was, he already seemed like an adult. I've always felt like a kid around him. *Always*. And that's probably why everything that happened was so overwhelming. There he was so big and powerful. All grown up as he headed for thirty and the sexiest man in D.C. And I was the dewy-eyed kid with a brain full of romantic rubbish. There wasn't a single moment when I didn't agonize over being out of my league with him. He knew everything . . . and I do mean everything," she added sarcastically. "And I was so easily molded to his desires." She shuddered remembering.

"I get it," Meghan drawled. "The Major took me by storm. Well, actually . . ." she blushed—causing Angie to do a double take, "I took him first." She smirked as she dipped her head and looked away.

Really? Well, high five, Red! Angie thought.

"But I know what you mean about big and powerful and sorry because I know he's your brother and all, but sexy as fuck. He just . . ." She shrugged. "I don't know . . . he like owns me in some way."

"And you worry that you won't be enough?"

She chuckled. "Shit, Angie. I went from thinking sex was all about pulling back the covers and turning out the lights to being tied up and spanked. This is a learning curve for me."

Hmmm. Red was voicing Angie's hidden fears. She'd always wondered if when Parker had dissed her that day it had been because, with his voracious sexuality, he found her inexperience dull and boring. She and Red had a lot in common. Two simple girls and the domineering men who changed everything.

"Thanks, Red."

"For what? Acting like a lunatic? Telling you that your brother has a kinky side?"

She cracked up laughing.

"Both those things, actually. Your moment of lunacy *and* confirming that Alex thinks he's god in the bedroom, too." She snickered playfully. "I needed to hear that. Helps me put my predicament with Parker and where my life is heading into perspective."

"What do you mean? How do you figure?"

"Well, just now when I heard myself say that I've always felt like a kid around Parker, I realized that might be what's confusing me. I'm not even going to try and pretend to be uninterested. I mean, the man makes me twitchy all over. But feeling awkward and like, ridiculously young because he's so. . . . *unf.* Maybe it's time to turn the tables a bit. Up the ante, as Tori would say."

"So, what you're saying is . . . you're actually serious about coming home. Permanently. But before you make that decision, you need to get the good counselor sorted out."

She chuckled and sat back in her seat. "I would say that about sums it up."

Meghan started up the cart and continued toward the cabin.

"Tits and ass, señorita. Works every time. Take it from one who knows."

Angie howled with laughter as Meghan started enthusiastically belting out the song of the same name from *A Chorus Line.*

She felt lighter. Less weighed down. And why the hell not? I mean, might as well face it. The decision to make a life change and move home permanently—see what happened—was all but written in stone. And as for the hot piece of barrister ass known as Parker Sullivan, *Esquire* . . . it was time for her to stop acting like a lovesick teenager.

He fucked with her at Pete's, which he really shouldn't have—and totally pulled his man-god shit at the fondue restaurant. Both times he'd pushed her buttons. It was high time for some reciprocal button pushing. Remind him who the hell he was dealing with before this went any further.

She wasn't a wide-eyed twenty-year-old innocent girl anymore, and he wasn't the ambitious young lawyer burning up the hallways at the Justice Department. They'd gotten older, matured, and needed to be real with each other. And besides, she was pretty sure that was exactly what had been on Esquire Parker's agenda when he duck marched her to dinner and then proceeded to quite deliberately establish his, uh . . . domination. *Yeah, right,* she snorted.

As they pulled up to the front of Lacey's sprawling cabin, she waved Meghan on to go ahead inside—holding up her phone and mumbling, "I have to answer this. Be along in a minute."

Once she was alone, Angie leaned against the buggy and muttered, "'Kay then Mr. Sexy Badass Lawyer, let's see what ya got now, big boy."

Let me show you how the big boys do it. As long as she lived, Angie would remember him saying that all those years ago and since he seemed hell bent on poking her with the evocative expression now, it was most definitely time to throw it back in his face.

She stared at her phone a minute then swiped and tapped, bringing up a text message. The fact that he hadn't given her his number almost stopped Angie, but then she figured, *What the hell. This was part of being real.* Yeah—she had his number. His address, too. Even had the location of his office saved in her map app.

She also wrote Mrs. Angelina Sullivan on tiny scraps of paper and made elaborate sketches of gowns with a suspiciously bridal flair. "So, shoot me," she grumbled aloud.

Hola. Talk to your Mom and let me know when we can do dinner. My schedule is totally open. Any day. Anytime. Tell me and I'm there.

Her laughter split the air. He was, after all, a guy, and she knew how his mind worked. He'd read those words and think *capitulation.*

Well, now that she'd tossed one over the fence, there was nothing to do but go find Red and Lacey. See what they'd gotten up to. Ooooh, maybe they could take the baby for a walk.

She'd moved less than ten feet when her phone buzzed. *Ahhahahahaaaaa. That was quick!*

Great. Mom will be thrilled. Where are you?

Multi-tasking was one thing, but walking while texting had face plant potential. Sitting on the bottom steps leading to the cabin, Angie concentrated on the back and forth with Parker. He might be older and wiser, but she had a few weapons to unleash that would even the score.

The cabin. Where are you?

Driving back to the house. How's Meghan?

Thinking back to Alex's stunned expression when Red went off on him, Angie bit off a giggle. Might be the first time ever that she'd seen her almighty brother get handed his ass so neatly by anyone other than their mother.

I think she's moving in with the Cameron's. Says she's had enough of Alex's shit.

OMFG You're kidding. Please tell me you're kidding.

She let a couple beats of silence creep by. Taking a deep breath, she looked at the view from the front of the house and smiled. Cam picked the perfect spot to build his home.

After letting him squirm from the quiet, she answered. She bet by now his heart was beating out of his chest!

You DO know that I want the full story. Right?

Angelina Marquez. God-fucking-dammit, woman. Tell me what's happening with Irish. He'll kill me first and ask questions later if what you say is true and I'm not wearing a bulletproof vest.

Oh, poo. He had a point. Alex could be so . . . volatile.

Chill your pecker.

Angie snorted laughter as she typed. He'd told her to chill her tits at Fon Do Me, and she'd almost smacked him for it.

Just messing with you. She's fine.

For reals? Don't fuck around. You don't want to know what he's like when there's trouble with M.

"Hmph." No shit.

Honest. The wedding is still a go. Alexander may want to crank open his wallet though and shell out for something that says My Bad.

Stupid fucker. Can't believe what he did.

What can't you believe? That you two shared some pussy or that he admitted to it?

You said pussy.

His *Beavis & Butthead* comeback made her laugh.

Calm down, you old pervert. It's just a word.

Are you kidding? It's the BEST word ever—especially coming out of lips as sweet as yours.

The word came out of my fingers, not my mouth. So does that count?

It counts if those fingers came out of your pussy and not your mouth.

She roared. He was something.

How the hell did you do that?

Do what?

Change worrying about Alex and Meghan to discussing my, uh . . .

She frantically searched her Emojis for something to insert rather than the actual word. *Jeez.* Someone would clean up with an app for symbols to use when flipping the bird, sucking a dick, and discussing pussy.

Pussy, baby girl. The word you're searching for is PUSSY.

Angie cracked up. Damn! He had fast fingers and though she meant to refer to how quickly he'd texted her, a naughty flash of other things those fingers could do crackled in her head.

Red is right. You're a pervert. An old pervert.

And you, my desert Angel, are a very sexy, very hot temptation who thought she was going to work me up in a text message. Worked. And now you can enjoy the rest of your day knowing that if we went home together at the end of the night, you'd be face down over my knee . . .

Oh, my god! Whaaaat? She laughed. Angie planned to tease him a little then dash away giggling—and in no way expected to be the one heavy breathing over a taunt. A suggestive one. Snickering, she typed a reply.

Sorry. What? Message was cut due to maximum characters

Finally back at the house. Will you be here later?

Why? You going to wait around to spank me?

Fucker. Play with her and good luck, buddy. She could be relentless if necessary, something he should remember from her childhood. If Parker was a rebel, she was a spinning top.

Yes

Unf. He was killing her. Angie didn't remember ever seeing this side of him before. It was oddly thrilling. Parker liked to play. Was good at it. He brought out a side to her nature that felt so right. But he also made it very clear who would win in the end. Didn't mean she had to make it easy.

Thin ice, counselor

You asked.

That's how we got in this mess today. Red asked.

Good point. Change of tactic.

Closing argument-no rebuttal. The ladies await.

Will you have dinner with me? Please note that I made that a question and not a foregone conclusion. If you say no, I will, of course, force the issue but thought we'd pretend first that you have a choice.

"Hey senõrita," she heard Tori holler from the front door. "Get your Angel ass in here. Carmen brought over a plate of sweet empanadas that will melt your brain. If you want one, get moving!"

She shot to her feet and waved then pointed at Tori and deadpanned, "I will murder you if they eat all the good ones."

"Then get the fuck in here!" Noticing the phone in her hand, Victoria *tsked* and shook her head. "Tell that man to shut up and sit down."

"There's a ban on saying shut up at the Villa. Haven't you heard?"

The other woman hooted with laughter and went back inside, leaving Angie to tap out her last reply. *Hmmmmm.*

Keeping the arrogant know-it-all guessing by giving nothing away, she simply asked . . .

Dress Code?

Tits and Ass.

Angie laughed as she climbed the stairs and let herself into the cabin. There was SO definitely something in the damn water!

Chapter Twenty-Nine

Before Parker had gotten but a couple of yards from the driveway, Alex came thundering down the walk looking a little bit like a storm cloud with feet.

"She's not here. Goddammit!" the man bellowed. "Where the fuck did she go?"

Jumping into the storm's path, Parker slowed him down with a carefully voiced, "Whoa, whoa. Relax. She's fine."

Glancing over Parker's shoulder, Alex's eyes scoured the driveway. "How do you know? Where is she?" Alex barked.

"She went to the cabin, man, so chill. I talked to Angie," he added by waving his phone for emphasis.

Watching Alex stand down was like letting the air out of a balloon after the emotion of the last half hour. Parker felt for him, he really did. Being no stranger to having opened mouth and inserted foot at the worst moment possible, he knew exactly what was going on in his friend's mind and it wasn't pretty.

Slapping Alex soundly on the back, he steered him back into the house. "You lucked out, dude. Those women, with the possible exception of your sister, are one hundred and fifty percent on Team Alex. They'll calm the waters but I'd still prepare for a full frontal assault," Parker quipped. "Come on. Cheer up. Let's go talk to that motley crew of yours. Get some married man perspective. Those two shitheads are always good for a laugh."

"Are they around?" Alex mumbled as he jammed his hands into his pockets and shuffled like a prisoner walking the green mile.

If this were an installment of *Parker and Alex's Excellent Adventure,* they'd be going back in time to that summer trip to Colorado and telling their younger, hornier selves to enjoy it now 'cause some day what they were doing was going to fuck shit up.

"Man, you are a mess," Parker muttered, pushing open the heavy wood door. "Yes, they're here. And you do surveillance for a living? Wow. You just walked right past Cam's SUV and practically tripped over the pretentious pussy magnet that St. John drives. Shit. Is Meghan's middle name kryptonite?"

Ushering him deep into the Villa, they made for Alex's tech cave where Parker was pretty sure they'd find Butch and Sundance doing their ever-alternating straight man and jokester routine. It wasn't just an act, either. That was how they were.

"Knew you were here, St. John," Parker drawled, "when I stumbled over your penis envy car in the drive."

Draegyn and Cameron were sitting alongside each other on a workstation, remote controls in their hands, as *Grand Theft Auto* boomed loudly from a huge monitor. *Always working, those two,* Parker snickered.

Tossing his controller aside, Drae slid to the floor and gave Parker the fuck you salute. "My Lamborghini eats your Porsche for lunch."

"More like your Lambo sucks off my 911."

"And my Escalade crushes both your girly cars," Cam smirked. "What's with him?" he asked, nodding at Alex.

Pushing the silent, plodding man into a swiveling desk chair, Parker stood over him like an animal handler and announced, "Men . . . I give you one Alexander Valleja-Marquez. Warrior, gentleman, and genius. And just about the dumbest motherfucker who ever walked."

"Oh shit," Drae groaned. "What's he done now?"

"Raise your hand if you've ever done a threesome."

Parker, Drae, and Cam all raised their hands.

"Ever tell your wives?"

Cam and Drae exploded at the same time, talking over each other.

"Fuck no!"

"Are you nuts?"

Parker stepped back and crossed his arms, spearing the two with a meaningful look.

"Well, what you see here," he gestured to Alex, "is the aftermath of having told a feisty, badass Irishwoman that . . . well, I guess there's no use in pretending I wasn't also involved so here it is. We did a MILF together when we were teenagers, and for some insane reason, he told her about it."

Parker didn't miss the way Drae and Cam coughed and fidgeted. He was guessing those two assholes knew firsthand what he was talking about.

"Duu*uuude,*" Cam drawled.

"She asked," Alex mumbled for the hundredth time, still managing to sound stunned that she reacted the way she did when, after all, *she asked.* My god. What they said was correct. Men really were dumb as dirt.

Then, after a long, tense silence, Drae muttered darkly, "What the fuck are you all looking at me for? I'm not the one who went to confession."

"No," Alex agreed with a sigh. "But you would know more than us three put together about how to keep your sexual history a non-issue. Tori's not exactly known for keeping a cool head, and with your past, I mean. . . . it's gotta be tough."

Hmmph. Good point, Parker thought. Looking at Drae, he wondered how exactly the legendary ladies' man retained his balls while being married to a whirlwind like Victoria.

Draegyn scowled. "My wife has nothing to worry about."

"Neither does Meghan," Alex agreed. "That's not the point. C'mon, Drae. Throw me a lifeline. Are we talking flowers or jewelry? Or a car. *Whatever.* Help a brother out here, man."

Because Parker basically observed, for a living, people, body language, and words on paper, this moment was pretty goddamn funny because Alex, he, and Cam were all focused on Draegyn St. John as if he was teaching a Relationships for Dummies course aimed at a bunch of alphas involved with women who when pushed could quite literally kick all their asses.

Drae however did not seem amused. "Okay. You guys are a bunch of assholes. Cut it out."

Cam took the role of peacemaker and playfully started slapping at Drae until the other man slapped back with a laugh.

"Come on, St. John," he drawled. "Show us the way, O Wise One."

"Bunch of fucktards," Drae muttered chuckling. "You make it sound like you're all promise ring-wearing members of the boys' choir while I'm playing the part of Long Dong John. I'm not the only one in this room to walk a little on the wild side."

"True," Parker sneered. "But, then again, none of us ever made it to the *National Enquirer*."

High fives all around on that one!

Defeated by their humor, Draegyn St. John snickered and shook his head at them. "All right, all right. First of all," Drae jeered. "Get your heads out yo' asses! These are our women we're talking about. Gotta play from a fresh deck. Rule number one. For the big stuff? Don't *ever* open your wallet. Will only make it worse. The only thing that works is words. Oh, and yeah. There will be groveling, but if you play it right, there's not a lot of things better than apology sex."

"Hmmph," Parker and Alex grunted in unison.

"Flowers and 'my bad' gifts are best saved for the day-to-day shit we step in. But a major faux pas like a threesome? Major, I'd be breaking out the knee pads and sizing up Irish's ass so you'll hit the right spot when you're kissing it. And come ready with a good story. If it were me?" he sneered. "I'd blame it all on him," he said pointing in Parker's direction.

Alex snorted a laugh. "Yeah. That was going to happen anyway." The look he shot his way made it clear he thought Parker was ultimately to blame anyway.

Drae and Cam turned in his direction. "You taking this one for the team?" Cam asked.

"Sure. Why the hell not?"

"It's not like you could do anything that would make Angie madder, right?"

Butch and Sundance chuckled from the cheap seats at Alex's snappy comeback.

Drae got all serious looking and asked, "What's that all about, Sullivan? Rumor had it that Angie preached the gospel according to Parker, but she seems more likely to have you in the crosshairs these days. You shit in her cornflakes or something?"

Alex fixed Parker with a look. He'd been damn careful not to go into much detail about his past involvement with the man's baby sister. He liked keeping his head, after all. Admitting to having slept with her was bad enough. But explaining what a dick he'd been? That part of the saga was going to go over about as well as a church fart. How quickly could he change the subject?

"Uh, we had a misunderstanding. Trying to make it right."

"How's that working for you?" Cam asked.

Parker kicked Alex's chair. "It would be working a lot better if this butt fuck didn't keep making all sorts of problems for me."

Drae groaned and told them, "The wife texted."

Everyone looked at him.

"And I quote. . . . Irish on fire. Alex a dead man. Ask Cam why Lacey is acting weird and get back to me."

The attention shifted in unison from Alex to Cam.

Drae frowned. "Anything?"

Cameron sighed. "Come on. I need a beer. Anyone else?"

Parker was already on his way to the kitchen.

"Check this out," Alex drawled from a spot at the counter after they'd grabbed some cold ones from the fridge. "Brody sent us a digital picture frame with all these great shots of Zeus from the kennel."

They gathered in a semi-circle and watched the slideshow, making pithy comments as the pictures flashed by. The last shot was of Zeus and Raven posing protectively next to the babies in their car seats.

"Cool," Cam murmured. "Believe it or not, I think Ponytail is considering a pup."

"Well, thank god you brought Lacey up yourself, dude, 'cause I think all of us were standing here trying to come up with a way that didn't sound all jackassey to ask what's up," Alex said.

"That's one special lady," Parker added. "Is everything okay?"

Cam drained his long neck, belched like a pro, tossed the empty into the recycling bin, and looked at each of them.

"The *Hey, honey, your dad's living in Oregon and has a second family* part of our program did not go over well."

Drae whistled and his eyebrows shot into his hairline. "Oh, fuck."

"Ruined your anniversary, didn't you. Ya stupid shit?" Alex shook his head with dismay.

Cam shrugged. "Not entirely. Was smart enough to wait until we were on the flight home."

"Wait," Parker interjected. "What? Lacey's father is in Oregon?"

Alex turned to him and filled in the blanks. "Cam tracked the bastard. Told her when they went to Vegas for their anniversary."

"I'm your fucking lawyer, Cam. Were you planning on telling me this? I mean, shit! Didn't we just get all your family stuff sorted out? Lacey made it pretty fucking clear that her legal family begins and ends with you and Dylan. Nobody said shit about a living parent."

Cam shifted back and forth on his feet and rolled his neck. Tension much?

"My wife had the right to know first, and I didn't want to tell her after dinner one night like it was the day's current event. That conversation needed to happen on neutral ground when our son wasn't around so she could react without a filter."

Although unhappy to realize he was the last to know, Parker did have to admit that Cam had acted with remarkable understanding and compassion. As always, his natural take on family dynamics was extraordinary considering that until recently, he'd never experienced what having parents or an actual functioning family was even like.

Parker recognized Alex's protective Big Daddy impulse firing up and wasn't in the least surprised to hear him ask, "Do you want me to fuck with him? Tori and I can make his life a living hell, you know."

Cam grimaced. "Seriously? You really think it wasn't hard as fuck not to just have the bastard wiped from humanity once I found him?"

Drae tersely drawled, "Fucker's not worth it. I vote for emptying his bank accounts and screwing with his digital footprint over a dirt nap."

Parker was taking mental notes about dirt naps and digital footprints. These guys were balls out impressive. No wonder Justice was in such high demand.

It wasn't at all hard to imagine what these three men had been like serving together in Afghanistan. Although not on the battlefield with them, he'd done his part from inside the government to crush the bad guys and the systems that made their fuckery possible. Parker understood better than most how bloodthirsty and inglorious the fight really was. Their bond wasn't ambiguous.

"Actually," Cam added soberly, "there's more that I didn't tell you."

"Of course, there is," Drae spat out.

In a voice that sounded brittle and harsh, Cam told them the rest. "You pretty much already know that Lacey bolted when she was seventeen to get away from an abusive relative after her old man more or less abandoned her. The father is a dick. The uncle, a criminal. Didn't take much digging to find out that the gator-baiting uncle died about four months after she left. Drunk driving. Go figure, huh?" he sneered.

He didn't say anything for a minute or two after that. Parker was used to these stories. He listened to this shit for a living, so he was already ahead of the curve and jumped in with a legal question.

"Are you saying he was dead before she turned eighteen?"

"Yep."

"Oh, jeez," he muttered. "They were brothers?"

"Yep."

"And Lacey was legally in this man's custody? Was support being paid?"

"Yep." The tone Cam answered in told Parker he knew where this was going.

"Ho-*ly* fuck." In his mind, that pretty much summed it up.

"Yep."

"Next of kin?"

"Yep."

Drae, who liked facts, stopped their odd exchange and asked that Parker clue him and Alex in.

Making a disgusted face, he told them, "Fucker knew the brother had died before his daughter was of legal age. He would have gotten an official contact and had to make the final arrangements. Probably got any death benefits, too."

Alex sounded like he'd just learned the tooth fairy was bullshit. "He didn't reach out, did he? Didn't check on his kid."

"No, he did not," Cam answered testily, sounding just as crushed by this sad bit of news as Alex did. "I should kill the motherfucker for that alone."

"What do you want me to tell the wife?" Drae asked. "The ladies must sense a disturbance in the force."

"It has to come from Lacey. This is her story."

"Meghan's asked a couple of times. So has Angie. I've said nothing."

Drae tossed his empty beer bottle into the recycle bin and admitted drily, "Victoria is obsessing, and that's not good."

"They're all pretty tight, huh?" Parker asked.

"Family," Alex pronounced.

Chapter Thirty

"I THINK WE'RE GOOD TO GO for Saturday night. What do you think?"

"*Mmmm,* can we do that last shimmy shake thing again?" Angie asked. "I think I'm a half-step behind Tori."

"Good news," Meghan blurted out. "We go on last! Boom shaka-laka, we got top billing!"

Lacey looked around at the circle of friends clustered in her living room. It was a beautiful day so the sliders to the brick patio were wide open. This amazing house. These wonderful people. And in the nursery safe in his crib was her beautiful son. This was her life.

"What should I wear," Angelina asked. "Karaoke virgin so please be gentle!"

She liked Alex's little sister. In a word, the breathtaking beauty was fantabulous, and Meghan had really taken to her. Lacey was glad. She knew a little bit about Irish's insecurities when it came to the noble and impressive family she was marrying into. She also understood the jitters that came with having sisters when she'd never had them before. Irish needed Angie to be just exactly who she turned out to be . . . a Marquez through and through. Funny, irreverent, loyal, talented, pretty damn good looking . . . just like her brother.

"Red, you've got the boots covered, right?" Angie asked.

"Oh, yeah," she snickered. "And wait till you see them! I'm breaking in a new pair. Give that kinky bastard something to think about," she mumbled in the end.

"And I'm taking these bad girls out for a spin," Victoria snickered as she grabbed at her boobs. "It's hard not to love nursing when this is the result!"

All Lacey could do was shake her head and smile. The boots and the sass were covered so they all turned expectantly to find out what devious way she'd devised to highlight her ass.

Her mind went blank. She had an outfit. Was pretty sure, at least, but try as she could, she just had . . . nothing.

Meghan looked at Victoria, who raised an expressive eyebrow. Then Victoria glanced at Angie who was studying Lacey with an air of concern.

Um, had she had an out-of-body experience or something? Why were they looking at her like she was a science project? Then she looked down at her hands and realized that for the past twenty minutes or so, she'd been absently tying little knots in a long piece of ribbon that had at one point been holding up her ponytail.

"You were waiting me out, weren't you?" she said with a sulky twang. Why had she even tried to keep this from them?

"Yeah," Tori said softly. "You're scaring me, sweetie," she admitted.

Meghan walked over, pulled the knotted ribbon from her grasp, and sat down next to her as Angie pressed a glass of ice-cold water into her hands.

She looked into Irish's calm, reassuring eyes. Even after her upset earlier with Alex, she was totally focused on Lacey. Seeing Tori's unusual show of emotion and the way the newest member of their Justice clique was so clearly disturbed, she felt a wave of support engulf her. And just like that she began to cry.

"Oh!" Meghan cried. "No, no, no honey. No tears. Please! Just tell us what's wrong. Is the baby okay? Cam? What's going on with you?"

Crying wasn't something that came easily to her. Too many hard years trying to keep it together in difficult circumstances robbed her of the luxury of even having time for emotion as she struggled to survive. Now? Her life was so blessed it wasn't like she had anything to weep about so she was woefully out of practice and realized immediately that she was sinking into one hell of an ugly cry.

Hiccupping back the tears, she put the glass down and swiped at her nose wailing, "My father. Cam found him!"

The shocked gasps that met this announcement tore at her composure—what little she had at the moment.

Tori—the first real girlfriend she ever had—rose and stood in front of Lacey, growing in stature until she seemed ten feet tall and about as terrifying and imposing as any Medusa ready to turn someone to stone.

"You want me to ask Draegyn to have him suffer? I bet we could make that happen. Right, ladies?" she asked, looking at Meghan and Angie for reassurance.

God bless the little dynamo that was Victoria St. John. The crazy waif was better than having a pit bull. Without hearing anything else other than that he'd been found, the ladies of Family Justice were ready to kick ass.

"Tissue," she choked, sniffling as she tried to control the crying jag. "A box."

Angie flew off in search of some while Meghan shifted closer and put an arm around her, rubbing circles on her back.

"Does your husband know you're this upset?" she asked her gently.

Lacey nodded immediately. Cameron was freaking out more than she was about the whole thing. He was just better at hiding it.

Angie reappeared with some tissues and put them in her lap.

"Thanks," she tried to say in a watery voice. "I love you guys."

"Victoria?" Meghan barked sharply.

"Hold on. Almost," she heard Tori answer. Then, "Okay. Got it!"

Next thing Lacey knew, their tongue-in-cheek theme song sounded from Tori's phone as *We Are Family* filled the air.

It was just what she needed to bring her back from the edge.

Blowing her nose with a resounding honk, she went through a handful of tissues, ending with a swipe of her face that she knew damn well was probably blotchy and her nose all red.

As soon as she sat up straighter and took a couple of sips of water, Tori turned off the song and went back to hovering over her. Waiting. Meghan's reassuring presence pushed her the last step and taking a deep breath, she told them as much as she knew, ending her sad tale with, "Frank Morrow is a piece of shit."

She should have expected the group snicker, but it still took her by surprise.

"*Hehehe*. You said a bad word," Tori wheezed with laughter.

"Wow," Meghan eventually bit out in a none-too-nice way. "What a dick. And even after his brother dies and you're like what? M.I.A.? He does nothing?"

The fierce explosion of Irish outrage was like a balm for Lacey's soul.

"What are you going to do?" Tori wanted to know.

Something uncomfortable twisted inside her. No child should ever have to be put in this position. She'd never understood how her father could have walked away from her as he did—didn't matter whether they were close or not. He was her only parent. She was his responsibility. Now that she had Dylan, she had even harsher feelings. Becoming a parent hadn't mellowed her at all.

Lacey couldn't hate him because she knew her mother had loved him and that they'd been a happy family before she died. But he'd changed after that and the man she remembered was nobody she'd choose to know. And certainly no one she wanted anywhere near her family.

"At first, I was so shocked that there were a few moments when I wondered if . . . well, you know—Dylan changes everything. And then I thought about his other kids and I asked Cam to find out whether or not they or his wife knew about his former life or me. I figured knowing that one thing would tell me a lot."

"And?" Tori drawled.

She half-smiled. "There's no evidence that his new family knows anything about his life before the time he spent in Alaska. Maybe, if he'd told them about me then I'd feel different. But he hasn't and so they don't know they have an older half-sister. Speaks for itself, huh? Thanks Dad, you fucking asshole."

She laughed first. Couldn't help it. Meghan cleared her throat and tried not to join in, but Tori's bellowed, "Ha!" got Angie giggling and next thing she knew, they were all on the floor laughing.

Every time she said, "Fucking asshole," it started all over again.

At one point, Lacey was pounding on the floor screaming, "Stop! Stop!" since the body-wracking laughter was killing her. "You're making me pee my pants!" Eventually, they fell into a giggling group hug that took a long time to break apart.

"Shit," Meghan sighed after they'd freshened up, visited the bathroom, and grabbed something to drink. "Look at us. I'm behaving like a crazy person morning, noon, and night. Today's freak-out being only the latest. Angie threw her bad self into the deep end of the pool—on purpose! Lacey has an unwanted family reunion. What the hell is next?"

"Thank god Tori's not swinging from the rafters, too. Somebody has to be the safe and sane designated driver." Lacey chuckled.

Took her a good minute to realize that Tori hadn't reacted or said anything.

Angie teased in her easygoing way, "Silence is never a good thing with her, is it?"

Lacey heard the telltale rumblings over the baby monitor of the little guys beginning to stir in the nursery. Time to shift into mommy mode.

"Well, since my tits are killing me," Tori said as she pressed on her chest, "and I can hear my greedy little St. John sucker gearing up to demand feeding, I'll give you the four-one-one in the shortened version."

"Works for me," Meghan said.

"Okay. Here it is," she snickered sarcastically. "Hold on to your dildos, ladies, because a certain Mr. and Mrs. St John have expressed a desire to visit Arizona and meet their grandson."

"Get the fuck out."

Tori looked over at Meghan and grimaced.

"What did Draegyn say?"

Victoria St. John's mocking expression said it all. "He's building a spaceship out in that shop of his so we can leave the planet. Apparently, that's the only recourse we have should they plan an invasion."

A husky cry sounded from the monitor. "I'd know that hungry bear sound anywhere," Lacey laughed.

She looked at Meghan and Angie, who were already gathering their stuff to head out. Tori, she knew, would wait to leave until after Daniel nursed.

"Irish—go easy on the Major. You know he's a mess on his best day but that man would rip his own heart out before he'd intentionally hurt you. And Angie? To answer your karaoke wardrobe question, I bring the ass so my question to you is . . . whatcha got, sister?"

Angie laughed and said, "Desert Angel has legs that go on for miles y'all! And I know just what to wear!"

"Think they'll be back soon?" a morose and out-of-sorts Alex asked Parker. They were in his study, sprawled out on two enormous leather chairs in front of an ancient fireplace that Alex had wisely converted to a closed gas unit. Far as ambiance went, it was just what they needed.

So far he'd managed to keep the worried man away from the bar. No way was having a drink going to be helpful in this situation. Best they meet what was coming at them head-on. But wiling away the time as their wait stretched on was fucking nerve wracking.

Angie hadn't contacted him again, but he hadn't expected her to. They were playing a game to see who had control. He wanted to laugh at how absurd it was because she had all the damn control but didn't know it.

He glanced at his watch. *Let's see.* She'd need at least an hour to get ready if she was going with him to dinner, so yeah, they'd probably be back soon. Plus, he'd heard Carmen earlier coordinating dinner with Ria so he knew Alex and Meghan were set for the evening. Maybe now was a good time to tell Alex that he was taking Angie out.

"I imagine they'll be along soon. It's getting late and Drae and Cam are probably heading home about now. You nervous?"

Hmmm. I would have thought he'd have a quick answer.

"Not really. More worried than nervous."

"'Cause you think she's mad?"

This time, Alex answered instantly with a loud snort.

"No! Because she's hurt. You know I can't have that shit."

He exhaled heavily, put his head on the back of the chair, and closed his eyes. "It sucks when you hurt somebody you love."

Parker heard Alex's deep answering sigh. "Is that what happened with Angie?"

He might as well tell him the whole thing. Wasn't like it was going to be a secret much longer. Once their respective families weighed in, all sorts of hell were going to break loose.

Sliding forward in the chair, he rested his forearms on his thighs, clasped his hands between his legs, and stared at the fire.

"Straight up. No bullshit. In no way a revisionist retelling okay?"

"I'm listening."

"No matter what you think, there was nothing going for two years after she came to D.C. I treated her like my own sister. We did everything together, and I did my best to keep an eye on her and make sure she didn't get sucked into any university stupidity."

"I know. She told me. Constantly. Her letters were like a private investigator's log. Parker ate a corned beef sandwich. Parker did his laundry. Parker bought tomatoes at the farmer's market."

He chuckled. Angie. She was so young then, and he'd been such a fool.

"And then, shit got real and well, you know that part."

Without warning, Alex reached out and socked him forcefully.

Startled, Parker grabbed his arm and hissed. "Ow, dude. What the fuck?"

"You slept with my little sister, you shithead."

"Yeah, and I told you—I happen to be in love with her too so cut me some slack, okay?"

"Continue; although, I reserve the right to punch your fucking lights out with no warning whenever the hell I want. No expiration date, either. You being in love with Angie is all well and good now. But you slept with her then which makes you a giant piece of shit."

"Your sister disagrees."

"That remains to be seen. Finish your little story before I forget how much I like you and take out my frustrations on your ugly face."

Gritting his teeth, Parker dropped the rest of the tale and waited for Alex's reaction.

"It was early days and we were figuring it out when some prick in my department started giving me shit about hanging out with a hot piece of coed ass. There was no fucking way I was going to let that dickhead think shit like that about Angie. Seriously, man," he sneered, "didn't give a rat's ass what anyone said about me but going after her? Uh-uh. A step too far."

"Fucking gossips," Alex muttered.

"Exactly. So I jumped in without thinking about what I was saying and pointed out to the bastard that the girl in question was family with a Special Forces brother off killing bad guys. To drive home my point that he was a dick who should be ashamed of himself, I made light of her age, said watching out for her was a pain in the ass. You know. Dumb shit."

"Unless it was a videotaped deposition, I don't see where this is going."

"No video necessary. Unfortunately, Angie overheard my part of the conversation. *Just my part.* Before I could explain, she cut me off without a word and until she showed up here, I hadn't spoken directly to her since. I figured she was mad as hell and rightfully so. Turns out I was wrong on that, too. She wasn't mad. She was hurt. It took me a long time, *too long,* to see that."

He let Alex digest what he'd said then brought the story forward into the present day.

"I've apologized. Explained. She's calmer and you see we're trying, right?"

"I thought you two seemed pretty chill earlier and said so to Meghan. That's how our conversation turned to you. She remembered you saying our Colorado trip was a summer of firsts. She asked. The rest you know."

"Angie texted when they went to the cabin. She's agreed to go to dinner with my folks."

Alex looked surprised. "For real? Aunt Wendy's on the ball, huh? Wonder if my mom has anything to do with that."

"And, um, I sort of got her to agree to have dinner with me. Tonight. Just the two of us. So when they get here, we'll get out of your way as soon as we can. Give you and Meghan some privacy."

Alex looked halfway impressed. "She agreed to go out with you? Like on a date?"

Parker knew he hadn't given her any choice whatsoever and couldn't help but chuckle.

"Actually, the girl makes me so crazy that I asked her in a way that made it impossible for her to say no."

Alex clapped his hands together and bawled, "Snap out of it, you fucking idiot. There's your goddamn problem right there. You still think of her as a kid. Wake up and drink the sherry, my friend. That's no little girl and if you think playing her like she's a toothy, braces-wearing twelve-year-old is going to get you anywhere, you need your head examined."

Chapter Thirty-One

MEGHAN STAYED SILENT ON THE ride up to the big house. What a bizarre day it had been. The musical morning picnic she thought would be so much fun turned into a shit show. Lacey was in the middle of an emotional meltdown, and Tori suddenly had in-law problems where five minutes ago there had been none.

"When we get home, I have to go get changed. Parker is taking me to dinner. That way you and Alex can be alone without an audience."

"Oh," she murmured. "Dinner? That's nice. Whose idea was that?"

"His," Angie answered. "He thinks he didn't give me a choice." She had to laugh.

"Ah," Meghan chuckled. "The alpha way of inviting a woman to dinner." She grunted comically and said in caveman style, "Woman. Eat. Now."

They each laughed and shook their heads.

"Sadly, it was something exactly like that. Joke's on him, though. You're right, Red. Time to give that man a taste of the real me. Not the little girl he remembers."

"I like that plan. It has great merit."

They drove on a bit and she asked, "Have you got something to wear that will melt his eyeballs?"

"I'll figure that part out when I shower."

"Want me to work him over for you while you get ready? Maybe scare the shit out of him a little? "

Angie laughed sarcastically and teased, "Oh, you mean like accusing him of being a pervert because he asked for your panties?"

"Sure," she answered enthusiastically. "It always pays to keep a man thinking. I can tell him you're designing the launch campaign for the latest must-have sex toy that's all the rage in Europe. Custom-made floggers maybe?"

Floggers?" Angie shrieked hysterically laughing. "Red. You're killing me!"

"Just trying to bring the giggles. Lighten things up."

"Hey," Angie said gently. "Don't worry about Alex. I know my brother. He's probably curled up in the fetal position and sucking his thumb because you're upset."

"I know and I feel bad. He caught me off guard. I'll talk to him, don't worry. Everything will be all right."

Boy, she really hoped it was that easy. Lately, she'd begun to put some stock into all that eyeball rolling about wedding jitters and crazy bride antics. Meghan was inwardly cringing because she felt all she did was careen from one emotional freak-out to another. There was too damn much noise in her head.

She was barely sleeping—the same for eating. A bottle of Zantac had taken up residence in her purse and not even the calm serenity of her normal yoga practice brought her much peace. And poor Alex. She was really doing a number on him. The man was dancing as fast as he could trying to stay out ahead of her craziness. *Dammit,* Meghan sighed. She really needed to find her center again because this shit wasn't working for her at all.

"Parker's here," she muttered absently after leaving the buggy for Ben to take to the garage and weaving through the usual clusterfuck in the driveway. "Oh, right. I guess he's waiting for you, huh?"

"Listen," Angie said in a jumbled rush. "As soon as we're inside, I'm running upstairs, okay? Don't wanna see him just yet. Have a plan. Knock him sideways. Show him what's what."

Meghan grinned. *Ah, the dance of love.* Wasn't all that long ago that it was her and Alex driving everyone batshit with their push-me, pull-me routine. She hadn't seen Angie in action yet, but she was so much like the Major that all she could do was bite back the hysterical laugh that threatened to erupt each time she imagined the ass-handing

Parker was about to experience.

"No worries," she assured her. "I'll entertain the men while you put your battle plan into action."

She could hear the smile in Angie's voice when she mumbled, "Stupid fucker," as they approached the front door to the Villa.

"Indeed," Meghan snickered gleefully as she pushed the wooden masterpiece open.

They playfully fist bumped and did this hilarious boob shimmy that Tori had them all mimicking where you bend forward, give the girls a good shaky-shake—she insisted this sets the boobs comfortably inside your bra—and then stand up straight and arch your back. "Ta-dah!" they cried then giggled and said, "Shh, shh, shh," to each other a dozen times.

Meghan pushed Angie up the stairs with a shooing motion and then took a deep breath. Smoothing her usual riot of curls, an action that usually did nothing because her hair rather insisted on itself, she pressed a hand against her tummy to stop the nervous flutters and metaphorically put her big girl panties on.

Go find your man, her inner voice demanded. *Do not pass Go and do not collect two hundred dollars. Get moving!*

She found them finally. Coming from behind, they didn't realize her presence right away, giving her a rare opportunity to catch the two alphas in repose. Had Alex's admission about the threesome with Parker been a shock? Of course. But over the course of the day, she'd been connecting the dots and thinking about the close, long-standing friendship between the two men.

Understanding the Major's relationship and bond with Cam and Drae was easy. All that soldiering stuff had a way of forging intense bonds. But Parker had been a harder read from the start. All the men were dynamic in their own way, but there was something different about the camaraderie between the old friends. Because Parker was the older and most probably when they were kids every inch the big dog, she had to wonder. Had he been the influence to shape Alex's unique, um . . . needs? All signs were starting to point to yes.

While Meghan hated labels, she couldn't ignore the simple fact that Parker Sullivan personified the capital D in dominant and gave it a kick in the ass. She sure hoped Angie knew what she was doing 'cause right now? Right this second? Before they realized she was right there? Meghan could feel the intensity rolling off both men, and yeah, most of it was sexual. Neither of these men was for the faint-hearted.

She saw Alex's head raise and knew he felt her presence. Meghan shivered slightly. He was in beast mode—waiting for her to come to him, as he knew she would.

Not pausing even a heartbeat, she immediately crossed the room. Leaning over the back of his chair, she said, "Hi,," then put her hand on his shoulder and swung sideways to his front for a quick kiss.

The minute she connected with Alex, Meghan felt his tension. Just as quickly, she felt it fade away when their lips briefly touched. With that one gesture, she let him know that they were all right. He reached up and patted the hand on his shoulder then slipped his fingers into hers. She left her hand where it was. Through that simple touch, they were communicating, and for now, it was enough.

As soon as Parker realized she was present, he jumped to his feet and came to her with his hands held open like a conscience-stricken penitent about to beg for forgiveness.

"Miss O'Brien," he said soberly. "I swear that whatever he told you was nine-tenths bullshit."

She thought it wise not to say anything, preferring to defuse the anxiety her earlier outburst had caused by not adding any more fuel to the fire. And besides, she was curious where the good lawyer was going with his mea culpa.

"First of all, this threesome? If it lasted ten minutes, I'd be amazed. I was fifteen. Fugly here," he said, pointing at Alex, "was barely fourteen. And we were admittedly high-times baked and then some. The whole thing was nothing more than two teenage boys with hard-ons, swaggering around the woods like god's gift to the world and a one-time encounter with Stifler's mom. It was dark. We were, as I said, completely out of our minds. And in case he didn't make this clear, I'm the one plowing the Mom, although at fifteen, plowing was a stretch. Poking maybe," he shrugged, "while Robin to my Batman kept it together for less than five minutes once she started blowing him. Hardly a wild sexual escapade."

Well, I'll be damned, Meghan thought. She had to give it to Parker. That was one hell of an example of what falling on the sword looked like. And the explanation? Award-winning because yes, she had immediately envisioned some raunchy bacchanal with naked women and all sorts of fuckery that upon reflection would not have been something two horny teenage boys could possibly pull off. She coughed back a snort of laughter knowing that the Two-Minute Man was a better description of what happened.

Didn't stop her from wanting to rattle both their alpha cages just for the hell of it, but right then, she needed Parker to wander away quietly so she could talk to Alex.

Deliberately arching a single brow, she pithily drawled, "Stifler's mom? That's your story? Five minutes with Stifler's mom?"

The hand on Alex's shoulder picked up the slight movement he made coughing back a chuckle. She guessed that until that moment, the expression *Stifler's mom* had probably never been part of the story. Typical lawyer. Fast thinking on his feet.

Sensing the storm had passed, Parker grinned that damn toothy smile of his and winked at her. "Debated between Mrs. Robinson, Stifler's mom, and Dean Wormer's wife, but some of those references were too obscure so, yeah, Stifler won by a knob."

Meghan rolled her eyes at the jesting innuendo.

"We're even now, counselor." She chuckled. "I know you thought you were going to get me back for the panties joke, but . . ."

Alex cut in tersely. "Excuse me?"

Meghan squeezed her fiancé's shoulder. "Oh, didn't I tell you, darling? Parker wants a pair of my panties to play with."

Parker exploded, "Meghan! Shit!" He jumped into Alex's line of vision and bellowed, "She's fucking kidding, dude. I swear."

She was gently kneading Alex's shoulder letting him know without having to read her expression that she was fucking with Parker.

"Who's your mama now?" she asked with a giggle.

Seeing the lawyer's stricken expression as his eyes swung from her to Alex and back again, she smirked sweetly and stuck her tongue out.

"Oh, by the way . . . Angelina's getting ready for your date." Meghan made sure to put just the right amount of taunt into the last word.

Alex pulled on her hand until she swung around and fell onto his lap. Cocooned in the big leather chair, feeling her man's thick, muscular thighs under her ass, Meghan melted. Yep. Parker needed to run along now. She had other things on her mind.

Drawling mockingly at his friend, Alex said, "I believe that was your cue to run along, counselor. Meghan and I need to talk and your presence is a sad reminder of what a dick you are."

Parker glared at Alex, which only made her smile.

"Remember what I said earlier?" Alex asked. "About snapping out of it?"

"Yeah."

"Go wash up, man, and get ready 'cause I'm pretty fucking sure after an afternoon with the ladies of Family Justice filling her head with all sorts of ball-busting ways to make your life hell, my sister is about to clean your clock. Help yourself to our shower and it's pretty obvious which sink is mine. Use whatever you need."

"Wow. Did Mom and Dad just send me to bed without dinner and tell me to take a bath first?"

Meghan smiled sweetly. "No. Mom and Dad just told you to get your shit together because there's an angel about to come crashing from the heavens right at your dumbass, and if you don't catch her, I will personally rip your face off."

"I like that," Alex told her with a grin.

She looked at him and laughed. "I know, right? It works somehow." She leaned close to his ear and whispered, "When we karaoke Saturday night, we go on as Boots, Ass, and Sass featuring Desert Angel. Shhhh. Don't tell!"

Alex laughed and shook his head. "Pinky swear."

Parker looked a bit bemused at their playful teasing. Maybe he was expecting them to read him the riot act? Threaten to dust Angie for fingerprints later?

My god, she thought. *He really doesn't know!* How fucking funny was this? Parker Sullivan was just like the rest of the clueless males of his species. Somehow the stupid fuck had missed the memo about Angie adoring his ass. *Pfft.* Some big bad dominant he was!

"All right, all right," he grumbled. "Once the whispering, secrets, and pinky swears start, it's time to give you two some privacy. Thanks for the shower and a chance to change. Can I grab a shirt, too? I have a feeling flannel and sun sweat aren't going to quite fit the bill tonight."

"In his side of the wardrobe, top drawer, left side you'll find clean stuff. And take your pick on shirts," Meghan added. "May I suggest something . . . dark."

Parker looked confused. "Dark? What does that mean?"

She snickered. *Men.* Who taught them to dress?

"See those black jeans and boots you have on? Well, a dark gray button-down or even matching black shirt will do nicely. And don't shave." She chuckled. "Bitches like that badass rebel look."

Alex's bark of laughter at her mention of bitches forced a laugh from her throat, too. She knew it was one of his favorite mocking expressions.

"Come on!" she yelped. "I'm trying to be serious here!"

"I'm sorry, my bad," he drawled. Turning back to Parker, he all but forced him from the room. "You. Upstairs. Shower. Now. And close the fucking door on your way out."

Meghan laughed as Parker saluted them with a leer and moonwalked his way from the room, calling out as he closed the door, "Okay. The door is shut and the clock is ticking."

"Suck my dick," Alex yelled.

"Maybe later," Parker laughed in response and then they were alone.

Chapter Thirty-Two

HAD SHE EVER SHOWERED THAT *quickly before,* Angie wondered. Probably not. She had a long-standing love affair with her modest tile shower in the gatehouse she shared with Sophie back in Spain. Some of her best thinking and planning took place as water streamed down on her.

But this wasn't the time to dally. She had a mission to complete. Operation Esquire was underway and she had every intention of staking a claim, starting tonight.

Rifling through the closet, she studied every outfit, every possible combination of clothing, and made some snap decisions. Quickly grabbing stuff off hangers, she tossed the outfit she decided on toward the bed and headed back to the bathroom to fix her hair.

Some twenty minutes later, as she stood in front of a full-length mirror, she knew her choice was spot on. The sophisticated looking woman staring back from the mirror was a far cry from the teenager in blue jeans he had stuck in his memory.

As only a woman could—and she knew that was a horrendously sexist remark, but there you have it—Angie scrutinized absolutely everything, deciding if this was what she wanted to do because there was no doubt about it. She was making a bold statement with her appearance. Once she issued this in-your-face challenge, she just knew that she was taking a huge chance by unleashing a force she'd been unprepared to deal with before. She had to be certain she could this time around before she let the door peek open.

"Couple of deep cleansing breaths," she muttered quietly as she rolled the tension from her shoulders, wiggled her fingers, and blew lungsful of air in and out.

"Okay." Focusing on her reflection, she sighed and started at the top.

While Alex and Soph had gotten their mother's coloring, which stretched from the middle of the road to California blonde, she had taken after her father's side of the family tree.

Blessed with spectacular hair, she loved her glossy dark tresses. Not quite black as ebony but damn close, her long mane had a subtle blue-black ombré added to the ends that played off the color of her eyes. She left it all to tumble about her shoulders. As she moved this way and that, when the veil of hair parted and swayed, she caught glimpses of the blue and gold of the delicate earrings she wore.

Except for a last-minute application of lipstick, her make-up was perfect. She smiled. Looking carefully at her brows to make sure the arch was the way Angie liked, she made a little pout in the mirror just to see how it looked.

Not only was her make-up perfect, goddammit, but so was her outfit. She'd chosen well. A vampy long line black corset bustier with a *Hey Look at Me* neckline, showcased her curves. The way the garment was fashioned accentuated her long torso and let her cinch the waist tight enough to really emphasize an hourglass figure.

Smirking at the sight of her boobs spilling perfectly from the scalloped top, she adjusted the necklace hanging right at the peak of her cleavage. The unique design featured an infinity loop and a knot sparkling with diamonds while a delicate sapphire hung underneath. She'd picked up a bit of sunglow from the amount of outdoor time she'd enjoyed since coming home and the fine gold chain and tiny diamonds sparkled against her skin.

One of her favorite wardrobe essentials from the collection of shrugs and camisoles she had with her was a skimpy, sheer, silk and gauze bolero in a beautiful shade of deep blue that coordinated beautifully with her eyes, jewelry, and even her hair. All it really did was offer some covering for her shoulders and a bit of modesty to even out the flagrant boob showcase going on. It was also sexy as hell.

Angie nodded approvingly as her eyes drifted downward to continue her inspection. This corset fell almost to her hips. She loved the long line it gave her. Bringing the D cups out for the evening was enough, she figured, so instead of a skirt that would have him wondering all night what color her panties were, she went with a pair of skintight straight leg pants that molded to her body like a second skin.

Yep. She looked fantastic. Sliding her feet into a pair of suede pumps, her favorites, the ones with a red bottom that coordinated with the rest of the blues in her outfit, she giggled. Oh, my god. He'd most definitely never seen her look like this!

Grown-up Angelina laughed at her in the mirror. When all was said and done, she knew without a second's pause that she looked hot. And available.

Grabbing some lipstick, she rolled several coats of *Undress Me Red* on her naturally pouty lips, then did the mandatory perfume spritz with the last one shooting into the air to drift down onto all of her as she twirled happily.

Get ready, 'cause here I come.

"Oh, for god's sake," Parker repeatedly mumbled as he rummaged through what was essentially Alex's underwear drawer. He really was going to kill Irish for putting him through this. Maybe he should just go commando because there was no fucking way he was putting on any of the briefs he found.

For about ten seconds, he wondered at his friend's taste in undergarments then shut the snide judgment down when he remembered Alex's injuries. He swallowed hard and felt the boom-boom-boom in his chest that happened every time he thought about the years of agony his friend endured knowing full well that almost one entire side of the man's body had been shredded, leaving behind a patchwork of angry scars and puckered flesh. Of course, he'd favor the least amount of fabric possible that close to his skin.

But Parker was more the long cotton brief kind of a guy. So, commando it was. He hesitated half a second then shook off the thought.

Nah. No way was he getting naked tonight. It still remained to be seen how combative Angie would be after his arrogantly forced invitation so gearing up for anything intimate seemed like a waste of time.

In the end, he followed Meghan's welcome wardrobe advice. He was a guy. What the fuck did he know? Match the tie to the suit was about as deep as he got. But teaming up a black button-down with the black jeans and boots was pretty effective. Rolling back the sleeves of the shirt, he strapped on the all black Tag Heuer watch his folks had given him for Christmas.

"Seems like a theme to me," he muttered looking in the mirror. He was either Steve Jobs or an undertaker. *Meghan better be right,* he thought. She also said not to shave, so he hadn't. Day three of not shaving and he was starting to look like a pirate.

Quickly reviewing his plan, he decided to take her out to the Roadhouse for a cowboy dinner. What she needed was some Southwest home cooking. They'd pick apart an appetizer, talk, and relax. She'd close her eyes and get all dreamy when she took that first bite of steak. He'd try not to flatten her to the table and . . . yeah.

If they made it to dessert, they'd each get something different and share. Just as they used to from the time she was a kid until later when they sat naked in bed after fucking like animals, indulging in something sweet.

It was clear to Parker he wanted all of that back. The history. The closeness. The feeling you got when the person sitting next to you lit up the darkest corner of your thoughts.

He'd fucked things up before. Molding her innocent desires to his had been the chance of a lifetime to build the type of fully formed relationship he knew was the only kind he'd ever be able to commit to.

Things were different now, yeah. Alex was right. She wasn't the kid he remembered or the coed he fucked. This time, if he wanted her, Parker was going to have to step up his game. One of his mistakes before had been not telling her what was going on in his head and heart. Stupid move. She would have reacted differently when trouble came if she'd known it was more than just sex for him.

Angie was still going to make him pay for having been such a monumental dick and for letting their estrangement linger. She wouldn't be able to stop herself, and really, he didn't want her to. This was part of what he meant by a relationship that was fully formed. He wasn't interested in superficial bullshit. Couldn't be satisfied with shallow nicey nice as the price for getting laid. He wanted it real. And raw. Fierce. Open. Honest. If she wanted to kick his ass, he'd set up the scene himself.

A minute ticked by after Parker shut the study door. Then another one as Meghan cuddled against his chest.

Alex didn't want to say anything to ruin the quiet, effortlessness of the moment. Her laying on him felt so right.

They'd weathered another storm, but he was sorely aware that he needed to be careful with her. She was a lot more fragile than even she realized. Their playtime out in the desert had left an impression on Alex. They hadn't really talked about it, which he feared had been a lost opportunity, and that kind of bugged him because they really should have. He'd taken them on quite an intense journey that day. And not just because they'd made love so many times and fucked in so many different ways that there didn't seem like much else they could do and survive.

Long before then, he'd been thinking about something a woman who he'd dated briefly had told him. She was an architect. A busy, highly paid professional at the top of her game, a Type A personality who struggled to relax and was a heart attack waiting to happen.

She told him of discovering a unique release that was like an emptying of whatever part of her held all her stress and worry. The release? Everything he and Meghan had been exploring—particularly the domination scenarios, light bondage, and the sensory play they regularly enjoyed.

It was hard not to notice that his sexy Irish fuck goddess had grown quite fond of having her ass pinked on occasion. Same for anything that he called *balls out excess kept tightly controlled.*

So he started doing some research and after having his eyeballs singed and his balls shriveled from the crazy and sometimes sadistic kinkiness to be found online, he'd stumbled upon a resource of straightforward information about some of the things he thought might fit into their playtimes.

And that research led him to the fascinating world of sensory flogging. None of that *beat her ass till she's screaming and covered in welts.* To him, that shit was insane. To each his own, but that just wasn't his taste. But the more sensual aspects of it intrigued him. The ballet of it drew him in. The different strokes. How and when to administer them. The slow warm-up and the important aftercare. Supposedly, the whole thing could be really cathartic.

So, he took a chance. That day in the desert, after she was completely broken down from their lust-filled explosion, he took her on that first step to something different. And that was when he fully came to understand how vulnerable Meghan was right now. She'd shattered completely during the simple scene. So had he. She was so beautiful and her need for him so great that they'd probably pushed it a bit too far that first time. But it had been worth it. When she fell apart in his arms afterward, he finally grasped just how on edge she'd become.

Nothing had really changed since that day. The storms still came and went, and until the wedding was behind them, he feared she'd continue to be a bundle of nerves and anxiety. But now he knew without any doubt that his woman was struggling.

Tucking a finger beneath her chin, he lifted until her bewitching green eyes looked at him.

"I have never loved anyone but you. I will never love anyone but you."

Kissing her tenderly, Alex held her close to his heart.

The sweet kiss became less gentle, more demanding. Her, not him.

Squirming on his lap, Meghan pressed against his chest as she went on a voracious exploration of his mouth that turned Alex's cock to stone.

Her hot breath and wet mouth were everywhere on his face and neck leaving kisses, licking, moaning, and nibbling. He could feel the fire burning hotter and hotter till her skin heated and a gorgeous pink glow spread across her fair skin.

Meghan pawed at the front of his shirt while kissing him furiously, managing to undo the top few buttons, but from her position on his lap, that was all she could reach.

She boldly explored his lips and the inside of his mouth as their tongues did a sexy slow-dance. Gasping for air, he searched her expression, found her gaze wild and hungry, and crushed her to him for a kiss that went nova, exploding around them in a cascade of firelights that shone only slightly less bright than the glory of their love.

Pushing off his lap, she sank to the floor between his knees and started tearing off his shirt. Alex felt like a fucking god among men when she gasped, eyes aglow as his chest was exposed. And then she fell on him with a wantonness that actually surprised him under the circumstances.

Alex had expected to do the appropriate amount of sucking up and groveling for his earlier faux pas and was looking forward to making his formal apology in the form of tender lovemaking that would obliterate her fears.

The woman gazing lustfully at his muscled torso, who was lightly skating her fingertips over his exposed flesh, however, had a completely different agenda in mind. Wasn't he supposed to be the one on his knees?

"Meghan," he groaned. The warning growl he meant to make must have gone on vacation.

"Be still," she whispered softly. His heart fluttered. *Be still*—that was usually his line.

Oh. My. God.

Chapter Thirty-Three

Unable to hold back, he gave himself over to her passion—groaning from the exquisite arousal washing over him as she devoured his skin, neck to navel. Alex's breathing was labored and heavy as he watched her bite at his nipples, growling dangerously when she bent and put her mouth on the skin above his waist, biting and pulling until he shuddered all over.

Her hands were on his belt at the same time that she rained a path of wet kisses across his abdomen. Alex sat absolutely still, his arms at the sides of the big chair. His head rested on the back as he watched mesmerized through hooded eyes.

Belt undone and hanging open, she slowly lowered his zipper and reached inside his jeans to scoop his balls and cock from the confines of his clothing. Her eyes shimmering with desire, she licked her lips and gazed admiringly at his male form.

Biting her lip repeatedly, she ran her fingers up the underside of his cock several times as it lay proudly upon his stomach, smiling each time his flesh twitched at her touch.

Her gentle fingers examining his balls almost pushed him over the edge faster than either of them would be happy about.

A long, drawn-out, husky, "*Mmmmmmmm,*" rumbled from her when she took hold of his staff with both hands. His eyes closed momentarily. Seeing his hardened cock in her grasp was too much. So was the agonizingly slow way she went about stroking him.

Alex's mind blurred. With a firm grip, she slowly caressed him using both hands in an exaggerated motion that set him on fire. Up and down, squeezing and stroking. She was worshipping his cock.

Time stopped when she took him into her mouth. Just like with her hands, everything she did was at a snail's pace.

He watched trancelike as she opened wide and eased her mouth onto his turgid flesh until he nudged the back of her throat. And then she moaned and he felt the sound along the whole length of him buried in her mouth.

He smoothed his hand down her hair, petting her as she sucked him into a sensual thrall. Alex willingly welcomed his enslavement to the voracious greediness of her sexy mouth.

And through it all—she never changed the pace. Never gave in to the impulse to go wild. It was hot, wet, slow, and decadent.

When the muscles in his thighs started to quiver, she slowly drew back and let his throbbing cock slide from her mouth. Holding it like a precious object, she dropped tiny kisses on the sensitive head and all down the underside, paying extra attention to the ridge of flesh at the crown that made him moan desperately.

"I love you," she murmured huskily. Feeding even more kisses on his manly flesh, she kept on murmuring, "I love you. I love you."

Alex was beyond moved. This was what being totally owned body, mind, heart, and soul felt like. He'd hurt her earlier, but by every word and with every action, she was the one expressing her unconditional love for him. There was something mystifying about how all that upset vanished to be replaced by this interlude of incandescent passion.

She looked into his eyes and time stood still. Tears threatened, and he made no effort to stop them. He loved her that much. Would always freely bare his soul to her so she would forever know and never doubt how very precious she was to him.

He leaned down, took her face in his hands, and kissed her with all the love in his heart as his tears wet both their cheeks.

Afterward, he sat back and let her finish, and holy mother of god, nothing he'd ever seen before in his life had ever been as heart-stoppingly captivating.

The agonizing slow rise and fall of her mouth took him swiftly toward the edge. His balls tightened unbearably, and Alex's head briefly thrashed from side to side as she drove him insane.

With his cock buried in her mouth, she twisted her head slowly, the hair around his manhood brushing against her cute little nose and causing him to growl lustfully.

And then she did, well . . . he was so deep in a fog of lust that he didn't know what the fuck she did. Swallowed, or something like that, which caused her throat to tighten around the engorged head of his cock. A deep, throaty groan that told him of her desire vibrated along his length and that was all he could take.

On a bellowed howl, he called out her name and exploded in her throat as she slowly and methodically sucked him till nothing was left. Overcome with a fierce possessiveness, Alex grunted as the last pulses of his thundering orgasm ripped through him.

Meghan," he growled. "Nobody but you will ever taste me, baby. That's all yours."

She looked up at him, her eyes a smoky green, his dick still stretching her lips. *Shit.* Had she ever looked sexier?

Sometime later after readjusting his clothes, she resumed her position on his lap, cuddling close to his heart as if she hadn't just dropped to her knees and sucked him to completion. On some level, it was amusing as hell.

Parker found them like that not long after. Knocking loudly on the door, he called out, "Knock, knock," before cautiously peeking into the room.

Woulda served the fucker right if he'd found them ten minutes ago. If it weren't for the fact that he'd have to kill Parker, friend or not, if he ever had a firsthand visual of Meghan with his dick stuffed in her mouth, he would have rubbed his nose in what had just gone down in the study.

Meghan never moved from her relaxed position. How come that made him feel good? Was it because seeing her barely react to the presence of another man fed Alex's primal needs? She was his. Period. He liked that it wasn't even in question.

Seeing they were in the midst of a moment, Parker nodded at Alex and spoke quickly, "Shower, shirt, and no shave. Thanks. I'll wait for Angelina in the main hallway. Meghan," he muttered, "I hope we're okay, you and I. And Alex? I'll have your sister home at a decent hour."

Meghan raised her hand and twinkled her fingers to acknowledge Parker's comment but said nothing. Alex could feel she was still completely focused on him . . . as it should be.

"Angie's a big girl," he told Parker sternly. "She knows what's best for her. Don't fuck this up, man."

He saw his friend glance at Meghan with clear concern on his face. Alex met his gaze and nodded slightly to let him know that everything was all right and not to worry.

"Lock up on your way out," Alex murmured. "Angie has a key."

Parker was backing out of the room, half bent, hands in supplication in front of his chest as he mouthed the words, "Thank you."

Alex watched him go, wondering what having the man as his brother-in-law was going to be like, and chuckled slightly because he knew damn well Parker was fucking clueless.

Personally, he was going to love watching the ever-a-big-handful Angelina Marquez run him ragged.

Join the club, dude, he thought with a laugh.

As Angie made her way along the upstairs hallway toward the balcony overlooking the main hall, she actually giggled softly. She loved shoes. Who didn't? They were almost her second religion. Well, shoes and lingerie, of course, and the Louboutins she had on made her walk with a suggestive rock 'n' roll to her hips that had her cracking the hell up.

She saw the back of Parker's head seconds before she emerged from the shadows to head for the stairs. He must have heard her approach because he looked up and glanced around till he found her.

When she was sixteen years old, her parents had made her do this old-fashioned cotillion thing during their annual trek to Spain. Soph had done it and though Angie nearly went dizzy from all the eye-rolling she gave her folks, the unusual experience did have some value. She remembered the hastily barked instructions to each of the elaborately dressed debutantes. Walk to the stairs and pause facing forward. Turn slowly either right or left and then pause again while you visualize descending the stairs. As you step down, push your shoulders back, head held high and shine as you take your place in the spotlight. In other words, Diva 101.

Stopping at the top of the stairs, she locked eyes with a stunned Parker, who seemed to be having some sort of problem keeping his mouth closed. Pausing to let him get an eyeful, Angie stifled a snicker as she pretended a last second check of her tiny clutch while keeping him in her line of vision because, lord have mercy, his expression was mind-blowing.

Hehehe.

Grasping the handrail, she stepped off . . . shoulders back, girls front and center, confident tilt to the chin. Angelina Marquez was in the house, bitches—lock up your men because she was dressed to quietly kill.

As she vamped her way down the stairs, the girls were doing a full bump and grind while her hips swayed, her hair bounced, and tiny jewels sparkled against her exuberant breasts. No red blooded, right thinking man was going to be able to ignore the performance she was putting on.

A prickling sensation that was both ice-cold and red-hot crept along her spine, settling in her neck. At the bottom of the steps stood a very big man with a serious expression who was putting off so much powerful energy that it filled the big open space. She swallowed. Her pulse picked up tempo. Angie knew that look.

Fighting back a jolt of nerves, she kept moving with an air of confidence she didn't really feel. His staggering masculinity always did this to her. *Ugh.* Suddenly, she didn't care what she had on or how sexy her shoes were because all her mind could handle was the overload of excitement she felt looking at him.

Holy something. Take your pick. Crap. Fuck. God. Shit. What the hell with the man-in-black thing? He looked dangerous. And friggin' hot as the bonfire raging out of control in her center. She was in trouble and hadn't even reached the bottom of the stairway yet.

Shaken by her reaction to the unrepentant look of longing that she saw in his eyes, Angie quivered knowing all it took was one covetous gaze from him to send her flying high. When her outrageous blue suede heels hit the floor and she found herself dwarfed by his size, she had to give a mental shake before falling on him like a lovesick fan girl.

He came close, stepping right into her personal space. She could feel him breathing her in. Angie barely managed to cut off a whimper. Unnerved by the involuntary step back she took, a purely female reaction to the subtle aggressive tactics of a predatory male, she felt the end of the curved railing press into her lower back. Damn. Trapped.

She swallowed—hard. He was looking at her so strangely. His fierce gaze pinning her to the spot. He wasn't touching her—not exactly. Just standing really, really, *really* close. For an eternity, neither of them moved, only inches apart. He, so big and imposing, stared down at her upturned face as he caged her in with his body, and her, quickly turning to liquefied Jell-O.

Just when she thought he might close the space between them and kiss her, his jaw clenched and she heard a faint rumbling growl that wrapped around her nerves and squeezed tight.

Um, whoa. The predatory sound was new.

His forehead lowered and almost touched hers. She was barely able to breathe as it was—maybe the corset hadn't been such a good idea, after all—so when his face got closer, Angie couldn't stop the whimper.

He stayed close, unnerving her, and picked up one of her curls and played with it against the plump mounds of her breasts. She was panting and close to hyperventilating. "Is this how the big girls do it?" he husked, his eyes gleaming with something that went way beyond simple arousal.

She'd thought to call him on his shit. Put the domineering lawyer in his place. What had she been thinking?

He really needed to access the conscience of his inner civilized man because the chest-thumping beast she roused from hibernation was fucking with Parker's plan.

The second he saw her wicked female swagger as she came to the top of the stairs, he knew he was in a shitstorm of trouble. There was no fucking way he was going to be able to downplay the audacious challenge she was clearly throwing down.

Fuck. So much for calm, cool, and controlled. And by the time she reached the bottom of the steps, he seriously regretted the *go commando* decision. It was all he could do not to rearrange the immediate hard-on she inspired so his jeans didn't do him permanent harm.

For as long as he lived, Parker knew he'd never be able to forget the way she looked at him once they were standing toe-to-toe. She was practically glowing with triumph. This was why she'd so effortlessly given in to his dinner demand! The move was pure Angie. Even as a kid, she refused to be cowed by any situation, was naturally competitive, and forever trying to prove her worth to him and Alex.

But a little girl no longer, she was making quite the grown-up statement that he heard loud and clear. She was deliberately trying to wind him up and it was succeeding more effectively than she imagined.

After taunting her with the *big girl* comment and seeing her flustered reaction, he was flying without a net. Fuck his plans. This was what he craved. That wild, exhilarating, *oh my fucking god* feeling that he only ever experienced with his Angel baby.

She wanted to rev his engine? No fucking problem. Wanted to show him she wasn't a little girl anymore? Message received.

Bring it on, baby girl. Bring. It. On.

Chapter Thirty-Four

CAMERON PEEKED INTO THE NURSERY with Dylan, who was busily working on a binky, perched on his hip. She was still curled up on the loveseat in a dead sleep so he pulled the door shut quietly and headed back downstairs.

"Okay, son, looks like it's just you and me. I think Daddy wore Ponytail Mommy out." He chuckled.

Planting a kiss on the baby's head, Dylan rocked in his hold and smacked his hands on Cam's chest like he was high-fiving Daddy for taking care of Mommy's needs. *If only he knew what that really meant.*

What a fucking day it had been. There wasn't any activity in the compound, not with the construction underway and coming off a long out-of-town-on-business stretch, he'd been taking it easy since he and Lacey came back from Vegas. Had earned a short break.

Thank god because, since the bombshell revelation that her bastard of a father was alive, well, and living life as a happily married family man, his wife had been in an emotional freefall. And he didn't know quite what the hell to do about it. In a way, he was powerless. Lacey's history was complicated and then some. Made his story seem like a joke. This was one path she had to walk alone and though he was right behind her, ready to catch her if she stumbled or fell, it was hell knowing that was all he could do.

Settling his son into his high chair, he laughed at Dylan who pounded his little hands on the tray in protest when Cam popped the binky from his mouth.

"Ah . . ." He chuckled while dropping two of Dylan's favorite toys in front of him. "An impatient guy with an oral fixation. Yep, that's my boy!"

Switching on the Bose sound system that he'd given Lacey to a station pumping out soft rock, Dylan nodded his approval by wiggling enthusiastically in a series of baby dance moves that just about melted Cam's heart. He knew exactly where his son learned to boogie to the beat and couldn't even count the number of times he'd come upon his precious Ponytail entertaining their adorable son with her amazing voice and goofy-mom shimmies. Lacey filled his once empty home with love, laughter, and music.

Poking around in the refrigerator as *Thinking Out Loud* wafted from the speakers, he heard the words and sighed. *Yeah.* He was starting to like listening to Ed Sheeran and made a mental note to add this song to one of his playlists.

Finding a container of Ria's Chili Caliente that he knew was too hot and spicy for Lacey, he grabbed it along with a block of cheese and used his hip to shove the refrigerator door closed. He smiled thinking about how peeved his wife would be when she woke up and found out he'd scrounged for dinner. His Ponytail took that wife and mother shit seriously. *Like, capital S serious,* he thought, snickering.

Far as she was concerned, Cam's participation in any culinary activities was to be confined to commanding the enormous grill they'd had built on the patio. Breakfast, lunch, and dinner for her boys? Yeah—that was all her and do not be fooled by the freckles and pout. Lacey Cameron was large and in total charge when it came to their household.

A loud clattering drew his attention. Dylan had mastered grabbing toys, and when they weren't in his mouth, he was happy to bang them on the tray of his high chair while making cooing and gurgling sounds in a symphony of baby delight.

The boy was growing so fast! Just last night he and Lacey reacted like two certifiably crazy people when, after much prodding and encouragement, the little guy had turned over and grinned at them as they screamed, clapped, high-fived, and basically lost their shit at Dylan's developmental achievement.

Confetti practically poured from the ceiling and a marching band stomped through with every baby milestone. Becoming parents together had made the connection he shared with his young wife even deeper. Sometimes they lay face-to-face with their son between them in their enormous bed and marveled quietly at all of it. Their life together. Their son. The profound love they found with each other.

Settling in a chair by Dyl's side with an overly large bowl of chili that he'd covered with a huge handful of cheesy goodness, it was that love he was thinking about as he ate.

His mind churned, knowing how devastated Lacey was about this news of her father. That was what had spurred him to tell the guys everything. They knew he found Frank Morrow, but he hadn't filled in the blanks. But Lacey's pain and his anxiety over it made sharing his concerns with Alex and Drae a priority. And Parker being there helped, too. Knowing he had their support and understanding kept Cam from losing it completely.

Bottom line. He could NOT handle seeing his Ponytail upset, unhappy, worried, or in any way afraid. They'd come too damn far for that, but short of sending the despicable bastard to the morgue, he had no clue how to make this better for her.

Coming home late afternoon, he'd expected to find Lacey either out in the storage shed that he and the guys had converted into a classroom office or hanging out with Dyl, waiting for Daddy to make an appearance. But what he found once he was through the door wasn't even on the list of scenarios he'd imagined awaited him.

Dropping his keys in the bowl by the front door, he noticed how quiet it was and, assuming the baby was napping, quickly toed off his boots so he didn't wake the lad up. For a guy who'd been a loner his entire life, he sure as shit converted quickly into a well-trained husband and daddy.

Looking around, he saw evidence of the girls having hung out and shook his head, grinning. When he'd built the cabin, the multi-bedroom home was probably overkill considering he didn't have any family and likely never would, but ever since Lacey entered his life, the rustic hideaway at the end of the lane had become the unofficial ground zero for the women of Family Justice. Of course, the theater room helped as did the massive hot tub and gazebo he and Drae had installed.

But hot tubs aside, it amused him that **HIS** house, where his wife and child waited for him at the end of every day . . . *that* was where the ladies chose to hang. Not in the opulent Villa and not at Drae's massive architectural masterpiece. Casa Cameron . . . built to the manly expectations of a single, brooding, lonely guy . . . had morphed into female central.

Not wanting to call out and possibly wake the baby, he figured he'd go search for Lacey—probably check the nursery first. Before he got to the foot of the steps, she appeared out of thin air and came at him. One second he was getting ready to climb the stairs, and the next, a half-naked woman was plastered to his front embracing him fiercely before his brain had time to register what was happening.

At the second his mind caught up, she unwound her arms from around his neck and took his shirt in both hands, ripping it open with a single mighty tug. Buttons flew everywhere, some falling with a thud onto carpet and others hitting the wood floor with a clink.

Whoa! What the fuck?

Deftly yanking the shirt from his shoulders to halfway down his arms, she abandoned that effort and applied the same forceful handling on his jeans while his arms were tangled up, bound by his own shirt. Struggling to get it off only made it worse.

Too much shit was happening and too fast. Cam was quickly applying pressure to the gas pedal trying to get up to speed, but as soon as he closed the distance, she leaped out ahead again.

He took a couple of steps backward because his legs still worked, disrupting her feverish attempt to get his pants off, and finally got a good look at her. She was naked except for those unimaginably sexy panties she liked so much. They were pink, feminine, and very pretty. Her hair was down, no ponytail in sight, and except for her wedding rings, that was all she had on.

Her breasts had always been magnificent, and motherhood only enhanced their loveliness. A single glance told him that he wasn't misreading her desire. Beautifully puckered nipples on each heavy globe seemed to pulsate with need right before his eyes.

Cam had less than thirty seconds to process all this when she simply leaped on him.

Tearing his shirt the rest of the way off, Lacey dropped it and immediately tugged on the zipper of his jeans. Before he knew it, she was forcefully yanking the pants and his briefs down his legs, having dropped to her knees to aid the effort.

Naked, he let instinct take over, going to his knees too and reaching for her. He didn't give a shit where they were. Didn't care that a bed was nowhere in sight. Far as he was concerned, this carpet right here by the fireplace was just fine because Cam could feel her need; he was nearly drowning in it.

Lacey was rarely, if ever, aggressive in their intimate life. She preferred, and so did he, that his prodigious sexual appetite have free rein, which admittedly zeroed in on her like a laser guided missile morning, noon, and night. Since he was insatiable when it came to his lovely wife, she didn't have much chance to assert herself even if she wanted to.

Of course, she did at times, but never anything even remotely like this. Nope. Something other than lust was fueling this inferno. Whatever it was had seriously jacked her up, so he let her have the reins—to take control. He was hers—totally.

She went to him willingly but immediately took over, twining her arms, one around his neck, and the other boldly stroking his ass. Kneeling face-to-face, their bodies pressed together, he felt a drugging heat coming off her body that made him groan. The way her fire wrapped around his nerves gave him a rush like nothing before ever had.

Lacey's soft hands greedily massaging his ass made his butt clench tightly as his cock hardened in the cocoon created by their connected bodies. Surrounded by her heat, his shaft filled, responding to the fierce waves of desire she was emitting. His heart went haywire.

"I need you," she groaned.

When she emphasized that need with a brutal squeeze of his ass, Cam answered her groan with a sharp grunt. "I can see that," he husked.

He was disappointed when she stopped grabbing his butt but didn't have time to be bummed for more than a second after she ran her fingers through his hair, scraping his scalp with her nails, pressed her naughty mommy tits against his chest, and dove onto his mouth.

Uh, *yeah* she needed him. Holy fuck. He'd never seen her like this and even though he sensed she was being driven by wild emotions that she had little control over, he was getting off big time because shit—

what she was doing was hotter than hell.

Cam's life sometimes felt like an embarrassment of riches since this glorious creature entered his world and one of those riches was his wife's mouth. Knowing her lips had only ever belonged to one man, *him,* was the core of their relationship. Lacey hadn't just been a virgin. Despite all the fuckery that made her life hell on Earth, she was a true innocent.

Loving her mouth as he did, Cam found her inexperience charmingly seductive and thanked his lucky stars from the start that his Ponytail was so sweetly responsive and just as eager as he was to lose herself in a kiss.

The greedy sounds she made devouring him turned not just his dick to stone but every inch of his entire body as well. Cam crushed her against him and pressed his swollen sex into her stomach. He could feel the slippery softness of her silky panties on his skin.

Oh god—her ass. He had to have her ass in his hands. With a deep grunt, he palmed the mind-blowing cheeks while she tangled her fingers in his hair and dominated his mouth with her tongue. Then with one of his big hands cupping her bottom possessively, he pulled her into direct contact with his cock. She fed a desperate whimper into his mouth that made him growl with pure male satisfaction.

The sensual quivers and the mindless shimmies as she rubbed against his body felt so fucking good. Cam hissed with pleasure when white-hot lust slammed into him while Lacey deliberately scraped her distended nipples across his skin as her whimpers became greedy grunts.

Without warning or slowing down beforehand, she quickly ended the kiss and pushed back off him. He instantly missed the warmth of her aroused body and was sorely tempted to seize control of the proceedings—grab hold of her and fuck her where they were. But he managed to squash the urge just in time.

Surprisingly forceful and impatient hands immediately pushed him down to the carpet, an unspoken command he willingly followed. And then she stood over him and he was rewarded with a sight so achingly beautiful that Cam simply went blank.

Seriously. His luscious young wife in nothing but a sexy pair of pink panties, with her long blond hair tumbling down her back as she stared down at him where he lay at her feet was making his insides do crazy thing and his cock want to explode.

As she hooked her fingers into the sides of her panties to take them off, he stopped her with a deep growl.

"Turn around when you do that. Show me your ass, honey."

Her eyes blazed at his command.

"That's right, wife. Turn the fuck around and let me see that fine ass I married."

With her fingers still grasping the sides of her panties, she dropped her gaze to his cock and a small, wicked smile curled her lips.

Cam grabbed his swollen shaft and surged his hips upward. "All yours, darlin'."

Like a delicate ballerina, Lacey pirouetted gracefully until her back was to him and her pink silk covered bottom squarely in his gaze.

She bent forward slowly pulling the scrap of pink down her legs. There, right before his eyes, was his very own erotic pin-up girl on full display.

Holy. God.

Since Dylan was born, she'd surprised him, this innocent wife of his, by keeping her pussy bare. As much as he liked the natural look, he had to admit that her sweet mound was sexy as fuck when he could see all of her. And right now she was intimately exposing herself to his view with the naughty way she bent over.

Cam squeezed his cock and slowly stroked as he got an eyeful of the pouting pink flesh glistening with the evidence of her arousal.

When she turned back to him, his eyes stayed fixed on her mound. He fucking loved Lacey's pussy. He liked looking at it as much as fucking it. One of his favorite pastimes was to sit on his feet and pull her ass up onto his thighs, spread her sexy legs and feast on her perfection. Playing with the sensitive flesh, running his fingers everywhere, tracing the puffy lips, watching as her clitoris swelled, spying the creamy evidence of her arousal as it leaked from her opening—nirvana, man. *Fucking nirvana.*

Right now though, he watched, mesmerized as she stepped close, and took up position, straddling his hips so he really did have a beautiful view of her dripping pussy.

And all the while? She was massaging her tits. Balls out playing with them. Even tugging on her nipples as she bit her lip and took shaky breaths. Damn, but he was a lucky man.

When she reached a hand between her spread legs and stroked her pussy, he'd had enough.

"Are you going to fuck me or not?" he gritted out.

With a hand kneading one tit and the other cupping the mound he'd been leering at, she looked straight into his eyes. Searching her face, he saw a wildness in her expression that excited him.

Putting one of her dainty feet on his chest, she pressed him against the floor, and then much to his dismay stopped fondling her sweet nubile body and told him in no uncertain terms. "Yes. And you're going to do nothing."

He smiled. "So, it's just this cock you want," he taunted as he stroked.

Straddling him once again, she knocked his hand away and slid to her knees. His dick throbbed as she ground her wet pussy back and forth along his length, anointing him with her pleasure.

With her hands planted on either side of his head, they locked eyes as her pussy continued to drive him wild.

Her voice was deep and husky sounding. "Oh, make no mistake about it, husband. I want more than just your body. This is my choice," she murmured. "You. *Us.* I made my choice before all of this," she told him with an edge of fierceness that held his attention. "Before the baby. Before the wedding. Before seeing this beautiful house. Before we even made it to Arizona. You were my choice, Cameron. Before all of this—what we have now—my choice."

He wasn't entirely sure what she was getting at or where all this was going and he knew he'd be asking later, but right now, he wanted nothing more than all she had to give.

Wrapping his arms around her, he asked, "What do you need, baby?"

"I don't need anything but you."

She reached between them and fondled his twitching sex before guiding him to the entrance to her sweet body.

Rising, she spread her knees wider and began sinking inch by throbbing inch onto his shaft, her hands on his biceps in a death grip. The intensity with which she looked at him seared his soul.

"I loved you first . . ."

Staring up, everything blurred except her. She was magnificent. His heart hammering like a bass drum, Cam watched, panting as she rode him with a sensuality that belied the fierceness she was giving off.

They were wild. Uninhibited. Ferocious. Earthy. Untamed.

Fondling her breasts, neck arched, head thrown back—her hair long enough that the ends tickled his thighs—she moaned with each movement. Undulating and writhing as he fought for sanity.

The demons chasing her were mighty and it took a while for his wife to cast off everything except what they were doing. He felt when it happened. Groaned at the way her body softened, melting into his.

Kissing him fiercely, his cock buried deep while she ground her wicked ass on him, forcing him as deep as possible, she became wild and demanding. By that point, Cam was so overstimulated and downright drooling with a thundering lust demanding satisfaction that all he could do was try to hold on.

She was drenched in sweat after having quite actually done all the heavy lifting, when he felt her begin to falter. The muscles in her thighs quivered and she dropped onto his chest unable to stay up any longer.

His wife's desperate groan made him shudder. Taking hold of her hips, he shifted, spread his thighs and dug his heels into the carpet for leverage. She groaned again and writhed on top of him. His body heard the plea in her sweet, sweet whimpers, and his cock answered her need.

Surging into her, he set an energetic pace—enough with the buildup. She was finally in the moment, dripping with arousal, their hearts pounding out a rhythm.

"You are my only love," he growled.

"Oh, Cameron," she cried.

He felt her tighten. Heat flooded her core. Arousal leaked from her body and covered him.

His thrusts became mighty. She ground her pussy on him and his heart did a double beat. Pushing her up so he could play with her tits, Cam tugged and kneaded while his Ponytail moaned with abandon. The sound of her pleasure was music to his ears.

And then she began to fall apart. Her eyes went blank, she cried, "Love me, Cameron. Please love me."

His heart seized. *I loved you first.*

Oh Ponytail, he thought. *My love for you is so big it'd scare you if you knew.*

Pulling on her hips with a ferocious grunt, he slammed into her a final time as she screamed and shook head to toe, her hips jerking as she came.

It was so fucking beautiful that he surrendered to the skin-prickling pleasure and released inside her. His beautiful wife's magnificent pussy demanded all of him and he gave until there was nothing left.

Chapter Thirty-Five

SHE WISHED THEY COULD CONTINUE to lie there forever, staying in this wonderful place of quiet bliss, but Lacey knew that wasn't going to happen. As the heat of their passion cooled, the air chilled her sweaty body and though Cameron had eased the pressure on her hips by shifting her into a sprawl, she was uncomfortable and suddenly conscious of where they were.

Some of her reluctance to move came from not wanting to confront the questions she knew were on his mind—the ones he'd ask the moment the cuddling ended.

Earlier, after the girls left and Dylan had gone down for his late day slumber leaving her with nothing to do, she felt restless and not just a little frazzled. Falling back into old habits if something was bothering her, she got busy. One, because doing something helped burn off excess energy, and two, because she did her best thinking while on task. Any task.

So . . . off she went to the laundry room. Always something that needed doing in there. After starting a load, she impulsively pulled off her dress and tossed it into the washer.

It was while she'd been folding a stack of her husband's things that she started churning mentally. Though glad she'd told the girls what was going on, doing so had ripped the lid off the containment she'd fooled herself into thinking would take care of the problem. Emotional lockboxes, once opened, could be a bitch.

Lacey had survived years on the street, totally alone, vulnerable and always fighting. Fighting for a chance to get out of the bottomless pit her father and uncle had dropped her into. She was damn proud that she never let anything knock her down. One of the ways she managed that was realizing early on that she couldn't waste time, energy, or resources on the past. Regrets, thoughts of revenge, the endless what ifs . . . all of that was useless. She didn't have the time for such things.

Letting her father clog her thoughts was inviting problems. She was losing her way inside a maze of endless *if only's* and didn't know how to get out.

Knowing her husband would be home soon, she thought running upstairs for a quick shower to relax would cut off the anxiety.

Switching off the light to the laundry room, she pulled the door shut and remembered that she didn't have anything on except her panties. While not a prude, Lacey had a reputation for being quaintly modest. She found vulgarity amusing but not something she was comfortable with coming from her own mouth. And she was always the one to suggest at least *some* restraint when hijinks and off-the-wall stuff happened.

But in private? Cameron had encouraged her to feel totally at ease with being naked in her own home. Having a home sanctuary of comfort and total seclusion was important to him. Didn't matter why; whether a result of his abysmal childhood, the miserable years that followed or the ones spent trying to survive in an unending war—the end result was evident in every inch of the home Cameron designed and helped build. Everything was open but private at the same time. The walls of windows and sliders opened to miles of natural open spaces in a heavily secured location. There was also an unwritten protocol that was the rhythm of daily life for Family Justice.

Early mornings were more or less sacrosanct and uninterrupted for each of their households, but once the day got started and people were working, they had an open door habit. Everyone came and went with nothing but a courtesy, "Howdy Do," shout-out. If you got caught with your pants down, so to speak, it was your own damn fault.

This being the Southwest and all, the Villa also customarily observed a late afternoon siesta. She snickered. *Uh-huh.* More like an opportunity between the workday and when dinner happened for the alpha patrol of Justice men to recharge and refresh for the evening.

It was that time of day so she didn't have to worry about anyone just barging through the front door. Feeling no reluctance whatsoever about walking around undressed, she headed to their bedroom. No big deal.

Plus, *after all,* she thought. I *am* wearing undies.

Her sexy brooding man might have taught her to be unashamed of being nude in front of him, but she made sure to put her own signature spin on it. It started one day when she'd strutted bare ass naked down the steps with a tie slung around her neck. He'd enjoyed her droll embellishment and teased her endlessly about it. From then on, a private joke was born and Lacey made it a point to always have *something* on. Anything! Just one thing and it didn't matter what it was since she was essentially playing for laughs.

She'd tied a ribbon around her neck. Worn a belly chain. The apron, of course, was a warm memory. One time she wore only a belt. Nothing but fluffy socks happened frequently and was her every day go-to. For important occasions, she wore lace top thigh-high stockings. On Halloween, she switched things up with a witch's hat. Christmas? Santa panties. She just got a couple of beautiful garters that she'd bought off Etsy that her husband hadn't seen yet. It was all good.

Plodding along the hallway, she heard the front door open and quickly close, and then keys dropped into the bowl, followed seconds later by the thud of Cameron's boots hitting the floor.

The delayed detonation of all that anger and regret toward her father suddenly exploded inside her. *That motherfucker.* She might not want to say the word out loud, but she had no trouble thinking it in her head.

No! She didn't want him there. In her head. *Fuck him.* Frank Morrow was entitled to no part of her. Not even her wayward thoughts.

A sudden desperation took hold. This was *her* life now and that dumbass wasn't going to mess up what she had.

Seeing Cameron at the end of the hallway as he turned toward the steps, she made a sharp detour to head him off. The minute she saw him, something inside her snapped.

Lacey wasn't the type to initiate—mostly she didn't need to. Their marital life was quite satisfying and full and her husband kept her occupied. But seeing him and then having all those crazy conflicting, unsettling feelings swirling inside her—the combination pushed her to action. Impulsive action. The sort that led to manhandling one's husband and demanding that he satisfy you. Not something she did every day.

She understood what was happening. Just didn't know how to explain it. How did you tell someone that they saved you—from a dark and dreary hell that stretched out ahead and had no end? And not because he'd physically rescued her and brought her to this beautiful place, giving her an opportunity to start a whole new life.

All of that was nice but came second. Cameron Justice saved her the moment he actually saw her. He saw her! Nobody ever saw her. She was invisible, thrown away, of no consequence.

But this beautiful man with the sometimes-fearsome scowl and dark, brooding intensity—not only had he seen her, he hadn't looked away. She felt like a real person for the first time.

He was her first in more ways than one. When she'd looked into his face and seen his unusual green eyes and those damn eyelashes, it wasn't so much his handsome face or that bad-boy sexiness that grabbed her—it was the way he looked at her. Knowing someone finally saw her was staggering.

She had to tell him. Had to show him. Let him know that no matter what—he'd been the first. The first free choice she'd ever made and that she would adore him to her dying breath.

After that? Oh, boy. Well, *that* had certainly never happened before. Of course, he'd have questions. He'd be insane not to. They'd been together more than a year—were married and had a baby. In all that time, she'd never ever been aggressive and demanding.

How the hell was she supposed to say, *The demons were chasing me and I used you and your magnificent body to get me out of my head.* Of course, maybe that was exactly what she *should* say.

Jesus. Her mind was working so hard, he could almost hear the gears grinding. Cam knew his delicate Ponytail so well. Sprawled and seemingly peaceful across his big chest, she was actually all but jumping out of her skin with her mind furiously churning as she tried to make sense of whatever was going on.

He could feel it in the tension hardening her luscious body that minutes earlier had been soft and warm and her still rapid respirations let him know she was back in her head and struggling once more.

Shit.

Waiting her out was his only option. Until she was ready to talk about what just happened, he was more than happy to remain as they were—naked and stretched out on the floor in front of the fireplace. Any time he could hold his woman tight and relax knowing she was where she belonged was more than all right with him.

A warm sigh drifted across his skin. *Hmph.* The waiting was almost over. He stroked her back gently but said nothing.

Before long, another sigh—this one harsher, more troubled. She was having a tough time.

What was that word Brody used in their recent video chat? *Waitience?* Yeah. That one. Patiently waiting. Well, enough of that shit. Maybe he should prod just a little to get her started. See where that took them.

Kissing the top of her head, he tightened his arms, and quietly asked, "Did you tell the girls?"

Cam knew he did not need to clarify further. She would understand what he was doing.

And then, the long sigh before a deep breath that signaled she was ready to talk. Lacey raised her head off his chest, made a fist, and rested her chin on it angling her face so their eyes could connect.

Now that the wildness was gone from her expression, she looked rather bewildered and not just a little flustered. God, she was cute. Sometimes, like right now, he remembered that she was barely twenty-four—the youngest adult member of Family Justice and yet she held her own around a bunch of burly guys and kickass women. Earning not just their respect but their unconditional love and support as well.

Nodding in answer to his question, she winced at the same time. "Yeah."

"And?" he encouraged with a tiny pat on her bottom.

Lacey's sweet lips curled into a half-smile, and she giggled softly. "Well, there was talk of digital shenanigans . . ."

He couldn't hold back the bark of laughter. "Shenanigans? Oh, no! Someone threatened actual shenanigans?" he hooted jokingly.

She nudged him and feigned outrage at his teasing. "Are you making fun of me, sir?"

Her approximation of what a stern expression looked like melted Cam's heart.

"Abso-fucking-lutely," he drawled at the same time that he smacked her soundly on the ass.

Now that the tension had eased, she was talking and engaging in a bit of playful banter. She told the ladies, they'd threatened retribution. That was all he needed to know for now. She'd tell him the rest in due time.

"Come on, Mrs. Cameron." He chuckled. "Your very hot ass is turning blue from being chilled. I take it my son is enjoying a late siesta?"

She groaned quietly and nodded.

Okay, well they didn't have long, but they did have a window of opportunity he intended to take full advantage of.

"How 'bout we continue in the shower?"

A pouty smile lit up her adorably freckled face. She knew damn well what would happen ten seconds after they were under the steaming waterfall. The smile revealed her excitement. But her pout? That was another thing altogether.

She sat up and pushed some hair over her shoulder. He rolled to his side and leaned on an arm, watching her face.

"I love you," she blurted out awkwardly. Cam knew his eyebrows had shot up at the impassioned declaration and instantly reached for her hand.

He brought her knuckles to his lips, and with his eyes locked on hers, he pressed a slow, warm kiss there. Instead of speaking and interrupting her flow, he told her through his touch, the gentleness of his kiss, and the reverence in his gaze that he most certainly returned the love.

In a hushed voice, brimming with emotion, she told him, "My life began the day we met."

She said it with such utter sincerity that Cam had a hard time swallowing past the sudden thickening in his throat.

Pulling her long locks in front of a shoulder, she fussed, her fingers making a haphazard braid. The action was more habit than anything else. When she was finished and there was nothing else to keep her hands busy, she shifted into a cross-legged position and hunched forward with her elbows on her legs. Quite the fetching pose, considering she was naked.

"You know," she began quietly—her face scrunched in a mask of torment. "I don't remember ever dreaming after my dad left."

She shrugged and he clenched his jaw. No part of this should be reduced to a mere shrug.

"Certainly never after I ran from Florida. It was . . . weird," she admitted. "And not only that, I didn't really daydream. Maybe a little but mostly about things I take for granted now—like getting to take a shower or having clean clothes."

Cam wanted to hit someone. Or smash something. Or both.

"But . . . after you brought me here?" She looked around and smiled. "My dreams slowly came back."

Something fluttered in his chest. Her dreams came back. How come he felt like crying at hearing that?

"Baby," he husked on a voice choked with emotion. "I only had nightmares before you."

Lacey reached out with both hands and framed his face, her thumbs sweeping over his lips.

"I loved you before the dreams came back. You were first, Cameron. Before all that's come after. The first choice I ever made for me."

Ahhhh. He was finally starting to get it.

We make choices for Dylan every day. My mom made choices. Everyone does, you know?"

Cam nodded.

"Anyway," she murmured. "When my father had to make a choice, he turned his back on me and walked away. His choice. His responsibility. His legacy. Not mine."

Wow. For one so young, his wife had the depth and wisdom of an old soul. That was one hell of a heavy statement she was making. And one he couldn't find any fault with. Frank Morrow was a fucking bastard and he got what he deserved.

"I was nobody before you," she said in a hushed voice. "Nobody saw me."

It was hard to stay still when he saw tears shimmering in her eyes.

"But then this dark, brooding loner came along and invaded not just my life but my heart and soul, too."

This time it was his turn to blurt out, "I love you."

"It was you, Cameron Justice, who told me that the past might shape who we are but it doesn't have to weigh us down or define who we become."

Cam smiled. He had indeed said that to her a long time ago, and she had used the exact same expression on him to wake him the fuck up.

"This is my family. You. Our son. Justice."

Yeah. He totally got it now.

"This is my choice. You were first. Frank Morrow can go fuck himself," she muttered sarcastically.

He snorted at her use of profanity, earning him one of her hilariously faux-stern looks.

"It was also his choice to move on with his life as though my mother and I never happened."

"Lacey Cameron, you are one hell of a woman," Cam drawled.

"This is the last time we ever talk about this. Dylan's family is here, with Justice. Alex is already acting grandparent, same for Meghan. The truth is that he's got more aunts and uncles than he'll be able to count and I'm sure a bunch more cousins on the way. And those cousins? They'll be the next generation of Justice."

"So . . ." he asked, "I'm not on the shit list for tracking him down and opening up this whole thing?"

"You did what you thought was best, and I love you for that. We don't grow and learn by running away from difficult things. Now I know. And because I do know, we get to move forward without anything holding us back."

"Infinity and beyond?" he snickered.

"Yes, Buzz," she giggled back, "and the way beyond."

"I want another baby," he announced, startling them both.

"What?"

Grabbing hold of his wife who was looking at him like he'd grown another head, he playfully pulled her as he rolled onto his back, bringing her atop his torso.

"Yep. Daddy wants to make another baby with Mommy."

"Does Mommy get a vote in this?" she purred.

"Are you kidding?" he joked. "You always get the final say, babe."

Lacey smiled and scraped her nails down his chest. He growled.

"Well, in that case, I cast my ballot for . . ."

And, just like that, Dylan Henry Cameron let loose with a hungry, bellowing wail that hurriedly ended their discussion.

Chapter Thirty-Six

Feeling pretty satisfied that he'd made the right choice, Parker was congratulating himself for thinking on his feet and executing a total redo of the plans he'd made for their dinner.

Once he recovered from the erotic heart attack Angie gave him when she, in quite the symbolic way, put on her big girl panties and then wagged her ass in his face, he knew what he had to do.

So she wanted to challenge him, did she? Cool! He wanted to laugh and laugh big. God. She was exhilarating. He'd missed her. Missed the crazy fuckery that always seemed to accompany Angelina Marquez.

Instead of his Porsche, he'd driven his everyday ride, a big SUV with so much on-board technology and options that it was like a miniature spaceship. And big enough that Angie's sexy ass was seated much too far away as far as he was concerned.

Those shoes—the ones he was going to fuck her in some day—made hopping up into the big vehicle a challenge for her. A situation Parker was happy to remedy—which he did by picking her up as she squealed with surprise and deftly situated her, right down to engaging the seatbelt harness.

But right now he was annoyed as hell that there was so much space between them. He couldn't haul her closer because the seatbelt would prevent that. *Fuck.*

Grunting with frustrated displeasure, he turned and looked at his passenger and almost drove off the goddamn road because in profile?

Her tits were fucking mesmerizing. Barely contained in whatever the fuck it was that she was wearing, the plump orbs spilled over the black lacy neckline. Not that he was complaining. *Pfft.* Hardly.

"You sound like a bear," she drawled silkily, her lips curled in a quivering smile. Apparently, she found his displeasure funny.

"Whoever designs these vehicles is a champion cock blocker."

She turned in her seat and comically gaped at him. "Did you just call the car out for, um . . . blocking your cock?"

He growled and bared his teeth when he did—looking over at her with a leer so raw and lascivious, there was no way she could mistake the meaning.

"I want you close enough to touch. Close enough to smell."

To his utter surprise, instead of teasing him for being so forward, she shifted in her seat, crossed her legs the other way and leaned heavily on the console between them. Dangling her hand down his side of the console, she lightly touched his leg.

"Better?"

Instead of answering her question, to him the response was obvious, he asked one of his own.

"Do you like touching me?"

"Yes."

"Would you have moved closer if I hadn't complained?"

"I don't know. What do you mean exactly?"

A statement and a question. *Women.*

"If you wanted to touch me . . . would you? Without me asking?"

She reached down and this time kneaded his thigh before backing off.

"I don't know," she admitted as her head went back onto the seat. "It's hard with you and don't you dare snicker at my choice of words."

Snicker? Fuck no. She was opening up to him, and he wanted more of where that was coming from. "Hard, how?" he asked with real curiosity.

"I feel like I have to prove to you that I'm not a little girl anymore and feeling that way just sucks. I mean, you've always been older. You're you. The way you've always been, but me? I've changed, Parker, and part of that change is not understanding where the lines are with us. Are we family friends? Old buddies from way back? What are we besides the lead attendants in an upcoming wedding? What are we doing here?"

She certainly had cut right to the chase. Good for her. He was glad she wasn't a game player. Demanding he open up to her with his thoughts and feelings meant she wasn't just fucking around.

"Do you need me to spell out for you who we are and what we're doing, baby girl? Because I will."

He was telling her to think about what she was asking because he'd gladly lay it out for her line by fucking line—whether she was ready to hear it or not.

She sighed deeply. "No," she murmured hesitantly. "I like flying without a net."

Parker chuckled. Classic Angie.

"Fuck, Angel! Nobody knows that better than me. See these gray hairs?" he asked pointing at his temple. "All of 'em are from that time you made me watch you fucking tandem skydive. Worst forty-five minutes of my life."

She laughed gleefully and clapped her hands at the memory.

"Oh my god, that was so much fun! Do you remember, Parker? It was autumn and the trees were so colorful. I remember when I jumped out of the plane thinking that it was like parachuting into a picture postcard."

She smiled dreamily and reached out to feather her fingers along the side of his head.

"The gray suits you, counselor," she said huskily. Quickly sitting back after that, she turned her head and grinned cheekily, adding, "So I don't feel in any way sorry for giving them to you."

She didn't look away for a long time, and if it wasn't for the fact that he was driving, he would have gladly gotten lost in her gaze. As it was, he was cursing the car's interior for being so unromantic and was feeling uncommonly sulky because concentrating on navigating the SUV was cutting into this opportunity to indulge in some Angelina.

Alex, Meghan, and the limo suddenly made sense beyond the nudge nudge wink wink backslapping they all did. It wasn't just about indulging their trysts, it was more about cultivating every spare moment into quality time when it was just the two of them. Parker was quickly seeing a lot of things through different eyes.

"Do you mind if I play with the radio?" she asked—but, in typical Angie style, she was already fiddling with the controls.

Bypassing all the news stations, she studied his music presets like a research scientist on the brink of a breakthrough.

"Spa music?" she wondered aloud. "Doesn't seem like your speed."

Parker chuckled and nodded his agreement. "Blame Red. It's her damn fault. I listen to it on the drive home. That way, instead of dragging my work into my private life, I use the drive time to disconnect. Center, as Meghan would say."

The way she was looking at him gave Parker the tingles.

"What?" he asked.

She looked down for a moment, then turned her amazing flashing sapphire eyes on him. Right before he tore his eyes away to concentrate on the road, she smiled impishly and purred, "Work hard. Play hard."

The shameless reminder of what, for Parker, was his personal motto got an instant reaction from his dick because she left out what came after . . . *Fuck Hard.*

And just like that, the moment evaporated as she went back to scanning the programmed satellite stations.

"Ooooh, I like this song," she said so quietly he wondered if she was thinking out loud.

Turning the volume up, she was singing along and wiggling in her seat as she ramped up to a full in-car performance.

Hmmm. Girl singer. Sounds young but not a teen queen. He thought about it as she sang and then it hit him.

"Taylor Swift?" he asked—incredibly pleased that his old ass had put it together.

Angie beamed at him and kept on singing. They shared an easygoing love for all things musical. He'd never given it much thought because, well . . . because it had just always been that way. Both their families valued the arts and pressed all the kids into playing at least one instrument. And Angie, not only did she play most stringed instruments, she also mastered the piano and had a magical singing voice.

An odd warmth slowly crept through him. Music was such a huge part of his world and not only because he'd been in a band since he'd sprouted pubes. Hands down, one of the coolest fucking things about having baby boomer parents was the incredibly broad musical tastes they enjoyed. As a result, Parker's personal musical catalog included a mixed bag of wide-ranging sounds and genres from Elvis and Patsy Cline to AC/DC and Black Sabbath. Eighties rock was his go-to; he willingly admitted to enjoying the occasional musical and would still drop everything for a Foo Fighters show.

Right until this actual second though, he never considered how little of his real self he'd shared with the parade of women who romped through his life over the years. Unforgettable although highly energetic sexual escapades—nothing too heavy or serious—never amounted to more than some pretty shallow, superficial diversions.

But this engaging creature belting out a catchy pop tune? Shit, man. Shallow and superficial never had a ticket for admission to the Parker and Angelina show. She was inside him. She knew stuff. Their lives were inexplicably in sync—even though the age thing fucked things up.

He had to get them out of this car soon because he was on borrowed time now. Remaining polite and mannerly was almost impossible now that Angie was back to being Angie again.

The song ended which set her off again, searching the stations for something she liked. Instant gratification, much? Just like her tendency to act out, Angie's impatience was something he'd like very much to tame. Not too much—just a little. After all, her enthusiasm and joy for life was what made her so unique but sometimes she really and truly did rush in where other angels would fear to tread.

Lowering the volume back to conversational level when another song ended, she relaxed in her seat and giggled quietly.

"Sorry 'bout that but I love Britney. She's playing Vegas you know," she squealed with delight. "Maybe after the wedding when Mom and Dad stay at the Villa during the newlywed's honeymoon, I can talk someone into going with me. I'd love to see her show."

Storing that choice nugget of info away, he reached over and yanked on one of her curls. "You've got a show of your own coming up. Can't wait for Saturday night."

"*Aargh.*" Her groan was adorable. "I'm actually nervous! Those girls take this karaoke shit seriously," she told him emphatically. "Hey! It's not just remembering lyrics with them," she whined when he laughed. "They've got dance moves and stuff like that."

Parker knew all about those dance moves. Having seen the ladies perform previously, he was well aware of the T & A show they put on. Hell! They were smart as shit for playing it that way too because it made people love their shtick and got the crowd riled up and ready to party. Just what a good karaoke party was supposed to do.

"Fuck, yeah!" He laughed. "Those raunchy burlesque routines they do certainly pack the bar."

She looked slightly horrified at his description, and he nearly died laughing when she started sputtering furiously.

"Burlesque routines? They are not! What do you mean?"

Slowing for traffic as he eased the big SUV into the turning lane, he looked over at her and openly leered the impressive cleavage she was so obviously flaunting.

"Tell me, baby girl," he husked. "Will there be boob jiggles and booty wiggles?"

"Parker!"

"What?" He laughed affably. "Are you telling me that I'm not to look forward to you shaking those delicious tits in my face?"

She was full of sexist outrage—the sort that made his dick hard—trying to defend using her body to advantage . . . and failing miserably at it.

"There's nothing wrong with some simple . . ."

"Bump and grind?" he taunted.

"Fuck! Parker!" she yelled, clearly exasperated that he was tying her up in verbal knots. "That's not at all what I was going for and you know it."

They were pulling into the parking lot of the restaurant he'd decided at the last second would give him an opportunity to show off the little bombshell beauty he had on his arm tonight.

Their past relationship complicated the simplest things like going out to dinner because once they'd became lovers, they instinctively withdrew from making public appearances. The truth was that all they really did was fuck. Nonstop. He wanted to set that part of things right. Now that they didn't need to hide being together, Parker was filled with a desire to show her off. His Angel. Having her by his side was the most fantastic thing . . . like, ever.

"Come on, Gypsy Rose Lee," he teased with a big grin. "I'll let you entertain me . . . all you want."

Hopping out of the car, he made it to her door and pulled it open while she was still in mid-mutter about wanting to kick his ass or something like that.

Even though he knew the move would be seen as highly proprietary, Parker pulled her close with an arm around her waist, handed off his keys to the valet, and cracked a lame joke with the doorman as he ushered her into the restaurant.

So far—so good.

All joking aside, Angie had a sudden urge to talk to her mother. She could use her mom's Zen-like calm and snarky humor right about now. One look at the man-in-black thing Parker had going on and the always irreverent Ashleigh Marquez would be the first one to start wagging her eyebrows and fan herself.

She'd already decided that she needed to call home anyway. Once she had dinner with Aunt Wendy and Uncle Matt, the phone lines between Arizona and Spain were going to light up big time. She wanted her mom to hear about this thing with Parker, whatever it was, from her first. One thing her folks had drilled into all their heads was . . . *don't put us in a position of hearing things from other people. Always tell us first. Don't embarrass your mom and dad.*

Somehow, she'd find a way to explain and then she wanted to ask her mom what she would do in Angie's position. She definitely wanted to be with this man. Oh, hell yeah, she did. But what about him? Was she what was best for him? And how did she go about figuring all this out? *Help me, Mom!*

As they walked to the hostess stand, she glanced down and caught sight of his hand where it lay curved around her cinched-in waist. *Oh!* It looked so huge and his fingers seemed so long and sturdy.

Her shoulder rubbed against his side where he held her fast—she felt small and fragile next to his impressive size even though she was neither of those things. He didn't smell entirely like himself, though.

What the heck was that all about?

He let go of her as he spoke with the hostess, giving Angie an opportunity to glance around the lobby and really notice where they were. She knew the place of course, everyone who lived anywhere within a hundred mile radius had at least heard of Jim's Ranch—a steakhouse with a Michelin rating and the cachet of having been the former home of Gentleman Jim's, a legendary private club that catered to the bordello inspired.

The lobby was covered with pictures and newspaper clippings about the historic gentleman's establishment and all around were artifacts from the original club. Dark wood walls, beautifully worn by time, reflected the lights and flickering candles in every nook and cranny.

Large red leather benches and couches provided seating while unusual art nouveau pieces softened the severe look of the décor. It was eclectic and inspired and she was immediately enthralled.

When her eyes finished the three-sixty visual once-over, she turned toward her date and had to catch her breath. God. He was so handsome and there was something about the black clothing that made her feel excited and all tingly. It made him look solid, imposing—maybe a bit menacing. She liked it. *Very much.*

What she also liked . . . *very much* was the way he was looking at her. There was no mistaking exactly what he thought when she turned and saw him. His eyes said it all. She felt . . . *consumed.*

He didn't say a word—the demand in his eyes spoke for him. Angie's feet began moving in his direction before she consciously willed them to. A prickling sensation like flickering bolts of electricity spread from her neck out to her shoulders. He put out his hand—she homed in on it and basked in his silent approval.

As she slotted her hand into his, he pulled her close and pressed his lips to her forehead, whispering, "You look beautiful, honey."

That weird sound? It was her—melting into a puddle at his feet.

Chapter Thirty-Seven

THE MINUTE THEY FOLLOWED THE hostess to their table, Parker started questioning his sanity. Expecting him not to break down into a grunting, knuckle-dragging caveman with a thundering hard-on, as he walked behind what had to be the sexiest and most fuckable ass he'd ever laid eyes on, was laughable. The way Angie rolled her wicked hips with each step was enough to tip him over the edge from civility to lusty predator in record time. And those shoes? *Jesus fuck me Christ,* he moaned. The number of erotic scenarios he could imagine involving those shoes was pretty impressive.

When she'd drifted down the steps at the Villa, she'd stolen his fucking breath. At any other time and in any other place, she wouldn't have gotten out of the house without being thoroughly . . . *taken.* Exactly what her outfit begged for.

But, timing and opportunity being what it was, he satisfied himself another way by changing his previous dinner plan and replacing it with this one, where he swaggered through Jim's with a beautiful woman by his side. Hell, he wanted everyone and their sister's best friend's cousin's mailman to get a look at Angelina Marquez and then envy the shit out of him knowing who she belonged to.

Parker loved Jim's Steakhouse. It was where he and Alex came whenever it was just the two of them. He dined there two or three times a month enjoying not just the amazing menu but the distinctive setting which was just slightly shy of being a garish spectacle held over from the region's wild west days. Someplace perfect for showing off his lady.

The thing was though that as they walked along, it was Angie who swaggered and not him, as every male eye and not a few females as well, nodded appreciatively as she rocked on by. *Dammit.*

And what was he doing while she commanded the suggestive leers of all the men in attendance? Dragging his knuckles along the floor in her wake, snarling and green-eyed with possessive jealousy.

With none of the private spaces available without a reservation, they were seated in one of the smaller lounge rooms at a small corner table away from the foot-traffic pattern.

This time when they sat, Angie didn't scramble as far from him as she could get, moving to the seat next to his. The hostess quickly instructed the wait staff to rearrange everything before directing their attention to the menu.

"Karen will be taking care of y'all tonight," the bubbly woman informed them. "You need anything, just let her know."

She had taken a dozen steps away from them before Angie gushed enthusiastically, "I love this place! How did you know?"

His mind stuttered to a halt at her question. Huh? What?

Snap out of it! His mind barked. *The most beautiful woman in this whole damn place is talking to you. She's giving you your shot, you dumb fuckwad! Man up, dude.*

"Know that you'd happily fall face first onto a bloody steak?" he smirked playfully. "Easy. Where us carnivores are concerned, takes one to know one."

She managed to accentuate her already over-the-top cleavage by leaning on the table with crossed arms and smiled warmly at him.

"Thank you. This is a first for me. Did you know? I've never been here before but always wanted to."

"Sign me up as conductor of all your firsts, baby."

Balls. Parker had to wince. Had that sounded cheesy? He didn't have time to think about it 'cause she asked a question that floored him.

"Can I trust you, counselor? With my firsts, I mean."

What was the meaning of the word coy? She had it in spades, whatever it was.

He half shrugged and reminded her grittily, "You have no reason to think you can. Trust me."

She blinked at him in slow motion.

"But I'm going to change all that. We're starting fresh, remember? Gaining your trust would seem to me to be key. Yes?"

She didn't give him anything by way of a response—just continued looking at him intently.

"Can you even imagine how badly I want to trust you?" she asked so quietly that he had to watch her lips as a backup to make sure he'd heard her correctly.

Everything became a blur after that. They ate. Drank. Laughed. Ate some more. Drank some more. Laughed some more. It was perfect. And it was rooted in the present and not the past. They talked mostly about Family Justice and life at the Villa. As the night and their conversation wore on, Parker got the distinct impression that she was thinking about more than just an extended stay because of her brother's wedding.

"Today was like Mr. Toad's Wild Ride, huh?" she asked.

"You mean your stupid head brother and his wild Irish rose? Yeah!" He snorted through a big grin. "Wedding jitters make people say and do the strangest things."

Angie curved in his direction, crossing her legs and pushing some of her long curls over her shoulder. In a conspiratorial voice, she told him, "I think it's more than jitters."

"Oh, jeez. What have you heard?"

"Mmm, you know," she jested. "People talk. Comments are made. Apparently, my big brother has a kinky streak a mile wide."

Parker lifted an eyebrow but tried not to smirk. "Uh-huh. And?"

She let his non-surprise go with a mocking smile.

"Apparently, Drae needed an intervention after stumbling upon Meghan, um . . . I guess there's no other way to say it than she was tied up in the tack room and . . ."

A gruff sounding laugh rumbled up from inside him. He fucking loved this story. It always made him smile. Good for Alex.

"Sorry." He shrugged. "Didn't mean to interrupt."

Angie was looking at him as if she could see straight into his deepest thoughts. Should that awareness bother him? He considered the ramifications and concluded he was good with it because it was her.

Let her look. She needed to know.

"What's so funny?" Her breathy question brought him back from his private thoughts.

Maybe it was the brandy, or maybe it was the good company and the generally awesome way he was feeling—he'd actually never know what made him say it, but he took a hefty swallow of his drink and nudged Angie's leg with his.

Winking, he quipped, "The boy learned his lessons well, I must say."

The second he stopped talking and saw Angie's eyes flare, he knew he'd done a stupid. Alex wasn't the only one eating his words today. *Fuck.*

She looked at him with such wide-eyed incredulity he had to smile especially when he all but saw each and every light bulb in her imagination go off inside her head.

"What did you do?" she hissed.

"Uh," he croaked, stalling for time. "Do? I didn't *DO* anything."

"Parker Sullivan," she bit out sternly. "You and my brother were a nonstop, live action version of Monkey See—Monkey Do. I grew up hearing my mom lament this fact. Just because I'm younger than you two doesn't mean I'm stupid!"

Whoa. She worked up to a full head of outraged steam pretty fast. Something he'd better remember in the future. His Angel had a bit of a hot Latin temperament. *High five!*

"You tied me to your bed years before red rooms became all the rage so don't even try to act innocent. Not with me."

"Touché," he drawled with an obvious grimace. She fucking had him there.

"Was my brother your padawan?"

First he delivered a knee-jerk, "No!" followed by, "My wh*aaaat?*"

He was a lawyer, for god's sake. He knew how that double-sided response was going to play. *Fuck. My. Life.*

"Oh, don't even!" she scoffed.

Walloping him with a kidding slap on the arm, she shook her head at him in mock disbelief. "Says he who has a *Stormtrooper* coffee mug and a *Star Wars* shower curtain," she *tsked.*

Her mocking reference to *Star Wars* had him breaking out one of his absolute favorite movie quotes which, to him anyway, perfectly summed up his entire assessment of those years along the Potomac. The description—*a wretched hive of scum and villainy* was the perfect fit. Goddamn D.C. He learned far more than simply how laws got made and enforced during his tenure in the nation's capitol.

He suspected she was taking a shot in the dark without knowing it was a dead center bull's-eye. The girl was smart. Clever. She put it together in record time after nothing more than an off-hand comment. He liked it. She was going to keep him on his toes.

Sniffing, Angie crossed her arms and bit out, "And if you think about it, I barely reacted to the threesome thing."

Hmmm. Now that you mention it . . . she hadn't reacted. *At all.* He looked at her questioningly.

"I know you two. Better than you think."

Ha! She sounded so confident. So full of herself. Though she knew him, huh? Well, he decided, let's use some language intended to get a reaction and see what she did. Goddamn, this was exhilarating.

Staring her down, he spoke calmly, succinctly—like he would to a jury. Commanding the pulpit was something he excelled at.

"Well, if that's really the case let me clarify a comment you made. It's not a kinky streak. I dislike that term. What you're referring to is better described as the traits of a dominant."

She swallowed but didn't back down in her expression, gaze, or posture. Parker recognized his match when he saw it.

"And before your fertile imagination runs wild, since you already have a, uh . . . movie-themed understanding of these things . . ."

He did not miss the caustic glare she fired his way.

"Being dominant is not just about what happens in the bedroom. To some, it's a natural expression of who they are. You know damn well that Alex was born that way. Shit, Angie. Your family celebrates his dominance. Think about it. The man is like flypaper for control. If he hadn't almost gotten blown to kingdom come, he could have gone right up the military chain of command."

He'd struck a nerve. She sat back and her general posture softened. Parker took a last swallow of his brandy and watched the play of emotions and thoughts she was picking apart show through her expression.

"But you're right," he continued with a silky drawl. "Nobody knows us better than you do, baby girl. Sure," he chuckled, "I may have shared some . . . *technical things* . . . with your brother but the bottom line? The rest is all him."

The bill for dinner arrived, he engaged in a bit of friendly chatter with the waitress, even straightened up their area and started making moves to leave, all while monitoring Angie's silent analysis—wondering what she'd say when she finally spoke.

His legal mind was working overtime and seriously . . . he never thought the skills he'd acquired in a courtroom, taking depositions, even researching precedents . . . was going to come in handy trying to decipher the female mystery of the woman avoiding his gaze.

Finally—after she'd racked up god only knows how many assumptions in her head that he figured he'd be dealing with at some point—she came back with a surprising but very wise observation. Instead of continuing to focus on Alex and him, she had ended up on the other side of the divide.

"But what about Meghan. She doesn't . . . oh, I don't know." She shrugged. A confused frown made her expression almost pouty. "Doesn't seem the type."

Yeah. He had to shut that thought process down. She was looking at it the wrong way. A bunch of pre-conceived pop culture bullshit. He sighed heavily.

"Honey," he said roughly—something that he noted made her go quite still. "There is no type. Think about what you're saying. You're right about not fitting a Hollywood template but the truth is simpler than the play-acting. Where those two are concerned, Alex's natural control gives Meghan the freedom to grow. She surrenders but never gives up being the one with all the power. She *wants* Alex to be a beast. He's happy. She's more than content. Who gives a shit about *type* or what they do in the bedroom."

He snickered. "It could just as easily have been him tied up, you know. Quid pro quo and all."

"Quid pro quo," she mumbled as her head shook and she tried not to laugh. It was cool that she got the joke.

Truth be told, Parker was worried that some of the shit he'd subjected her to before, which he knew at the time went way beyond what an innocent twenty-year-old should be exposed to, might be coloring her perceptions.

What a fucking dick he'd been. In his rush to mold her into his ideal mate, he'd been a complete idiot. I mean, fuck—he'd known from the get-go that he and Angie had a volatile sexual connection. She lit him up and provided the fuel for the massive combustion they created together. Instead of letting that unique connection unfold naturally, at its own pace, he'd pushed and prodded until she was the perfect naughty plaything without fully understanding what that really meant.

Leaving out the emotional connection had been so huge a mistake that he was certain a page existed in some Alpha handbook somewhere with a subheading that read *How to Shoot Yourself in the Foot* with his picture alongside and a caption that read—Wanted for Grave Stupidity.

"Are you okay?" he asked gently.

She didn't hesitate to jump right in.

"Is that how you see yourself, counselor? As a dominant."

Parker snorted, amused. Instead of using his name, she thought to distance herself from the discussion with a shrug and the use of his lame ass title. He also noted she all but choked on the word *dominant.*

"I don't care for the emotional reaction that word evokes in people. And I don't . . . *appreciate* . . . the posers who hide behind the power implied and use it to manipulate and abuse."

He let that statement sink in as they drove.

She was fixed on him, and even in the darkened car, he imagined he could see flecks of gold swirling in her sapphire gaze.

"I'm a man who doesn't take shit. Am I controlling? You know damn well, I am. But not in an asshole way."

She made a noise . . ."*Hmmph.*"

"What's the real question, Angel? Are you asking me if I want that in a relationship? With you?

She gasped.

Parker smirked. "Oh, and I don't play word games. I cut to the chase. It's an occupational hazard."

Chapter Thirty-Eight

WHAT WAS IT ABOUT DRIVING through the dark that sent a person inside their thoughts? Maybe the nighttime was imbued with special powers that helped to clear away cobwebs and open the mind.

Did she want a relationship like that? Angie was surprised he was so direct, but at the same time, as the pieces began falling into place, she simply started seeing things she already knew, in a different light. This side of her brother's best friend had always been there. It wasn't new. Not at all.

Her thoughts were tempered by knowing that the last time she'd fallen under his commanding spell, she'd had been woefully unprepared for what she was getting herself into. This guy did not fuck around.

And she knew things that she probably shouldn't about his time in D.C.

Parker Sullivan was no altar boy. Or even a Boy Scout. He was big and powerful, and she wasn't referring to his physical presence. The guy could be one huge scary monster if he needed to.

He didn't want to play word games? Thought cutting to the chase was a viable strategy? Okay, then. Two could play at that.

She reached up with both hands, gathering her long hair at the back of her neck twisting it till it lay down her back in a loosed twirled tail. It was something of a nervous reflex. When she was finished, Angie dropped her hands into her lap and quietly uttered, "I know about The Cavern, Parker."

Glancing his way, she saw him clench his jaw and knew she'd taken him by surprise with her unexpected reveal.

Jesus. Guys were so dumb sometimes. I mean, what the actual hell? Just because she was most definitely naïve all those years ago didn't mean she'd been brain-dead.

Her first awareness of The Cavern had happened almost a year before she and Parker slept together. It was because of the fact that they hung out so much—literally most of their free time, when they weren't working or going to school, was spent together—that she knew anything at all.

They'd been on a hike in a suburban Maryland park just outside the District that had a wonderful trail around a lake marked with beautiful weeping willow trees. From her first weekend after she'd started at Georgetown, they'd engaged in a friendly competition to see who could make it around the lake in the fastest time. He always won, but she gave him one helluva run for his money, the fucker.

After one particular second best run, they'd gone to his apartment to change and clean up. While Parker had been in the shower, she'd wandered absently, gathering stuff into piles and making stacks of all the magazines laying around. She'd even replaced two of his guitars into their cases marveling that he didn't take better care of his stuff.

And that was when she saw it. A print out of an email for key holders about some event at The Cavern and Parker's name was clearly evident. She hadn't told him what she knew—until just now. Hadn't admitted that she'd done more research into the goings on at the private club than she put into her schoolwork that semester.

For lack of a better way of putting it, The Cavern was an exclusive establishment catering to the BDSM community. And that so-called community was, due to its unique location, full of high-powered people. Public figures, politicians, diplomats, lobbyists . . . you name it. Parker rolled with the big kids.

Had she made a mistake by telling him that she knew? He was awfully quiet and the way his hands were gripping that steering wheel, she was surprised it didn't snap off.

Cold, unease slithered along her nerve endings. Oh, shit. She should have thought that reveal through before acting on it. Clearly, by his reaction, she had trod on something private that he didn't want to be exposed. *I guess,* she thought, *it's a little like finding her vibrator in the nightstand.* Some things didn't need to be discussed.

"I'm sorry," she muttered. "None of my business."

How did she know he was bent out of shape? The knuckles on the hand gripping the wheel were now white and she could feel waves of something intense coming off him. Feeling horribly gauche for having embarrassed him, Angie considered jumping from the moving car, preferring to eat some road gravel to sitting beside him while he was furious at her

"Fuck!" he bellowed. She jumped half a foot and smacked her elbow on the car door.

"Angelina Marquez," he growled fiercely.

She swallowed hard. *Uh-oh.*

"I swear to god if you tell me you *ever,*" he shouted, "stepped even *one toe* inside that place, I will blister your ass until you won't be able to sit down for a month, young lady."

Hold on, hold on, hold on. What? He thought *SHE* was the one at the club? And he threatened to do *WHAT* to her ass?

"Ewww! No! What? We're not talking about me, counselor. And for the record? Me? In a sex dungeon? Uh . . . you've met me, right?"

Still hanging on to his anger, he yelled, "Met you? Are you fucking kidding? Yeah, I've met you and who better than me would know you'd be the first one to visit a place like that and pretend to be all ballsy and nonchalant about it, too."

"Well, I didn't so stand down. You're scaring me."

He groaned and turned to look at her, his eyes practically invisible in the dark confines of the car.

"Angie . . . goddammit. I don't know how you knew about that place, but it won't be pretty if I find out you ever go somewhere like that. If you're curious, you talk to me. Don't go off on your own. Some of those places have strict protocols and rules, and without realizing it, you could find yourself in a situation you couldn't handle."

"Okay, counselor," she snapped, cutting him off in mid-comment. "I get it. But don't think this little finger wagging lecture distracted me from what we were originally talking about."

"Actually, Angel," he told her in a tone that sounded all alpha-smirky. "The original question was whether you want a relationship with me. We only ventured into different territory when *you* brought it up."

She laughed. Lawyerly asshole. Getting the upper hand in a verbal conversation was going to be a challenge around him.

A surefire way to piss him off had Angie picking up her phone—she tapped on the screen and began scrolling away in that way that said . . . *yawn.* She knew he'd react to the provocation and bit her lip to keep from loudly snickering.

"You don't get your answer till I get mine," she answered dismissively.

"You didn't ask a question, baby girl. You made a statement."

"But the statement about The Cavern was after I asked if you if that's how you saw yourself. In the dominant role. So the question came first."

So there, she sniffed.

"I only said what I did about the club so you'd know I wasn't completely ignorant. I do know what I'm saying, Parker."

She could feel him collecting his thoughts. Oh, my. Maybe she didn't want to hear the answer. The explanation, whatever it was. They were in dangerous waters right now. There was personal and then there was . . . this.

Eventually, he gripped the wheel less forcefully and the tension inside the car eased off. She stopped fiddling with her phone and leaned on the center console giving him one hundred percent of her attention.

"Just say it. All of it. Out loud. I know what's at stake. We were the best of friends. Closer than friends. Then we were lovers. And then? Not enemies. Not friends. Just a horrible limbo. And now we're friends again. I hope," she added sincerely. "And unless that bulge in your pants is an optical illusion, it would be all too easy to fall into the lovers thing again."

He grunted. God, he was cute.

"I'm not interested in sleeping with you. What a waste of time that would be. Been there—done that, remember?"

"What the fuck are you saying?" he muttered darkly.

"Didn't you hear me? I know what's at stake." She let the importance of her words hang there in the air. "But unless we're talking about bigger picture stuff, I'm not up for fooling around no matter how much fun it would be. It's ironic," she murmured

"What is?"

"It took all this time to realize that I want more. I want everything, not some romantic, sanitized version of what a relationship should be. That is *definitely* a been there, done that," she griped. "But you have to spell it out for me first, Parker. This is all or nothing. You're too important to me and have been for all of my life, for what we've got to end up being friends with benefits."

She must have struck a nerve because he spelled it out for her then in pretty blunt and specific terms. If she had any questions after his speech, well . . . she must not have been paying attention; that was how precise he was.

"Understand this."

She shivered at the tone he used. What the hell was that? And why was there a fluttering in her chest?

"I'm not some character in a book. And you already know I don't fuck around. You want to know what I want? Who I am? Fine."

Maybe she should just jump him right now. Before he said anything. Leap across the inconvenient console and have her wicked, wanton way with him. It didn't matter what he said. She already knew. This was just the fine tuning.

"First, this is the only time I've ever had this discussion. With anyone. Until this moment, frankly, it didn't matter. But you're right. There's something huge at stake, and we have to be honest. Something superficial would never be enough with you. Any more than some cookie cutter, once on Sunday and a blowjob for my birthday arrangement."

"Birthdays should be special. When did a blowjob become special," she joked, trying to ease the tension.

"You're just making my point for me, you know."

Oops.

"Did I fuck around at places like The Cavern? Yeah. Do I see anything like that in my future? No. Not really. The group thing, the public thing—has no allure for me. Are my bedroom tastes a bit . . . demanding? You already know the answer to that. But that's not what this is about. Is it? You want to know what your place would be. What you could expect."

"Before you continue, there's something I should tell you. Please don't go crazy on me."

Angie heard his breathing change. *Ugh.* She hoped he didn't get mad.

"Aldo took me to an event last year. One of those debauched celebrity parties. Sado-masochistic theme. Fucked-up take on the whole shades of grey thing. The decorations, and I'm not kidding even a little bit, were live people, men and women, tied up, strapped down, hung from crosses, and locked in stockades. It was horrible. I freaked. Aldo, well . . . he showed a little too much interest in the S&M beating scenarios."

Parker pulled off the road so fast, a gravel and dirt cloud enveloped the car as they came to a grinding halt that made her snap back and forth in her seat belt.

"If that son-of-a-bitch laid a hand on you, I am going to fucking kill the little prick."

She shouldn't have smiled—but she did. He was all kinds of cute when he was jacked up.

"It's not fucking funny, Angie," he grated out. "I won't have it."

Awwww. How sweet. He had no problem threatening to spank her tushy, but suggest someone else might, and he was an instant caveman.

Unable to resist the temptation to poke him a bit, she pouted and squinched her nose up.

"He got a leather crop and wanted to experiment with it, but . . ."

"What?"

His roar was downright thrilling. She couldn't believe she'd actually asked if he saw himself as a dominant. What a farce! Just look at him. He was the personification of a commanding alpha with a bad-boy streak. And my goodness, was he ever on fire right this second!

"That's it!" he growled. "What's that fucker's name? Ronald? Ronald MacDonald? That asshole will be shitting happy meals into next year after I shove a ton of 'em up his ass."

Okay, now *THAT* was funny. She was struggling not to burst out laughing.

"A fucking riding crop? He's a dead man if he touched you with it."

A sudden vision of Alex and Parker doing unspeakable things to Ronaldo spurred her to ease him down off the ledge before he went off half-cocked.

"Actually, what he had in mind was the other way around."

She said it plainly. No inflection. How long would it take him to . . .

He threw back his head and laughed deeply. Apparently, it hadn't taken him any time at all.

"Oh, my god! For real? This is awesome!" He laughed. "Did he get you one of those leather and latex Dominatrix outfits as well?"

His laugh was infectious, and she had to admit, it *was* funny. That weekend it hadn't been funny, though. Not when Aldo all but begged her to experiment with him. She couldn't wrap her mind around any part of what he needed. The idea of paddling him, something he showed a particular interest in, just left her cold. There had to be a line somewhere. She was no sadist, any more than she was a masochist and if that was what he was looking for . . . well, they had a problem. One of many.

The laughter had broken the tension. All of a sudden, he unsnapped her seatbelt, reached, and hauled Angie half over the damn console and dove onto her mouth. It wasn't a kiss of seduction. Nor was it one of passion. It was a marking. A brand on her ass couldn't have been plainer.

Settling her back in her seat after the kiss ended, he leaned over her, one hand wrapped around her neck so she had no choice but to look straight at him.

"I want to be excited and challenged—outside the bedroom. I need a partner who is my equal. Not someone I control. *Dominate,*" he added for good measure. She was started to see where he was going.

"I won't pretend that I'd be anything less than what you already know I am in a relationship. Arrogant? Of course. But a partner who yields to her master," she saw the humor in his expression when he said it which was all that saved him from a punch in the gut, "gains more than she gives away."

"How do you figure?" She really wanted to hear his answer.

"Because, Angel baby, we'll both know that you'll *choose* to yield.

Such an honor can only be met with loyalty, protection, and affection. Your happiness would be foremost in my mind and present in every action."

Hmmph. Affection? She had to call him on it.

"Affection?" Her tone landed somewhere between *Are you fucking kidding* and *Please feel free to blow me anytime.*

He caressed her cheek. "The word was carefully chosen because though you smirk, I don't think you're ready for the other discussion. The one with the L word."

Well, he was right about that. A couple of weeks ago, they hadn't spoken in years and just hearing his name sent her into an emotional freefall. Four months ago, she'd been engaged to another man although she'd admittedly used the term *man* as a reference. Aldo was a toddler in diapers compared to Parker's panty-melting masculinity.

Did she want this man with a desire that was completely messing with her head? Yes. But that was sex. And she'd already thrown down the gauntlet that screwing around wasn't enough.

Beyond that, though? Was she ready to take that risk? The leap of faith it took to put herself totally in someone else's hands. Just the thought made her feel vulnerable and exposed so, no. She wasn't really ready to call the L word out from the shadows. Oh, she knew it was there—hovering just out of sight, but for now, that particular emotion had to continue as an understudy a while longer. Wasn't time for a starring role and it remained to be seen whether their admitted lust for each other was on life support or if it could flourish and grow into something deeper.

Chapter Thirty-Nine

THEY MADE THE LAST LONG drive to the Villa off the main road in loud silence. Parker glanced at the dashboard clock. Ten fifteen. Whew. For a second there he was worried they'd lingered beyond his self-imposed eleven P.M. curfew.

The wide circular driveway that curved around the front of the big house was always like a fucking parking lot and tonight was no different. Even when no one was really around, it seemed like there were a half dozen odd vehicles parked here and there. Betty's distinctive surrey-fringed buggy cart was there next to Meghan's green John Deere. He wondered briefly if she ever tired of the Irish green jokes and references.

He pulled alongside Alex's ranch truck because it offered a sliver of cover and privacy.

Their conversation had gotten so serious and heavy that he half expected Angie to bolt from his vehicle the minute he cut the engine. He was relieved to answer her questions and concerns freely and openly. It felt damn good and was exactly what he referred to by wanting a partner who challenged but was his equal. He felt completely at ease with her. But he was having a hard time reading her reactions.

Reading people was in the first paragraph of his job description and was something he was known for. But with Angie? Yeah, sometimes he could follow her thoughts like a paint-by-number project but only to a point. She was being guarded and while he hoped he was right about what was happening in the hidden part of her heart and mind, he didn't really know for sure.

To his astonishment, she did not leap from the SUV and run screaming from him. Was she making a statement by showing her fearlessness in the face of what they'd discussed? Heat rushed into his groin.

He heard a muffled click followed by the sound of her belt retracting. He unclicked his and let it reset as he pulled the keys from the ignition so the cab would go dark. Parker had every intention of kissing his Desert Angel to within seconds of an erotic meltdown and didn't need the glare from the onboard lights to throw a spotlight on what they were doing in the front seat of his SUV.

Her soft hand reached down and rested on his thigh as she leaned on the console. "Thank you. I enjoyed tonight, Parker."

"As did I," he assured her warmly.

"You've given me a lot to think about."

Huh. No shit. Just the little matter of every fucking thing rested on what she decided was best for her.

How could he press his case without forcing her hand or come off like a control freak?

Tell her to get her ass onto your lap and be quick about it if she wants to be kissed properly, his snarky inner voice quipped.

Okay.

"While you think," he husked, his fingers having reached out to play with one of her silky curls. "Do it from my lap."

"Um . . . your lap?" she asked, confused.

"Yep," he ground out. "That spot where your magnificently sexy ass belongs if you want me to kiss you goodnight."

"Oh."

Not sure how they did it, but a combination of seat adjustments and sheer ingenuity ended with Angie sprawled across the console, her ass resting firmly on his erection and her legs and feet, with those sexy-as-fuck shoes, stretched out on the passenger side.

She had an arm about his shoulder as he leisurely ran his fingers up and down her leg. The higher he went near the fleshy part of her thigh, the more he could feel the heat coming from her center.

Parker touched her face and smiled into her wide-eyed gaze.

"You are so fucking beautiful."

He traced her delicately arched brows and skidded a finger down the center of her nose then slowly outlined her lips with his hands like a blind man memorizing a lover's face.

He took hold of her chin and stared at her mouth, which was open as she panted shallowly. When her tongue came out and swiped her lips leaving a sheen of moisture behind, he groaned.

"Tell me now if sucking your nipples is possible with what you have on."

She blinked half a dozen times and he felt her head shake infinitesimally, confusion running riot on her face.

"I thought you were going to kiss me," she purred as her free hand started toying with a button on his shirt.

Parker's lip curled in a small lopsided grin. Kissing was his secret weapon with her. She surrendered so quickly once the kissing started that he knew withholding his mouth from hers, if only for moments, was driving her crazy.

Tilting her face up with a finger beneath her chin, when she was looking into his eyes, he casually took the same finger that had been on her chin and fed it slowly into her mouth.

She sucked on it and swirled her tongue all around as he lost himself in the image of her sultry lips closing around his sturdy finger.

In a deep, gruff voice he told her, "That's right baby. Suck it. And then get ready to have your mouth fucked."

Her eyes lit up. *Shit.* He said that wrong but knowing she took it like he intended to get off in her mouth and seeing her wanton reaction to the idea didn't help him keep control.

"All I want to know is, do I have a shot at those wicked tits or are your goodies locked up with no access 'cause once we start, shit's going to get fucking real and fucking fast."

"Oh, uh . . . it's a corset. If you unlace it from behind it will be loose enough to fold over."

He rolled his eyes. No guy should need an engineering degree to undress his woman.

"Sit up," he grunted as he pushed her up and shoved her shoulders so he could eyeball these laces. T-shirt, no bra. That was what he wanted, not some Victorian bondage accessory.

Making quick work of loosening the laces, he didn't bother with any sort of romantic gesture, just tugged on the cups of the bustier and freed her breasts.

Now, there was a sight to behold. The sweetly curved mounds were so damn perfect that he couldn't look away. My god. He knew the pale, pink tipped heavy breasts would feel like heaven under his touch. So creamy and smooth, they looked full and soft with nipples that tightened into hard nubs before his eyes.

He concentrated on the feel of her succulent body, groaning when his hand cupped a full globe and his thumb swept across a tender peak. Angie's corresponding whimper almost did him in.

Trapping her eyes with his, he squeezed her breast.

"Now we kiss and I tongue fuck your sexy mouth in between biting those badass nipples."

And he did. With fervor. Until she was writhing on his lap and whimpering with need. When his mouth moved onto her tits, she gasped sharply as his tongue whisked the throbbing tips and he had to remind her to breathe.

"Come on, baby," he murmured close to her ear. "I'm not finished yet. Big deep breaths. Feel my mouth on your tits."

She groaned low and deep. "Ohhhhh."

He nipped at one of her delectable nubs. Her fingers immediately went into his hair and the arm around his shoulder tightened as fingernails, sharp and insistent, dug into the skin at the base of his neck.

Aware that he was making greedy, sucking noises as he devoured her lush beauty, Parker made no effort to be someone or something he wasn't. He wanted Angelina Marquez. In his bed. Underneath him so he could fuck her with all the fierceness running rampant through him. Fierceness she and only she inspired.

Never had going commando been such a fucking nightmare as it was right now. Parker's cock felt like it was fighting to break free, desperate for the sweet release he would find in her body. If he didn't reel it in now, he'd have her clothes in tatters and his shaft buried inside her within moments.

Fuck.

Fuck.

FUCK.

With a dose of aching regret, he laved one last smoldering stroke of his tongue against a delicate tip and eased back.

"When you are mine," he growled lustfully, "you will bare your breasts to me whenever we are alone."

Her quivering, "Okay," was adorably sweet. Just then, she would have agreed to walk naked through the center of town if he'd asked her to. Did she even know what she said okay to? Probably not. All her attention seemed to be focused on the longing looks she gave his mouth.

She knew what she wanted. He had to give her that. "Kiss me again," she begged.

He put his forehead to hers briefly then kissed her nose. "Can't," he ground out. "Date night's over, honey. Have to get you inside before Big Daddy marches out here with his night vision goggles on and makes a scene."

Parker had to cough back a chuckle when she began spouting nonsensical oaths of retribution and vengeance against her brother as she struggled awkwardly to untangle from their sprawling embrace

The more difficult it was to sit up and get re-situated, the fiercer her petulance became. Some part of him dug the shit out of knowing that she was going to make his friend's life a living hell for being the impediment to what she wanted.

Not for the first and certainly not the last time, Parker considered what a relationship between him and Angie would do to the Sullivan-Marquez family dynamic. Alex would be forever able to bust his chops whenever he felt like it and would no doubt take enormous delight in fucking with him because he could. Asshole.

But really. Wasn't this the way it was always supposed to be? He had his years of lording it over his friend and now it would be Alex's turn to be top dog. Somehow it seemed so perfectly . . . karmic.

She was still grumbling as she pulled it together so when they walked inside it didn't look like a bear had just mauled her. He let her have all the time she needed, not out of any inflated sense of chivalry but because he needed the opportunity to coax the out-of-control hard-on he was sporting back to a resting state. Wouldn't be a good idea to find himself staring down the thundering anger of her brother should he catch a glimpse of the obvious.

Good luck with that his head snickered. Especially now that you actually HAD mauled her to the extent that her taste is in your mouth and her scent invading your senses. Sucker!

In time, he helped swing her down from the vehicle, not that she was incapable of doing so herself, and nodded approvingly when she hesitated and checked out the placement of her clothing one last time.

"You look fine," he assured her.

Halfway down the walk to the house, she started laughing.

"Oh, my god," she wheezed in a building giggle. "This is worse than when Mom would threaten us, *wait till your father gets home!* I'll take my father any day over Alex with his military bark and that disgusted scowl he does so well."

Parker laughed, too. It truly was funny because he also felt like a bad kid about to get an ass-whupping from an angry parent.

Grinning broadly he scolded her. "Behave yourself."

She jerked to attention and said, "Yes, master," then fell apart in an attack of squealing giggles.

What the hell was he supposed to do with her? Heaven help them if Alex overheard her say that even as a joke. He'd rip his balls off first and ask questions later. Maybe.

With a hearty thwack, he swatted her playfully on the butt before leaning in to nip her earlobe.

"Now I understand why Alex keeps score . . ." he muttered which only made Angie's hysterical laugh get bigger.

"Seriously woman," he drawled as they came to the door. "Pull it together before we go in or my balls may end up being on permanent display in the family archive."

"What is it with this fascination over your balls?" she hooted. "First Meghan threatened and I had to plead for ball-mercy. And now Alex, too? Sheesh. How 'bout I get you a cup to wear?"

The imp. She was openly taunting him.

He grabbed her hand and pressed it firmly against his crotch. Finally, a reason to be glad he was free-ballin.'

"Feel that?" he drawled with a leer. "Better make that a custom cup, baby girl. Don't want to restrict the family equipment."

She was saved from coming up with an answer when the door was suddenly jerked open and a stone-faced Alex was standing on the other side.

Quickly snatching her hand away, she flounced past her brother like he was the doorman at the Ritz and hip-swayed into the house.

"Be nice, Alexander," she scolded on her way in. "He told me all your filthy secrets so you better watch yourself, brother dear."

He caught Alex's instant scowl at the same time she winked at Parker and turned away laughing. Score one for the baby sister.

Ass. Blistered. Yep, yep. Looking like a definite possibility.

Meghan appeared at the top of the stairs wearing an expression that told him she'd be in his face in a heartbeat if Angie were unhappy because of him.

"Alex," Meghan said softly. "Come to bed. Angie can lock up after Parker."

Again—the look she speared him with was full of heavy meaning. If it was anyone other than Irish, he might have smirked.

"Where did you go?" Alex asked Angie, ignoring Parker completely. "What did you do? Was that asshole a gentleman?"

Meghan shook her head and rolled her eyes. Parker hoped she was taking notes 'cause this was exactly how Alex would be with a daughter or two to protect. Growl, bark questions, be a huge dick, and make dark looks.

Angie smiled so sweetly it almost made his teeth ache.

"Oh! We went to Jim's and I had a steak the size of your face. Then Parker forced me to eat this death by chocolate dessert that I swear came with a health warning." She rubbed her stomach and grinned. "And now I'm stuffed and need to get out of these clothes and put on some stretchy pants before I explode."

Meghan purred again, "Alex. *Enough.*"

For a second, Alex looked back and forth between him and Angie then back at his love who smiled and put out her hand. "Come on, Major. Angie's a big girl now. Let her handle this."

Angie went to her brother and threw her arms around him in a massive hug. His arms immediately came around her and he lifted her off the sexy heels for a brotherly squeeze. Parker saw her whisper into his ear a second before Alex looked him straight in the eye.

He held his breath hoping she wasn't saying anything stupid.

Putting her down, she thumped him good-naturedly on the chest and said, "Run along now, Alexander. I've got this."

Alex walked to the stairs then turned around for one more meaningful look in Parker's direction. When his best friend in the whole world used two fingers to indicate that he had his eyes on him, his balls shrank.

He loved Alex Marquez like a brother. No. Fuck that. They *were* brothers. But he loved Angelina even more. Keeping the respect of her brother and all the members of her family was vitally important to all their futures.

He politely took his leave of Angie not long after with a short, sweet kiss by the front door—just like they were kids at the end of a date.

"Don't forget," he chuckled on exit, "dinner with Wendy and Matt tomorrow. My mom is really looking forward to it and, be prepared . . . my dad has some crazy PowerPoint he wants to show you. Something to do with your dad and that's all I know."

Angie giggled. "I love Uncle Matt! And tell your mom that I pried two bottles of a rioja out of the Villa's wine cellar that will knock her booties off."

Chapter Forty

"So, we're good to go then for the seventeenth? I want this to be memorable, guys. The whole enchilada."

"Don't you mean the whole corned beef?" Drae snickered.

Cam crushed an empty soda can and tossed it through the air in a perfect arc that dropped dead center into the recycling bin, then swung his arms up and hooted, "Score!"

Alex petted Zeus's head when she looked up at him in that way that dogs had that felt conspiratorial. It was like she agreed with him that these two shmoes were an endless source of head shaking and eye rolls.

He leaned down and let her lick his face. "I know, right?"

"Did you give Sully his outfit? Motherfucker left me holding the phone on this one. Showed up for one fitting and then pulled a fuck-it."

"*Hehehe.* Not thinking straight, that one. He's blue balling," Cam sniggered.

"Shut the fuck up," Alex grunted. Goddammit. Why did his little sister have to be such a pain in his ass. The very last thing he wanted to think about was the state of Parker's balls.

"Hey man," Cam quickly interjected. "It's a fucking compliment. Show me a single time in that dude's whole life when one woman, and a small one at that, stopped him in his tracks. We all know he's got an ass-ton of available pussy waiting for his unique, uh . . . charms. My hat's off to Angie. She's one badass little lady for not taking his shit."

Drae chuckled. "It's not like each of us hasn't been exactly where he is right now. These women," he smirked with mock scorn. "They'll be our undoing."

"Hell, yeah," Cam joined in.

"Fuck that asshole. We have other things to handle, and no, I haven't given him his outfit yet. I'll take it tomorrow night when the girls do their thing. Pete wants the band to close out the night with a quick set so he has to be there."

Cam snickered mockingly. "Yeah—like he'd miss Angie's moment in the spotlight. Get fucking real."

"What-fucking-ever," he grumbled. "Back to the planning. Cam? You've got the playback thing figured out, right?"

"On it, Major. And I've got the best digital version of that movie you asked for. Consider the entertainment covered and my wife, along with Tori, is busy making all sorts of decorating plans. They're going to the party store warehouse in Sedona and I shudder to think what that means for Casa Cameron."

"Check this out," Drae said. "It's almost finished. It's for you guys from the rest of Family Justice.

Cam whistled approvingly while all he could do was mutter, "Holy shit," when he saw what Drae was working on.

Hanging out in the wood shop together was becoming a thing. With the compound shut down till after he returned from his honeymoon, Alex had less and less reason to putter in the tech cave . . . especially since Tori absolutely insisted she continue to work as his assistant three days a week. So most days he and Cam had taken to wandering to Drae's place after breakfast. Shoot the shit. Hang out.

Betty dealt with the office end of things and had the experience to handle the smaller Justice commitments that their B Team were working. Besides checking in on the construction and making sure things were moving ahead as swiftly as possible—something all three of them were anxious for—there wasn't a whole hell of a lot for them to do. It was completely weird to have so much free time.

Taking a long look at Drae's project, he was momentarily stunned. "Fucking, eh, Draegyn," Alex muttered. "I don't know what to say. Does Meghan know about this? I mean, wow. It's beautiful," he murmured.

Running his hand appreciatively over the heavy chest with the carved Celtic knots, he appreciated his friend's amazing talents and craftsmanship.

"I'm gonna make one for each of the girls," Drae murmured. "My sister calls these things a hope chest. Someplace to keep memories. I figure they all need one."

"For the keepsake booties," Cam quipped, nodding his approval.

"Exactly. Got a couple more coats of wax to apply but it'll be ready for the get-together. We can either place it in your bedroom without Meghan knowing or just haul it to Cam's and show it off that night then move it later."

"Drae, you have a gift, man. I want everyone to see this and know what you're doing for the girls. It's amazingly thoughtful."

"Did you just call me an insensitive jerk-off? Isn't that what amazingly thoughtful really means?"

They all cracked up laughing cause, yep. Pretty much what he said was absolutely true.

"Oh and listen up, men. Got an undercover mission. Highly secret. For our eyes and ears only, okay?"

"Jesus," Cam drawled. "What the fuck? Secretive? Need to know? We guarding the Commander-in-Chief or something?"

Alex half-smirked. "No, but once I explain, all will become clear."

"Oh, joy." Ha! He could always count on Drae for the dry wit.

"Team Justice to the rescue," Alex quipped.

He had to fill all this free time with something, so he'd been working overtime on a secret project of his own and it was time to execute.

"Buckle up your ball sacks, gentlemen, 'cause what we have to pull off will require skill and luck. And under no circumstances can your women know anything."

"Mom, seriously. Relax. It's fine. Really. Please!"

Ugh. Angie was beyond stressed. Pacing back and forth in the privacy of her room, she struggled to catch up with a conversation that had taken her by surprise. Knowing she had to tell her folks about her involvement with Parker before they heard it through the grapevine, she'd been gearing up to make the call when her mom rang her up. Before the hello was fully finished, she'd demanded that Angie explain herself.

Fuck. My. Life.

She wasn't surprised that Aunt Wendy couldn't wait to tell her BFF that Parker was bringing Angie home for dinner and how excited she was that at long last, her favorite niece, with apologies to Soph, was back home in Arizona.

While she'd never know what the two truly talked about—and she had her suspicions—the way her mom was telling the story, Parker's parents were treating her presence in the Southwest like the return of the baby Jesus and would be breaking out the good china for their dinner.

"Daughter of mine," her mother cooed in that way she had that always made Angie sit up and take notice, "kindly remember who you're speaking to and cut the horseshit young lady."

Ouch. As always. . . . a direct and uncomfortable hit.

Ashleigh Dane Valleja-Marquez was a law unto herself whose unique dance to a different drum had been what enchanted the American-born heir to an old Spanish family.

Petite to the point of being tiny, she was the quintessential California girl who still wore her blond hair long, had a wicked sense of humor mixed in with an appreciation of the absurd, and who, despite her small stature and soft voice, ruled her family with an iron fist that to outsiders must seem laughable.

The disapproving tone being applied from thousands of miles and a different continent away was very much the case in point.

"I'm waiting," her mom bit out.

Squeezing her eyes shut, Angie ran a hand through her hair as she pressed the phone to her ear. Moms. *Sheesh,* they could be scary.

"Uh . . ." Mother–of–god! When had she become so tongue-tied?

"Angelina!" her mom snapped. "Are you sleeping with that boy?"

That boy? That *BOY?* What the hell was this? High school? And how had her mom gone from discussing her having dinner with the Sullivan's to whether or not sleeping with *that boy?*

"Mom!" she yelled. "There's no sleeping going on."

Angie squeezed her eyes shut again and muttered, "Shit." She sounded like an idiot.

Her mom snorted. "Well, Daddy and I don't do much sleeping either and you know perfectly well what I'm asking so don't word game me, young lady."

Oh, god. The last thing she needed in her head was any reminder of her parents' sex life. Talk about raging seniors! For as long as she could recall, Angie hadn't known her mother to bother with a chair if her husband's lap was available. There was something adorably cute about a couple of sixty-somethings getting handsy and giggling when they thought their kids weren't looking.

But right now? There was nothing adorable or cute about her mother's line of questioning.

"It's dinner, Mom. That's all. Seriously, you guys," she whined, "what's with the gossipy phone calls?"

For the briefest second, she thought a bit of laughter could be heard in her mother's voice before she used that don't-even-think-about-it warning tone that parents did so well.

"I knew that boy was trouble where you were concerned. Had to forever shoo him away from your cradle whenever he was around. Him and your brother. They'd spend hours rocking you and reading stories. Boy stories!" she chortled.

"Parker would do the sound effects and Alexander would do the acting out. No cute fairy tales for you, my dear! Oh no. *Treasure Island. Tom Sawyer. Robinson Crusoe. Sherlock Holmes.* All the classics."

"*Whaaat?*" Angie squeaked.

Her mom was outright laughing. "Now, I'm going to have to look around but I know someplace there's a videotape that Daddy shot of their theatrical extravaganzas."

"Oh, my god. Are you serious?"

"Yes, I'm serious," she replied. "And your delighted reaction isn't helping make the case that this is no big deal."

Angie sighed. Wasn't she just thinking the other day that she wanted to talk to her mom? Why the hesitation?

"Mom," she mumbled as her pacing stopped and she folded onto the edge of the bed. "I don't want you to be mad. Or disappointed."

"Oh, sweetie," Ashleigh Marquez said in a soothing mom tone, "you're my baby girl. Daddy and I named you Angel for a reason, honey. We could never truly be mad at any of you kids. And I doubt you're capable of disappointing me so whatever it is that you're not saying . . ."

Scooting back, she pulled her feet up and sat cross-legged against the bank of pillows stretched along the headboard. There was a lump in her throat and that tingling sensation in her nose that signaled tears about to fall.

"He's not a boy, Mom. I didn't know him as a boy—I've only ever really known Parker as an adult. A grown up man. And before you say anything, I know he's too old for me."

Her mom *tsked* a couple of times. "Don't make assumptions, Angel. Nobody said anything about age. Was he too old for you when you were fifteen? Yes. There's a decade and more of water under that bridge now though, sweetie."

Wow. Her mom was friggin' awesome.

She took a deep breath. "I've loved him since I was old enough to say the words."

"I know."

The crying started. Not violently. Just a soft, steady stream of hot tears.

"He broke my heart when I was at Georgetown." Her voice sounded hushed and vulnerable.

An understanding sigh from her mother warmed Angie's heart. "We suspected as much. That was hard for his parents and us to watch. You were so happy and then suddenly, you weren't. And Parker, well . . . Wendy had a fit."

"I don't know what to do, Mom."

"I will snap that boy in two like a twig if he's pressuring you."

Seriously? Angie had to put a hand over her mouth to stop the bark of laughter her mother's description triggered. Picturing tiny little Ashleigh snapping beefy hunkster Parker in two was deliciously amusing. It could happen, too. She'd seen both her brother and father stopped dead in their tracks on more than one occasion by one of her fierce looks. Parker didn't stand a chance against her, no matter how big he was.

She snickered. "It's me who's the problem. Not him."

"What in the world does that mean?"

"Tell me first what you meant by Aunt Wendy having a fit." She needed to know. Had her aunt been upset by Angie's short affair with her son? Damn. She shuddered at the thought of upsetting so many of the people she loved.

Her mother's gentle laughter filled her ear. "You young people all think your parents are imbeciles. It's hilarious. I mean, after all—it's my generation who ushered in the sex, drugs, and rock 'n' roll era so why you act like we have no clue is funny as shit."

"I don't understand."

"Think about it, Angie. You have always been like a magnet for Parker and vice versa. Did you think we were all blind when of every college in the whole wide world that you could choose from—Georgetown was where you ended up?"

"Oh, my god," she groaned dismally. Had it been so obvious? The embarrassed heat made her cheeks feel on fire.

"Honestly, baby, it was more than Wendy or I hoped for when you two seemed to be so perfect together. And happy. Both of you. And then, overnight, all that stopped. You became quiet and distant. Almost as serious as your sister and Parker just shut down completely. A crystal ball wasn't really necessary."

"I didn't know," she murmured.

"Yes, well . . . when we realized something had happened, Wendy went off. She couldn't believe her son had been stupid enough to let you slip out of his hands."

"How do you know it wasn't me and not him?"

"Baby, you have a lot to learn!" She laughed heartily. "I have a son, you know. The one you're staying with. He and Parker Sullivan were cut from the same damn cloth. Why am I sure it was him? That's why!"

"He wants to start over."

"And here you thought you were going to the desert just to scratch an old itch. I bet he's playing for keeps this time, isn't he?"

"I can't believe you just said that," she told her mom. "Is that what you thought?"

"Sweetie, I knew the second you ended that farce with Aldo that

Arizona was your next stop. Tell me something . . . does Alexander know about this?"

"He knows and he's meddling so fast I'm surprised he hasn't hurt himself."

"Meddling in what way?"

"In that big brother pain-in-the-ass way he has. You know Alex. He throws us together, stirs the pot, and then threatens Parker to an inch of his life for reacting to the obvious provocation."

"Typical."

"He tried to intimidate Parker at the door when he was dropping me off after a dinner date, Mom! It was so embarrassing. They're grown men, for heaven's sake. It was worse than having Dad hovering at the door."

She heard a heavy, mom sigh through the phone. "Is he what you want, Angelina? Talk to me, sweetie. Is Parker why you went to Arizona? Are you ready to *carpe diem,* baby girl?"

The million-dollar question. Was she ready? To seize the day? She knew he was hers for the asking, but this wasn't a dress rehearsal this time. They really were playing for keeps which meant she had to know what the hell she wanted and also had to be prepared to give herself to the things he wanted. Whatever that meant—and she was in no way implying that cheering for the same sports team fit the requirement. But no way was she getting into that with her mom.

"Mom, I think I want to stay in Arizona. After the wedding, I mean. When we all come back to the Villa after Boston, I'm thinking about hanging here. Meghan's doing something amazing for the vet community that I'd like to help with."

"You didn't answer me about Parker."

"I know. It's hard to see clearly where that's going, Mom. But I wanted you to know that besides Parker . . . I think Arizona is just in my soul. I missed being here. Hey, did you ever hear Uncle Matt call me Desert Angel?"

"All the time, sweetie. All the time. And don't you worry. Daddy and I know you've carried those red rocks and that bright sunshine inside you while you've been with us at the vineyard. We were just waiting—giving you the time and space to figure it out for yourself. You scared us shitless when agreed to marry Aldo. There was no love there, Angie, no matter how perfect a marriage may have seemed. If you going home to Arizona is the price to be paid for coming to your senses, we'll take the distance with a grain of salt and thank our lucky stars that you were brave enough to chase your dreams."

Chapter Forty-One

"Uncle Matt!" Angie cried with delight when his dad flung open the front door and came rushing out to the driveway. She was unbuckled and scrambling the second he put the car in park.

He watched as his father swooped in and picked her up, twirling in a circle as she laughed and hugged him tight. Parker chuckled. Matthew Sullivan had a bit of a soft heart when it came to Angie. The old man adored her and had always treated her as though she were his own daughter.

Lowering her, she landed with a thud as her cowgirl boots hit the pavement, he held her out at arm's length and proclaimed, "I know it's been less than a year since we've seen each other, girl, but I swear you look even more beautiful here under the sun of the Southwest than you do at the vineyard."

Parker shook his head and groaned. The campaign to convince Angie to stay in Arizona was underway.

Angie beamed then made a wry, conspiratorial face. "There's something in the water at the Villa. I think Alexander has tapped into the spring of contentment at his little kingdom of desert land." She giggled.

Weaving her arm through his, she turned as if suddenly remembering who the hell she came with and smiled at Parker.

"Don't forget the wine, okay?" And with that he was forgotten.

Pushed aside to toddle in her wake as she bestowed her endless charms on his old man. "Nice going, Dad," he griped out loud.

By the time he made it into the house after stopping to grab her shawl and purse along with the carry-bag holding the bottles of wine, he was odd man out judging by the laughter and joyful banter coming from the kitchen.

They knew he was coming to dinner too, right? *Jesus Christ.*

He was an only child—used to undivided attention from his adoring parents—not virtually ignored as they jumped for fucking joy over a visitor.

But Angie wasn't exactly a visitor. She was family.

Shit. This was complicated.

"Made your favorite!" his mom crowed. "Cowboy Enchilada Pie." As he made his way toward them, his mom smiled sweetly and added, "And cheesy jalapeño biscuits for my boys."

"Hi, Mom," he drawled, dropping a dutiful kiss on the cheek she proffered. Taken aback slightly by the gleam he saw in her eyes, he looked at her quizzically, but she wasn't giving anything else away.

Pushing the handles of the carry-bag into her hands, he said, "Angie brought some rioja . . ."

"The one you like, Uncle Matt!" she interrupted.

His dad perked up. "Oh! Is it that one we got hammered on last year when we visited the Aragon finca?"

"The very one," she snickered. "Have you heard that Mom and Dad are giving the newlyweds the finca property as a wedding present? I guess after that visit, they decided it would be perfect for Alex and Meghan."

"Getting shitfaced does that to you."

"Oh, shush," his mom admonished her husband with a playful swat. "The four of us have been falling down drunk in half the cities of the world. Seeing the completed restoration through inebriated eyes may have had something to do with it, but I'm not surprised. Alex and his bride will love it."

"Haven't you met her yet?" she asked stunned.

When they shook their heads, she looked at him with astonished eyes. "Parker! What's the matter with you?"

Huh? What was the matter with him? Fuck. Nothing was the matter with him. It was not his goddamn responsibility to introduce Alex's fiancée to his parents. This one was squarely on his friend's shoulders.

"Me?" he barked. "Talk to your brother. I'm his fucking lawyer, not the keeper of his social calendar."

She looked at him strangely. The grumpy bark that was just this side of a snarl was a bit much even by his standards. Did it help that his dad was openly smirking at him? No, it did not.

"Well," Angie sniffed after giving him a dismissive look, "you must meet her before Boston. That way you can tell my folks how awesome she is."

"Why don't we do lunch in town?" his mother suggested enthusiastically. "Or go get a manicure. Just us girls."

"I think our manly importance in this matter has been pretty thoroughly spelled out, don't you, son?" his dad snickered.

Humph. Parker just grunted and stomped to the refrigerator. He needed a beer. Maybe a couple of them. When he turned around again after tossing the cap away, he was alone in the kitchen.

What the fuck? Really? Glad to know he was as important to the evening as, well . . . as what?

Laughter rang out from the family room. On reluctant feet, he headed toward the sound, grumbling the whole way.

He found Angie bending over his dad's shoulder as he showed her something on his laptop while his mom was nowhere to be seen.

"So you know how your dad and I have that Rube Goldberg Challenge?"

"Challenge?" Angie snickered good-naturedly as she nudged the older man's shoulder. "How about lifelong pissing contest?"

"And then there's that." His father chuckled. "Well, anyway—this time, instead of doing a video reveal, your dad's shipping his machine to the Villa so after the wedding while we get in a long, extended visit, we can complete the challenge together."

Oh, god," Angie muttered sarcastically. "My mother must love that!"

"Hey!" his dad teased. "Come on now. Be nice. We keep it within a set of restraints so neither of us can get too crazy."

"You call *no bigger than a big screen TV and can't use electricity* restraints?" She chuckled.

"Tell me, Angel, do you know what he's building this time?"

"Hell no, Uncle Matt! Sophie and I stay away from the mad professor's workshop and Mom only goes out there when she has to."

From his perch in the doorway where he leaned casually against the door jam and nursed his beer while eavesdropping on their conversation, Parker blurted out with a snarky snort, "Mad professor. Good one! Alex's apple didn't fall far from your old man's tree."

Angie, who had turned around the moment he'd made his presence known, laughed joyfully.

"Oh, my god! You're so right. What's that expression?" she asked with a questioning frown. "Two peas in a pod? Something like that."

"The Marquez men are most definitely two of a kind," his mom chimed in as she came into the room carrying a platter overflowing with homemade tortilla crisps, a mound of guac, and a carafe filled with fresh salsa. Apparently, it was southwestern night at the Sullivans.

"Dig in," she nodded at the pile as she put out individual salsa cups for each of them. "I kept the hot in the salsa to a slow burn." Turning a raised eye in Parker's direction, she noted the beer in his hand and said, "And Uncle Matt has a pitcher of margaritas ready to go, Angie. You ready to get your tequila on?"

"Don Julio!" his dad hooted. "None of that Cuervo crap in my house."

"I'm stuffed," Angie groaned. Laying her napkin over her empty plate like a tarp at a crime scene, she pushed it away and clutched her stomach. "Everyone look away." She giggled. "Have to let out my belt a notch or two."

Uncle Matt, who always had the best one-liners, made the perfect response to her comment by way of an ear-splitting belch that was met with a stern groan from Aunt Wendy and a quiet chuckle from Parker.

"Must you?" Wendy drawled.

"Better out than in," her uncle quipped with a wink.

Lord but she loved these two people.

"Need help with the dishes?" she asked politely, rising from her chair.

Angie was startled when her aunt pounded Parker on the shoulder and said, "See? That girl's been raised right. Not like that Allison person. Nobody bothered to teach her any manners."

What? Allison? Who the bloody hell was Allison?

"Mom!" Parker groaned.

"Man up, Parker," Aunt Wendy smirked. "The woman was a twit and you know it. No need to be embarrassed just because your girlfriend was brought up by hillbillies."

Angie almost choked to death on the margarita she was sipping. Girlfriend? Had the word GIRLFRIEND come out of her aunt's mouth? She was seriously going to murder that man. A girlfriend? Really? *Fuck.* Hadn't seen that coming.

"Oh, Wendy. I don't think she was a hillbilly. That's a bit harsh, don't you think? To the hillbillies, I mean," Uncle Matt drawled with a sarcastic bite.

As her aunt and uncle cracked up over what was obviously an inside joke, Angie glared malevolently at Parker. At least she thought her look was menacing. Was hard to tell. Tequila always made her face feel numb, but it was just so damn yummy when it came to her in one of Uncle Matt's crafted margaritas that before she realized the folly of her ways, she was double fisting the tasty drinks and pounding them down like ice water.

"Girlfriend?" *Shit.* Had she slurred that out loud?

Glancing at her then back at his mother, Parker griped, "Ma, let it go. That was a year ago and I told you. She wasn't rude—just . . . insensitive."

Wendy laughed and pushed the hair from her son's forehead. "Thank god you came to your senses."

"I need some air," Angie mumbled, scrambling awkwardly to her feet.

Learning that Parker had at some point been with a girlfriend was making the excellent dinner she'd just inhaled rumble menacingly in her belly.

"Why don't you take Angie out back, son?" Uncle Matt suggested. "It's a beautiful sunset. We'll all go out to the patio for a while. I'll just help your mom clear everything away and join you two in a bit."

"Go on, now," Wendy encouraged. "Matt, honey. Freshen their drinks. And Parker?" she added. "Show Angie my violets in the greenhouse."

There was a lot of hustling and bustling, chairs scraped on the floor, dishes and glasses clinked as they were gathered but all she could focus on was the term *girlfriend.*

Taking their drinks, Parker nodded solemnly, "Come on." Nodding toward the patio door with his head, Angie considered kicking him—like she would have when she was five years old—instead of going anywhere with him.

The sound her boots made as she stomped ahead of him seemed to mock Angie. A girlfriend changed everything, right? Who was she kidding? Remembering that she'd been cavorting with a fiancé around the same time only diminished her displeasure by degrees. How dare he have a girlfriend?

Flouncing dramatically across the patio, she dropped clumsily onto a swing bed hanging beneath a heavy wood frame and stared glumly at her date for the evening. Where five minutes ago she might have considered stretching out with him on the distinctive outdoor swing, at the present second she was considering pushing him down and jumping on him—to tear his heart out.

"Here," he drawled pushing the icy cold drink into her hands. "She wasn't a girlfriend. She was a lawyer in the Public Defender's office. Did I see her a couple of times? Yes. It wasn't serious, though. I swear."

"Oh?" She winced at the shrill sound of her voice. *Yep. Drunk.* Or damn close. Knowing that, unfortunately, didn't stop her mouth from continuing to snarl. "Then how come your mother met her? Usually when the parents enter the picture it's more than a. . . ."

"Nope," he muttered swinging his head side to side. "Nope, nope, nope."

Was that the tequila talking? She couldn't be sure.

"Whatever you're thinking . . . just, *NO.*"

"Did you sleep with her?" Oh, my god. Had she lost her mind? Never ask a question unless you were prepared to hear the answer.

"That's not fair, baby girl." His voice was deceptively calm though she saw the rigid tension in his spine.

"How do you figure?" Angie's tone? One hundred and ten percent courtesy of the tequila.

And then she saw his jaw clench and eyes narrow dangerously. Oh no, no, no! Wait. *Shitfuck.* Well, too late now. Open mouth—insert foot.

"I'm not the one who was engaged."

Having asked for the harsh rebuke, she gulped. No. Really. An actual gulp. His quiet voice was also ripe with a hostility that burned her like a brand.

Swiping her tongue along the rim of the salted glass, she tipped the tasty drink and swallowed a huge mouthful—probably a mistake, but hey, tequila and mistakes are bosom buddies, right?

The most awful hideous uncomfortable silence ensued while he stood in front of her as she huddled on the swing bed alternating between biting her lip and tossing back her drink.

"Were you really going to marry that asshole?" The emphasis he placed on *marry* sounded an awful lot like he was accusing her of contemplating something heinous and disgusting.

Okay. That was definitely the alcohol talking. Until now, he'd tossed off a few disparaging remarks where Aldo was concerned but this was the first time he actually challenged her outright. How come she felt like she owed him an apology?

"I don't know," she whispered miserably. She stopped from voicing the rest of her thought, which was that, at the time, she figured if she couldn't have what she wanted, well, she might as well accept what she had. Twisted, yeah. But there you have it.

And what she'd wanted? Then and now? He was standing there, inches away, glaring down at her sparking feelings that were making her uncomfortable. Part of her cringed—*How could she?* Another part, howled—*How dare he?*

This time, the alcohol helped her find some cocky bravado as she pithily informed him, "Don't you dare fucking judge me."

His head snapped back at her angry words.

"I still had one foot planted in my teenage years when you made me your plaything without any goddamn thought to what that was going to do to me. Demonstrate your mastery of my body? Mission accomplished. And congratulations for setting a standard that no other could ever possibly meet."

She saw his eyes flare at the bold admission and wanted to throttle the arrogant jackass.

"But what all that did to my head . . . well," she bit out. "Did you ever once stop to consider what you were doing to my mind? And my heart?"

"Shit, Angel," he muttered.

"I need a man who will pick me up when I'm down. Someone who will have my back even when I'm full of shit!"

Tossing back the end of her margarita, she downed it with theatrical precision and laid the empty glass on a side table.

Rising a bit unsteadily to her feet, she straightened her blouse and smoothed her skirt then fixed him with a pained frown. "Expressed clumsily . . . perhaps, but no different than hearing what you expect of me—if you think about it."

The intensity of his expression held her fast. A nerve had been tapped, she could see it in his eyes.

"So when you judge me, you judge yourself," she ended in a whisper.

He looked at her. Really at her.

"I want the master, Parker. Not the judge."

She saw when her words hit home. The air around them was crackling with static energy that made her skin prickle.

"Do you know what you're saying?" he asked sharply.

Angie shrugged. "No. Not really. Tequila brain and all."

A sound came from behind them. His parents were coming, and from the sound of their boisterous laughter, the party was just getting started.

"This discussion is not over," he growled a second before Uncle Matt smacked him soundly on the back.

"Help your mother, my boy," he said. "And let your old man enjoy this lovely young lady's smile for a bit."

Chapter Forty-Two

PARKER REALLY WANTED ANOTHER DRINK, but he was driving later and needed to start shaking off the buzz, not adding to it. But motherfucker, he was practically undone and feeling how he imagined someone who bungee jumped felt after being left hanging upside down for too long.

Watching his folks fawn all over Angie had been a test of his composure. He knew his dad adored her. Shit, the man was president of her fan club and he was his damn father, but that didn't stop him wanting to shove him aside and stake his claim of the sexy raven-haired woman with the naughty pout on her crimson lips and the sweet twinkle in her sapphire eyes. What the hell was wrong with him?

They were discussing some shared adventure from his parents' most recent trip to Europe that Angie was a part of. He listened impassively; his mind drifting from thought to thought. After a bit, his father wandered away and Parker focused on just the two women huddled together on the big swing.

The saints had blessed him with the most amazing mother. She was smart, funny, clever, irreverent, and Parker's first love. His father had taught him from the cradle to cherish this gift from the heavens and that his mother was the queen of the universe as far as his dad was concerned.

For the first time, he understood all those feelings and sentiments in a way he never had previously.

"Here we go," his father boomed a bit too loudly. "One guitar, as requested."

Parker jumped, sat up from his slouch and flinched when his dad shoved the instrument not into his hands, but into Angie's.

What the fuck?

Angie reacted just as startled as he felt and looked helplessly at his mom.

"Will you play that song, sweetie? The one you sing for your mom and dad?" his mother asked quietly.

"Oh, Aunt Wendy," Angie cried. "I can't. You know I can't," she wailed softly—giving him a hurried side-glance that grabbed his attention.

Song for her mom and dad? What song and why won't she play it?

"You're right, my dear," his mom said as she patted Angie reassuringly on the arm. "But play something else. You know Uncle Matt loves when you sing."

Angie giggled and shook her head no.

With a self-deprecating smirk, she asked, "Wouldn't you rather hear Parker play?"

Dammit if his mom didn't toss back her head and laugh.

"Aren't you cute," she teased Angie. Turning to his dad, she giggled and said, "Matt, honey. Isn't that cute? She thinks *your* son actually plays for us."

His dad snorted and held his drink aloft in salute.

"I take that as a no, then?" Angie quipped.

Settling the guitar on her lap, she crossed her legs and pushed her hair out of the way. She'd worn a simple white blouse unbuttoned to the top of her cleavage and tucked into a long, flared denim skirt that had a wide leather belt the same color as her lace-up ankle boots

She looked like a cross between a modern day Laura Ingalls and a denim-clad Megan Fox with overtones of Snow White. He almost laughed at the absurd thought until admitting the comparison was right on. She had Snow's delicate beauty and innocence blended together with the actresses hot sexiness all dressed up in some Little House on the Prairie clothes. *Fan-fucking-tastic.* He wanted to fuck Laura Snow Fox.

Okay. Definitely no more to drink 'cause that was funny as shit.

Laura Snow Fox. That one was a keeper.

Angie was quietly strumming the guitar, talking with his mom who sat by her side smiling warmly.

There was something about the way her long, delicately tapered fingers swept across the strings that made his blood heat. Remembering how it felt to lay still beneath those same fingers as they explored his body, and every grunt, sigh, and quiver her tactile inspection drew from him, sparked a lusty chain reaction inside Parker.

Out of nowhere, his father leaned over and drawled close to his head, "That's a special woman, son. Don't fuck around," he growled. "You hear me, boy?"

Could this get any weirder? The patriarchal threat of good behavior or else, he expected from Angie's father. After all, it was the man's right and as it should be. But hearing his own father admonishing him not to be a dick? Wow, that was eye opening.

The first few chords of a familiar song vibrated in the evening air. What was that? He listened a few more seconds. It was pretty. Melodic. She, of course, played beautifully.

He knew what the song was the second she started singing. Five seconds in his mom captured the harmony and the two women belted out a spine-tingling rendition of Sheryl Crow's *Strong Enough*.

Parker suspected she was singing the song to him, then knew for sure she was when on the last verse, she locked eyes with him.

How much plainer or clearer could she make what she'd said before? His angel wanted the master. Not the judge.

"I'm on it."

Alex saw Meghan tense all the way from across the room. He'd been on the phone with his father for the past half hour listening as the man went back and forth between dire threats and hopeful ramblings about the Angie-Parker situation.

Seemed like the cat was out of the bag and from what his dad was saying, it was Angie herself who confessed everything to their mother. He was going to kill her when she got back from Uncle Matt and

Aunt Wendy's for not fucking warning him that she'd spilled her guts. Maybe if he'd known that they knew, he'd have been better prepared to handle his dad instead of what was happening now.

He had to end the call and see about Meghan. Frankly, he was sick to death of the Angie-Parker dance. Knowing well where the man's tastes lay, Alex couldn't understand why he didn't just stop all of Angie's flightiness with a bit of caveman.

"Look, Dad," he muttered, scraping his hand against his skull and across his face. "Angelina's a big girl. I know she's the baby and everything, but we have to give her a chance to figure this out for herself. You know Parker's a good guy and I think she'll pull her head out of her ass eventually so just chill, okay? As I said, I'm on it."

After that last statement, he heard Meghan slam something onto her vanity followed seconds later by the distinctive sound of water rushing into the huge soaking tub in the bathroom.

Cornering her in a tub full of bubbles would make calming her down a whole hell of a lot easier. He knew exactly what was bothering her, making quick decisions on his feet as to how to proceed.

Promising to call with any news, he ended the call and tossed the phone onto his nightstand with a frustrated grunt.

It was time to tell her. He couldn't stand to see her bent out of shape—not that she didn't have a cause.

Reefing his t-shirt over his head, he wadded it up and tossed it into the hamper in a perfect three-point throw from the outside. Deftly undoing the heavy buckle on his jeans, he peered over his shoulder toward the doorway to the bath after yanking his zipper down and pushing the denim down his legs.

He picked up the scent of warm vanilla, one of his favorite for shared bath times and quirked a half smile. Surely, she realized the smell was like an invitation to join her.

Naked, he walked in her direction. Though it was something she didn't normally do, his woman was sulking—for good reason, and he was going to thoroughly enjoy making it all better.

She was already in the tub, her glorious red curls in a sexy mess atop her head. With her head tilted back along the edge, he admired the long arch of her neck and licked his lips. He wanted to bite her there.

Growling, he demanded that she make room for him, knowing his

Alpha bullshit would earn him a snicker and a leer. Her answering smirk reminded Alex how much she got off on his lord and master routine.

Settling in behind her in the tub, Alex put an arm around her waist and pulled her back against him. Taking the sudsy pouf from her hands, he swept it across her chest from shoulder to shoulder right above the water line.

"All right," he murmured when she sighed and relaxed against him, laying her head upon his chest. "Go on—I already know what you're going to say, but say it out loud, baby."

Some serious over-reactive shit almost went down when he heard a tiny quiver in her voice.

"Energy. Other people's. I love Angie, and though it pisses you off, I sorta love Parker, too."

Dickhead," he muttered for effect and because he knew she'd smile.

"But look what's happening. Your parents are in a tizzy about those two. And there they'll both be—standing by our sides at the altar and I'm sorry for being such a bitch but you know damn well Parker's parents will be hearing wedding bells for those two and from what I just gathered, your parents are on board with that."

No. She wasn't a bitch. He totally got where she was coming from. Those vows were the most important words either of them would ever speak out loud. She wasn't wrong or crazy for wanting nothing but love and light to surround them at that moment.

He continued to slowly wash her, raising one arm at a time and running the pouf across her skin.

"Baby," he started in a gravely voice. "I have something to tell you, and I want you to stay calm and just listen. Okay?"

She went absolutely still. *Well, fuck.* At least he knew he had her full attention.

"Breathe, Meghan," he admonished softly.

Her head turned on his chest until she could look up at him, those alluring green eyes drawing him in.

"Don't say anything until you kiss me," she whispered in a small voice.

Ah. She needed some reassurance before he spoke. His heart thudded. This was the way it was with them. Nothing came before this—the connection. Seeing her need gave him dick butterflies.

He put a finger beneath her chin for leverage and lowered his mouth to hers kissing her tenderly, never letting the passion that was ready to explode take control. One thing at a time.

"Better?" he asked with a smile after thoroughly kissing her until the tension left her body.

She nodded and relaxed in his wet embrace.

Discarding the pouf, Alex reached into the water and found her hands, twining his fingers through hers and resting them on her stomach below where her breasts bobbed weightlessly.

"I wanted to wait a little longer and surprise you with this, but we're close enough anyway," he told her. "You'll be jetting off with Angie sooner than we realize and after that, we won't have any privacy until after the wedding."

He liked the way she sighed. What a pair they made!

"You saved me, Meghan O'Brien. The day you walked through my door, I felt like my life came back after a long journey through a dark hell that nearly destroyed me. You are my *only* love, and I would do anything to see you happy," he told her.

Her fingers squeezed his. "I know," she whispered.

Alex took a deep breath. He hoped to god she was on board with what he was proposing 'cause, if she wasn't, he was screwed in more ways than one.

"I've been thinking. You're right. Our families would be crushed if we eloped, but maybe there's another way to have the private, spiritual moment we want while still giving everyone who's supported us what they want, too."

She shifted in the water and looked at him. Her hands were like two tense blocks so he kissed the tip of her nose and grinned.

"What have you done, Major?" she asked warily.

There was something enormously fucking cool about knowing he'd get to hear her ask that question a zillion times in the years ahead of them. He was always going to be fucking shit up and she would always shake her head and use that tone—call him *Major* for good measure and do her best to keep him in line.

Letting go of her hands, he placed his over her floating breasts and gave a gentle squeeze.

"How does this sound? The day after St. Patrick's Day, which I specifically chose so you'd always remember," he snickered. "You and I wander out to Amor Vórtice. We'll get dressed up, take some flowers, whatever you want. And we'll have our own private ceremony. Say the things we need to say—the way we want to say them."

She turned in his arms so fast that water sloshed from the tub.

"Are you serious?"

Yeah, he was serious, but he hadn't even told her the best part yet, and maybe he wouldn't have to. Perhaps he could keep that one secret a bit longer.

"Would that make you happy, baby?" he asked cautiously.

"Oh, my god! Alex!" she cried. Throwing herself on him, she started pressing feverish kisses all over his face while her hands gripped his head.

"Yes! Yes! Yes!" She laughed joyfully. "Oh my god, yes!"

He laughed, astonished his half suggestion of some dress-up time out in the desert and the promise of some pretty words was apparently enough to make her content. God, but she was ridiculously easy to please and boy, was she in for a surprise. The rest of his laugh was for Carmen who was going to want to kill them both because he had no doubt they were about to make one holy hell of a mess in that bathroom.

With nothing more than the promise of a pretty dress and some flowers, she was all over him.

I'm a lucky man, he thought. *Luckiest son-of-a-bitch alive.*

Chapter Forty-Three

"YOU OKAY TO DRIVE, SON?" Matthew Sullivan sternly quizzed. Parker had to smile. He didn't take shit from anyone because he learned the trait from his father. The warm and fuzzy teddy bear side of him might have been on display this evening, but his old man could be a complete nightmare. Not as much now after his heart scare, but the guy had serious balls. Parker wouldn't even try to fuck around where his father was concerned.

"I'm good, Dad," he assured him. "Am well acquainted with those death-by-cocktail pitchers of fun you mix up, so I knew when to back off."

"Don Julio, my boy. Will kick you in the ass every time!"

"Indeed," he drawled.

Where the fuck was Angie? She trotted off after his mother a good twenty minutes ago. Women. Jesus. Didn't they ever look at the damn time? They had a long drive in the dark back to the Villa and he wasn't looking forward to Alex sitting by the door with a shotgun in his lap waiting for his sister to be delivered safely from Parker's lecherous clutches.

His dad snickered at Parker's restlessness. "Get used to it," he quipped.

Hmph. "Uh, Dad," he half-blurted. "You don't have a problem with me and Angie, do you?"

"I have a huge problem with you and that little girl, son, but I'm counting on you being the man I raised. You do right by her or heaven help you."

"She's making me nucking futz," he muttered. "Didn't talk to me for years, ignored my ass completely despite how close our families are. And now that she's here and in my face? You'd think I'd never been with anyone before."

"That bad, huh? Welcome to the club, son. Y'know, I was seeing somebody else when I met your mom, but all it took was one glance followed by a double-barrel unloading of her wiseass mouth and that other girl may as well have been invisible—it was that quick and that overwhelming. The family curse, my boy." He laughed. "Just like my dad. We fall hard, the Sullivan men do. When they meet their match, there's just no other."

"Do you think it's creepy?"

"What do you mean?"

Parker sighed and searched for a way to express his worries. "She's like my sister."

Matthew Sullivan roared with laughter.

"No, she's not! I hear what you're saying but look at it this way."

Parker searched his dad's smiling face and prayed he had some words of wisdom 'cause no matter how anyone spun this thing, it was right on the line.

"You've always felt protective of her, haven't you?"

Well, it would be fruitless to deny it. Between him and Alex, they'd all but investigated each of her teachers when she started school and even as teenagers would have gladly punched out any sniveling five-year-old brat on the playground who wanted to act the bully.

"Yeah," he mumbled.

"And, after a while, that protective impulse got a bit blurred. Started feeling more possessive maybe?"

His eyes swung to his dad's. Uh . . . that was exactly what happened.

"You believe in destiny, don't you, son?"

Hmmm. Did he?

"I think Alex and his bride are a great example of how that destiny and fate thing works."

Good point, Parker thought with a slight head nod.

"Maybe what you've been experiencing all these years isn't so much brotherly as the stirrings of your destiny. With that girl. Something for you to think about."

"There you two are!" his mother cried as she ushered Angie out of the house to where he and his dad were standing by his car. "Sorry about the delay but I wanted Angie to have some violets to take with her."

Parker chuckled. His mom's newest passion was growing violets and exotic plants in her hi-tech greenhouse off the garage.

"Look," Angie gushed, holding up a little pot of the purple flowers. Throwing an arm around his mom's neck, she hugged her tight. "Thanks, Aunt Wendy. I love them!"

"Do you know what the symbolism of the little flowers is?"

He and Angie shook their heads.

"Violet folklore says the little flowers depict a simple, delicate love. The kind that needs plenty of care to thrive and bloom."

Good lord. Were parents always this obvious?

"All right, all right," he teased as he went to his mom for a good-bye hug. After kissing her dutifully, he murmured low so only she could hear, "Give it a rest, Mom."

She smiled sweetly, patted him like a good boy on the chest, and shooed him into the car. His dad had already handled getting Angie settled, effectively robbing Parker of the chance to get close and touch her. *Balls.*

After one more round of good-byes through the open windows, he rolled the car out of the driveway, turned the wheel toward the highway, tooted the horn, and off they went into the night.

Whoa. *How much had she had to drink?* Angie wondered. Feeling as if she was enveloped in a cloud of soft warmth, she let out a deep sigh and turned to look at Parker. With her elbow resting on the door, she fingered a long curl while contemplating how seriously hot he looked.

Had he looked that yummy when he picked her up earlier? She couldn't remember because Alex had been a complete asshole, hovering about, playing the overprotective brother. Seriously. She wanted to smack him—and especially so if his bullshit had distracted her from noticing the drool-worthy hunk sitting next to her.

The serious, formal lawyer-esque thing he usually did was not in evidence this evening. Nope. Tonight he was rock 'n' roll Parker with his inner rebel on clear display and she loved it.

Because their evening had been dinner at home with his folks, everyone had been super casual. Another thing she enjoyed about the rhythm of life in the Southwest. There was a time and place for dress-up and doing things properly but a relaxed family get-together wasn't it.

And tonight, Parker looked like all the best things about every drool-worthy country boy rock star rolled into one. Faded t-shirt? Check. The close-up inspection would reveal it was an old and well-worn Garth Brooks concert shirt. *Hmph. Made sense.*

The jeans? Well, they were old too and fit him perfectly. Too perfectly, molding to his thighs and butt while challenging her to look at the zipper area and not blush.

Keeping the pink tinge at bay was made harder by the oddly breathless reaction she was having to the belt he wore. Nothing special, it was dark leather, looked well-used and probably soft to the touch . . . something her fingers itched to discover on their own.

"You're staring a hole through my brain, Angel."

Dropping the curl she'd been absently twirling, Angie snickered and for some insane reason reached out and pushed the hair off his forehead with a rumbling sigh.

"Sorry," she grimaced with a smile. "I was just admiring your attire," she mocked.

"My attire?"

"Yeah." She chuckled. "Guess I'm just a little astonished that at your age . . . well, you know. That you can still carry off the jeans and t-shirt thing."

He started to sputter at her jibe, just as she knew he would, but she was already off and running in another direction before he could say anything.

"Oh! Let's have some music!" she cried gleefully.

Making herself at home with the controls of his car, she cracked the moonroof, adjusted the dual temperature settings, and commandeered the satellite radio, scanning stations until she found something she liked.

She was killing him. First, she subjected him to an visual pat down that got his blood boiling and thoughts racing. He might be driving, but Parker knew when his junk was being checked out and had glanced over to find her seemingly hypnotized by his crotch while she toyed with a long curl and chewed her lip.

Being looked at like he was about to become her main course, after a long fast, sorely tested him. He was only human, after all, so, of course, he contemplated pulling over because there certainly were plenty of remote roads to park along but that would have only ended with him dragging her tipsy ass from her seat and slam fucking her from behind on the hood of the damn car.

Mmmmm. Probably not a good idea.

Ordinarily, he could make the trip between his folks' house and the Marquez Villa in forty-five minutes if he was flying, which meant it was really an hour long trip. Thoroughly enjoying himself and the company he was keeping, he slowed down. Big time. At best, they meandered down a dark sparsely traveled road as Parker relaxed and got his groove on with the Angel show happening in his passenger seat.

She was singing along and bouncing in her seat having proclaimed that she was "car dancing" at the top of her lungs over the sound of some Jay Z song thumping through the speakers. If she got any more adorable, it would be criminal.

"Take me dancing sometime?" she husked breathlessly between songs. She was leaning on the console between them scanning satellite stations, completely unaware that he was hanging by a thread.

For as long as he could remember, Angie barreled through life with a full head of steam at all times. It wasn't even a little unusual for her to ask a question or make a bold statement and then seconds later be off on to something else. Keeping up with her was exhilarating.

"Hey!" she chirped happily. "Will you dance with me tomorrow night at Pete's? You know what this car needs?" she asked waving her hand at the displays and the dashboard.

Lord. Talk about a complete about face.

"A bar. Like right here," she pointed where the GPS screen was. "Fuck that navigation stuff. A bar though would be *so* cool. With those little bottles, you get in a mini-bar. I love those little bottles. They're so cute!"

He chuckled. A bar? Really? "Don't know how practical that would be, baby girl. With the driving and all."

"Oh," she mumbled settling back heavily in her seat sounding miffed.

Parker was biting back a laugh when she suddenly blurted out, "That's what the limo is for! Oh, my god! Red was right."

Looking at him with a solemn expression that completely belied how absurd the conversation was, she drawled, "We should have used the limo."

"Is that the alcohol talking?" he asked with a smile.

"Maybe a little," she shrugged with a hair toss worthy of an Oscar. "But I assure you, counselor," she told him pointedly, "I am far from drunk."

"My dad's margaritas are a legend, you know. And he prides on having experimented with a whole slew of different tequilas. They sorta creep up on you."

"Don't let me forget the little pot of violets in the backseat. I love your mom," she sighed and just like that they were talking about something different.

He made sure to take his good ol' time getting her home and knew a bit of regret when he turned down the long road onto the Marquez property.

Truth be told, he loved the feeling he got, especially at night—like now, when he'd pull into the big circular drive that curved outside the vine-covered iron gates leading up to the winding walkway leading to the massive hacienda's front door.

Rather than bathe the house with glaring outdoor lights, Alex had gone with subtle ground lighting carefully hidden among the plantings and trees that gave the old distinctively Spanish architecture a warm, romantic feel. He understood why everyone loved this place so much.

It was special, unique, and had for generations been the home base of a family he was proud to know.

As he was lifting Angie down from her seat, she started whispering like it was two hours past her curfew.

"Sh, sh!" she breathed with a finger to her mouth. "Come on," she whispered. "We need a drink."

"Do we, now?" he smirked. Oh man, what was she thinking? "What about your violets?"

"Pssh, I don't think they like tequila," she burbled nonsensically.

Ooookay.

Grabbing his hand, she started dragging him away from the hacienda and toward the barn. Following along dutifully while she dramatically tiptoed, he was trying not to crack up laughing.

Did she really imagine that they were actually sneaking around? Surely, she knew that all the common areas on the property shared by Justice were under twenty-four-hour surveillance. There were cameras everywhere and while he didn't know what Alex was doing this exact moment, he was pretty sure if he wasn't aware that they were there, he could review the security tapes and have a great laugh watching his best friend and little sister skulking about like naughty teens.

As they neared the barn, she waved her fingers again and sternly shushed him, "Shh! Gush is closing up," she whispered-slurred. Pushing him down to the ground, they crouched beside a long water trough while old Gus switched off some lights and ambled slowly away to a nearby truck that he climbed into, started, and drove away.

"Good! He's gone. Come on!" Angie commanded after springing to her feet like a cat and dashing for the side door to the old barn. "Hurry up."

The renovated barn was huge and part of the original Villa. Though it was heavily in use for Justice purposes, it still housed a private section, maintained just for the family, of stables and tack rooms where the vaqueros traditionally gathered.

Switching on a row of lights that lit a long hallway, she quickly skirted into the room behind Parker, as he watched, bemused, wondering what was happening in her mind.

"Help me," she called out so he followed her into a mess of a room littered with old leather sofas and heavy wood tables along with a kitchenette in one corner. She rummaged through a couple of cabinets, whipped open the refrigerator, pulled something out, then whispered conspiratorially, "Carry this and don't drop!"

In short order, she pushed a bottle of Cuervo into his hands, shoved a plastic container of god knows what under his arm before taking two shot glasses and putting one in each of his back pockets, something she took her damn good time doing. He didn't miss the sexy little sigh she made when she was finished—like she wanted to go on touching his ass and was disappointed that she couldn't.

"Wait a minute," Parker drawled. "What are you carrying if I've got all this?"

She held up a container of salt and a bag or pretzels, stuck her tongue out at him, said "Nyah, nyah," laughed and scooted out the door.

Okay then. Fun times ahead.

Chapter Forty-Four

"They're back," Alex informed Meghan when she came from the bath.

He was sitting in an easy chair, the French doors leading to their small vine-covered balcony were open. The cool nighttime air spiced with mesquite and acacia filled him with peace. Knowing the love of this lifetime was within his grasp made a moment like this seem perfectly perfect.

She was wearing a short, white robe that was soft and silky—one of his favorites *because* it was simple and showcased everything he found alluring about his fiancée.

Meghan stopped for a moment at the open doors where he heard her take a deep breath, before turning around.

Sliding a rubber band from her hair, she pulled on it until her glorious auburn curls tumbled across her shoulders and down her back.

"How do you know?" she asked, eyeing his present state of undress with a raised brow. "And please tell me you weren't prancing about in your skivvies where everyone could see."

"First of all, woman . . ." He smirked as he reached out and grabbed hold of the tie on her robe and yanked her forward.

"I do not prance."

Smiling, she chortled lightly. "Aw, it's so cute that you think that!" she teased with a wicked leer.

When she was standing at his knees, he untied the robe and patted his thigh indicating exactly where he expected her to plant her bottom.

As she gingerly sat down, he continued talking at the same time that he pushed the robe fully open. When she was situated with her legs crossed and her hair a red halo about her naked shoulders he appreciated her abundant curves up close and personal—the way they were meant to be.

"And second, *skivvies?* Is that really a word?"

"It's not?" she asked, instantly showing her puzzlement. "I thought it was military slang."

"Let me guess," he drawled teasingly as he casually ran his fingers around the dusty pink areola of a perfect, erect nipple. "You Googled it?"

He found the way her nose and cheeks pinked to be utterly charming.

"It's a teacher thing," she mumbled. "Now, tell me how you know Angie's back."

Alex laughed and flung his head back on the chair. "Oh, my god," he groaned. "Is this how I'll be with a daughter?"

Meghan leaned down and quickly but quite soundly kissed him with a satisfied-sounding smack, then sat back and grinned. "I'm counting on it, Major," she smirked.

"Well, good to know because right now I feel a little bit like a fucking voyeur. I programmed the gate sensors to alert me by text when a vehicle entered. Not long after an arrival, Gus called to let me know he was finished in the barn and was on his way out. Said he saw Parker and my sister skulking about in the shadows."

"If they can't make it work . . . I think it'd be almost tragic," he continued after a long pause. "And I don't think either of 'em would be truly happy." He shrugged—like an afterthought and breathed deeply. "I know this is hard for you, babe."

Uncrossing her legs, she pulled in her knees and shimmied on his lap until she was curled against him, breasts pillowed on his chest, her face buried near his neck.

"It's not hard, Alex," she murmured. "Life doesn't stop for us when we need it to. There are seven billion souls on this planet, and they all come with their own shit and stuff. Our wedding is important to us, but that doesn't mean everyone else's life takes a backseat."

He ran a hand up and down the silky fabric on her back. "How did you get to be so understanding? *Hmmm?*"

She hooted sharply. "Understanding? Ha! Give it a week and then you'll be shaking your head and wondering how to survive me being hormonal."

"I think I'm fucked up in the head," he murmured.

Her face popped up on his shoulder and she stared at him, wide-eyed. "Why would you say that?"

"Because, my wild Irish goddess, you've brought such happiness into my life that I just want to prance about tossing handfuls of fairy dust on everyone so they can be as happy was we are."

"See!" she barked playfully with a sharp swat on his chest. "You just admitted that you DO prance! *Ahhahahahahaaaaa.*"

"In here!" Angie urged Parker, as she pushed open a heavy wood door. Instantly, sensory memories flooded her emotions.

The smell of leather, wood, earth, and straw assailed her senses sending fireflies dancing in her stomach. This was a magical place—old and filled with memories gathered over time. Angie treasured that her DNA was part of those memories.

Didn't matter that she was an American girl-next-door—raised on ice cream and burgers on the grill. She was a Valleja-Marquez. Her people had lived on this land and been part of ten thousand sunsets and seasons. This very room had been used for well over a hundred years by vaqueros and patricians alike. Angie could feel the unique energy vibrating off the walls . . . like murmured passages of a story, her family's history—whispered over time.

Excited by the blatant masculinity of the room, she ran her hand along a long leather daybed with tufted arms rolled at each end accented with nail head trim. Her imagination running wild, Angie nearly nibbled her lip off as a burst of triple X-rated images involving the distinctive furniture stole her breath.

"I love this place," she told him softly. "Did you know I had my first job—right here? I was eleven that summer and had the time of my life."

"I remember it well." He chuckled, surprising her.

Turning quizzical eyes on him, she quipped, "Uh-huh. I'm sure you do."

"Seriously!" he barked.

Dropping the salt container and pretzels onto a rustic wood slab large enough to have housed the Knights of the Round Table, she crossed her arms, made a doubting squint, and waited.

"I have an elephant's memory," he drawled with something barely this side of a leer. "Not only do I remember that summer, I also remember that you wore your hair in pigtails and had a pair of bright pink work gloves that your granddad gave you."

She gasped. Her pink gloves! Oh! She remembered them. Her abuelo had presented them to her that first day when he introduced her formally to the other stable hands. How wonderful to think that Parker remembered something so meaningful that had in all honesty been lost in the shadows of her memory.

Hoisting her bottom onto the big wooden table, she gestured him over and motioned for him to turn around. Reaching into his back pockets, she slowly extracted the two shot glasses, making no effort whatsoever to hide her appreciation of his ass.

Lifting his elbow, the plastic container he carried dropped with a thud onto the table.

"What is that?" he asked.

Beaming, she wagged her eyebrows, declaring, "Limes!" as she peeled back the lid of the bowl. "Crack open that Cuervo and make a toast."

While he started setting up their drinks, Angie looked around the room. Several antique saddles were displayed and all along an entire section of wall, tack hung. Everywhere she looked, there was gleaming silver, burnished brass, wood, and leather.

Leaning back on a hand, she crossed her legs and watched him pour the shots. *My goodness, this table is big,* she mused. Why, she could stretch out, her arms wide and still have plenty of room.

Suddenly, the table and just about every other object and piece of furniture in the room became part of some vividly erotic scenarios that had her clearing her throat and sitting up straight. *Oh, my.*

That padded sawhorse looking apparatus over in the corner? She could think of several interesting ways to put that odd piece of equipment to very good use. So too the array of leather crops in a short barrel by the door.

"Okay, Angel," he quipped. "One tequila shot as requested."

Thinking she could drown out the lascivious thoughts crowding her mind with alcohol was downright stupid, but that was what she did.

"How's this go?" she said aloud. "I don't remember. Oh, wait. Yes, I do. It's lick, salt, shot, and then lime. Right?"

She looked at Parker for reassurance and found him nodding as he licked a spot on the hand in which he held a lime wedge. Pouring a stream of salt onto the wet skin, he wagged his eyebrows at her, said, "Salud," put his lips onto the pile of salt, then tossed back the shot and immediately stuck the lime his mouth.

Shaking his head with a deep growl, he slammed the empty shot glass down on the table.

"Okay, baby," he taunted. "Show me how the big girls do it."

Did he? Oh, no he didn't! Well, she'd show him. Grabbing her glass, she held it up in silent salute and challenged him with mocking eyes.

Mimicking his technique, she licked, making sure to do so slowly with a hushed moan as her tongue laved her skin before sprinkling the salt. Holding a slice of lime, she blew out her breath, licked the salt, downed the shot in one gulp, and then put the lime wedge into her mouth as she bit down to release the fragrant juices.

"M*mmmm,*" she moaned. And then the alcohol burn marked a trail from her lips, down her throat and into her belly where the heat spread. "Holy fuck!" she hollered, surprised that she wasn't breathing actual fire.

Parker chuckled and smacked her on the back. "Not as smooth as Dad's Don Julio but tasty nonetheless."

Angie sputtered and laughed. "Oh, my god. I think my eyes are watering."

"Tequila is good for the soul," he joked. "Ready for another?" he asked. "It's best to go balls out and knock 'em back pretty quickly," he stated emphatically. "That way you can't pussy out too early."

"Did you just accuse me of being a pussy?" she choked out with mock outrage.

He looked at her. First, with laughter, and then, with something else. A challenge maybe.

Chapter Forty-Five

"Wanna try something different?"

One shot and she was already starting to float. And now he wanted to . . . try something different? Sure! Why the hell not.

She looked at him expectantly and found herself biting back a groan of raw female appreciation when he abruptly whipped his t-shirt over his head and threw it aside. Goddamn, but his chest was a work of art. Smooth. Muscled. Broad.

He poured two more shots, grabbed a hunk of lime and smiled wickedly at her.

Taking two fingers, he held them to her mouth and drawled huskily, "Lick."

Swiping her tongue across his skin, she managed to fight a whimper when he then wet the spot where his neck met shoulder with her saliva and quickly dropped a big pinch of salt on top.

In a voice that sounded gruff and demanding, he commanded her to, "Lick," as he tilted his head to the side to give her room.

In a trance, she leaned into him and laved the flat of her tongue on the salt, pausing to suckle at the spot . . . I mean, after all, she DID want to get all the salt, right?

Now, the truth was she would have happily kept on just like that, her mouth on his skin, sucking, but him pushing the shot glass into her hand reminded Angie what she was supposed to be doing.

Quickly huffing out a deep breath, she knocked back the second shot and before hyperventilating from the burn, destroyed the lime wedge while she swung her head back and forth. "Fuck!" she yelped again as the alcohol tore a hole through her core.

Through watery eyes, she found him grinning broadly as once again, he patted her on the back to help her catch a breath.

Oh, my dear sweet lord! she thought. Maybe this stuff should be illegal.

Murmuring silkily, he said, "My turn." Eyeing her from head to toe, he kind of smirked then shook his head. "You're all covered up," he objected with a disgruntled bark.

Angie giggled. *Yeah. Tequila was the shit.*

"Sorry," she confessed with a pouty frown intended to get a smile—which it did along with an eye roll and a head shake that acknowledged he knew how easy she had it when it came to charming the shit out of him. Winning!

"I didn't want my ass hanging out in front of your folks."

She wasn't sure but when she said ass, it might have sounded more like ash. He didn't react, so either he didn't notice or he wasn't listening to her anyway.

Now, where were they? What had they been talking about?

Angie saw his eyes flare. Oooh. Likey! What made him do that?

"I'd like to bite your ass and then lick a tequila shot off the dip in your back."

Oh. That was why he flared.

"All covered up. Remember?" she said, pointing at her head-to-toe outfit.

"Lay back," he commanded.

"Uh. What?"

The skin on her neck prickled when he fixed her with a meaningful look and said roughly, "My turn. And since I can't have your ass, your stomach will have to do. Now lay the fuck back."

She didn't know why she laughed, but the dark scowl on his face and the way he was sizing her up hit her as hilarious.

Giggling wildly, she scooted back until her legs weren't dangling and teased him, chirping away, singing, "Ooooh, look at you! So big and bad. Dommy, dom, dom, dom! Knock, knock. Who's there? *Can't have your ass,*" she mimicked him growling then fell back laughing until she was, as he asked, on her back.

"Ready, Mister Dommy, sir. Sir Dom-your-great. *Sir*dom. Sir*dom,*" she grumbled mischievously as she nodded to him with a drunken salute.

He stood over her where she lay sprawled on the big table. Remembering her earlier thought that she could probably spread out and still have plenty of rooms got her flinging both arms wide. He didn't say anything so Angie picked up her head and looked at him. He was just standing there—staring at her. The whole thing suddenly felt very virgin sacrificey.

"I like this," he said. Waving his hand for emphasis, he indicated her laid out before him. "Works for me." He chuckled deeply.

He reached for the buttons on her blouse, just beneath her breasts and started undoing them, pulling the tails from her skirt until he could fold both sides back and expose several inches of her stomach.

Nothing showed. Not her bra and not even her belly button. Sensual modesty. Just enough skin to titillate without being vulgar.

Sliding onto the table, he rested on one hip and turned toward her, giving him complete access to her body. Angie shivered.

This time, instead of asking her to lick his fingers, he inserted them into her mouth. Briefly shocked—probably the tequila slowing down her responses—she recovered and swirled her tongue around his fingers, sucking on them. His eyes devoured, watching every expression and reading her responses.

When he wiped the saliva from his fingers onto her stomach, her skin quivered with anticipation.

A quick pinch of salt and then he leaned over her and his mouth was on her stomach. *Oh, my god. Oh, my god. Oh, my god. Oh, my god.* His breath was hot, his lips soft, and his tongue . . . wet and slow against her skin.

When he threw back his head for the shot, she watched his throat work as he swallowed then drifted her eyes down his bare torso imagining the tequila moving through his system. Through an expression blazing with desire, he looked into her eyes as his mouth made greedy sucking noises on the lime.

She watched, fascinated, and involuntarily licked her lips. *Mmmm.*

His lips probably tasted real good.

Had she said that out loud? The look on his face and the fire in his eyes told her that, yep, she most definitely had.

Tequila mouth. Speak first and then deal with whatever you said later.

Parker grabbed hold of her chin and hovered over her for a second then swooped straight onto her mouth.

She was right. He tasted divine. Salty. Sweet. Tangy. The flavor of the tequila clung to his lips and tongue, driving her wild with the beguiling aftertaste. *Mmmmm.* Maybe tequila was their drink. Angie was certainly enjoying the warmth creeping along her nerve endings, and though she was definitely a bit lit, she was far from drunk.

After kissing her with a deliberately slow thoroughness that rendered her stupid, he eased back and feathered her hair away from her face. The way he was looking into Angie's eyes made her quiver.

"I didn't treat you right before, Angel." The deep roughness in his voice gave his words gravity. "Can you forgive me?"

Acting on tequila time, which basically meant she had no damn idea how long it took her to reply, she put a hand on the powerfully big bicep that caged her in and sighed.

Forgiveness wasn't the issue. Or then again . . . maybe it was.

When she said something, Angie was surprised by how small and uncertain she sounded. Parker did that to her. Made her feel vulnerable. Nothing and nobody else had ever made her feel this way.

"I make it too easy for you."

"How?" he growled, his face a mask of confusion mixed with concern.

Running appreciative fingers on the warm skin of his muscled arm, she attempted to shrug and looked away—unsure how to explain.

"I don't find any of this easy, Angelina," he told her emphatically.

Pfft. Did he really have no idea? How was that possible?

"Yes, well . . . ," she murmured self-consciously. "Truth is, I'll always forgive you. No matter what you do—I can't help myself."

She continued to stroke his arm while he silently considered what she said.

"And you imagine this gives me some sort of . . . power? Advantage?"

She could hear him trying to make sense of her statement.

Swinging her eyes to his, she thought, *Well, it does* . . . but didn't say the words aloud.

"It means," she eventually told him quietly, "that you could hurt me. And I'd let you. That's scary shit, Parker."

He was quick to respond to her bold statement.

"I did not mean to hurt you. What I said that day was not meant for you to hear and my words, though chosen poorly, were an attempt to shield you from malicious gossip."

"I know that now," she whispered. "But I *did* get hurt and knowing I'd forgive you anything—even tearing my heart out—is what kept us apart. I had to stay away from you just in order to stay sane. You do realize that, right?"

He grimaced. "As you say, I know that now."

Her most secret inner thoughts and fears broke loose—thanks, Cuervo—and she blurted out one of the big ones before she could bite back by the words.

"I'm afraid I won't be enough for you."

"Shit," he barked as he jerked upright, pulling her with him. "Sit up. Let's get this out in the open and put it to rest so we can move on."

There they were, sitting on a huge wood table, having scooted to the edge, they sat side-by-side, their legs dangling toward the floor.

"Okay look," he bit out sharply. More sharply than should have been possible after a couple of healthy shots. Oh, sheesh. She'd hit a nerve.

"We can fuck around and play word games till hell freezes over, which I admit can be fun, but let's cut to the chase."

He eased off the table and moved to stand in front of her—so close his thighs almost rested against her knees. When he did, his big body blocked the light behind them and made him seem huge in her field of vision. Her mouth went dry.

"When have I ever given you the impression that you're not enough? And don't give me that tired shit about what you overheard. Just show me one fucking time when . . ." He was yelling and clearly frustrated. Running a hand through his hair, he growled and looked at her with pleading eyes. "Dammit, Angel. What the fuck? I can't defend myself against something I don't understand."

"Don't be upset with me," she implored, frowning. With a bravery she hoped was real and not just fueled by the liquor, Angie put her hands on either side of his handsome face.

"Is this the age thing?" he asked.

"Partially," she admitted.

"And . . . ?"

Dropping her hands, Angie saw something flash in her mind. "Can I ask you a question?"

"If it relates to this, yes. Don't change the subject, okay? I need to understand what's happening in that head of yours."

"Oh." Was she changing the subject? She didn't think so. Biting her lip, she fidgeted, looking anywhere but at his bared torso, even going so far as to shove her fingers beneath her bum to keep from tracing the definition of his muscular chest.

"Um, before we get into this, I think I need another drink."

Parker's eyebrows shot into his hairline. She didn't give him long to ponder her sudden detour thinking that by taking him by surprise, she'd have some sort of advantage.

Pulling on his arm until he was close enough to touch, Angie bent over and swirled the flat of her tongue on and around one of his nipples. Taking a clumsy pinch of salt between two fingers, she dropped it on the wet spot her tongue left and then thoroughly sucked and licked the area clean.

Not resting on ceremony, she grabbed the Cuervo bottle and upended a stream of tequila into her open mouth. Sputtering as she swallowed, she slammed the bottle down and scrambled quickly for a lime wedge shoving it into her mouth for relief.

"Mother of god," she choked out through her burning mouth as tears blurred her eyes.

His expression was unreadable. The only thing that indicated he was alive was the fists clenched tightly at his sides and the slight vibration she felt coming off him. Come to think of it . . . he hadn't so much as taken a deep breath or moved a single muscle since she licked his chest.

Suddenly whirling away from her, she saw a hand go into his hair and a low, steady rumble come from his mouth. Took her a couple of seconds—in tequila time—to figure out the rumble was actual words being growled. She heard *tied up* and *behave herself* and Alex's name thrown in there but . . . oooh, wait! That was her tequila brain babbling—wasn't this where, according to the talk around the Villa, her brother tied up his fiancée?

Taking a sudden interest in the ceiling, she was peering upward, and had completely missed whatever Parker was mumbling when he took her by the arm and gently shook her.

"Are you even listening?"

Mmmmm. She liked the growl. Remembered it well. *Knees up, angel, and hold on tight.* I bet the hooks and hanging rings for the tack were what he tied her to. Oh, look at that! Her shirt was almost completely unbuttoned. Angie sighed and looked at Parker, who was openly scowling at her. Okay, NOW she was starting to feel tequila fuzzy and had to admit her thoughts were a jumbled mess.

"Ask your question, woman, or by god, Angelina . . . I swear your ass will be bright red when I'm finished with you."

What? How the hell had they gone from licking each other's skin to a spanking?

"That's what I'm talking about," she whined. "You want to spank me?"

"Oh for god's sake," he barked two seconds before yanking her off the table and hauling her ass to sit on the long leather daybed bench. She'd like to imagine she sank gracefully to her seat but knew she actually dropped like a rock and sat there staring up at him, her mouth open, eyes wide.

Uh-oh. In the low lighting, standing over her bare-chested, eyes blazing—he looked like . . . well, shit. He looked like a dangerously sexy cowboy wearing nothing but a pair of jeans that knew his body well and some boots that for some reason were giving her the swoons.

"How drunk are you," he demanded. "Maybe we should do this another time."

"No!" she blurted. "I know what I'm saying Parker and being a little drunk only means my fillers are off."

"Your fillers?"

She licked her lips, aware that she had to concentrate when she spoke. "Fill-*ters*. Filters are off."

Without warning, he picked up the tequila bottle and downed a mouthful, his eyes never leaving her.

"I'm thinking I may need that if we do this sans filters."

He might be right.

She suddenly fell silent. How should she start?

"I'll help move this along," he grumbled. "You're going to tell me why you think you're not enough for me and somewhere in that jumbled mess is a question."

"Can you sit down, please?" she begged, patting the space next to her. "You freak me out like that."

"Like what?"

An excess of energy, fueled by sexual tension and Cuervo Gold, burst free inside her. She manically shook her hands and pouted. "Oh god, I don't know."

Parker snickered softly but sat next to her.

It was now or never, she thought. He was halfway smiling—because, as usual, he'd found something to tease her about—and there'd never be a better time to just say it all out loud.

"You frighten me sometimes," she said in a hoarse whisper.

He went absolutely still.

"I don't mean I'm afraid. From the very beginning, I felt so young and dumb and . . . and . . ." She paused and frowned, searching for the right words. "Um, unsexy or something. And you, well, you were the one who knew, who had all the experience, and were so matter-of-fact about everything."

She shrugged. "I don't know, Parker. That always confused me. And even now, I don't know what to call that whole weird time. We weren't dating. It's not like we were involved. Was it an affair? To say we slept together just sounds tacky but what else was there? I mean, would you even call that a relationship? I felt then and even a little now like a dumb kid that you were teaching the ropes to."

He moaned. At least he was listening so she added one last thought to her mini-tirade. "Just like you taught my brother."

Chapter Forty-Six

THERE WASN'T ENOUGH TEQUILA LEFT *in the bottle to get him through this conversation,* he thought glumly. He'd asked for this years ago. Maybe he didn't know the actual words she'd use but he knew what was at the core. Had even alluded to it earlier when he admitted he hadn't treated her right before.

Everything they did together was a series of firsts for her, but he'd given zero effort or thought to what that meant. There had been no romance. No slow seduction over a carefully planned dinner, never a chance for her to indulge her girly side by taking her out and showing her off someplace where she could dress up and feel special.

Feel special. What a dumbass motherfucker he was. Never once had he made her feel like a priority. From her standpoint, of course, it must feel like there hadn't been a relationship at the core of what was going on.

Oh shiiiit, his mind screamed. Shit, shit, shit. Clarity was a cruel bitch. By tying in her conflicted feelings from before with the knowledge that he'd been something of a mentor for Alex, she'd arrived at a conclusion that pretty much damned his sorry ass to hell.

Buck up, counselor. Now was not the time for glib so grab your balls, shithead, because that little lady hanging her head like she had anything at all to explain or apologize for had bigger ones than you!

Lowering his head into his hands, he rested his elbows on his thighs and groaned. He was older and supposed to be smarter, wiser.

He had to say something significant. Immediately. Sooner than immediately. And then he had some serious explaining to do.

"When I made love to you," he began cautiously, sitting up and angling toward her, "I . . ." He stopped cold at the angry look on her face.

"Do not call what we did making love. Don't do that to me, Parker."

Whoa. He never wanted to hear that tone again—Angel had teeth. And maybe claws. *Okay then.*

He dipped his head to acknowledge her objection and pivoted to a rewording of his previously interrupted statement.

"Okay, maybe a bit blunt, but if that's how this needs to go, so be it. So, the first time we had sex, I was such a fuckwad that until it was too late to change course, I was clueless on the state of your um . . . innocence."

He heard a faint intake of breath on her part. "Are you saying you didn't know I was a virgin?"

Jesus. Even now, he still cringed at the memory. Didn't know. Wasn't prepared. Reacted badly. Fucked her viciously. Guilty.

"I did *not* know, to my great shame, by the way. And then once I did, instead of telling you how I felt, well . . . you know." He shrugged.

"Said nothing."

"Right. I was embarrassed and yeah, I admit . . . my embarrassment trumped your innocence."

"Oh."

Yeah. Oh.

"Which brings me to the bullshit you have in your head about me and Alex and all that BDSM crap. You knowing about The Cavern only makes it worse. And honestly, most of it I can't explain—especially not with half a bottle of tequila in me—but ask yourself this, baby. If I really saw myself as some all-powerful being who just wanted to take and be in control, would I just have admitted to being embarrassed? Don't you think if that's all I wanted, you'd be naked and on your knees with my cock buried inside you?"

"I don't understand what you want," she wailed softly. "I can't just be a sex toy. I need more than that, but you never asked for anything else. Never wanted more than just that."

Ouch. That fucking hurt.

"Fuck, Angie! Don't you see? We already had all that other stuff. You were closer to me than family. We didn't have to explore whether we shared interests. Shit. Please tell me you see that. I swear to god it wasn't just about the sex."

Fear, regret, desire, tequila—all roiled in his gut.

"Tell me what you want," she pleaded again. "Tell me exactly where you see this going. I'll always worry I'm not going to be enough unless you spell it out."

He wanted to yell and maybe break something. Oh, dear god—she thought she wasn't enough. What the fuck? She was *everything.* And all that other stuff? Time to set the record straight.

"I want *you.* All of you. No-holds-barred. I want you to speak your mind and be exactly who you *are*—not someone you think you *should* be."

It bothered him that she had her arms crossed so rigidly that it looked like she was trying to keep from falling apart. But, at the same time, he saw a warmth in her eyes that was enough to keep him talking.

"Don't believe all that shit you see in the movies," he said and then quickly amended the comment. "Actually, I'm wrong. Believe all that shit because it does happen but I promise you—whatever you're thinking about me and Alex is all wrong. Can I explain, please? About The Cavern, at least?"

Giving him a shaky nod, Angie sat quietly with a slightly defense in her posture but it was still there.

"Look, this may sound like a ton of horseshit, but it's really the simple truth. Ninety-nine percent of anything that happened during that time can be chalked up to one thing . . . Washington. The other one percent was normal curiosity."

"You told me once you hated it. All the phoniness."

Had he said that? Thank god because maybe having that as a reference she'd listen to what he was trying to say.

Not able to sit still any longer, Parker lumbered to his feet and moved aimlessly about the room. It helped him think. Like pacing back and forth in front of a jury.

"What I did there, well. . . . that shit never lets you go," he told her. "It's been a couple of years, but that doesn't keep me from being involved. Still."

He was uncomfortable making the statement mostly because he hoped if he didn't say that stuff out loud maybe it really would just go away. But for guys like him who had been heavily involved on the legal end of the early days of the war on terror, they'd be tied to it forever.

"In that type of environment, where the reality is so horrific and gruesome that you become numb to it, people tend blow off steam in unusual ways."

The time he spent in the nation's capital had been formative years for Parker professionally. With a little effort, he'd found himself on a fast-moving, inside track. Almost overnight, he was in with the power hitters and superstars—lobbyists, politicians, the FBI, military. With Washington being ground zero for doing everything legally, his sharp mind and impressive verbal skills got him noticed quickly. Everyone wanted to either be his friend or have him as one of their entourage. It was a heady time during which he'd seen history being made first hand. He'd also seen way too up close and personally the darker, grittier side of the power town.

"The Cavern was a particular favorite of the special ops guys, the security contractors. The badass motherfuckers who didn't have time for downshifting to hearts and flowers. For them . . . well, it was different. Each time your brother came statewide, he always did a long stay-over in D.C. That's how either of us even knew about that place, so for real . . . Alex brought me into it. Not the other way around."

She snorted and rolled her eyes, but there was the hint of a smile near her lips.

"Hey! Don't be hatin'!" he teased. "I coulda' been blowing rails off some high paid hooker's ass." He actually shuddered at the thought. "So a sex dungeon that was all watch and no play doesn't seem all that bad now, huh?"

"All you did was watch?" she asked.

"Yep."

Even though half the room was between them, he saw her facial expression shift as she considered what he said.

"You never . . ."

"Fuck, no. Angie. Do I seem like a *do it in public* kind of guy? Or someone who'd find the presence of another dude even remotely okay?"

Finally, she changed position. Loosened up. Tucking her feet beneath her, she sat on them, her long skirt completing covering her legs. Adjusting the unbuttoned blouse, she pulled her clothes together while he watched.

The tension of a frown marked her face, but by the time she was buttoned up and had pulled her hair into a single tumble over one shoulder, she looked remarkably less troubled.

"So that's not what you want? I always thought because of some of the stuff we did that . . ."

He cut her off as quickly as he could. "No! And that's my point if you'd let me finish."

She sat back on her feet with a startled flash of shyness.

"No, that's *not* what I want but I see where you'd get that impression. I'm not a dominant," he growled, making air quotes and saying the word with as much sarcasm as possible. "And I'm not in the market for a submissive. No contracts. No crazy rules. No need to inflict pain. Understand?"

Parker gritted his teeth—he hadn't meant to raise his voice. He also broke out the cross-armed, naked chest, feet wide apart stance that generally made mere mortals quake.

Shaking his head, he muttered, "Shit," and uncrossed his arms. "Sorry for yelling."

"Oh no," she choked out. "Feel free to yell all you want."

What did she say? Go ahead and yell all he wanted? Wait a minute. Parker walked over to the leather bench where she sat perched on her knees to get a good view of her face to try and read her expression.

What the hell? She was literally bent over in half, her face on her knees, slapping a hand on the leather as her screams of laughter split the air.

"I'm sorry," she wailed a bit hysterically as a fresh wave of uncontrollable giggles left her flailing uncontrollably.

Parker couldn't help but laugh. She was completely undone with laughter. Full throated, tears rolling down her cheeks, hysterical shrieks that filled up the room with her joy.

Play-acting with a deep scowl on her face and a comical gruff voice she said, "I like it when you yell and do that caveman thing. *Rrrroar!*"

And then she giggled some more. "Especially when you play all badass—try to distract me with the killer chest and are you fucking kidding me jeans."

He was grinning like an idiot. Just like that, they were officially too drunk to know what they were doing so no more serious discussion and now that she brought it up, he thought, *maybe I should put my shirt back on.* The very last thing they needed was a tequila injected sex romp in the Villa tack room to help them navigate this weirdness.

He bent to pick up the t-shirt and she was suddenly all over him like an eager puppy anxious to play.

Swaying ever so slightly, she told him emphatically, "You told me what you wanted so now I have to say something . . . about that, I think. I should say something, right?" she asked.

He nodded solemnly knowing he was egging her drunk ass on.

"Well, wouldn't you like to know?" she taunted while he laughed at her inebriated state.

Straightening as tall as she could muster and with all the dignity of a drunken duchess, she tossed her hair back and stuck her cute little nose up in the air.

"I may be a lady, sir," she told him with a weak wristed wave, "but I like it dirty."

Parker blinked. Did she say dirty?

"You did that, you know. Taught me from the start that dirty was what I did best."

Once the words were out there, they both froze.

A freight train of emotion derailed inside his chest. He couldn't prevent what he said next.

"Were you dirty with him? That motherfucker you were going to marry?"

He knew damn well that he shouldn't have asked—he didn't have the right, but he didn't know he was going to say it until the words came out.

They stared at each other.

"No," she murmured softly.

She wouldn't look at him, but he saw the deep blush that crept up her neck and across her face. So . . . the smarmy Spaniard hadn't floated her boat. *Interesting.*

"I think we need another drink, don't you?" he asked. Slinging an arm loosely across her shoulders, he gathered her close for a sloppy hug then pushed her toward the table.

"Set 'em up woman," he barked as he swatted her on the ass. Her comical yelp of surprise and the little dancing two-step she did to escape his hand made him laugh.

Like a good western saloon gal, she quickly poured two ridiculously generous shots and pushed the container of limes close.

This time she did him Arizona proud—made a fist, licked the fleshy portion around thumb and forefinger, poured a healthy amount of salt onto it, licked, exhaled, and then threw back the entire shot. She used the lime like a mouth guard, getting all of the juicy goodness.

After watching her flawless performance, he followed suit but after destroying his lime, tossed it aside and immediately grabbed Angie by the neck so he could then devour her mouth.

They were drunk—that last shot wasn't going to help matters—and he really did know they shouldn't be doing this, but she tasted so damn good. Like tequila and Angie and limes and stuff.

So he kissed the living shit out of her. She didn't resist. Mostly she clung and moaned and rubbed all around on him as he kept her tight against his body.

Eventually, they ended up back on the huge table after covering it with a stack of riding blankets they found, giggling like naughty children as they made a nest.

"I want a room like this," she sighed, snuggling against him, one of her legs thrown casually over his thigh.

"A tack room?" he asked, confused.

She chuckled. "No. Just a room with lots of leather and wood. I like the smell and the way it feels."

"I have a study in my house in Sedona," he told her. "Lots of wood. Big pieces of furniture. And leather. Even the top of my desk is leather."

She didn't say anything right away so he asked her before he lost his nerve. "Would you like to see my home, Angel? Come to Sedona for the weekend maybe and let me spoil your baby girl ass a bit?"

"What is it with you and my ass?" She giggled. "One minute you want to spank it, then I believe there was a bite it in there someplace, and now you want to spoil my ass?"

"Is that a yes?" he asked hopefully. Spending the whole weekend with her would be amazing. Give them a chance to keep building on what they'd started.

She laughed and kissed him soundly with a loud smacking noise. "My brother would kill you. Come to town for the day? Yeah. For a whole weekend? You're dreaming."

Alex. Shit. Sometimes it was easy to forget the stone in his shoe that was Angie's brother.

"I'll take whatever I can get," he drawled. Hauling her close in their cushioned nest of blankets, Parker feasted on her with his mouth, lips, and tongue. That was pretty much the last thing he remembered—the voracious kissing and then the tequila took over and everything became a huge blur.

Chapter Forty-Seven

"Gus did an amazing job re-thinking the space Brody wanted to be changed."

That was high praise coming from Drae, and Alex did have to admit the guy was right. With the animal program expanding, they needed to maximize the existing kennel space and an area in the barn that was available because of the new construction. Brody had been working with Gus to make that happen.

So he, Cam, and Drae were coming from an inspection after one of their early morning conference calls with the dog guru who was still back East, when something so fucking funny happened that Alex almost shit himself.

They were walking back to the house, talking quietly because it was still early even though nobody was around, making their way from the rear of the big building when in front of them many yards away, one of the walkway doors to the barn opened wide with a tremendous bang as it slammed into the side of the wood structure.

The three of them awkwardly shuffled to a halt waiting to see what happened next and in the blink of an eye, sure as shit, something did.

Stumbling like prisoners released from the hole after a long confinement, Angie and Parker stepped from the barn into the daylight, each of them instantly groaning and covering their eyes. Angie was using the other hand to swing back and forth in front of her as she walked like a blind man wielding a cane. While Parker looked a lot like the

Hunchback of Notre Dame.

They stumbled into each other, she snapped something at him, he growled something back, and then gave her a mighty shove along the path. Off they went, like two hung over sailors after an all-night drinking binge.

As they walked on, Alex felt his blood pressure soar when he saw that hanging from the back pocket of that motherfucker's jeans was an unmistakable pair of pink panties.

Why, he was going to have to kill that son-of-a-bitch! The only thing stopping him was the sound of Cam and Drae whooping with laughter.

"That looked like the morning after I married Victoria," Drae guffawed merrily. "Same hung over stumble, same snapping female. Ah, the memories!"

"There really may be justice in this world if that grinning poster boy met his match. And leave it to a Marquez to be the one to hand him his ass." Cam seemed to think this was especially funny, then sobered, muttering, "I hope this doesn't mess up tonight. You know how the girls get. They want that karaoke trophy bad!"

"Fuck my life," Alex grumbled. "Now I have to kill that asshole."

More grist for the comedy mill because his foul temper and the ridiculously fucked-up situation with Parker and his sister was giving his two counterparts a serious case of the shits and grins.

"There's comfort in this, though," Cam sniggered. "None of us had to deal with another dude. Like in the flesh."

Drae muttered, "Fuck that shit."

Truth. The three of them were alike in that way. He could easily imagine blood being spilled should a contest to win their women had been part of their stories. They played for keeps and people were generally wise enough to respect them due to their physical presence alone.

Parker was all that too, only he was something of a lone wolf out there in the big city. Drae wasn't kidding with the snide poster boy remark. It was true. Guy looked like he stepped out of an underwear ad. The kind the women lick their lips over. He could have all the strange he could ever want, but Alex was aware that there actually hadn't been any notches added to ol' Parker's bed post in quite some time. Probably the reason why he hadn't drop kicked the man before now.

So what was Cam's reference to another dude? Was he missing something?

"Yo," he barked. "Cam. Wait up," he grumbled because he'd fallen behind while lost in his thoughts.

"What'd you mean about another guy, in the flesh? Angie's not interested in anyone else," he snorted. "Believe me."

Drae planted himself in the middle of the path and did that hands-on-hips silent visual appraisal thing he excelled at. "Indeed," the analyst drawled a touch mockingly. "She's Team Parker, according to my wife."

Alex nodded his agreement. "C'mon, I mean—that's why she's here. To resolve their thing, whatever that thing is, once and for all. I don't see how another guy figures in."

Cam smiled. It still knocked him back a second when a genuinely warm expression replaced his usual glower.

"Do you ever even look at that hi-tech surveillance grid you've got going on or was that just another toy you've lost interest in?"

Drae roared a mocking, "Ha!"

Alex couldn't be bothered not to laugh. They had him there. He was the king of gadgets, tech toys and nerd projects. His fiancée only made things worse. Sometimes he could tell what her mood was by how many Amazon and QVC boxes were piled by the door. Just last week she'd giddily passed out every imaginable make, model, and style of drone she could find. The ultimate boy toy. It was hilarious too, all of them, running around the property with their flying gadgets, dive bombing the dogs, bothering Gus whenever he was outside the barn, acting like a bunch of twelve-year-old kids at summer camp.

Yeah. He liked gadgets. The surveillance system was a necessity and hardly one of his tech toys, but Cam was correct. He hadn't bothered with it much lately. With all the construction activity, it became impossible—even cutting out separate work entrance hadn't done much. It was crazy town out here some days so yeah, he had indeed dropped the ball on that.

Apparently, Cameron had seen something so he asked, "What'd you pick up?"

Pulling his phone out, Cam tapped and swiped away then cleared his throat like he was announcing a royal birth or something.

"You can do this too, by the way," he said sarcastically, waving his phone in Alex's face.

Another less boisterous "Ha!" came from Drae.

"Anyway—at approximately eight-oh-five A.M., an airport limo accessed the keypad at the main entrance. The license plate was scanned and came back as a valid operator."

An airport limo? It was too soon for the surprise he had for Meghan and besides that, a limo service would be unnecessary so who the hell had turned up on his doorstep? Suddenly exasperated, he snapped at Cam. "*And?* Jesus, dude, spit it the fuck out. Who's here?"

Snickering with delight, Cam pocketed his phone and started back along the path, elbowing Drae out of the way as he passed.

"I predict more fun times await inside the Villa, fellas. The silent approach," he drawled with a winking sneer. "Best to watch and wait. Let things unfold organically, okay?"

"What the fuck is this," Alex muttered tersely. "What's going on?"

"Oh," Cam chuckled. "Just you wait!"

It would have been kinder just to put a pillow over her face and let her die a slow painful death than what she was going through now. *Oh, my god.* Her head weighed a ton and seemed to be filled with explosive marbles swirling about that detonated on contact.

Gripping the towel bar in the powder room off the big kitchen, Angie steadied herself and peered into the mirror. *Oh, no.* It was worse than she thought. Good lord. She looked a fright. How the hell could she fix this? Turning the water to a slow trickle, she dragged her fingers through the stream and splashed a smattering of droplets onto her face.

A face, which was pale as death, crowned with a mass of wildly tangled hair, with eyes that looked sunken due in no small part to yesterday's make-up which was now a smeared and smudged mess. The bride of Frankenstein looked better than she did.

And her mouth? Oh, dear god. Her mouth felt slimy and tasted like roadkill left too long in the sun.

Slowly turning back her sleeves, she had to take it easy or her head might topple from her shoulders. Angie let a groan out from the taxing effort. Fucking tequila.

By the time she'd washed her face and done what she could about the horror happening in her mouth, her head began to clear a bit as well.

What—the—hell—had—they—done? She wasn't sure. Not only was their evening after they'd returned to the Villa a blur, what she did remember was confusing at best.

Waking up to a sound that made her want to kill something, she knew the second one eye cracked open that she'd fucked up big time. Instead of finding herself all comfy and cozy in her huge wood bed in the familiar hacienda, she was staring up at a rustic beamed ceiling with all sorts of stuff hanging about. The barn. She was in the damn barn.

And then that sound happened again and she had to groan as mightily as she could to drown out the obnoxious racket. What the hell was that?"

Groaning again, she tried to shift to her side but couldn't. She was restrained somehow—unable to do more than wiggle. And she tried to do as little of that as possible because every movement caused a thunderous boom in her head.

Checking to see if her legs worked, she stretched one, knocked something over with her foot that sounded like an empty bottle when it fell.

A new noise joined the growing racket in her head. A roar. No, a growl. Sounded animalistic and not just a little menacing.

"Stop fucking wiggling," an angry, muffled voice demanded.

Parker. Shit. It all came rushing back. Dinner with his folks. Uncle Matt's deadly margaritas. Driving back to the Villa. Sneaking around in the barn. Polishing off more tequila. With Parker.

Why did it seem like she was cocooned in some sort of man-shroud with half his body covering hers and the other half weighed down by something else. Struggling to untangle from him, she started pushing at his dead weight. Feebly, but she tried.

"Get off me!" she groaned. "You snore and I need to pee."

It took a couple of minutes of heavy effort to get them both upright where she realized they'd passed out cold on the big round table in a bed of riding blankets. Nice.

But the icing on the cake? Although they were both dressed, when she managed to pry both eyes open at the same time and looked at him, she was horrified to see that dangling from his arm were the pink panties she'd worn last night. Somehow, and she shuddered to think how, they'd gone from being on her body to his entire arm in a leg opening as the pale pink against his cowboy heartthrob denim mocked her.

She and Parker seemed to notice those damning panties at the exact same moment, both of them letting go simultaneously with a tortured sounding groan.

"What did you do?" she croaked—the words causing shards of hung over agony to pierce her brain.

"What did *I* do?" he ground out indignantly. "I'm not the one with no underwear on," he snapped.

She needed a bathroom—like stat. Not only did she desperately need to pee, now she had to hope she could tell just how fast she was going to hell. The suspicion that they might have succumbed to an interlude of drunken sex made her stomach gurgle.

With a strangled, "Ugh," she slid carefully off the table relieved to discover that yes she actually could feel her feet. Unfortunately, the room chose that moment to spin. Clutching her head, Angie closed her eyes and swallowed down the embarrassing vomit threatening to join the proceedings.

Unable to deal with Parker while she felt like the walking death, she wobbled carefully toward the door only to find him hot on her heels.

"Move it or be carried," he grunted, crowding her from behind with his big body.

Instinctively, just like when she was a kid, Angie shoved him with her shoulder. "You're not the boss of me," she gritted out, not caring that she sounded like a peeved five-year-old.

Thinking she could stomp away, leaving him in her high-and-mighty dust, was a joke. Instead, she stumbled and lurched awkwardly, her hand on the wall of the barn for support as she made her way along.

At the door, she fumbled with the heavy latch and snarled when it didn't immediately open.

"Move," he scolded on a throaty growl pushing her hands away and attacking the latch himself. "Don't want you to break a nail."

"Oh, fuck you," she scolded.

His response was a husky croak.

Note to my bad self, tequila was most certainly not our drink. Maybe a couple but not enough to get falling down shitfaced because the other side of that? Well, she didn't know about separately, but together they were one snarling, mean-spirited unit of tequila excess. Not their best look.

Angie tripped over the door jamb but managed to keep from face planting as the door swung open and bright sunlight smacked 'em both dead on.

Groaning, she covered her eyes and headed for the house on auto-pilot until he practically knocked her down in his haste.

"Back off, counselor," she ground out.

"Move your ass or . . ." he drawled then gave her a shove along the path.

How they made it into the house was a blur, but they had with Parker quickly dropping onto a stool at the kitchen island, his head cradled in his hands.

"Do I smell coffee?" he mumbled to no one in particular.

Leaving him to figure that part out himself, she scuttled away as quickly as she could and barricaded herself in the powder room to assess the damage.

Chapter Forty-Eight

WHAT FUCKING DAY WAS IT?

Ugh. His head felt like Satan's crypt. Full of dark shit and ready to burst into flames at any moment.

Coffee. He needed coffee. And some Advil.

Luckily, he knew the kitchen well so he was able to bumble through the steps of pouring a generous mug of the hot brew without making too much of a mess. Back on the stool, Parker kept one foot on the floor as an anchor and hunched over the mug of steaming coffee while massaging his temples.

Slowly, the fog cleared. It was Saturday. That was good. No one would be looking for him. That was one problem out of the way. Which left that other thing, the waking up with Angie pressed against him and her underwear looped around his damn arm. *That* thing. *Ugh.*

The hot coffee tasted bitter as it washed over his tongue and down his throat leaving behind a burning trail of leftover tequila vapors. The only thing keeping him sane at the moment was the relative certainty he was clinging to that he hadn't done anything too horribly stupid despite the evidence of the pink silk presently pushed into his back pocket.

Nothing much from the end of their drunken frolic remained in his memory, but he was pretty damn sure there was no fucking way he'd had the ability to perform considering how trashed he was. That and the fact that he awoke fully dressed, boots still on, and as far as he could tell, still wearing his briefs, went a long way to keeping him from overreacting.

The panties, though. That bothered him. How the hell had her panties ended up wrapped around his arm? He suspected they'd never know for sure.

"Thanks for pouring me one, too," he heard a voice gripe.

Slamming a mug onto the counter loud enough that he grimaced at the jarring sound, Angie got herself a coffee and joined him, only from the other side of the island.

"What time is it?" she asked before taking her first sip.

With his head still in his hands, Parker peered between his fingers at the clock on the wall. "Nine ten," he told her.

She nodded but didn't say anything else or look in his direction.

Parker looked her over, searching for clues. She'd done a damn good job of pulling it together although the buttons on her blouse were out of sync, making the fabric gap at just the right spot to give him a clear glimpse of the sheer bra she had on and a peek-a-boo vantage point for a dusty pink nipple.

He should probably tell her, but the view was so enticing and offered a distraction from the bass drum pounding in his head so he said nothing—just sat there, sipping his coffee, slowly coming back to life while flat-out fantasizing about licking the tiny nub and nibbling at it while she thrashed and moaned.

"I want my undies back," she snapped. Was that indignation he detected in her voice? He didn't know exactly how he came to be the one in possession of her panties, but he was certain he hadn't wrestled them off her. She had nerve playing the outraged innocent.

"The fuck you say," he drawled sarcastically to her stupid request. "You gave 'em to me and I'm keeping them."

He had no idea if any of that was true. He just liked needling her.

"You're an asshole when you're hung over."

He snickered. Yeah. He was. "I'll make it up to you tonight."

"How ya figure?"

"'Cause I'll be the one cheering the loudest when y'all take the stage at Pete's."

Flashing her his very best although decidedly hung over, Tom Cruise style toothy grin, he added, "And if you're a good girl," he paused when he saw a flare that threatened the safety of his testicles move across her expression and grinned broader, "I'll invite you to the mic at the end of the night."

"Why would you do that?" she asked.

"Because Pete asked Desert Thunder to close out after karaoke."

"You're playing tonight, too?"

"Uh-huh."

He watched a slew of emotions shift on her face and waited for her comeback. Would she sing with him in public? She had to know the significance of him making such an offer. There'd be no doubt what his fucking intentions were if he ever got her next to him on stage.

A soft but getting louder by the second commotion was building behind him making Parker swivel in his seat to see what was going on. He heard Red's voice and someone else.

From a different angle, he saw that Alex, Cam, and Drae had appeared, standing off to the side across from him and Angie and away from where Meghan was coming from.

What the hell was going on? Those three looked mighty suspicious over there—almost like they were waiting for something. And how the hell had they managed to creep up on them without being noticed? *Fucking hangover.*

Meghan's gentle laughter filled the air. As she came closer, he heard her say, "Can I get you anything? Coffee? Tea? Some water? We can wait in the kitchen. I'm sure Carmen will find her shortly and . . ."

As she rounded the archway into the big open room, Meghan stumbled to a halt when she caught sight of him and Angie, a look of worried tension all over her face.

"Oh, my! Angie. There you are. We were looking all over for you."

The look Meghan gave him made his skin prickle. Parker sat up straighter. Red's tone signaled something was up. He glanced sharply at Angie, her mouth hanging open and a look of pure shock that slammed into him.

What the fuck?

Following the direction of her gaze, he turned back toward Meghan and felt the bottom drop out of his stomach. *You've got to be fucking kidding.*

"Uh, Angie," Meghan tittered nervously. "You've got a visitor."

Last year, an up and coming turd in the D.A.'s office had blindsided Parker with a surprise witness at the eleventh hour of a trial that left him flabbergasted and flat-footed. Two things he did not like. This, right here, felt a little like that.

For Angie's part . . . she became a statue. One made of cold marble because whatever color she'd regained after washing up and having some coffee had quickly disappeared. She was pale as death and looked like she saw a ghost.

Not surprisingly, this so-called visitor had a slimy sounding, unctuous voice that set his nerves on edge.

"Querida. Why do you seem so surprised? Surely you knew how impossible you are to give up."

Was this douchebag kidding?

"A-Aldo," Angie sputtered. "What are you doing here?"

A deep, red haze seeped into Parker's vision. So this little fucker was that Esperanza prick. Prepared to hate him on sight, the puny hipster didn't disappoint. Wearing a blazer so blindingly white it looked fake, he had a fucking navy blue pocket square that matched his slacks and the polka-dotted tie that perfectly complemented the medium blue of his dress shirt. The red haze turned dark and dangerous. Fucker was wearing skinny jeans. Who the hell wore those things? They were fucking undignified if you asked him.

All in all, Parker thought he looked perfect for target practice. What in the fucking fuck had she ever seen in this pretentious poser?

He watched silently as the one-dimensional stick drawing masquerading as a dude, skirted around the island and went to a still speechless Angie.

"Darling." He chuckled.

Parker already hated the asshole's heavy accent.

"What is this you are wearing? Is this how the horse girls dress?" he asked as he went in for a two cheeked Euro-hug. "You do know there's a hole for every button, hmmm?"

The minute the shithead touched her, Parker was on his feet. Uh, he didn't think so . . . but before he could take a step, Meghan was right there with her hand on his shoulder and a warning look in her eyes.

She gasped and looked down. Seeing her blouse gaping open, she glared at Parker as she fixed the damage. When Angie found her voice, she took a hasty step backward and crossed her arms in front of her. She couldn't say back off any louder, but the stick figure didn't seem to notice.

"Um, it's cowgirls and I am not your darling."

He'd had enough. Moving from Meghan's restraining grip, he started in Angie's direction only to find Alex coming at him from behind. He felt him yank on his pocket, sending him off balance so he had to plop back down, followed by his hand doing something else in the area of the pocket.

Whispering so only Parker could hear, Alex drawled, "Pink isn't your color, shithead."

His hand immediately swung to his rear and slid inside the pocket where Alex had stuffed Angie's panties deeper where they wouldn't be seen.

He glared at his friend with frustration and escalating possessiveness that he knew Alex would understand. Was he really expected to just sit here and let that limp-wristed pansy ass touch his woman?

Once Alex made his presence known, Meghan dragged him forward for an introduction.

"Ronaldo Esperanza, this is my fiancé and Angelina's brother, Major Alexander Valleja-Marquez."

That she used his formal title said a lot. Meghan wasn't going to take this guy's shit either.

Transforming before everyone's eyes into the undisputed Big Daddy of Family Justice, the Major—and Parker used that term snidely—extended his hand and spoke in a voice he'd known him to use when scaring the agency's recruits.

"Mr. Esperanza," the Major said smoothly. "I didn't expect we'd be meeting."

Snap. Parker wanted to high five his old friend. Subtle putdown. Perfectly delivered.

Ronnie's handshake was exactly the type of phantom creep out that guys like him and the Justice brothers generally mocked. The bony hand came out but just as quickly slithered back—like he was afraid of being touched.

From the shadows, a duet of comical snickers told him Cam and Drae had seen and were also marveling at the fuckstick. Shooting them an eye-rolling look, he was relieved when they came forward—ready to engage.

At the same time, Carmen bustled into the kitchen from the back door, saw Meghan, and immediately started jabbering that she looked everywhere but hadn't found Señorita Angelina. This was turning into a circus.

Angie started awkwardly and put her hand in the air like a kid during roll-taking. "I'm here, Carmen," she mumbled. "Sorry. I was . . . um, in the barn earlier."

She looked at him, but her face was almost on fire whether from embarrassment or anxiety, he didn't know. Perhaps both.

Drae was almost at Parker's shoulder when he exclaimed, "Who's your little friend, Ang? I don't think we've met."

Cam cleared his throat when Drae referred to the stranger in their midst as Angie's little friend. Those fuckers. They were going to be laughing about this later. Goddammit.

It took Parker a good minute to realize that Alex, Cam, Drae, and Meghan had positioned themselves in such a way that he was effectively caged in. They obviously knew how close he was to losing it. Might be funny any other time. Now? Not so much.

"Oh," Angie said peevishly. "Right. Everyone, this is my . . . uh, friend. Ronaldo Esperanza. I had no idea he was coming," she insisted. "Aldo, um . . . obviously you've met my sister-in-law, Meghan, and my brother, Alexander."

"Not a sister-in-law just yet though, eh?"

The asshole looked at Meghan like she was a threat to humanity. Probably because she could bench press the skinny little bastard in her sleep. If Alex didn't smack the shit out of this fucker, he would.

"Yes, well . . . a mere formality, I assure you," Angie snapped defensively. "Close enough."

"As you say," he simpered with a derisive smirk.

Motherfucking asshole. Parker looked at Drae and Cam and pleaded with his eyes. *Come on, guys. Let's kick this shithead's ass.* They didn't react, but he could tell both of them were ready to snap.

"And who might these others be? Ranch hands?"

Ranch hands? RANCH HANDS? Okay, that was it. He was going to chew this fucker up and spit him out. Breakfast special style.

Alex's mouth opened like he was about to say something, but Parker beat him to it. Sliding between his two handlers, he made straight for the obnoxious turdage in their midst and approached him like a hostile witness he was about to destroy.

Pointing at Cam and Drae, he dug out his Supreme-Court-Judge act and laid it on kinda thick. The Garth Brooks t-shirt and jeans probably didn't help so he relied on his physicality to make an impression.

"Yeah, ranch hands—those two," he emphasized as he crowded Angie's little friend with his size.

Without bothering to put out his hand, he nailed the white-jacketed pussy to the spot with a baleful glare.

"Parker Sullivan. *Esquire*," he added with a sneer as he speared Angie with a quick look. "I am the Major's personal attorney."

He saw the flare of concern in the other man's eyes. Finding out there was a lawyer in the mix usually made the weak go silent.

After he was sure his words had made an impression, he arrogantly pushed the pretentious prick out of the way and went right up to Angie. Pressing a kiss to her forehead, he slung an arm casually around her shoulders and added, "My firm has handled all of the Marquez family affairs for years. And Angie, here?" He smiled at her, but he made sure she saw the challenge in his eyes. "I've known her long enough to have changed a few of her diapers."

Carmen snickered.

Meghan outright laughed.

Angie groaned.

Drae muttered, "Dude," with a choked laugh, and Cam nudged Alex's shoulder when the man snorted out loud.

Parker had absolutely no doubt he was going to pay for that speech.

"I see," Ronnie said.

Yep. He just bet he did.

"Why are you here, Aldo?" Angie muttered anxiously. "And where are you staying? How did you find your way to the Villa?"

Looking annoyed as all hell, clearly Mister Skinny Jeans wasn't up for an audience, he made a lame attempt to convince Angie they needed to speak privately.

"We should talk, querida. Your father thought we might clear the air, too. That's how I knew where to come," he said sanctimoniously as if that particular grenade had any real explosive power.

What an idiot.

"My *father* sent you?" Angie made no effort not to shriek when she asked.

Meghan chewed the inside of her mouth, and he saw the unmistakable curl of laughter on her lips. Do not mess with a daughter where her daddy was concerned.

Turning blazing eyes on her brother, Angie angrily barked, "Dad did this? I swear, Alexander—if you knew and didn't tell me . . ."

Alex jumped like he'd been shot. "I just talked to him the other day, and he never mentioned any of this." The look he gave Esperanza didn't bode well for that man's life if he was lying.

Carmen, knowing full well she was stirring the pot as evidenced by her comic tone, turned to Meghan and politely inquired if she would like her to have Ben take the luggage of Miss Angie's guest to the casita.

At the mention of luggage, Angie looked around frantically as if she suddenly realized that a visitor from Spain wasn't just hanging out for fifteen minutes and then hitting the road.

When Parker heard the word casita, he went apeshit. *Over his fucking dead body.* No romantic and very private little hacienda-bungalow was in that ass munch's future. Thank Christ, Cam jumped in and saved the day.

"No can do, I'm afraid. My wife is redecorating the casita in preparation for guests when the Marquez clan descends after the wedding," he informed everyone like what he was saying was even remotely based on fact.

Parker knew better. Nobody was using the casita because the Villa was big enough to house everyone. He knew this because his folks were making all sorts of plans for Ashleigh and Cristián's extended visit. It was one big happy and the family would be staying under one roof.

"The apartment Victoria used above the business center is empty right now," Drae offered as an alternative.

Good. That was settled. Parker didn't rest on ceremony nor did he let Alex or Meghan handle any of the details. Acting like lord of the fucking manor, he instructed Carmen to freshen up the small studio and told her to have Ben take care of the luggage.

Throughout all of this, Angie didn't say much. Or move. She seemed frozen like she was watching from an out-of-body perspective.

Fuck. He should have made love to her last night whether they'd been trashed or not. If he had, this whole ridiculous conversation would be moot.

Chapter Forty-Nine

GALES OF LAUGHTER FILLED THE cramped dressing room at Whiskey Pete's as Angie readied for the big night ahead with her new friends. They were going on after the group presently belting out a bunch of stage hits and after having seen what everyone else had to offer, she and the girls were going to bring the house down.

"Beside the sore nipples, these baby boobs are bangin'!" Tori hooted gleefully. Wearing a completely see through lace blouse with a black push-up bra visible underneath and a pair of indecent Daisy Dukes, Draegyn's wife looked every inch the naughty MILF. The lace-up ankle boots that added several inches to her tiny stature gave vampy a run for the title.

Meghan roared with laughter. "I heard Draegyn refer to them as a double handful."

Tori giggled. "Why am I not surprised my husband was discussing my boobs with the Major?"

"Cam was there, too," Meghan added with an apologetic hand gesture to Lacey and an *Oops, my bad,* smirk.

Lacey shook her head and laughed along. Working on putting in an earring, she cocked a hip at Tori and told them all rather drily that, "You know damn well once we hit that stage, they'll be high-fiving each other about the tits and ass."

"Holy crap!" Meghan yelled. "Did my ears hear you correctly Mrs. Cameron? Did you just utter the expression *TITS* and *ASS?*"

Tori gasped dramatically and clutched at her heart. "Oh, my god. Has hell frozen over?"

Angie was the first to break apart in giggles. Teasing Lacey and her sometimes-prudish behavior was their go-to comic relief. In the simplest of girlfriend terms, Lacey was their Charlotte, a reference anyone who ever watched *Sex and the City* would understand. There were some people who were just naturally sweet.

"Do I look okay," she asked with a hurried twirl. "This outfit seemed like such a good idea a few days ago, but I'm not so sure now."

Meghan *tsked* a couple of times. "Now, now sweetie. You look fantastic—absolutely perfect for the part you're playing."

God, Angie thought. She hoped so.

"You certainly did bring it, girlfriend!" Lacey cooed. "Nicely done."

Victoria winked at her. "That's what we call a fist fight outfit, Angel. I'm thinking that dress—or lack thereof," she snickered as the other two laughed, "and those *I-Dare-You-To-Fuck-Me* boots are going to unleash the Kraken."

Unleashing the Kraken. That was what she was afraid of.

What a friggin' shit show this whole day had been. First waking up with the evil stepmother of all hangovers and discovering she and the hunky lawyer had passed out dead drunk in the barn, and then Aldo's surprise arrival and all the complications that brought. And then, the uncomfortable conversation with her dad because she hadn't been able to stop from calling him with a demand to know what he'd been thinking.

She'd been out of her mind, of course, to take a tone with her father, and he'd let her have it with both barrels. Threw down a slew of uncomfortable truths—told her to get her shit in order, and without actually saying so, alluded to being on Team Parker should it ever come to a vote.

After Aldo had gotten settled in the studio apartment, she'd gone and talked to him, leaving forty minutes later before she lost it and throttled him. She'd broken their engagement. Ended the relationship. Moved on. What part of that didn't he understand? And why did he keep insisting that she just needed to *get this out of her system.* What exactly was *this?*

And then Parker. He'd flat out refused to leave the Villa and Alex, that jerk, had just shrugged and said nothing. He'd cornered her in the courtyard and given her a raft of shit, which she promptly served right back to him. She hadn't asked Aldo to come and Parker could go fuck himself with a donkey dick, she believed was how she put it, for handing her a pile of grief over something she had no control over.

The part where he grabbed her, growled something about belonging to him and how he didn't share, then kissed her senseless . . . well, somehow that tawdry little interlude was the high point of her day.

With an angry, frustrated lawyer hovering about and Aldo behaving like a royal fucknut, she was unraveling fast. He'd protested and bitched like a spoiled brat about the group outing to Pete's—even going so far as to express an objection to her performing in public.

Apparently, any potential for public embarrassment was to be avoided at all costs—even if you were in on the joke. When had he become such a stick up the ass?

The drive to Pete's had been a nightmare. Because there was no way in hell Parker was leaving her alone with Aldo, Alex had decided the five of them would ride together in the limo. Overkill, for sure, but somehow Angie was relieved. She needed her brother to referee if things got ugly.

Inside the big car, Meghan and Alex took the seat at the back while Parker—who spread out and took up an entire bank of seats—sat at the opposite end. She and Aldo were awkwardly together along the side with both Parker and Alex cross-armed, glaring at her unwelcome companion as he launched into a running and uncomplimentary commentary about her outfit. What was the big deal? She wore jeans and an old t-shirt because they'd dress at the club so she really didn't get what his objection was.

By the time they pulled into Pete's, she was a bundle of nerves and wondering what the hell Aldo was wearing. All she could hope for was that some drunk cowboy didn't try to use him as a Q-tip.

He'd recoiled in horror while walking across the rough, rocky parking lot, making ridiculously snotty remarks and condescending noises about everything from the preponderance of pickup trucks to the rowdy noise coming from inside.

The minute they had their hands stamped and were through the door, Lacey and Tori came running up to her, anxious to meet Aldo after having no doubt gotten an earful from their husbands.

They were dressed similarly to her, which only amped up Aldo's dislike of the casual, informal honky-tonk atmosphere. What had she ever seen in him? He'd always been pretentious. Trust fund kids couldn't avoid it most times, but he used to be at least a little bit of fun. Hadn't he?

Introductions over, everyone split up for various reasons—it was some time till they'd get their turn in the dressing room and there was schmoozing and drinking to do. So Aldo deftly swept her off to a remote table in the far back of the bar, away from all the action. *Oh great,* she'd grumbled. He was going to start whining. At the table, he dropped like a bratty kid into a chair, leaving her standing, which was not a smart move on his part.

Say whatever you want about Family Justice and all the good ol' cowboy types driving those expensive trucks lined up out in the parking—they knew their damn manners and treated women like ladies. She'd rarely had to navigate her own chair whenever anyone else was around.

Dropping her bag on the table with a thwack, she thought, *What a dick,* then yanked her chair out only to loudly slam it on the floor for emphasis—not that he noticed.

And then it started. *Wah-wah-wah.* This place is a nightmare. Tacky. Dirty. And the injustice of being sneered at when he ordered a glass of white wine at the bar. The horror! My god. How would he ever get over it?

When they'd gotten their drinks, just to be perverse, she went with a Corona because he deemed the brand piss-water. *Moron.* Corona and lime were practically a requirement growing up. Taking a long draw from the ice-cold beer, she watched Aldo nervously fiddle with a pinky ring as he bitched. Angie listened impassively noticing a hundred different things that had nothing to do with his childish tirade.

Informing him that the evening's outing would be casual, she figured he'd dress appropriately. Who in their right mind traveled halfway across the globe to the American Southwest and not have a pair of jeans with them? Ronaldo Esperanza, that was who.

The standard dress code for guys at Pete's was pretty basic. Flannel, leather, t-shirt, denim, boots, cowboy hat. Some half-flaming poser in a pair of shiny looking light gray slacks with a button-down shirt, tie, and vest stood out like an agent in SWAT gear at a kid's birthday party. Oh, yeah. And he had on yellow socks. Something about a pop of color. And the glass of white wine? Really? Would it have killed him to have a beer? Embrace the culture maybe?

What. A. Douche. And she'd actually thought marrying this guy was a swell idea? Her parents should have held an intervention.

"Querida," he drawled unctuously. "This slumming, it's beneath you. These cowboys," he spat out derisively, "is this a phase, my dear? Big muscles and tattoos?"

Peeved with his attitude, Angie attacked her beer and sat back staring at him while he went on and on and on and. . . . oh, for fuck's sake. "When did you become such a pretentious snot?" she finally asked.

"I beg your pardon," he barked with outrage. "I am not a snot, Angelina, but I do know my place, and until today, I thought you knew yours as well."

"What is that supposed to mean, Aldo?"

He looked at her like she had two heads. "You ask when I changed and I ask when you became so obtuse. Why must you be so friendly with everyone? The workers at your family home, these . . . people," he indicated with a wag of his head toward the whole room. "You're a Marquez, my dear. That may not mean anything more than a clean glass and a cold beer here, but at home, you are the product of an old, proud family with deep roots in Spanish society."

She wasn't obtuse, nor was she a product. He was an asshole and she'd had enough. Unfortunately though, he was correct about one thing, although he was expressing himself so clumsily, it was a miracle she hadn't decked him yet.

He was right. The truth was that the Marquez thing actually did mean something in Spain. But here? No big whup. Being part of Family Justice carried more weight than her birth name. And while she'd like to kick his ass to the curb and forget this unfortunate situation had ever happened, she knew she'd have to tread softly. Her behavior would reflect on the winery and her parents. *Shit.*

"Aldo, for the tenth time—why are you here? I spoke to my father and he tells me that he at no time suggested you come after me so please don't insult me or my family again by pretending this surprise visit was sanctioned or in any way thought of as a good idea."

He fiddled with that stupid ring some more and adjusted his tie, looking around at the unfolding bar scene with clear distaste. "I want you to come home, Angelina. We were good together and a marriage between our two families is advantageous on both sides. I understand your need to return to the scenes of your childhood, but our life is in Spain, my dear. We have invitations to Cannes and Monte Carlo."

Again, his disparaging glance around the bar made her furious.

"Why would you want to remain here, dressed like a homesteader when we could be enjoying the life we were creating at home?"

"We weren't invited to any of those things," she bit out. *Pretentious fuck!* "You have clients . . . talent, that are booked for those events, so don't make it seem like we were some Euro power couple. That's bullshit and you know it."

She sneered when he jerked in response to her words. He disliked swearing. Thought it was unladylike. *Bah!*

The two sides of Angie's life clashed head-on. Her life in the States versus the things expected of her at her other home in Spain. It saddened her that the two couldn't play nice with each other but that was the way it was. Until she let one place or the other claim her once and for all, she was stuck in the middle.

"I have to go join the girls."

He didn't react. She'd wondered if that was because if he did, then he'd have to admit that all this was real. That she was real and he didn't belong here.

"Look, Aldo—I don't want to argue. We are not getting back together. I made my decision months ago and you've been silent all this time. But you're here now, at least for a couple of days, so loosen up and try to have a good time."

She grabbed her bag and started to leave, then turned back for a last comment, "And try not to overreact when we take the stage. This is a bit of harmless fun and I'd appreciate it . . . actually, fuck that. I demand that you not embarrass me."

She turned on her heel as he sputtered, outraged, at her language and got the hell out of there fast.

Parker's eyes narrowed and the dark, dangerous thoughts he was nursing along with his beer got even uglier when he saw that slimy shit put his perfectly manicured fingers on his Angel and lead her into a back corner of the bar.

Fucker. You could slink away into the shadows, you spineless prick, but you can't hide. I'm watching. And joke's on you, shiny pants, 'cause I know her ass and the language it speaks better than anyone alive and that tight hipped, boxed in stomp she was doing? Yeah—that didn't bode well for Ronnie-boy.

Parker did his own sliding into the shadows, making his way around the dark perimeter of the room until he was almost close enough to hear their conversation without being seen.

Minutes ticked by. His beer emptied. They kept talking and he kept studying her body language. Lawyer habit. Besides the fact that she looked as relaxed as a rattler about to strike, Parker was intrigued by her choice of clothes. All the ladies were in jeans to start because they would be changing into stage clothes, but it was her outfit at a *closer look* that tantalized him.

She was wearing a pair of jeans that surely had to be illegal in some countries. Old, well-worn, and dangerously tight, they gave her ass a moment in the spotlight. But it was the t-shirt that stopped him short. Was she sending him a message? Had to be. No other reason for her to wear that shirt or even have it in the first damn place. The minute he saw it, he knew he'd been right to absolutely refuse to head home earlier and meet up with everyone later.

No fucking way was he leaving her side. Not while she sported a faded Blakely & Hughes V-neck that had seen better days. Blakeley & Hughes was the law firm he played baseball with during the D.C. years. Angie had spent many a Saturday afternoon cheering him on from the stands.

"Yo, Parker," a deep voice boomed, startling him from his reverie. "What up, bro?"

"Hey, Barry. How's it going?" He responded with a friendly handshake. "I didn't see you behind the bar. You working or here to see the show?"

The tattooed guy chuckled. "Slamming drinks tonight and happy to do it, too! Make a crapload of dollars when your girls hit the stage. Look at this crowd, man." He laughed. "I swear this is all for them," he snickered. "Oh yeah and for Desert Thunder. You're doing the close out, huh?"

Parker grunted. "That's what they tell me." He held up his empty, "We'll see how that goes after a fuckton more of these."

Barry frowned and shook his head. "It's your gal, huh? She still running?"

Oh, jeez. Running he could deal with. This other? He wasn't sure.

"Nah. Pinned her down . . . well, got her to slow her fucking roll and we were making progress and then . . ."

"The little prick in the sweater vest?"

Sneering, he nodded. "Ah, I see you've noticed."

The burly bartender studied the object of their derision. "Bet he shaves his balls," he murmured.

"Yeah, and gets his ass bleached," Parker added.

Cue the guy laughter.

"Dude," he growled. "Any way to put that asshole on the floor? What's he drinking?"

"Ah, fuck. Wine." And then Barry laughed like hell. "Jesus. I wonder if he realizes he's drinking grape from a box? Don't worry, man," he assured him. "I'll keep an eye on him."

After Barry had walked away, Parker did a double take when he heard Angie's voice start to rise. He wasn't actively trying to eavesdrop, but she was making it hard not to. *Ooooh.* He knew that tone. Snarky Angel was spreading her wings tonight. *Ah hahahahaaa!*

He clearly heard her say, "We are not getting back together." Would anyone notice if he broke out some Michael Jackson moves in celebration? He looked around. All he saw were people on their way to being shitfaced. Even a bit of comic moonwalking would end up getting his ass kicked.

And then she let loose with a pithy, "Fuck that! I demand you not embarrass me."

Laughing quietly, he rose from his chair and eyeballed her tight-assed retreat. Judging the performance, he'd say she was hovering somewhere between *What a dick* and *Imma' kick his ass.* Shiny pants might not realize it yet, but he was toast.

Chapter Fifty

AS THE YOUNG KID WHO took care of the equipment ran around setting things up for them to take the stage, the ladies gathered in the wings waiting to go on. Angie was a bundle of nerves. Meghan, Lacey, and Victoria? Cool as could be.

"Relax!" Meghan chuckled, giving Angie a hearty side hug. You look ah-mazing," she drawled. "Prepare for the house to go wild when they get a look at you, sister!"

"My god, ladies, if y'all weren't spoken for by that troop of Justice ghouls, I'd be refereeing a bar wide fist fight tonight. Your men know you leave the house looking like this?"

"Pete!" Tori squealed. Leaping into his arms for a quick hug, he dropped her down and shook his head looking at them.

So this was the legendary Whiskey Pete. Lacey warned Angie to expect him to show up tonight. Apparently, it was quite the honor to have the venerable old man walk you out to center stage. According to legend, he was a battle-scarred Vietnam Vet with nothing more than a bad ass chopper and a backpack to his name when he opened the ramshackle honky-tonk.

He had an enormous soft spot for the Justice crew, occasionally working with the agency on veterans' issues. Carmen told her that before Justice was even Justice, Alex had been involved in investigating a charge of drug running that was hanging over the bar's head and ruining Pete's spotless reputation. Lots of folks attributed that one event and the guys saving Pete's ass with giving eventual birth to the current day Justice Agency.

And the man himself? He had a case of the grins where Victoria St. John was concerned. It was Pete who declared the little spitfire to be 'sassy' and the moniker just stuck after that.

"And who do we have here?" the old man asked as he zeroed in on Angie. She liked him on sight. He reminded her of her dad; they were probably close in age with the sort of deep, expressive eyes that had stories to tell.

Victoria jumped in with an introduction as Pete snagged her hand and, quite simply, wouldn't let go. Angie giggled and shook her head—a little embarrassed.

"Pete Allen," Tori intoned somberly. "Allow me to introduce Senõrita Angelina Marquez." She put quite a bit of meaningful spin on her last name, which earned the appropriate eyebrow arch from Pete.

Smiling impishly at Angie, Tori continued the impressively grave introduction. Hollywood missed out with her!

"Senõrita Marquez, this is the whiskey man himself, Mr. Pete Allen of Bend-You-Over-the-Bar, Arizona."

Looking at Pete, she drawled in a smart-alecky voice, "She has that lovely baby sister look, doesn't she?"

Angie giggled and blushed as the old man continued smiling warmly at her. With a twinkle in his eye and a lopsided grin, he said, "Now that I've met you, Lovely Angelina, I can forgive your mother for that sorry piece of shit you're saddled with as a brother."

As far as gracious opening lines went, that one was an instant classic.

He dropped her hand as they all laughed and scooted out of the way while some people squeezed by.

Chortling he drawled, "You ready? Time for this old man to hog the spotlight." He touched his bolo tie and ran a hand over his impressive, gray mustache.

"Oh, wait!" Tori chirped and ran to his side. Rising up on her tiptoes, he bent to the side to listen as she whispered something in his ear.

Laughing, he straightened and bellowed, "Understood! Boy, I hope this old place can handle you four," and with that, he wandered out to the main stage spotlight.

"Ready, girls?" Lacey chuckled. "I don't know about you, but I want that ugly trophy so let's blow the roof off this joint and show these good ol' boys how it gets done . . . Justice style."

Justice style. Perfect. She was a Justice now. Remembering Aldo's scowling presence, she grunted dismissively. She'd made her decision.

"Okay, okay, okay. Settle down boys and girls," Pete boomed into the microphone as catcalls and thunderous applause greeted his arrival on stage.

"Thanks for sharing the love, but you're nucking futz if you think that's gonna get y'all any free beers!"

The cheers and laughter suddenly turned to good-spirited, "Boos," and cries of, "You suck!"

Grinning, he taunted his customers with practiced lines that were met with raucous applause. Angie's smile as she listened was so big it almost hurt.

"There's a mark on the floor and a sign outside my door that says . . . *Dick Suckers Line up Here.*"

The crowd erupted with laughter, and she could hear people saying, "You first, Brad," and, "Down on your knees, pal."

Nothing like working the shitfaced crowd into a frenzy.

"Now that we have that settled," Pete smirked, "let's get down to business. Moving up in the brackets with a firm showing in the early competitions is a Whiskey Pete's favorite . . . the ladies of Justice. Now ya'll know them as Ass, Boots, and Sass . . ."

Wild applause broke out.

"Well, kids, got a real treat in store for you tonight. I want you to give these little ladies a thunderous welcome okay? So get ready to rock the motherfuck out. Bringing it red rocks style are Ass, Boots and Sass with a special appearance tonight-for the first time anywhere-*Desert Angel!*"

It sounded like a football stadium the cheers were so loud as the four of them strolled hand-in-hand onto the little stage. Familiar faces were in the crowd, and right down front, like bouncers forming a perimeter, were Alex, Draegyn, Cameron and . . . Parker!

She'd remember the look on his face till her dying breath. In the simplest of terms? His expression suggested he was on life support. Heat exploded inside her and she secretly gladdened that she'd chosen to wear self-adhesive nipple pasties rather than go braless under these stage lights. The minute she saw him her damn nips puckered tight and the last thing she needed was the whole audience getting a detailed picture of her tits.

Wearing what is best described as a little black dress, she suddenly worried that it was too much. Too edgy. Too right on the line of being slutty. Short—too short, it was an off the shoulder slouchy thing that molded to her breasts. She'd pushed the arms back to her elbows and slid on a bunch of brightly colored bangles that twinkled under the lights.

With her long black hair, ruby red lips, and the exaggerated stage make-up, she looked like Snow White trolling for her Prince. But it was the boots she wore that made the outfit. And they were outrageous with a capital O.

Thigh-high suede with platforms and fuck-me-till-I-scream heels that made her walk with a hip rolling swagger got the cowboys on their feet in a hurry.

Sass immediately commandeered the microphone, adjusting it to her height. Slapping her hands on her hips, she stood there in her Daisy Dukes and grinned broadly at the enthusiastic crowd.

Someone yelled, "You look fucking hot tonight," which got Tori laughing.

Snickering, she jeered, "Hey, I remember my first beer, too!"

The room erupted in cheers and applause.

"Pretending to read from an imaginary piece of paper, she chirped into the mic . . ."Okay, kids. I've just been handed a note here from Pete. Apparently, some dumbass peckerwood built a statue of his horse in the men's room toilet and clogged the pipes."

Screams of laughter filled the air.

"So, gentlemen . . . from now till closing . . . y'all are instructed to hold onto your shit!"

Tori was a natural. Who knew? What was the definition of vamp? Because Mrs. St. John needed her own one-woman show to showcase her theatrical talent. Her mama sure would be proud.

In full cowgirl-diva mode, Sass fluffed the exaggerated hairstyle she had going on, then put both hands on her girls and gave them a good wobble, which was met with thunderous approval from the rowdy crowd.

In the voice Tori said was her very best *Southern Gal twang,* she worked the crowd over like a pro.

"Now, I know some of y'all are wondering who's who," loud catcalls and whistles split the air, "but before we take care of all you, uh . . . cowboys," she drawled so cutely, Angie had to giggle, "to all you ladies out there? Girls, while your men are staring at us. . . . relax! You can stare at our men while yours act like idiots. Gentlemen, where are you?" she called out.

Roaring with good-humored laughter, Alex, Cam, Drae and Parker swung around, faced the crowd, and raised their hands. A comic low rumble of discontent from the men in the bar met this announcement while a distinctive, appreciative hum from all the ladies got louder and louder.

Tori was a genius. She'd hilariously defused any bullshit coming at them from the women in the audience and effectively brought them in on the joke. Which in turn guaranteed that all the men could feel free to go hog wild without paying a price later. Win—win!

"Okay, so who's ready to get their karaoke on?"

More wild applause.

"Well, get ready to dance your panties off. Without any more yackety yak, let me introduce to you . . .

"Ass!" And with that, Lacey sashayed forward, her blond beauty shimmering in the spotlight. The tight blue sheath that clung to her from collarbone to mid-thigh looked adorable from the front but when she turned around, shit got real. The entire back of the dress was open from the collar down to the top of her butt and was cut in a way that totally accentuated the woman's outrageously perfect ass.

Settling into a flirty pose, she blew a kiss to her husband and beamed at the enthusiastic response from the crowd.

"Boots!" Tori hollered next as Meghan came forward and quite literally knocked socks off in an emerald green lace dress—one of those stretchy things that could stop traffic. Especially so since this one showed off her voluptuous attributes with a choker style neckline that opened to a heart-shaped bodice.

Angie noticed Alex down in front throw up his hands like he was shooting, "Score!" as the guys smacked him on the back and roared with delight.

Meghan had applied a soft sheen of glitter to her ample cleavage which replayed down the front of her toned legs, but the icing on her sexy cake were an outrageous pair of high heeled, cowgirl boots complete with rhinestones and crystals that caught the stage lights, and frankly, made her look like a million bucks.

Acknowledging the booming applause, Meghan also moved into an exaggerated pose, next to Lacey, with a foot up on a wood box at the edge of the stage.

Tori giggled into the mic. "And I, of course, would be the Sass!" she proclaimed with a stripper shimmy that would rival that of the most seasoned pole dancer.

Parker and Drae high-fived, which only made Angie laugh more.

"Which brings us to a very special appearance tonight by the newest lady in our modest sewing circle." That comment was met with loud guffaws and a number of pithy shouted comments.

"Hold on to your privates, boys, 'cause this one comes with not only a big brother," Angie heard Alex let out a thundering, "Boo-yah," "but an ambulance chasing boyfriend as well!"

Loud boos and groans filled the room. Angie giggled knowing that Aldo was probably shitting himself by this point and hearing Parker referred to as her boyfriend, well . . . fuck it. Wasn't far from the truth.

"So let me hear a supersized cowboy howdy for the spicy senõrita known as Desert Angel!" With that, Tori backed up and took her spot next to Meghan and Lacey in what was now apparent as their own version of the Charlie's Angels pose.

Showtime!

Striding confidently into the spotlight, Angie knew she had this and that they were gonna have the time of their lives.

At first, she pretended to be shy and embarrassed by the attention, going so far as to strike an innocent, pigeon-toed pose as she twirled a curl and hid her eyes while the men went apeshit.

Softly speaking into the microphone, she used a little girl voice and started speaking in nervous, rapid, breathy Spanish. The whole room got quiet to hear what she was saying.

When she had everyone's rapt attention, she laughed loudly, waved a hand at the audience and joked, "Nah, I'm just messing with you! Arizona proud! Born and raised right here in the red rocks."

The room erupted with regional fervor and appreciation. She grinned. Drunk cowboys were so easy sometimes!

"Who's ready to rock?" she asked . . . nodding at the dude handling the impressive karaoke setup and moved into her assigned spot in their group pose. Flashes from cell phone cameras twinkled and she heard Lacey compliment her, "Nicely done, Angel!"

Yeah. No shit. When she took her place, and stood, legs wide in a pose she'd practiced that paid homage to every comic book vixen every imagined, Angie knew the thigh-high boots and the barely-there dress held in place by her breasts, were a provocation she'd have to answer for later.

And then the fun began. She wasn't spouting nonsense when she said these girls needed a record contract. All of them were natural singers and took to the playful stage acting to sell their performances like fish to water. In short, Ass, Boots, and Sass kicked the butt and then some.

The competition rules say each group chose four songs and then a song from the house list that had tunes from every imaginable genre and time. For their last number, the crowd got to request a song and the karaoke DJ made the final choice. Half an hour of spotlight hell!

Lacey got things started with a spirited rendition, sexy mama style, of *Hit Me with Your Best Shot.* One of their advantages was the fact that Tori grew up watching her mom organize beauty pageants so she knew a thing or two about talent competition. So while Lacey sang her heart out, strutting back and forth across the stage with a rock swagger Pat Benatar could be proud of, the girls ran through a series of bumps, grinds, dance steps, and synchronized shimmies that thrilled the crowd.

It was exhilarating, being on stage with her friends, enjoying the response, and watching their guys down in front actually getting into their performance. She couldn't wait to tell Soph how much fun she was having.

Though she didn't say it out loud, Ang was hoping that by embracing what she really wanted out of life, she'd set an example for her big sister—hoping that she'd find the courage to do the same. Sophie had some shadows in her personal life that had made being happy a hit or miss proposition.

"That was great!" Lacey gushed when the song was over. "Did you see Cameron?" She was giggling and peeking at her husband over Meghan's shoulder. "It's not often that he looks so . . ."

"Shit kicked?" Tori interjected playfully

"Mmmm," Lacey murmured. "Your turn to kick some butt, Mrs. St. John!"

Playing to the crowd, Tori danced up to the microphone and asked, "Where are all the good girls in the house?"

A host of arms waved in the air and female shrieks filled the house. "Well, this one's for y'all!" Tori purred with a wink before ripping into a boot stomping, bring the house down, open-throated version of Carrie Underwood's song, *Good Girl*. She might be little, but she sure did pack a serious wallop when throwing down a vocal. The crowd, of course, went wild.

When it was Red's turn, she vamped in her sexy boots up to the microphone, with her glorious mane of hair looking like fire under the lights. Gripping the stand, she shimmied slightly and it struck Angie that she looked like a red-haired modern day version of Marilyn Monroe, flirting with the crowd while displaying a stage presence that was mesmerizing.

With a half-moon tambourine that had a zillion colorful shimmery ribbons hanging off it, she playfully shook it close to the mic to get everyone's attention—as if every male eye in the room wasn't already firmly fixed on her boobs.

Smiling coyly, she told the crowd, "Help me out here, what's that expression? Rock out with your . . ." She didn't finish, just let the crowd fill in the rest with an approving roar.

She tilted her head back and laughed then mocked the audience, saying, "Yeah. .that! Get ready!"

To Angie's thrilled delight, Meghan chose a classic Stevie Nicks song, *Enchanted*, that gave all the girls the perfect backup harmony opportunity. Borrowing from the rock out—cock out category, they ripped into the song with Meghan providing an exuberant, growling vocal and some kickass tambourine moves that got the crowd on its feet. She smiled to herself. One day real soon, Meghan was going to fully understand how funny her fascination with the legendary rock goddess really was.

Why . . . this was more fun than a Friday night at home in her pjs with a quart of Haagen-Dazs and a chick flick!

And then it was her turn to take center stage.

Chapter Fifty-One

HOLY FUCKBALLZ. PARKER WAS A little stunned at the wild exuberance the girls ignited in the crowd. Honestly? It was awesome.

Lacey with her beguiling sweetness that spoke of something smoky and sultry just below the surface.

Victoria—the ultimate contradiction. Tiny and delicate, her feminine outer shell belied the vulgar-tongued, independent, genius within. In her case, smarts did not take a backseat to beauty.

Meghan. *Unf.* Seriously. Alex was so fucking lucky. He'd hit the damn jackpot with that lady. She was the perfect mate for his friend. With the type of curves he knew Alex drooled over, she was the ultimate sexy librarian.

And his Angel. Her dark-haired loveliness against the soft, pale beauty of her flawless skin and those sweet, kissable lips gave her a fairy tale quality that also contradicted the strong-willed woman she grew into.

Totally getting off on the whole vibe, it was fun as shit to be in the crush of bodies closest to the stage. Nothing like a packed room of people having a great time! And he was having the greatest time of all.

Abundantly aware that there was a scowling baby-faced pussy with an annoying stuck-up attitude hovering in the shadows, Parker relished being the one publically marking his territory.

He wasn't stupid. He got why she hadn't caused a scene and tossed the ex out on his ass. It was complicated by who he was, where he was from, and how their connection affected the Marquez family and label. The little turd could cause trouble so she was playing nice.

Didn't change the fact that he was a loser.

It was Angie's turn to take the lead and as she stepped up to the microphone, his heart almost stopped. From this vantage point and with the courtesy of her barely-there dress, he could almost make out the color of her undies. Glancing anxiously left and right, he checked out the reactions of Alex and Cam—relaxing when they didn't seem to notice. Maybe he should get his damn mind out of the gutter. Ha. Fat chance of that.

He missed the first few words she said, so mesmerized was he by her long, curvaceous legs in those wicked thigh-high boots. He noted when she was dancing around that they laced up the back. Since then, he hadn't been able to banish from his mind what she'd look like dressed in only those bad girl boots, bent over one of the padded saddle horses in the tack room, butt ass naked, being pounded from behind by his hungry cock.

"So, yeah . . ." She was chuckling. "I know all about the legend and lore of Whiskey Pete's!"

Hoots and hollers met her comment. Straining to catch up on what he'd missed, Parker figured she must have been playing the hometown girl card.

"And now I'm back," Angie chirped happily with a wink and a little ass shimmy, "and ready to show y'all . . ." She looked directly at him. "How the big girls get it done."

Boom! His heart exploded in his chest and no exaggeration at all . . . Parker thought his dick might have just grown another head. Right up until that actual second, he wasn't sure. But the big girl comment that went straight to his groin and his heart in a double shot that pretty fucking much made him feel like king of the universe.

She nailed her song—totally making the Taylor Swift tune her karaoke bitch. Singing about spaces or something like that—he didn't know and honestly didn't care . . . so focused was he on planning out his next move that she could have been singing about giant hairless balls, and he would barely have noticed. The ladies in the club on the other hand, sang along, dancing enthusiastically.

The boisterous bar crowd and the enthusiastic response to the girls made an energy that filled the room and filled him with an exhilaration that felt like pure adrenaline. Just about the time his fantasies started running wild, he felt a cold chill creep up his spine and tingle along the back of his neck.

Goddammit. That fucking cretin finally got off his worthless ass, did he? Parker did *not* feel like playing nice. In fact, he wanted to vault onto the stage, growl menacingly, and beat his chest at the audience, pick his Angel up, toss her sexy ass over his shoulder and drag her into the first dark, secluded, and private space he could find so he could claim what was his. Until he was buried balls deep in her sweet little body and he made her come all over his cock—she still didn't fully belong to him. Which gave the pretty little pansy ass crowding near his shoulder a foot in the door.

Meghan noticed the minute Ronaldo crept out of the shadows and moved toward Parker. The pissing contest over who got to claim the sexy señorita singing her ass off was about to begin. The fun was about to get real.

Truly, nobody was more flabbergasted than she was when the man made his surprise appearance at the Villa. He was nothing that she expected for the ex-fiancé of her almost sister-in-law. *Nothing.*

Totally unremarkable, Ronaldo Esperanza was barely *meh,* in her book. What the hell had Angie ever seen in him? He was little and smarmy and had an obsequious arrogance that creeped Meghan out.

Catching the Major's eye was easy enough. He looked like a card-carrying super fan, hanging at the front of the stage, watching her every move. He was so friggin' cute with his big smile and that messy hair he kept running his hands through.

One meaningful look from her though and he changed the direction of his attention, looking back over his shoulder at Aldo before elbowing Parker and giving him a chin nod. She was glad Alex was right there; in case something physical broke out, he could handle it.

Angie was playing with fire where the two men vying for her attentions were concerned. Parker had been well on his way to staking his patently obvious claim when the surprise from Madrid appeared on the scene.

Meghan executed a couple of bumps and shimmies along with Lacey and Tori while their Desert Angel started bringing the song home. They'd done a bang-up job so far—enough that Aldo's scowl of clear disapproval made her want to scream. It wasn't all that difficult to feel bad for Ang. She hadn't asked for this weird complication. But it was here on their doorstep—and right royally fucking with Meghan's bridal chi.

From her backup singer-dancer spot behind Angie, she watched while the Major wisely insinuated himself physically between Parker and Aldo, also moving Cam and Drae to anchor spots on either end of their grouping. If something broke out, the Justice boys were ready to contain the mayhem.

She couldn't see everything going on—the stage lights made that kind of difficult—but she noted that words were exchanged. Judging by Parker's posture, the words hadn't been friendly. Alex had his hand on Aldo's shoulder. *Jesus.* She hoped the stupid shmuck wasn't foolish enough to actually challenge *any* of Angie's protectors.

The song ended to rapturous applause. Their four numbers over, it was time for the DJ to announce the wild card song. With a quick five-minute break coming, the girls huddled together giggling and high-fiving—well pleased with their performances.

"This is fun!" Angie chirped happily. "Who knew?"

Tori roared with laughter. "We've got ourselves a convert, ladies!"

Not wanting to rain on their happy parade, Meghan wasn't going to say anything about what the men were up to. There'd be plenty of time for that later. But she didn't expect Lacey to bring it up, groaning when she did.

"So, your boyfriend looks like he's sizing up your fiancé for a butt kicking."

Meghan shook her head. *Ugh. Men.*

Tori found this statement ridiculously funny, falling apart into a fit of giggles. "More like your boyfriend looks like he's sizing your fiancé's ass up for a DFP."

Lacey looked confused. "DFP?"

Did she not know what a DFP was? Meghan groaned louder and added an eye roll at what she knew was coming. Another way that growing up surrounded by brothers and the entire Boston first responder community gave her the inside track sometimes.

"DFP," she drawled. "Disciplinary Fudge Packing."

It took Mrs. Cameron a good few seconds to put it together, but when she did, an amusing blush crept up her neck as she grimaced comically and said "Oh. Yikes."

Yikes, indeed.

Studly McStudlerson waved them over to his DJ perch to give them their next song. The girls bestowed the snarky nickname on him because he was one of those man-whore cowboy types who made no effort to pretend he was anything except a pretty face with a hot bod and an available cock.

To his credit, however, he treated them with well-mannered deference. The Justice cachet extended far and wide. Nobody in their straight mind would dream of messing with any of them.

"Reaching deep into the archive for this one, ladies," he boomed jovially. "Don't want any finger-pointing or cries of favoritism when y'all dance away with Pete's trophy. Can't make it too easy, right?"

He thought they were gonna win? Hell to the yeah!

"Bring it on," she smirked. With a wink at Angie, she pointed out, "Now that we've pulled out our secret weapon, I think we can make a go of whatever you throw at us."

Lacey and Tori snickered at the challenge and burbled, "Ooooooh."

Angie, who it turned out was fucking priceless when it came to yanking chains, put on that pigeon-toed little girl lost shtick and actually twirled a goddamn curl at Studly. From the corner of her eye, she saw Alex throw up his hands in defeat as Parker all but leaped onto the stage, ready to destroy whatever man was on the receiving end of her naughty songstress act.

Making matters worse were the two grinning hyenas, Cam and Drae, who had a grim-faced Aldo boxed in. They clearly loved the macho drama.

"Easy isn't any fun," Angie purred at the DJ.

Oh, god. Meghan wanted to kill her. Now was *so* not the time to play sex kitten.

"Hard is so much better . . . don't you think?"

Thank god the DJ laughed her off. No doubt the stern warning glare being directed his way from Angie's glowering brother made an impact.

"My mom's a nut for sixties girls groups," he told them. "This one had a remake in the eighties, if that helps. I've loaded the tracks into the system; you can use the headphones to give a listen. Once I make the announcement, the clock starts ticking and you've got four minutes to pull it together. Got it?"

They all looked at the screen, and in unison, she and Angie quipped, "I've got this." Of course, they did! Their mothers were probably the same age.

She quickly set up everyone's part. Tori threw together some moves, and they were good to go.

While their four minutes ticked down, Studly was amusing the crowd and he honestly looked a bit relieved when they stepped back into the spotlight. Hurriedly handing over the mic, he whipped up the crowd then retreated to his control panel.

The lights dimmed a second and then bam! The song started, and they got everyone dancing and singing along to *You Can't Hurry Love*. The Supremes did it first, so they went with that arrangement and basically tore up the stage.

Exhausted and running low on adrenaline, their last number was a request and once again, Studly counted the votes and made the final decision. This time though, there'd be no practice time. It was a cold start and these last songs usually ended up being comic masterpieces of faking it till you make it to the end.

"Oh god," Tori moaned. "Anything?"

"*Hmph.*" Angie looked like it was a maybe.

"Oh!" Lacey blurted out. "Wait. I know this. Yeah," she said shaking her head enthusiastically. "It's in one of Cam's playlists."

"Are you sure?" Meghan was drawing a blank. Maybe she'd know once the tune started and she saw the lyrics.

"Yep. Totes," Lacey assured them. "You'll know it too. It's a straightforward ballad. Love song done country style. Rocks a bit."

"Oh, you mean like your husband?" Tori snickered.

"Hush, you. I'm saving our bacon! Least you could do is rub my shoulders and give me some encouragement. You want that fugly trophy . . . right?"

They laughed together and went in for a group hug.

"Let's do this," Meghan drawled as she nodded to the DJ.

Just five more minutes and then she could collapse in Alex's arms.

Lacey looked illuminated from within, standing in the spotlight at the microphone. The crowd hushed—her lovely sweetness had a way of doing that. She took the mic off the stand and addressed the audience.

"Great request! Whoever snuck this one in . . . I like your taste in music. Challenge accepted. A little off the radar but a fabulous tune. If you're not familiar with it, fire up your iTunes immediately and get *This Kind of Love* by Sister Hazel. We hope you like our version."

Before taking her spot, Lacey turned back to the crowd and said sweetly, "And we're dedicating this to the four gentlemen standing in front."

A kiss got blown and she pirouetted, giving the audience a full view of the outrageous backless dress and the ass which was fast gaining legendary status.

The ladies of Family Justice ruled the house!

Chapter Fifty-Two

THIS HAD TO BE ABOUT *the* most bizarre circus the Justice brothers had ever found themselves embroiled in. Was it weird that he felt a sense of pride at how deftly and evenly the three of them still worked together as a team?

When his sister's slimy ex-*whatever-the-fuck* slithered into their midst and foolishly poked at Parker by calling him an *old man,* Cam, and Drae were on that shit in a nanosecond—so fast that Parker barely had time to react which was a damn good thing 'cause Alex had no doubt the taunt was going to get the smarmy little shit's ass annihilated. Parker could do it, too. And never break a sweat.

But his team's swift intervention kept the furious boil over about to happen to a slow bubble . . . *for now.*

Alex smiled to himself. It was what they did. They kept the shit to a minimum. Some things never changed. And while the fireworks simmered down here on the floor, up on the main stage was where the circus was at peak performance. His smile changed to a shit-eating grin at what was happening under the stage lights. Same grin that Cam and Drae sported.

Watching their women own that stage, the crowd, and the air they were breathing was exhilarating. They were secure knowing that Brad Pitt could have walked naked through the room and while each of their women would have looked, the look would end with a giggle-shrug then they'd go right back to what they'd been doing. They were lucky bastards.

But Parker, *hmmm*—there was another issue altogether. Alex wasn't dumb and he knew all too fucking well what a hell raiser Angelina could be. From her youngest days, if it meant getting his or Parker's attention, she'd have readily put her own safety in jeopardy just to prove a point. That quality in a grown woman was beyond scary. No way did he envy his friend on that. The truth was that he was secretly enjoying watching his old pal jump through hoops and grovel on command. He just hoped his sister knew what the fuck she was doing.

As if keeping their Justice drama contained wasn't enough, the crowd was on fire. Their women were fucking dangerous. They could incite a drunken cowboy barroom brawl with two shimmies and an ass shake. Which was almost exactly what happened when some beer-soaked fucknut in a two-dollar cowboy hat shouted, "Lemme fuck that ass, honey!"

Cam reacted instantly. Without missing a beat, his hand shot out—a direct hit sent the guy flying to the floor. With the asshole at his feet, he kicked him and growled, "That's my wife, you loser. Show some fucking manners if you want to walk out of here alive."

The guy's beer buzz had to have vanished in a hurry. Scrambling awkwardly to his feet, he hung his head and mumbled something. Cam grabbed him by the front of his shirt, grunted into the guy's shocked face, and then let him go with a vicious shove.

Aldo watched all this play out. His naturally pasty color showed through the fake tan, his eyes guarded and slightly hooded. The douchebag was almost shaking in his polished loafers. A good head shorter than all of them and dressed like the fashion police, Alex mentally opined . . . *one of these things doesn't go with the others.*

Seriously though, the guy was lucky he survived the *old man* barb without losing some teeth. The age thing was Parker's Achilles' heel so the Esperanza creep certainly chose a good weapon.

Weapons, circuses, and drama aside, all that shit flew out the window anyway when his Irish goddess was on stage. Good lord, she was magnificent. The lace dress and the dangerously sexy cowgirl boots made it hard to think. Especially when his cock was trying to burst out of his jeans to get to her. The smiles and wicked looks Meghan shot his way let Alex know she was fully aware of and very much on board with whatever his dirty imagination conjured up for later.

It sucked that other passengers in the limo eliminated any possibility of doing her in the car before they even pulled from the parking lot. *Damn.* But anticipation was a powerful tool in seduction, so he watched her strut across the stage, her voluptuous breasts dancing in time to her movements and imagined his fiery redhead in those sexy as fuck boots, bent over, dress hiked up to reveal her fantastic ass, moaning for all she was worth as he slammed into her wet heat until sweat poured off both of them and their screams and grunts filled the air.

Leaving his erotic musings on simmer, he enjoyed the rest of the show, knowing that it was drawing to an end. Whatever they were performing was pretty and gave them a chance to show off some beautiful harmonies. Lacey was on lead and from the expression on her face as she purred the lyrics, the whole crowd might as well be invisible. The sweet freckle-faced beauty saw only her adoring husband making the public performance a private love note.

He caught Meghan's gaze. She noticed the touching moment, too. Tori was smiling broadly with obvious tears sparkling in her eyes. No matter what else was going on, there was something about the pure, unabashed innocence that the married couple created from the power of their feelings that moved everyone. Cameron and Lacey were love's touchstone. They were all blessed for knowing them.

When it was over, the crowd went wild, begging for an encore, but the DJ pulled the plug and said it was against the rules. Promising a close-out set after some re-staging, he directed everyone to the bar. After congratulating all the karaoke acts on a fabulous event, he started up a playlist of thumping rock, and went about his business.

Parker looked at him. Alex tried to read his expression, noticed at the same time that Drae was having a hard time keeping the pussy boy in check, and knew just what to do. Giving his old friend a quick nod, he focused on Aldo. Taking one for the team, he plastered on a smile and tossed an arm about Aldo's thin shoulders.

"Drinks are on me while the women hit the dressing room! Cam! Get Aldo a glass of wine and grab a basket of tortilla chips while you're at it."

Becoming the life of the party, Alex quickly organized a mini-gathering in the back of the bar that drew a crowd of friends while Cam and

Drae stood watch. Aldo had no choice but to hang there with the guys and wait for the women to turn up.

Fucking Parker better make this good, he thought. Babysitting Angie's throwaway was hardly Alex's style but just this once he was going to be nice.

Sprinting, Parker hurried after the girls as they drifted, one by one, into the darkness behind the stage, making their way to the shitty little dressing room he knew so well.

He was on a one-man mission to tame an angel. Enough dancing around the subject. If she thought for one second that he wasn't going to make love to her until she couldn't move—well, . . . really? I mean, she was all but begging. He was good with that. More than good.

He found her leaning against a wall behind the stage in a long narrow hallway lit only by filtered blue light that made her appear fragile. Vulnerable.

She looked at him—her eyes dark but wide and filled with something he dared to hope for.

"I'm sorry."

"For what?" He couldn't imagine what she needed to apologize for.

"Aldo." She bit her lip and looked away.

"He called me old. Said you're too young for an old fart like me." Parker said the words before he thought them through. He had to see her reaction. Needed to know how she really felt. *Yeah, that's right.* He was fucking insecure, too.

"What?" she wailed. Stumbling in the dark, she pinned him to the wall, her hands tightly gripping his forearms. "Please tell me you're kidding."

She sounded pained and upset. Just like him.

"Baby," he murmured. "You know I can't kid about this. It's true, honey. I *am* older and . . ."

She moved her hands to his face and forced him to look at her. "I've waited forever to be old enough for you," she husked. "Don't you chicken out on me now, counselor."

Fair enough. Taking her hand, Parker dragged her behind him down the hallway to the lounge Pete kept for his personal use. It was good to have connections everywhere.

Pulling her into the cramped room, he shut and locked the door, then without any pause whatsoever, yanked on the top of her dress. When he uncovered her amazing breasts, he groaned. Soft, weighty, and capped with . . . *what the fuck?* Expecting to find rosy areolas waiting for his attention, he saw something entirely different.

Pushing her shoulders against a wall, he barked, "What the hell?"

Angie looked down and giggled. "Oh," she exclaimed. "I forgot."

"What in the hell did you do?"

"Oh, settle down!" She laughed, smacking him playfully on the arm. "They're just nipple covers! They *do* come off."

He studied the odd little fabric patches affixed to her creamy skin. Why would she do this? He didn't understand. Parker lusted after her nipples and felt a peevish annoyance that she was keeping them from him.

Reading his expression—he wasn't doing much to hide how he felt—she smiled so sweetly. "Six weeks ago, I wouldn't have thought twice about getting caught in some revealing light with my boobs on display."

She had the cutest flustered look on her face. "But I was pretty sure," she confessed while doing a number on her lip, "that my, uh . . . *boyfriend* . . . wouldn't like others seeing what was only for him."

Holy. Fucking. Shit.

No, no—for real. Holy! Fucking! Shit!

She just called him her boyfriend and attached these things to her tits because she knew he'd freak at others enjoying what was only his? *Fucking, eh.* He didn't care for the nipple blankets or whatever the fuck they were, but the fact that she considered him at all was huge. Bigger than huge. This was major shit, man.

Parker grinned. "How do they come off?"

She started picking at one of the corners, trying to unstick it from her delicate skin. "I've never worn them before, but I think all you do is peel."

"Let me do that," he husked, pushing her little hands away. Her tits were *his* job.

As gently as he knew how, Parker pulled the adhesive edge off her soft skin, both of them watching intently. She moaned a little, and he jerked to a stop.

"Did that hurt?"

"No," she assured him, her hand resting on his arm.

"Why the moan then?" he asked sharply.

"Because I like seeing your hands on me."

Her answer was so quiet—so earnest. Parker's heart thudded.

Uncovering her beautifully puckered nipple, he cupped the full, firm breast and squeezed; then in a swooping motion, he leaned down to suck the dainty nub into his mouth.

Her hands went immediately in his hair, soft groans rumbling in her chest, and a leg in its naughty thigh-high boot wrapping around his. Greedy for more, he tore the cover off her other breast.

Bending his knees for perfect access, he cupped and kneaded both voluptuous breasts, alternating between licking, nipping, and sucking on the delicious mounds until she quivered head to toe.

In the distance, her name was called. Dammit. Sounded like Tori was looking for her. Their time was up.

Covering her, he pulled the dress into place and smiled into her eyes. "You please me very much, baby girl."

Parker didn't know where those words came from. The thing was that she looked . . . *delighted*. When had any woman ever given a shit about whether he was pleased or not?

Taking her small hand in his, he raised it to his lips for a soft kiss. "Thank you," he drawled. With her other hand, she ran her fingers through his hair, pushing it back off his face.

"For?"

"Caring what I thought."

She laughed at him. "Fat lot of good it did me. Now when we leave this room, my headlights are on high for everyone to see."

"Yeah," he smirked. "True. But you'll be right by my side and believe me, no one in their right mind will as much as look twice. Not if they want to keep on breathing."

She grinned but chuckled. "Promises, promises."

Pushing her against the door, Parker shoved a thigh between her legs, pulled down one side of the dress, cupped a breast and sucked on it till she cried out. An instinct, something old and primal, made him mark her skin. Satisfied, he looked at her flesh in his hand.

"Remember that time I made you come just from sucking your nipples?"

She gasped and slapped him on the arm. Hard. "How can you tease me so when you haven't even kissed me?" she pouted.

Parker roared with laughter. "Easy. Because you and I both know if I kiss you, neither one of us is getting out of this room with our clothes on."

He rearranged her dress again but spent a good long time massaging her boobs through the fabric. My god, she had the sexiest tits ever.

"There," he drawled, tweaking a nipple. "Perfect."

"Men!" she growled, shoving him away with a laugh and yanking open the door scant seconds before Tori tried the knob.

"Oh, there you two are," she jeered. "No time for the pantsless intermission, kids."

Angie sputtered, but nothing came out, so Parker did the honors. "Something you would know about, Mrs. St. John. I'll bet fifty bucks your fingers have been all over someone's zipper."

Tori giggled outrageously and nudged Angie with her shoulder. "Performance high. Stage adrenaline." Gesturing, she said, "I heard the stagehand say they'd be ready for y'all in about ten so you better get out there before they send a search party."

Right. He still had a short set to play. Looking down at the beautiful señorita at his side, Parker knew just how that part of the night would pan out. She'd be his in the most public way and Aldoriffic and any other buttfucker eyeing her up could eat shit. After tonight? To get to her, you'd have to go through him. Good luck with that.

Alex grabbed him the second he reappeared in the bar. "Well?" he barked. "She packing her bags or can Uncle Eduardo pencil you two in?"

"I've got this," he assured his friend. "Buttfucker Yellow Socks over there is complicating things, though. What's his deal? Why is he still here?"

Alex laughed, but the sound was more malevolent than reassuring. "Ignore him and focus on the set."

"What do you want me to do?" Parker replied. Alex was right. Time for music.

Alex grinned. Big time. "Mmmmm," he drawled. "Obviously, we open with *Coming of Age*. After that? You lead, I follow. And seriously . . . if you can't make that song work, you are one sorry fuck."

Parker threw back his head and roared with laughter.

"Team Justice!" Alex hollered. "Assemble, gentlemen."

Game on.

Chapter Fifty-Three

SHE HADN'T CHUGALUGGED A COLD beer since college when stupid shit like that happened all the time, but that was exactly what she did while Aldo ran off at the mouth, rather belligerently scolding Angie for what he described as a *poor showing* that he declared slutty.

Oh, my god. The nerve of him. How many times had she bit her tongue while he gallivanted all over Europe with a tribe of questionable celebrity types who were essentially sluts for money. What a dick.

Angie was sure she'd completely lost her mind when, after draining the bottle, she slammed it onto the table top then expanded her gut and gave power to a mighty beer belch that deserved an award.

Aldo looked at her in horror. "What is wrong with you, querida? Has this place made you forget who you are?"

The subtle insinuation that her behavior was somehow off was shot to hell before the words left his mouth when two guys and a woman walking by gave her a thumbs-up like a lady burping one out in public was an everyday occurrence. Tori and Lacey shouted from a few tables away with approving hoots, claps, and boisterous laughter. So, what exactly was *this place* doing to her?

"This is about that cowboy lawyer, isn't it?" he goaded her. "I understand," he added silkily.

Ewww. Was he kidding? Angie shuddered.

"These things happen all the time, my dear. The allure of something so different. If you must fuck him, please get to it so we can go home to the life we planned."

That sleazy comment was so far over the line that she, well . . . she knew exactly what she was doing and couldn't blame the adrenaline or the beer for what happened next. *Nah.* That was all her.

In a major league move, her arm bent back then arced forward as her small hand flattened and tightened—aiming directly at Aldo's smirking babyface, she walloped him good. Hopefully, the hand mark she left would be more visible than a tattoo.

Damn proud that she was now a true Whiskey Pete's gal, having slapped two different men on two separate occasions, she stowed her smacking hand, and tried to hide a smirk.

Like fruit flies descending on an overripe peach, Family Justice was all over them in the next heartbeat. Angie knew there was no way she could haul off and whack Aldo without them seeing. And reacting. But she wasn't quite finished yet.

Sizing Ronaldo Esperanza up for a burial suit was looking easier and easier. *Little man.* He'd always been pompous, but he'd never pulled this holier-than-thou nonsense—she wouldn't have put up with it. Angie guessed what she was seeing was the real Ronaldo. Gone was the practiced gentleman with the continental airs. And in his place was a small-minded cynical sack of shit. She sensed he still wanted something, this trip had a purpose, but she was done being nice. *Fuck that.*

"Your language is rude and offensive," she ground out. "And your insinuation that fucking a cowboy was something you'd ALLOW is beyond disgusting. You are a pig, Aldo, and I demand an apology."

"Are you okay, sweetie?" Lacey asked as her arm snaked around Angie's middle.

Little Tori came and stood right in front—between her and Aldo—crossed her arms, and stared at him. Behind them, she could feel Cameron and Draegyn's ominous presence. Angie knew with one word she could have the man gawking at her ripped to shreds.

The house lights dimmed and the air came alive with the hum of guitar amps. The crowd moved closer to the stage. *Alex and Parker were going on.*

Since Aldo didn't seem in a hurry to apologize, she threw up her hands and stomped away in a huff, supremely conscious the whole time of her bouncing breasts and the way her nipples peaked. *Great.*

"Angelina," Aldo squawked. "Do not walk away."

Angie whirled around as Tori gave him a hearty shove and walked past. Knowing or rather hoping that her parents understood, she flipped him the bird then went to find her man. If Aldo tried to mess with her through the winery or her folks, she'd deal with it but more than that? He really could go fuck himself.

They found Meghan where she always was—right by the stage ogling her Major and making sure he wasn't overdoing it. Parker, of course, was right where he always was. Up front. In the spotlight. Larger than life. Hotter than a dozen heart-throb country singers rolled into one very sexy package and staring right at her.

Adjusting his guitar, he grinned and started talking to the crowd while his fingers picked out a chord. "Helluva show earlier."

His meaningful leer and the wink that followed got her all tingly and way too giggly for her own good.

The crowd cheered.

"Heard some good shit tonight, right?"

More cheering.

"Well, me and the boys are here to close out the stage and you know how Pete is about sending a bunch of rowdy motherfuckers onto the roads after a night at Whiskey's."

Now the cheering was raucous and over-the-top.

"So," he drawled with a sneer as he fiddled with a guitar pick, "that old fucker made us promise no head banging. Ballads and soft rock only."

A smattering of, "Boos," were heard, but for the most part, people laughed and nodded like it was a good idea.

"Now most of you know our part-time drummer . . . another old fucker, my good friend Thunder Foot of the Justice Clan . . ."

A titter of good-natured laughter rippled through the room.

"But what you might not know is that one of tonight's performers is Thunder Foot's little sister."

Oh shit. Angie wondered if she'd get arrested for throttling him.

Tori nudged her playfully and Cameron whispered, "FYI, little sister. Grown men play for keeps."

The color started creeping up her neck. *Little sister.* Someone was going to die.

After a bit more boisterous applause and shouts of, "Who?" Parker nailed her with a look that was all challenge. *Grrrrrr.* Damn him. She never could say no when he did the taunting. Alex's smirking, know-it-all expression made it clear he was in on this little performance.

"What do you say we get her up here to share the stage—make it a family affair?"

People went nuts with applause. She was doomed.

In full smirk, Parker locked eyes with her and called out, "Desert Angel! Get your ass up here and sing with me, sweetheart. Let's show 'em how the big kids do it."

Aww, shit. She absolutely couldn't hold back her laughter. Lacey smacked her butt and said, "Come on, sister! Get up there in those nasty boots and wipe that smile off his face."

Tori rubbed her back. It was like they were in her corner, psyching her up to enter the ring.

"Uh, Angie?"

"Yeah?" she answered.

"What happened to the pasties you had on earlier? Your high beams are lit up, Angel baby." Tori giggled.

Angie quirked a lopsided grin. "Yeah, about those," she drawled. And then she walked to the side of the stage and took a deep breath, hearing Lacey and Tori's shrieks of laughter as she walked.

Parker immediately came over and extended a hand to help her up the short stairs, then pulled her to center stage where he put his nose in her hair and breathed deep.

"Tell me something," he asked sounding serious. "Did you mean what you said about me being your boyfriend?"

She snickered. "Who knew you were so needy, counselor?"

He swatted her behind for not answering and left her standing in the spotlight. Angie didn't need to ask what song was coming. Alex's ridiculous gotcha smirk only confirmed what she already knew. Spying Meghan's fancy tambourine near the drum kit, she grabbed it so at least she'd have something to do.

Back at the mic, Parker riled up the crowd a bit. "If you like eighties rock, you'll know this one. It's our all-time favorite little sister song. Another playlist standard! Check it out—*Coming of Age* from Damn Yankees."

A whoop of approval rose from the crowd when he soberly added, "Please observe a moment of silence for all that awesome eighties hair." The mocking reference brought the house down.

Proving she was up for anything he threw at her, Angie rocked out with glee. This time when she heard the song, instead of it igniting memories and yearnings she'd rather not face, she let it seep into her senses until a huge bubble of joy grew.

Yeah. She absolutely was the little sister and glad for it, too. And now that she actually had come of age? Parker Sullivan, Esquire belonged to her. All that other noise? The years of self-doubt and confusion? Even letting herself believe she could ever replace Parker with . . . well, with anyone? All that was the past. It was him or a life of yearning and regret. No in-betweens.

Arizona was in her blood and Parker was in her soul. This was the right choice for her. She'd been an idiot long enough.

The first time he and Parker played this song with a band and for an audience was during college, and over time, it grew into one of their go-to numbers because it rocked, had a catchy tune, and was a favorite of both sexes. Just the sort of thing any decent cover band had ready to go.

Fast forward to Angie's high school graduation. Alex was stateside for a time and had retreated to Sedona—mostly to sleep and lay on a lounger by the pool. It was just by coincidence that he was around that June. Same for Parker, who by then was already up to his nose hairs in terrorism stuff.

Surprising his baby sister was no easy task since she had some sort of weird sixth sense where he and Parker were concerned. But for that occasion, they managed to pull off the mother of all surprises by showing up at her graduation party. In addition to simply being there, they cranked out a pretty kickass rendition of the song. *Coming of Age.* Huh. Seemed appropriate then and was a little like waving a red flag now.

Props to Angelina, he thought proudly. She was truly a Marquez. Even if she was completely rattled, she'd never show it and certainly performed gamely enough, making quite a statement of her own with those boots and Meghan's tambourine.

As the song ended, she came to the front of his kit, dropped the tambourine to the side, and *tsked* at him several times.

He answered with the big brother grin.

"Some brother you are," she snarled gleefully.

The contradiction was pure little sister. He arched a brow and widened his grin.

"I don't know, Alexander. Letting that old pervert," she taunted with a barely concealed laugh, "take your little sister. How could you help him?" she wailed laughingly.

"Take?" *Yeah, right.* Laughing, he *tsked* right back. "More like *took* and zip that mouth, kid, before it gets you into trouble. Behave and do as you're told."

She stomped her foot and grunted, just like she did when she was six. He was sure as shit glad that Parker knew what a handful she was.

"I think your boyfriend wants you," he quipped dryly. "Oh, and I hope you like Lady Antebellum."

Angie's head zipped in Parker's direction at supersonic speed. Dude was smiling, only Alex knew the expression was more *Get your ass over here.* She must have known it too 'cause she swaggered over to him, taking her place behind the microphone he indicated, and unless his lip-reading was woefully insufficient, said something along the lines of *bite my ass* with a dazzling Angel baby smile on her face.

Shit, this was fun. Alex glanced in Meghan's direction. She was also watching the interaction on stage with avid interest. Meeting his eye with an expression of loving amusement, she eye rolled and quirked a little grin. They were both relieved that Angie finally stopped running and was standing her ground.

About fucking time, too. He had a wedding and a fiancée to focus on.

Chapter Fifty-Four

"Go easy on me," he joked into the microphone, his eyes trained on the stunning beauty sharing the stage with him. "This being my first time and all." He snickered as whoops of delight greeted his declaration.

"That's right! You heard me," he growled at the audience. "I'm a virgin. Never done it in public with this pretty little girl before. Sing with her, I mean."

Angie crossed her arms and cocked a hip at him mockingly. "Give it a rest!" she quipped with a bit too much glee. Pointing at him, she wagged her head like a know-it-all and proclaimed him, "The Almost Forty-Year-Old Virgin."

Desert Angel easily got everyone laughing with her dry, sarcastic delivery. The tits, short dress, and thigh-high boots helped. Everyone was watching. She was roped in and knew it. This was almost more public than jumbotron kissing at the sports arena. No turning back now.

Running his fingers across the strings of his guitar, he nodded to Dave, his bass player, and Dave's wife, who was doing keyboards, 'cause no way could they do this song right without them. Then he gave a quick glance to Alex. This was it.

Let's see what she does, he thought on a deep inhale. Saying a quick, silent prayer that this was the right thing to do, he leaned over and whispered in her ear.

"Angel girl, I need you now."

It was a statement first and a song title second.

"And," she murmured softly, "I can't fight you anymore."

How long did it take to sing that song? He didn't know. Not long enough. Not nearly. They'd harmonized together in their younger days hundreds of times but never like this, in public with an audience.

Parker picked this song for a reason. Besides the haunting melody, he liked the lyrics. They said everything he couldn't. And she wasn't fighting him anymore. If there weren't several hundred eyeballs watching them right now, she'd be naked and underneath him instead of just beyond his reach.

But make no mistake about it, she was making her feelings abundantly clear anyway. Angie sang from the heart. Every sway, every movement, each breath was loaded with emotion. Her eyes never looked away and on the harmonies, she shared his mic. It felt uncommonly intimate even with so many watching.

He'd be so fucking lost without music in his life. It was his drug of choice. The magic they were creating as they sang to each other felt effortless, almost trancelike. As if they'd been singing to each other forever. And maybe they had.

When the song was ending, Parker felt a wave of emotion wash over that almost wrecked him. He'd loved this girl from the first time they locked eyes. What had she said? That she'd waited forever to be old enough for him? *Jesus Christ.* He wanted to cry.

When the final notes faded, all he wanted to do was drag her somewhere private and kiss her silly. She was certainly looking at him like her thoughts were running along the same lines. Fuck it if Alex didn't pull the plug on such insanity by pounding out a count on his sticks and immediately ripping into their closing number.

Angie laughed when Dave leaned over and told her what they were playing and dashed for the tambourine. Another duet with some country style harmonies, they rocked out singing about going home and being a rolling stone. Bon Jovi was compulsory for any rock band worthy of an electric amp, and just like with the Lady Antebellum song, this one was tailor-made for him and Desert Angel.

Alex got in on the rowdy vocals and right away it turned into a joyful musical interlude for the three of them. Parker would remember this for a long time. It was good stuff. The shit you made room for in your memory.

When they were finished, what was left of the crowd was enthusiastically appreciative. Especially after Alex announced that the next round was on him. Nothing like causing a stampede for the fucking bar!

In a way it was good that everyone except Team Justice was distracted elsewhere because in one of those slow motion *are you fucking kidding* moments, Mr. Spanish Shiny Pants leapt onto the stage making a straight line directly at him. Parker saw him coming and decided not to do a fucking thing. *Piss ant motherfucker.* He shit turds with more character than this annoying bitch.

When the little prick swung, he was reminded of the cartoons where the puny loser tried to mow down a muscle-bound Goliath and struggled not to collapse laughing.

In his peripheral vision, he saw dumbfounded expressions on Cam and Drae's faces and figured they must have gotten caught flat-footed when Aldoriffic bolted from their custody. *Well, at least there were eyewitnesses,* the lawyer in him noted.

The other thing his eyes caught was Barry the Barkeep's beefy hand shooting out to stop the bouncer from coming over. Good man. He knew what was going down was a private matter. A Justice matter. No interference necessary

Now, to be honest, he grudgingly admitted—the punch pussy boy threw was fairly effective. And it would have been ten times more effective if Parker didn't have about five inches and several layers more brawn and pure muscle than his challenger. But the puny fucker did put his heart into it, no matter how laughable the effort so he had to give the dude *some* credit.

As he swung, Esperanza shouted something in Spanish most of which went right over Parker's head, but he most definitely picked out the word *grandpa.*

Why, that little fuck. Was there a particular noise right before shit started hitting the fan? Seemed like maybe there was, this time anyway, because, all of a sudden, several layers of grunts, growls, and barking yelps rang out. And *then* the yelling started.

Angie went nuts, shrieked and actually jumped on pussy boy's back, beating his shoulders. "Are you insane?" Her screams were shrill and furious sounding.

Okay. Come on. Seeing her, dressed as she was, literally brow beating this guy's ass was entertaining as fuck. He probably shouldn't have laughed. But he did.

His mocking laughter enraged Esperanza, who had yet to shake Angie off.

Alex appeared in their midst like he'd transported via some hi-tech nerd teleportation gadget and started threatening the dumbass if he didn't take his hands off his sister.

Aw, man. This shit was classic home video gold! Why wasn't anyone shooting it? YouTube was being robbed if you asked him.

Next thing he knew, little Tori in her outrageous barely-there short shorts materialized, also out of nowhere, and ran across the stage to peel Angie off the guy she was now clearly assaulting. Fuck. This was getting funnier by the second.

"Don't you *ever* touch him," Angie screamed as she pummeled his head.

Well, this was certainly interesting and a spot he'd never been in before. Considering that the punch that started all this barely left a red mark, her frenzied defense of him really struck Parker as downright fucking adorable. It wasn't like anyone doubted he could have put that fucker in the back of an ambulance with one hit, so her coming to his aid as his avenging angel . . . how could this possibly work out any better for him?

Shiny Pants wailed like a little girl, "What is wrong with you, Angelina? How can you let this man use you like this?"

Tori finally managed to get Angie on her feet again and was physically restraining her from going in for round two.

"Use me?" Angie barked. "Ha! That's funny coming from you. Wasn't using me and my family name what our engagement was all about? Be honest, Aldo. For god's sake—what the hell is wrong with you?"

Parker loved this part. He'd been on the receiving end of the sort of fire she was spewing and knew all too well how uncomfortable it was. Bitch better be wearing an asbestos suit if he hoped to survive without third-degree burns.

"This is my home. My family. My friends. I don't want you here.

Go back to Madrid, Aldo. Stop pretending we had a relationship. We didn't."

Alex, who seemed to have grown and looked to be about eight feet in height of angry, menacing badass took Angie by the hand and pulled her beside him. Snarling in a voice that was intended to intimidate, he added his two cents.

"I've now heard my sister tell you several times to buzz the fuck off. She does not want you here. What part of that exactly do you not understand? Need a translator? Let me know, 'cause I'm done playing nice."

Tweedledee and Tweedledum growled.

"Don't fuck with Justice," Draegyn drawled darkly. "It won't end well if you do."

And then Meghan did something that blew Parker's mind. With Lacey playing the sidekick, the ball-busting redhead stepped into the upheaval and effectively stopped everyone in mid-motion.

In her most ladylike tone, she stated, "I'm sorry, Mr. Esperanza, but Family Justice is by invitation only and yours, I'm afraid, has been permanently lost in the mail."

Was this what was meant by—you could hear a pin drop it was so silent?

Parker understood why Alex had such a soft spot for Lacey. She defined sweetness but had a tough inner core that took no prisoners. Woe to anyone who thought the freckles and cute face meant she was an airhead. Lady had balls. *Big 'uns.*

"And," Mrs. Cameron added saucily. "We just don't like you. *At all.*"

Tori smirked. "Did you really imagine you'd be good enough for Angelina Marquez?" She snorted an inelegant, "Bah!" and shook her head.

Parker was enjoying this immensely. In the perfect world that was his mind, he'd pulled up a chair a couple of minutes ago and sat down with a cold beer to enjoy the show that Team Justice was putting on.

Outmaneuvered by a bunch of women, Shiny Pants looked like he was close to busting open a vein in his head. Whatever lunacy existed in this guy's mind about Angie wasn't tethered to reality. Maybe she'd been different before, he didn't know, but as far as he was concerned,

Ronaldo Esperanza had worn out his already thin welcome.

"Angelina," the guy mumbled. It seemed to finally be dawning on him that he wasn't among friends.

"No!" she barked, and then stomped off, her boots thudding across the stage followed quickly by her posse of women as they made for the backstage area.

He'd give it a few minutes and then go after her. She needed some ladies time. Plus, Parker already understood how the Justice women worked. If they were moving in a pack—stay the fuck out of their way. Peeling 'em off one by one was the best way to maneuver if you really had to.

"What the hell is he even doing here?" Meghan quizzed once they were ensconced in the cramped dressing room. The perfect place to have a bitch session. "Angie, seriously," she snapped. "You just say the word, sweetie and he'll be toast by morning."

Lacey wiggled up onto a long countertop underneath a bunch of tacky band posters from another century and nodded her agreement. Crossing her long legs, she picked up one of the bags she had with her and started fishing around.

Pulling out something small, round, and blue, she handed it to Angie. "Here. Lip balm. It helps calm the mind."

They all cracked up. It was just the release they needed. Despite her young age, Lacey was what Meghan's ma would call an old soul. You could see it in her eyes. She relied on her amiable personality as a sort of rudder for their group. In a way, Lacey Cameron was their moral compass. A badass one, but still . . .

Cramming things into a floppy shoulder bag, Tori remarked that she had a bad feeling about Aldo. Something didn't seem right to her.

Hmmmm. Funny. He was a bit off and not just because the man was a poor representation of testosterone. It had been hard not to judge Angie's friend by his appearance. I mean, after all, they were in what was essentially a den of alphas—there just wasn't any other way to describe the Justice men—and Ronaldo was so . . . *inconsequential* in comparison. It was the only word that fit. This guy was nobody. He just didn't matter. But . . . he *WAS* up to something.

Angie finally spoke. "I know, you guys. I know." She shook her head and pursed her lips. "You're right, Tori. It's like I can smell it on him or something, but honestly . . . no clue. When we ended things, I didn't leave the door open—believe me. There was no ambiguity on my part."

Tori snickered. "Had one foot out the door and on a plane here. Not much ambiguity in that!"

"So, does he have anything on you?" Meghan asked.

"Of course, not. He's nobody. But in Madrid? The family name has importance. Old Spanish society. I think they wanted me in the family more than they wanted him. Something of an embarrassment when it comes to work ethic."

Tori groaned. "Oh fuck, Angel. Been there, done that. Now there's a tale I know all too well." She shuddered dramatically.

"True that," Lacey commiserated. "But with Aldo, know what I don't get?" Lacey muttered. "Why does he keep taunting Parker? Seems a bit odd. Like he's trying to force a confrontation."

"Yeah," Lacey agreed. "The man's got a death wish. Cameron told me that he called Parker an old man. Can you imagine that?"

Angie groaned and visibly shook. Startled, Meghan went to her for a supportive hug. "Don't worry, he kept his cool."

Angie tensed. "The age thing is an issue for us. Always has been."

"Oh, so calling the sexy lawyer a grandpa probably didn't help things, huh?"

"Tori!" Meghan barked with a stern frown. Dammit. Sometimes she wanted to pull the plug on Victoria's mouth.

"What?" she asked with a look of genuine confusion. "I was just kidding . . . I mean, Parker's not really freaked out by this right? I've never seen him rattled by anything. Maybe *you're* the one with the age hang-up?"

"It's always been an issue," she admitted quietly. "Nine years . . . it's a lot when you consider how long we've known each other."

Lacey grunted but didn't say anything. *Hmmm. Bet I know what she's thinking.*

"I told Parker that I've waited my whole life to finally be old enough for him."

"Wow," Lacey chimed in. "Interesting choice of words."

"So . . ." Meghan pondered aloud, "do you think maybe Parker saw you as a kid? Until recently?"

"Maybe," Angie shrugged then after a second, she grunted, "No. If I'm being honest—no. I did that. It was all in my head."

"Do you think Lacey's too young for Cameron?" She hadn't known how bothered Angie was by this or she would have said something sooner.

"*Whaaaat?*" Angie squawked. "Good lord, no! Why would you even ask that?" She was looking back and forth between her and Lacey. Tori chuckled softly.

Smiling, Lacey cocked her head to the side so her ponytail brushed against her neck and shoulder. "How old do you think I am?"

Angie looked like she was swinging between flabbergasted and horrified. "I don't know. I figured we were all like, the same age or close. Actually, aren't I the one hitting the big three-oh first?"

"Well, actually," Lacey deadpanned, "ya'll are gonna get there *waaay* ahead of me. You'll hold me a spot though, right?"

She and Tori chuckled through a flurry of fist bumps. Meghan saw the light bulb go on over Angie's head when the point she was making hit the mark.

"Are you fucking shitting me?" she asked.

"Nope," Lacey chirped gleefully. "The wife with the most seniority," she quipped mockingly, "is the baby of the group."

It was funny watching Angie frantically doing the math in her head. Every doubt about her and Parker's age difference was crumbling to dust. A more perfectly matched pair than Cameron and Lacey could not be found. Screw that age nonsense.

"Please tell me that you're at least twenty-five."

"Sure," Lacey cooed. "At some point. Not yet, though. But soon," she added impishly.

Tori drawled mockingly as she used her elbow to point at Angie. "Got a hand crank for that jaw of hers? It keeps hitting the floor."

"So, what did we learn tonight, ladies?" Meghan bawled, choking on laughter from Tori's comment.

"Tits and ass rules!"

Lacey groaned and threw something at Tori's head. "I think she meant in the bigger picture, silly."

"Age is a *state of mind*," Angie emphasized with air quotes.

"Yeah," Tori kept on teasing. "And you'll get the senior citizen discount before any of us!" she hooted.

Meghan laughed.

"Justice has been served!" Lacey giggled.

"Boom!" Tori added, feigning a dramatic mic drop.

Chapter Fifty-Five

ONE BY ONE, THEY GATHERED their crap and dragged everything to the parking lot. It had been a long night after an especially difficult and trying day. Angie, feeling shit kicked, seriously wondered how she'd managed to keep it together.

Starting the day off with missing panties, a hangover, and the unexpected and upsetting kamikaze appearance of her former fiancé hadn't been enough. Oh, no. Competing in the karaoke challenge. Aldo's craptacular attitude. Yeah. Great day. Awesome. Let's do it again. Not.

Her exhausted mind was considering what she'd just learned about Lacey and Cameron. Mind-blown, she wondered if this was a paradigm shift in her thinking. For years, she'd believed that she and Parker hadn't worked out that first time around because she'd been too young. She was certain he had certain needs that an inexperienced, unsophisticated college kid couldn't possibly satisfy. It was no wonder that at the first sign of problems, she'd run and didn't stop until so much silent time and geographical space lay between them that any sort of resolution seemed improbable.

And now here they were and by some stroke of luck or maybe because of that destiny and fate thing her mom referred to, he still wanted her. Had he waited for her to return and claim him?

Angie heard his approach and stilled. Aware of him closing in on her from the sound his boots made crunching on the hard packed dirt and stone of the parking lot, a shocking surge of wet heat dampened her panties. Her breathing became uneven as adrenaline spiked in her system.

And then he was right on top of her. Angie's heart thudded. Some part of her wanted to run. A sensation . . . primal and not a little frightening ran along her nerves. Just the suggestion of his powerful masculinity held her in place.

Trembling like crazy, she waited, unable to turn around, immobile like prey boxed into a corner. Then she felt his breath on her bare shoulder. Angie bit back a frightened cry and gasped when his big, warm hand slipped between her legs.

The urgent possessiveness in his voice rocked Angie. "You are hot and sexy as fuck when you're angry," he said running his hand firmly up the inside of a thigh, grabbing the soft inner flesh just beneath the line of her panties.

He made her want things that shocked and excited, taking Angie to a place that tested her emotions. "Don't play with me," she whispered in a voice just barely audible. "You don't know . . ."

"What?" he growled an inch from her ear. "What don't I know? That you're on fire for me?"

He squeezed her flesh as a reminder of where his hand was. Burning heat surged between her legs. Instead of surrendering to the desire, she felt like crying.

I'm tired, she thought. Tired of thinking. Tired of worrying. She'd give Sophie a call in a couple of hours and have her sister do some digging. Find out what Aldo was really up you. But beyond that? She had nothing.

"I'm . . . drained," she admitted after a slight hesitation. "Played out."

He sighed, turned her and pulled her in close. "Let it all go, Angel. I've got you."

How did he know that was all she wanted to hear? With a quiet whimper, she melted into his embrace. Fitting so perfectly it made her heart ache, she burrowed as best she could and did what he said. Just let it all go.

Time stilled, they stood there, wrapped up in each other. For Angie, the quiet interlude felt perfect—just what she needed. But all things good eventually come to an end.

"Where's Aldo?" she asked reluctantly. The idea of the return trip in the limo with all of them crammed together was making her nerves fray. She wasn't so sure she could do it.

"Hey," Parker murmured, the concern heavy in his voice. He dipped at the knees so he could see directly into her eyes. "Did you really think I'd let him near you again?"

She blinked at him. Tears threatened and her nose stung from the effort to hold them off.

"Or your brother? Or Red for that matter?"

That broke her.

"Talk to me," he pleaded. "Don't keep it inside, honey. This is you and me now and we talk to each other this time, okay?"

She nodded and flattened her hands on his chest, needing to feel his solid strength.

"I didn't make a mess of things, no matter how this looks." She was pouting, and nobody was more surprised by that than her.

"Are you worried that I think you fucked up somehow?"

"Of course!" she cried. "How could you not think that?"

"Because I know you, sweetheart."

He said it so somberly that she stopped in mid tirade. Of course, he did. Parker knew everything about her as a person.

"I really did do things the right way." She wasn't sure if the reassurance was for him or her. "When I knew for sure that marrying Aldo wasn't what I wanted, I told him right away. There weren't any games. I didn't run away from what happened, Parker. I learned my lesson."

He let her see his belief in her. It shone in his eyes giving her the strength to continue.

"I gave him the ring back and even went and explained things to his parents. I didn't want there to be any doubt whatsoever about my decision. It was irrevocable and I thought everyone understood that. I needed there to be absolutely no doubt. No strings left hanging."

Angie leaned against him, biting her lip as she flexed her fingers on his muscular chest. "I knew, you see," she murmured quietly, "the moment the decision was made that the only thing for me to do after that was come here."

She felt him catch his breath and his hands tightened where they held her arms.

"What are you saying, Angelina?"

She didn't need to be afraid. He'd catch her when she fell. Trembling, she looked into his handsome face. "I came back. It took me a long time to stop running and when I did, well . . . there was only one place I wanted to be. One person I needed to see."

Angie held her breath. What she'd admitted was huge. It was all out there now. Their journey back to friendship forced them to face hard truths and personal failings. He'd accused her of running. She had. He'd admitted to handling their relationship like an idiot. That was also true. And yet, neither of them had ever genuinely moved on.

"Oh god, I'm so sorry. For everything. Please believe me. I didn't want any of this. Why does it have to be so fucked up?"

He gathered her close. She hadn't fallen—not exactly, but he still managed to catch her.

"Here's the deal, Angie," he said after a bit. "We agree, about this, right?" he asked. "It's you and me now. We're going to figure out what *we* want."

"Yes," she agreed.

"You have nothing to be sorry for, so I don't want to hear you say that again. Understood?"

Oh, my. She liked that growly thing he had going on. If he kept that up, her panties were going to melt right off.

"And then you don't leave my fucking sight. Plain and simple. As long as that fucknut is at the Villa, so am I."

She smiled and bit the inside of her mouth to keep from giggling. This was one of those moments she wanted to remember. It was not every day that a badass rock 'n' roll rebel, Alpha, ninja lawyer staked a claim.

"Okay," she replied meekly.

Mmmm. The flaring nostrils and the way his eyes darkened at her easy submission gave her an unbelievable thrill. Definitely something for future reference.

"You and I are riding back to the hacienda with Cam and Lacey. Your brother and a very pissed off Red are in charge of pussy boy. It's been decided. His Angelina privileges have been permanently revoked."

Oooh! She liked the way that sounded. Liked the way he said it as if someone was in danger of getting their ass kicked. And speaking of ass kicking, putting her and Parker under the same roof might get a little . . . dicey.

"Um . . ." she started jerkily.

"Don't worry." He chuckled. "Alex is cool, but that doesn't mean he won't be dusting you for fingerprints."

His tone changed. "I told you before, that I didn't treat you right and that's not happening this time."

Angie tilted her head so she could better see his face.

"Am I going to fuck you senseless? Yes. Count on it. Frequently, in fact. But we're doing this the right way and jumping into bed isn't a great way to start."

"But . . ."

He gave her this stern look that must have thought was his Tarzan expression. Wow. He wasn't joking.

Shit. Be careful what you wish for, huh? She wanted more than sex, but that didn't mean she wanted to live like a nun. Was her own damn fault for letting him think he had to prove something. How come there wasn't a middle ground that would satisfy them both?

Lacey and Angie were talking quietly together in the back of an enormous Escalade while he sat in the front passenger seat next to Cam. Traveling along nearly desolate stretches of road that led them away from town out into the desert, Parker considered some of the thoughts whirling in his head.

Something wasn't right about any of this. Esperanza's belligerent outrage in the face of being clearly outnumbered, overwhelmed, and tied up in Justice knots didn't add up. He was a self-serving little prick, so discovering what he hoped to achieve with his continuing combativeness was at the top of Parker's priority list.

That decided, he zeroed in on the sound of Angel's voice coming from the backseat. He was relieved that she was as together as she appeared considering that twenty minutes ago she'd been in avenging

Angel mode. A scuffle had come close to breaking out when they were assembling in the parking lot to work out who was riding with whom.

The girl was mighty impressive when she was worked up! It was funny when she went off, which had been the case when Alex tried walking Esperanza to the limo without incident. Ha! Fat chance of that happening once he hurled a few insults in Parker's direction. At least he thought they were insults—Spanish never came easy for him—but Angie certainly understood whatever he said and went after the idiot in the space of a single breath with some pretty fabulous flashes of badassery in that parking lot.

The whole incredible scene was nearly indescribable. They'd been talking quietly to Draegyn and Victoria, leaning against the side of a truck, waiting for everyone else to catch up. Not knowing what was coming at them next and feeling unusually protective because he knew damn well their whole situation was in motion, he'd been guardedly scanning the parking lot while attempting to stay in the conversation.

Distracted for seconds, he hadn't seen Alex and Esperanza come around the corner of the building until all hell was breaking loose.

Finding Parker standing with his arm languidly draped about Angie's waist with a hand possessively on her ass must have been Esperanza's last straw cause next thing any of them knew, the little shit started freaking out in a different language.

Angel immediately went into fuck-off-and-die mode and began arguing with him, also in a different language. There was a bunch of hand gestures and her posture evolved into something more dangerous than friendly.

He actively held her back from tearing the man a new rectum, while Alex kept a firm hand on her antagonist's shoulder. Parker knew if he slacked up on his hold, she'd be on the fucker in a heartbeat.

Drae tried to step between them as they furiously screamed and yelled at each other but quickly backed off with his hands up in surrender when his wife rather sternly told him to let Angie deal with it.

Shit was racing to an eleven as Angie just got more and more furious. Whatever they were saying to each other could not have been pretty. He almost lost his grip around her waist when she suddenly went completely batshit and began kicking. He probably shoulda let her stomp the motherfuck out of him. Those boots she was wearing could have left some permanent damage.

Barry appeared on the scene, asking if they needed his help. Parker really couldn't answer. It was taking all of his concentration to keep Angie in check.

All the while, Esperanza was still shrieking like a girl.

"Dirty old man? Grandpa? Is that fucker kidding?" Barry yelped when he heard what was being said.

"Are you fucking serious?" Drae barked at the translation.

Thanks, dude, Parker thought. *Owe you one, man.* Now that everyone knew the little fucker was basically standing there calling him names, he'd had enough. And so had Angie. It was cute as shit that she was so eager to defend him but enough was enough.

"Alex," Parker bit out. "Shut that motherfucker up or I will."

In what could only be described as perfect timing, Cam and Lacey pulled alongside them. "Get in," Cam grumbled darkly as he kept an eye while Alex shuffled their unwelcome visitor toward the limo. Ben, who knew better than to get involved, was already wisely in the car with the engine running.

Dragging a still sputtering and wildly gesturing Angelina to the passenger side of Cam's vehicle, he helped Lacey slide from the front then hastily pulled open the backseat door so he could deposit his snarling lady inside and out of the line of fire. Lacey hurriedly climbed in beside her and shut the door.

Before taking a seat, Parker let the explosion that had been building inside go off. Leaning over the hood of Cam's big SUV, he pointed at the retreating shithead who got his woman all worked up and bellowed, "One more word out of your fucking mouth and you go through customs in a body bag."

When he slammed the door after getting seated and Cam started to drive off, it took less than five seconds for Angie to crack up laughing. Followed by a clearly relieved Lacey. Eventually, Cam started sniggering and Parker had to admit the dust-up *had* been pretty comical. Who knew Desert Angel was such a wild woman?

Lowering the visor and flipping up the lighted mirror, Parker adjusted it until he had a clear view of Angie behind him.

"You okay, honey?" It wasn't too late to turn around and go back to Pete's—teach that sniveling jackass a thing or two.

The bewitching sapphire eyes that had captivated him from the time she was a baby focused on him in the mirror. Pissed him off that couldn't read her expression in the dark.

Parker regretted putting her into the back seat—away from him. Not that he'd had much choice. Despite the other couple present it would have been impossible not to make out with her in the moving car if they'd been sitting together

All the tension inside him melted away when he felt her small hand touch his shoulder. He peered more closely in the mirrored visor. Of all the times to be serious, she chose this one to be an imp.

"Are we there yet," she whined jokingly. "How much *looooonger?*"

He smiled. Turning his head, he reached for her fingers and kissed them lightly. Before he could return her playful banter, Lacey got them all laughing when she yanked a Dylan toy from the seatback. A colorful ring with noisy plastic shapes hanging from it. Shaking it in front of Angie's face like she was distracting a grumpy baby, she cooed, "Who wants to play?"

Chapter Fifty-Six

*U*GH. IT WAS TOO DAMN early for her. With dawn still an hour and a half away, Angie made her way silently from her bedroom down into the kitchen. Coffee was the only thing capable of saving her. Hot. Stat . . .

Waiting for the pot to brew, she wandered around the huge space on bare feet, wishing she'd had enough sense to put on a robe. It was chilly overnight and with her short nightie barely covering her legs, she needed that hot drink.

Spying a plate of shortbread on the counter, she snagged a couple of hunks. Angie groaned with each bite, using her tongue to wipe crumbs from her lips. Meghan was teaching Ria how to make the O'Brien Family recipe for the butter sweetened biscuit, so there seemed to be an endless fresh batch available for taste testing. And these? Oh, my god. Bliss.

Grabbing a mug, she poured a large serving of java-energy, stopping at the frig to add a tremendous dollop of heavy cream then made her way quickly into Alex's study—where she could shut the door and have a bit of privacy.

Very, very glad that her brother had wisely converted the hacienda's secondary fireplaces to gas, she got the flames dancing, snatched a soft throw blanket off the love seat and curled up in one of the matching leather chairs facing the hearth.

After a couple of sips of the hot coffee, she felt clearer—which was absolutely necessary before she got on the phone.

Mentally calculating the time difference, Angie glanced at the clock, and figured it was just after lunch at the winery—perfect time to get Sophie alone for a chat.

"Hi, sweetie!" she chirped enthusiastically when she heard her big sister's voice.

"Angie!" Sophia yelled happily. "Oh, my goodness. What time is it in Arizona?" She laughed. "Hold on," she quickly added. "What's wrong? Are you in trouble?"

Good lord. Being the little sister really could be trying at times. Not that she was complaining. After all, it was kind of cool knowing there were these other people in her corner who loved her unconditionally and would always have her back.

Angie chuckled and hunkered down into the throw blanket, enjoying its softness and warmth. "Why's it gotta be this way?" she teased. "How come the first thing you ask is whether I've screwed up or not?"

Her sister mockingly bawled, "Because we've met before, remember?"

"Ah. Good point. Score one for the big sis."

"Speaking of big," Soph joked, "how's that muscled lug masquerading as our brother? Arizona declare him the official state hulk yet?"

"Wait till you meet Meghan, Soph. She's just like she is on the phone but when you see the two of them together? Oh, my god, hon. It'll melt your heart. The way he looks at her . . ."

She couldn't continue. Sophie knew what she was getting at. Being emotional about their beloved older brother was something the two sisters shared. Alexander was their hero—almost losing him had deepened their bond of love.

"Mom's shitting herself," Soph jeered. "Did she tell you we're stopping in New York before going to Boston? Shopping spree. With dad's blessing, no less!"

"Cha-ching," Angie quipped.

"Exactly! She got all worked up about meeting the O'Brien's. Got it into her head that the Valleja-Marquez clan needs classing up. Something about old hippies and sweaty desert rats. According to Mom, the only way to deal with this is by shopping till we drop."

Angie roared with laughter but quickly bit off the sound remembering how early it was. Or how late. Depended on your point-of-view.

With a bit of mockery, she told Sophie, "On the other side, we have the O'Brien's who think that we're some venerable European dynasty! What a laugh, huh? Red says her folks have practically redecorated their house attic to cellar so they don't come off as lowly colonials."

"Well, if it all means I get to flounce around New York and park my ass at Barney's Madison Avenue with a personal shopper before dropping some cold cash at FAO Schwarz before they close . . . the folks can freak out all they want!"

Hmmm. "Are you really going to FAO?"

"Absolutely! You want me to pick something up for you?"

Angie's mind swam with ideas before settling on something giggle worthy. Laughing quietly, she instructed Sophie with precisely what she wanted her to be on the lookout for.

"Does this have anything to do with a certain rock 'n' roll lawyer?"

"Oh," Angie muttered in surprise. "You know about that?"

Sophie laughed—she had one of those outrageously huge cackles that seemed incongruous coming from someone so serious minded.

"For real?" her sister quipped dryly. "Ya do know that after you spilled your guts to mom, she started gathering a trousseau, right?"

Aargh! Parents. "And let me guess—she's burning up the phone lines with Aunt Wendy, too."

"Bull's-eye," Soph drawled. "I'm happy for you, sis. Parker's amazing and it's not like both families haven't been secretly cheering you two on. I knew after Ronaldo's skinny knees bumped the curb that you'd have to finally resolve the issues between you and the lawyer."

"*Pfft,* well it's not completely resolved although we're trying. And here's the thing, sweetie," she added. Taking another sip of coffee, she sat up and frowned. "Aldo is here." No use in stating anything other than the facts. Soph would start tossing off questions anyway.

"Excuse me?"

"Yeah. You heard me. Showed up yesterday morning."

"In Arizona?"

She chortled hearing the confusion in her sister's question.

"Yep."

After a slight hesitation, Sophie asked for more clarification. She didn't blame her. "Arizona as in Arizona in the USA?"

Was there another one? Angie smirked. Sophie was just as flabbergasted by this turn of events as she was.

"You heard right. Turned up out of the blue at the Villa. Piss poor timing, of course, but yeah. There you have it. My former fiancé has traveled to the foreign land of cowboys and Indians supposedly to fetch me home."

"Er, uh . . . what?"

Angie sighed. Her sister's reaction confirmed that nobody had seen this coming. Somehow, she was relieved.

"That's why I'm calling, Soph. Look, he's up to something. There's not a single, solitary reason why he should have flown all the way here. That door was nailed shut, if you know what I mean. And since he arrived, pretty much all he's done is insult everyone in sight and act like a pretentious snot."

"And Alexander hasn't served him up for dinner?"

"Not yet but Aldo's being such an insufferable shit that it could happen at any moment."

"*Hmph,*" Sophie grunted. "Interesting. A man you dumped months ago follows you to the States and figures antagonizing your Terminator-like sibling seems like a good move."

"See what I mean? Doesn't that sound like he's got an agenda? And not only that! He tried to throw Dad under the bus by insisting that's how he knew where to find me."

"I remember he called into the winery about five days ago. Dad simply said you were with Alexander helping get things ready for the wedding."

"Check things out for me, Soph. I have a bad feeling about this."

"Hey, no problem, Ang. You know I never liked that guy. Sorry sis, but you would have chopped Aldo up into little pieces if things went further than they did."

She snorted with laughter. "I nearly smacked the holy crap out of him last night. He started an argument with me in Spanish and . . ."

"Oh, crap Angie. I gotta run. We have a tour starting in ten minutes, and Mom isn't here, so it's all on me."

The conversation ended rather quickly after that, leaving Angie quiet and thoughtful in the silent, still sleeping hacienda.

Feeling better for having touched base with home, she knew her sister would move mountains to find out what Aldo's agenda was. The sooner she ended this farce and got him on a plane, the better for everybody.

A soft sound in the silence drew her attention and she turned toward the door in time to see Parker moving swiftly through the dim light. Wearing only sweats that hung dangerously low on his hips, he came straight to her, scooping her and the throw blanket into his arms so he could steal her seat in the big leather chair. Her hushed squeal of shock and surprise was the only sound in the room.

"What are you doing up," she asked.

He kissed her forehead and cuddled her close, pulling the blanket over them.

"You left your bed," he murmured quietly.

Had he been camped outside her room and she hadn't realized?

"Oh." There didn't seem to be anything else to say.

Angie curled into his big, warm body and sighed. When she put her cheek on his chest, it felt so natural and so right that she swiftly pressed a kiss on his shoulder, then went right back to snuggling against him.

"Who were you talking to?" he asked.

Angie yawned and rubbed her nose on his skin. He smelled like happiness.

"Angel?" he prompted again.

'Sophie," she mumbled. "Time difference . . ." And then another yawn.

Being held so close, the feel of his naked chest under her, the way he was gently stroking her hair . . . *mmmmm.*

Letting sleep overtake her felt deliciously sublime . . . so she did.

Chapter Fifty-Seven

He must have dozed off because one minute he'd been enjoying the simple delight of watching Angie sleep and the next he was struggling out of a dream that threatened to push him further than he wanted to go.

Pretty much the last thing this situation called for was an erotic fantasy involving Angie's legs, his shoulders, and a pillow bunched up and shoved under her ass. Not good. Not good at all. There was only so much control he could cling to before something like that tripped him up. And no way was he going to fuck this up by getting naked with her in Alex's house.

Inhaling deeply to try and shake off the dream's aftermath, he ended up groaning when all that did was fill his senses with her alluring scent.

It hit him like a freight train rolling eighty miles an hour. Had he ever been fully present with anyone but her? He didn't think so and was damn sure he'd never given two seconds of thought before to how anyone smelled.

A soft sigh drifted across his chest and she squirmed slightly in his embrace. It felt so good to hold her close. Something was happening inside him. No. Not the ever-present hard-on he lived with twenty-four seven. This was different. Feeling immersed in her smell. Caring about her feelings. The simple pleasure of holding her close. These were not things that existed in his world before. She was changing him.

The angel sleeping in his arms sighed and quite adorably, rubbed her face on his chest with a quiet moan—settled, then sighed again.

"Mmmm." Her voice rumbled slightly and sounded husky. "I was dreaming."

Pushing off him with a murmured, "Oh," she moved the hair from her face and looked at him, her teeth worrying her bottom lip. "Did I fall asleep?"

Parker smiled and thought, *Ah yes—that moment when you wake up and ask the obvious.*

He glanced at the clock on the bookcase. "Just for a few minutes. Was it a good dream?"

When she sat up the blanket slipped off her shoulders giving him his first really good view of what she was wearing and oh, dear god, what was it about silk and lace that made a guy's dick throb?

He knew precious little about what women wore to bed. Sleeping wasn't an activity that mattered much when all he'd ever done was hook-up. Sex was sex. There was an established protocol . . . all superficial. Drinks or dinner. Occasionally a show or a social engagement. No strings attached fucking.

Lather. Rinse. Repeat. Nighties and practical shit? *Yeah, whatever.*

Gathering her hair into a tail, she told him with innocent surprise, "You were in it."

He chuckled. Well, he'd been dreaming about her as well, but he bet his mental picture was a fuckton lustier than anything her sleep-drunk mind had conjured up.

Running his finger over the swell of her breasts above the flimsy silk nightie, he husked, "Did I behave myself?" Not even the dim light of the room could conceal the prickling of her skin beneath his gentle touch.

She actually thought about it! *Hehehe.* Un-fucking-believable. Someone else might have been ready with a practiced line and played a part in an attempt to gain his attention. Angie didn't have a coy bone in her body. When she was shy or reserved, it was genuine and not some pretense.

At the sound of a muffled chuckle, he dragged his hungry gaze from her flesh and found she was giggling with a hand firmly over her mouth. "Oh, you were very well behaved."

Ooookay. Pulling on a curl, he kidded her tenderly, "Are you saying that you weren't well behaved? I find that hard to believe. Your performance earlier at Pete's was perfectly well behaved!"

Her whole body moved causing nearly permanent impairment to his manhood when she adorably crossed her arms and huffed dramatically. "That was not the time to be ladylike, sir," she snarked with a frowny face.

Unf. Control was becoming an intention rather than a requirement. Supremely conscious of their circumstances and where they were had Parker struggling. Need was a mighty opponent—one he was losing to.

"The fiery spirit you have is a good thing, Angel."

She stopped frowning. And breathing.

"Your passion excites me."

They stared deeply into each other's eyes.

In a small voice, she asked, "Do you want me, Parker?"

"How is this even a question?" He growled and rolled his hips beneath her, driving his steely cock against her bottom for emphasis.

"I think I needed to hear you say it," she admitted.

Not sure where this was going, he issued a muttered warning, "I absolutely want you, but that doesn't mean I'm making love to you in this house."

Better to get that out there and be firm about it. He'd deal with the disappointed fallout if there were any.

The stunning smile that made her face glow rattled his ability to function and the suspicion that he'd somehow just handed her the upper hand made him twitchy.

Wiggling her naughty ass on his lap, she wrenched the blanket from beneath her and tossed it aside with a hearty grunt, "Ugh."

Without missing a beat, the sexy nymph stood then gracefully sank down, pressing open his thighs as she did, ending on her knees between his open legs. Her hands immediately went to his chest, landing with palms flat on his shoulders.

Grinning wickedly she dug her nails in and firmly clawed her way down to the top of his waistband. "I'm so glad you're clear on what *you* won't do. It's good to have that spelled out."

Drawing figures on his naked stomach, she smirked at him from time to time with a pout that made him nervous.

No. No. No. No. No. No. Uh-uh. Nope. No way.

"What are up to?" he asked warily. The effect her nails had on his flesh was shocking. It was a miracle he didn't embarrass himself by coming right then and there.

"That's odd," she purred. "You asked the same thing in my dream."

She's trying to kill me, right?

"Cut it out. Stop messing around, Angie." There. He told her!

She snickered and moved her hands up to caress his pecs. "Said that, too."

"Behave yourself," he grunted.

Leaning close, she asked him in a husky voice, "Are you sure that's what you want?" She punctuated the question by rubbing his hardened manhood through the sweats. *Unf.*

Parker swiftly grabbed her hand. This was getting ridiculous. He had to make her stop. "Angelina," he growled.

"Parker," she answered with a mocking growl of her own.

Only thing was, while he'd grabbed her hand, he also made no real effort to remove it or stop her from rather boldly fondling him. With one hand thoroughly mapping his erection, she took two fingers of her other hand and tapped them lightly on her lips.

"Kiss, kiss Parker."

He froze. She used to do the same thing as a little girl, always asking for kisses. During their torrid liaison, she'd turned the gesture into a private intimacy.

Her hand upon his straining flesh and those words still clinging to her lips pushed him to the edge. Grabbing her face in both hands, he pulled her into his mouth and went deep. A kiss wouldn't hurt, right? Just one kiss. Maybe a really, really, really long kiss. With lots of tongue. Something wet and slow and sensuous.

Yeah. He was cool. They'd just kiss.

And kiss.

And kiss.

And kiss.

Moaning, she welcomed his mouth and wound her arms around his head, rubbing her silk covered tits on his bare chest while her tongue dueled lustfully with his.

Banding an arm about her torso, he held on, grabbing a handful of her sweet ass to knead and massage. Their faces were getting wet from the saliva and each time the need for air forced them apart, she licked his lips and whimpered until he returned and ravished her mouth some more.

Parker hung in there as long as he could. She was just this side of insatiable and so demanding that the kiss threatened to go supersonic until a point was reached that tested his limits and he knew they had to back off.

But each time he tried to peel her off and put some space between them, she protested and pushed him further.

Finally, when he was hanging by the thinnest of threads, he shook her off with a frustrated grunt. "Enough."

She sat back on her feet and frowned sullenly. Running her hands over his thighs, she made a plea he was unprepared for.

"Please don't make me leave here without having some part of you."

Her words stunned Parker. "What is it you want, baby girl?" he asked. In a way, he dreaded her response.

"I think you know," she replied, her busy hands making it difficult to think.

"We can't," he declared vehemently.

"But I want you."

Why the hell did she have to lick her lips like that? "Angie. Please. This isn't a button you should push."

"I. *Want*. You."

She wickedly squeezed him in a demonstration of her want and that was it for him. Giving up, he sat back heavily in the big chair, gripped the soft leather upholstery on the arms and tilted his head back. Growling a terse, "Fuck," he pinned her in place with a look. "You'd make a shitty submissive."

She beamed at his scolding tone. *Dammit.*

Once he surrendered, she went into overdrive, swiftly divesting him of his sweats. His shaft exposed, she gasped and exclaimed, "Oh, Parker!"

Keeping his hands on the arms of the chair was torture. Through eyes at half-mast, he examined the expression lighting up her face as she studied his bared flesh. His cock was a self-centered bastard, used to the admiring glances of women. Thick and long enough that he was accustomed to the thrilled sighs accompanying an unveiling, Parker was bowled over by the immense satisfaction he got from her obvious delight.

She got busy damn quick after that. Putting those soft hands of hers to good use, she thoroughly fondled and stroked his swollen flesh, making little noises that read like erotic shorthand in his mind.

Showing a particular fascination with the fat head of his sex and the ridges of sensitive flesh that ached for her attention, she created a mesmerizing sensual ballet out of handling his pulsing cock. By the time she bent forward and added her lips and tongue to the effort, he was so far over the edge that freefalling was guaranteed.

No stranger to a blowjob, Parker was nonetheless spellbound watching as Angel feasted on his manhood. She was on fire, greedily licking, nipping, and kissing the length of him.

It was a fucking given that he very much liked what she was doing. The wildcard was that she so obviously did, too. An adrenaline rush thundered through his body and he grunted along as she began taking him deeper and deeper on a journey of such exquisite pleasure, he ended up closing his eyes, his head thrashing on the back of the chair as she sucked him into an erotic trance.

He was so close—yearning for release—but not wanting to end the torture of pleasure that she was creating. Forcing his eyes to open, he watched through the ravenous craving clouding his vision.

Parker pounded his fist on the chair's arm, grunting wildly at the sight of her luscious lips stretched around his swollen cock. Oh, *fuck*. It was too much. When she looked at him, half his dick in her mouth, eyes glazed with desire, he cried her name lustfully.

"Angelina!"

Plunging up and down on his staff, she worked his flesh until an orgasm of such intensity overtook him that he gave up his determination not to touch her and grabbed her head.

She welcomed his rough handling with eager moans as he pushed her to take him deep. *Deeper.* Until he felt her throat working the head of his cock.

When he exploded, she groaned and accepted the pulses and throbs of his wildly jerking flesh as he released in her mouth. She hadn't wanted to leave without some part of him. Well, she certainly got what she wanted.

But he wasn't happy about it.

Chapter Fifty-Eight

Angie crept silently from the study a while later, hurriedly making for her room. She shuddered to think what would happen if Alex found her sneaking around the downstairs in a nightie. Especially since there was no way to disguise the rather telltale aftermath of the oral seduction she'd lavished on the body of a certain lawyer. Biggest clues? Her hair was a total mess, and she had what Tori called BJ Lips, a polite way of saying her mouth had that puffy, swollen post blowjob look. *Eeek*. No way to hide that.

Safely back in her room, she threw herself onto the bed and hugged a pillow close. There was no way to explain what she'd just done. One minute, she'd been enjoying a hot spicy dream, and the next, she was demanding things from Parker she never had before.

All she knew was, when she woke up from a deep doze, surrounded by his heat and incredible smell and with the remnants of a highly erotic dream still in her thoughts, the first thing that occurred to her was *this man is mine*.

She was done with all the bullshit and decided on a sleepy, sexy whim that no matter what it took, she was going to make Parker Sullivan love her. Luck didn't happen to those who stood on the sidelines. If he was what she wanted, well . . . men, y'know? She'd be waiting forever for him to get a freakin' clue unless she took matters into her own hands, or mouth, as the case might be.

Angie rolled into the pillow to hide her face and groaned loudly.

What had she done? It wasn't the balls-to-the chin, blowjob that was the problem. It was the expression on Parker's face after. She'd struck a nerve, and it didn't look like a good one.

Dawn had finally come but Parker had yet to return to the tiny room adjacent to Angie's that he'd settled in despite a glowering frown from Alex. Nobody said fucking shit when he declared that he wasn't leaving Angie's side while Esperanza was still around, but that didn't mean any of them were stupid. Putting him and Angie in nearby rooms was sexual suicide.

So he'd made a vow on the fly that no matter what, he'd show the proper respect to his friend and behave. He was a guest in the man's home and sleeping with Alex's sister while they were under his roof just wasn't going to happen.

Why the hell did everything keep getting more and more complicated? And fucked up?

Flipping the fireplace control to off, he plodded on bare feet to the tall arched window looking out over an expanse of Villa property. He was at war with himself and needed the calm that the bucolic vista brought.

Ready to jump out of his skin at any second, Parker remembered other times he'd felt this unhinged. Months after he and Angie fell into their deadly silence, he and a small team of government lawyers and a handful of agents fresh from Quantico had been quietly dispatched into the middle of two fucking wars. Every goddamn thing the military and the government did was under constant legal scrutiny. It had been a busy time.

He'd bounced around to more black and special op compounds than he cared to remember. Brutal shit went on around him morning, noon, and night. Dropping into the middle of a war zone wasn't unusual for him right up until he left Washington.

During a couple of those trips, he'd hooked up with Alex and learned a new term . . . *feral anxiety*. The conditions those guys lived under was staggering. What they were doing was terrifying. To say he developed a new level of respect for his friend was the understatement of all time. And he couldn't even think about how much deeper that respect and gratitude went after the bombing, which nearly killed him.

Guard-dogging Angie had been his reason for staying at the Villa. Parker was a lot of things, but a total dog wasn't one of them. His intentions had been genuine. Keeping that jackass Esperanza on a short leash and away from her was his primary motivation.

But he also had an itchy conscience because Alex trusted him to . . . well, he trusted him to keep it in his goddamn pants and remember where the hell they were.

Vigorously scraping both hands back and forth through his hair until his scalp tingled, Parker tried valiantly to rein in the angst eating him up. Never intending to disrespect his friend and supremely conscious of the privilege afforded him not only as a guest at the Villa but as a card-carrying member of Family Justice, his loss of control with Angie felt like a tawdry betrayal. *Ugh. Fuck.*

The morning view was beautiful, but he was still jumpy and off balance. And it didn't help at all that his inner beast complicated this emotional turmoil. The knuckle-dragging caveman was threatening to break free so he could thunder upstairs, push open her door, scoop her badass up and toss it over his shoulder—take her away from here where they could be alone and figure out what the fuck they were doing.

The figuring out part was admittedly second on the to-do list. First up was some bone-melting lovemaking and once and for all, he was going to tell her how he felt. That he'd loved her for her whole life and could never love another. And that he was more sorry than she will ever know for the years they lost.

Humming happily to herself as she ambled through the big hacienda, Meghan stopped to chat with the portrait of Alex's great-great grandmother that hung in an upstairs hallway. She liked the beautiful señora's enigmatic smile and knowing expression. Must be a family trait because she often saw the same look on the Major's face.

"Morning, Abuela," she chirped. "Did I say that right?" she chuckled. Shaking her head in mock annoyance, she teased the silent portrait, "Your great, great grandson dropped the ball, I'm sorry to say, when it comes to learning the language. But don't you worry! I'm on it."

Fussing with the bowl of fresh flowers that Carmen religiously maintained on a table beneath the large ornately framed canvas, she assured the distinguished-looking ancestor that the next generation of the Valleja-Marquez family born under the Arizona sun would most definitely be bilingual.

Smiling, she continued on, making her way to the kitchen for a cup of the coffee she smelled wafting through the house. Meghan truly loved the hacienda. There was something about the history of the Villa and the surrounding land that spoke to her. And lately, she'd felt it speaking back.

She was still unsure and nervous about how she'd handle being the mistress of a legacy so grand, but with Alex at her side, she knew they could handle anything . . . as long as they were together.

Skipping lightly down the wide staircase, her dress swinging as she moved, it was all Meghan could do not to explode with contentment. She had a great life. A man who adored her. A growing family and a vision for the future that was really exciting.

Softly giggling as she smoothed some wayward curls, she had to admit that the off-the-hook lovemaking the Major lavished on her at every opportunity didn't hurt. Why, just this morning he'd taken her so sweetly and tenderly that she cried after and clung to him while he held her tight, whispering lovingly until the demands of the day forced them to leave their bed.

But that wasn't the only reason for the incandescent happiness lighting her up from the inside. Alex's quirky solution for alleviating her growing concerns about their wedding being overshadowed by the circumstances and judgments of others was so damn cool and exciting, she was dancing on air.

Her mother had gifted her a stunning dress finished with vintage lace that was short with a flared skirt and a wide satin ribbon around the waist that jumped out of her closet earlier when she'd been looking for something. Almost shitting herself was the only way to describe how she reacted. It was perfect and exactly what she wanted for their private celebration.

Lost in her happy daydream, Meghan was ninety percent oblivious to anything going on around her when she bounced into the kitchen on feet barely touching the floor. Her happiness was so big, she wondered if she could contain it.

Pouring a glass of OJ, she'd just taken a sip when she turned around and got a good look at what was going down in her kitchen. *What the hell?*

Parker and Angie were present but by the look of things, must not ever have been formally introduced because they were completely ignoring each other. A better description of the scene she stumbled on might be that a bent-out-of-shape lawyer was hunched over the island bar nursing a steaming cup of whatever while a lip-biting and discernibly uneasy Angie, stood to the side picking on a bowl of grapes, occasionally glancing Parker's way.

Well, this looks like shittons of fun!

Three seconds after that wry observation, Alex came bustling into the kitchen with an armload of packages, a couple of which fell to the floor as he struggled to dump everything on the island.

Chuckling, he smirked at Meghan. "Honey, you keep this up and I'm going to have to hire that poor driver to be your personal delivery service."

All Meghan could do was laugh. He was right, of course. During the months she'd been in Arizona where their location made a shopping excursion something of a long-distance slog, she'd become a champion at ordering. Her days of mall crawling, looking for whatever caught her eye, were now relegated to specially planned and executed occasions. With QVC and Amazon being her main bitches, she had that one-click thing down pat!

His eyes glowing with pleasure, Alex came around the island and kissed her quickly. "You look lovely," he murmured.

Words? What words? Her smile said it all.

Snatching the glass of OJ right out of her hands, Alex tossed it back with a loud grunt then slammed the empty down. "Ahhhh, I needed that," he kidded while she arched an eyebrow at him.

"Uh, one of those smaller packages has Ria's name on it . . ."

"I've corrupted her, I'm afraid," she snickered, interrupting whatever he was going to say. "Ben wanted a whatchamacallit-thingy for the garden and . . ."

Alex barked a laugh. "Whatchamacallit-thingy?"

God, he was adorable when he teased her. Reaching out, she grabbed his shirt and pulled him forward. "I want very much to tell you to shut it." She grinned—thoroughly enjoying his eyes flaring at her obvious attempt to manipulate the no-no expression.

Did he even realize Angie and Parker were present, she wondered or was he simply ignoring the drama this morning? Frankly, she didn't care. Those two would figure it out. Just like Cam and Lacey had. Just like Draegyn and Victoria, her and Alex, and hell, even Stephanie and Calder had, although that sitch was still a work in progress.

Following the direction of her gaze, he turned his head, first studying Parker's impersonation of a mute as he sat nearby. The look he gave her was just short of an eye roll. Meghan choked off her laughter with a hurried cough.

Glancing the other way, he checked his sister out and this time he really did roll his eyes and shake his head. Kissing her quickly one more time, Alex leaned close and whispered, "Remember baby . . . just you and me. Fuck this shit, okay?"

She didn't need reassurance. Not anymore. When Meghan explained how she felt, Alex hadn't hesitated. Not for a second. He didn't ask for more detail or try to talk her out of her concerns.

Was she glowing? Probably. That was how this man made her feel.

"I'm good," she deadpanned with a pouty smirk right after eyeing the ominously restrained couple. Chuckling deeply, her Major helped himself to some of her ass. "Oh, and I found the perfect thing to wear."

"It better be white," he muttered. "Your mom's right. You look angelic in white." Then, quickly changing the subject, he sighed heavily. She couldn't agree more. C'mon," he nudged her shoulder, "Looks like it's intervention time."

Mentally reviewing the checklist of things he still needed to do, Alex made a quick note on his phone before pocketing it then hustled himself a mega mug of coffee. Satisfied that Meghan was okay with whatever the fuck it was that was going on around them, he felt a hundred times less stressed now that he'd included his fiancée in at least a portion of the special day he was planning for them.

It still cracked him up that she was so easily satisfied with what she imagined was nothing more than a picnic in the desert. Jesus, was she ever in for a shock. Only a couple more days and then she'd be his forever.

Truth? He was starting to get nervous. Not groom jitters. More like a guy trying to surprise and please his lady jitters. There was always the chance that he'd fuck shit up or had read her signals wrong.

No, *uh-uh,* wait a minute. Read her signals wrong? As if! He had this situation by the short hairs and as long as he didn't let the cat out of the bag too soon, he was going to pull off the most epic, romantic, guy gesture of all time. Shame they had to keep it a secret.

Taking the stool next to Parker, Alex noticed that Meghan made no effort to engage Angie. Perhaps that was because his little sister looked like she was gearing up to admit to the crime of the century. What the hell had gone on between these two morons after he and Meghan went to their suite last night? Whatever it was, well. . . . it didn't look good.

"Mission Control to jerkbag," he murmured.

Nothing. *Oh, great.* Taking a healthy sip from his mug, he pushed a plate of glazed blueberry muffins toward his friend. Even Alex had to admit they looked delicious and with Parker's inability to resist anything from the bakery, he felt sure a muffin would be a good icebreaker.

Still nothing. Really? *Shit.* Tempted to wave his hand in front of the guy's face to see if he was conscious, Alex sent Meghan a look of bewilderment. She shrugged and sipped her beverage.

Well, this is just fan-fucking-tastic.

As the four of them lingered in silence, he wondered what the hell he was supposed to do. The uncomfortable gathering was on the verge of getting ugly when a phone rang. Comically, everyone reacted by reaching for their cell.

The call was for Angie and the instant she answered, Alex knew something was up. The immediate shift in her demeanor and a dramatic change in body language sent up a red flag that he noted but did not react to. Justice was known for offering top-notch surveillance. Being watchful was *Duh 101* in the training manual.

Wondering whose call could affect so quick a change in his sister, his answer came swiftly when she caught his eye and gestured to the phone.

"It's Soph. I've gotta take this but say hi."

"Hey, Squirt," Alex boomed as Angie held the phone up. "Love you. Miss you. Can't wait to see . . ." he got out before she hastily fled the room.

Meghan snickered, then went back to fiddling with her iPad in a less-than-genuine way that told him she was actually paying close attention to every little thing. She would have made a great operative.

With Angie now out of the room, he swiveled toward Parker and punched him in the arm. "What the hell did you do?" he barked.

"Ow, you asshole. What the fuck was that for?"

Alex laughed. He had to. All of this was so bizarre. *What the fuck was that for?* Was he kidding? Actually, no he probably wasn't. Upon closer look, it was apparent that Parker was distracted, bothered, and generally bent.

Changing his approach, he sat back and eyed his friend, saying, "You look like shit." And he did. Like total shit. And not too much to drink shit. Or stressed at work shit. Or even feeling like shit. This kind of shit looked damn serious.

"Wanna talk about it?" he asked.

"No." The answer was immediate, forceful, and tinged with something else. Unless he was mistaken, the man was sulking. Full on, kicking the dog brooding with a double dash of moody bastard thrown in.

Well, whadaya know? The great and mighty Parker Sullivan sent crashing to Earth by a bratty angel. Circle this date on the calendar!

Chapter Fifty-Nine

"Are you okay?"

Angie didn't know if she was okay or not. Surely there had to be some suffering or impairment after the world tilted or, in this case, came to a jarring halt.

"Uhhh . . . sure." *Liar, liar, pants on fire.*

Sophie grumbled, "Dad's going to filet his miserable ass. This is so far over the line, he won't have any choice."

Oh no. Dad knew about this? Holy crap. All she could do was groan and drop her head into her hand.

"Sorry, Ang. I had to tell him. The story is about to go wide and he needed to know in case someone asks for a comment."

"I know, sis. It's fine. Really. Just a lot for me to take in, y'know?"

"Shit, Angie. I am soooo sorry."

She chortled bitingly. "What do you have to be sorry for? It wasn't you who knocked up some club circuit slut while engaged. To me. *Ugh, god!* How could I have been so blind?"

"Sweetie, don't take this on yourself. You didn't do anything. Aldo did. He played you dirty, Ang. No other way to put it. All signs point to him figuring you guys would have a modern arrangement which is arrogant asshole code for he wanted a wife to make him socially acceptable while he behaved like a privileged pig on the side."

"Sniveling dumbass."

"You're taking this better than I thought. Does Parker have anything to do with that?"

A tiny flame, the one that never really went out, flashed inside her. Her heart smiled.

"We sang together on stage, Soph." She was going to say more, but her sister's sharp gasp left her speechless.

"Oh, baby . . ."

Was that the sound of tears edged with sniffling she heard coming from the phone?

"The heavens must be in perfect alignment!" Sophie exclaimed tearfully.

Her reaction warmed Angie. "We're going to give it a try. See what happens," she anxiously muttered. Saying it out loud to another person was a bit scary. Made it awfully real.

"I'm thrilled for you. I love Parker and you know the 'rents on both sides are gonna go apeshit."

"But it's weird, huh?"

Sophie loosed her wonderful laugh. "It's weird for two seconds and then there's nothing but love, baby. In a way, I think maybe we've all been waiting to see if either of you was ever going to come to your senses. You freaked a lot of people out over the years, but now that it's all coming out, you're gonna find that you two being together is what everyone figured was your destiny all along. Think Mom and her hippie-dippy nonsense."

Angie's mind was whirling. She wanted to sit there and chatter away with her sister. Gush about Parker. Lose her shit over a boy. But that had to wait. First there was the Aldo mess to clean up.

"One last thing and then I'll let you go. Is all of this why Aldo's been trying to create a scene? Does he hope to deflect attention from a European scandal with an American one?"

She practically felt the warmth of Sophie's breath as she heaved a deep sigh. "Bingo and here's where I have to drop the final part of the bomb. It's worse than you think. The girl is about to pop any day."

"Excuse me?" The fine hairs on the back of Angie's neck felt like spikes with exposed nerve endings. The math was pretty easy to do.

"Soooo, what you're saying is, when I ended the engagement four months ago, she was already obviously pregnant?"

"Yes, and there's more."

She grimaced and snapped back, "Of course, there is. Just give it to me."

"His folks brought the hammer down when they found out. Cut him off without a dime. The person I heard from says he talks incessantly about you. How if he could get you back, he'd be respectable again and his parents would back off. So he did some research after he found out you were with Alex. They think he decided to go to the States and convince you of whatever. But when things didn't go as he imagined, Plan B went into action. Nothing like a nice juicy lawsuit, maybe some paparazzi nonsense to make headlines and line his pockets."

Angie couldn't believe how stupid this guy was. "Soph, can you even imagine how lucky he is to still be walking? He poked at all of us, nonstop. He actually punched Parker in the face!"

"Seriously? And Parker didn't serve him up with a side of guacamole?"

"Actually, all the guys have been pretty restrained because they thought tiptoeing around him was better than a confrontation. It was me who got physical."

"Did you smack him, I hope?"

"No, but wish I had. Parker held me back and Alex had Aldo by the scruff of the neck. If we'd been let at each other, I would have ripped his throat out."

"Well, thank god Justice knows how to keep the calm. If any of them had gone off and assaulted him, Aldo was ready to sue the shit out of everyone. Clearly, you can see what an excellent and caring daddy he's going to be. A great way to secure a future for his kid!"

They actually laughed. On some sick and twisted level, what she said was true.

"What are you going to do?"

Oh. Angie knew exactly what to do. No doubt about it.

"Yeah, I think it's trash day."

"*Bwahahahahaaaaaa,*" Sophie barked gleefully. "Don't get your hands dirty and make sure you wear shit kicking shoes when you do it!"

"Put it on speaker," Alex told Meghan when his phone chirped. She reached over and tapped the screen then went right back to what she was doing.

"You're on speaker—go ahead."

Parker recognized Ben's voice immediately. "Uh, boss . . . we have a situation."

Puzzled, Alex croaked directly into the phone. "Define situation."

"Um, well, you see, Gus called me over to the garage."

"Uh-huh," Alex looked at Parker like *what the fuck?* "And . . ."

"Yeah, and uh, he had a vehicle request."

"Oh, for god's sake," Alex muttered. "And why am I involved?" he asked with an edge of frustration in his tone.

"It's Miss Angelina, boss. She wants to take out one of the SUV's for the day."

Parker froze. Meghan looked up.

"She going somewhere?" he asked.

"Gus says it didn't seem like his place to pry, but that's why he called me and that's why I'm calling you. There's no problem giving her any of the cars, but I figured you'd want to know she was on the move."

"What the fuck is she up to?" he griped out loud. To Ben he said, "All right. Give her whatever she wants and maybe find out what's going on, okay?"

"You got it, boss. Thanks."

Parker didn't know what to think. He was with Alex on this one. What the hell was she doing that she needed an SUV for the entire day? Half an hour ago she'd been in sweats lounging in the kitchen and now suddenly she's behind the wheel and going god knows where.

The damn woman was hell on wheels. Now, what the fuck was she up to?

She sang *Here Comes the Sun* as she walked from the house deep into the compound to the big garage where all the vehicles, carts, scooters, ATVs, and general riding toys were kept. The song felt right for the beautiful sunny morning.

Stomping along, she had to congratulate herself on her outfit choice for the errand she was on. Going full Desert Angel, she put on an old pair of beat up black western boots and wiggled her butt into a wickedly slutty pair of cutoff denim shorts that had seen better days—like five years ago. One good washing and the fabric of the well-worn jeans might fall apart, which only made her love them even more.

A plain white tank top under an ancient flannel shirt with the sleeves rolled back was innocent enough until a closer look revealed she was braless. Aware that her boobs were bouncing as she walked only made her gurgle with laughter.

Jiggle away, girls, she thought gleefully.

When she was growing, this was her daily uniform. Parker would love it, but she knew her appearance was going to send a statement Ronaldo wasn't likely to forget.

Rounding a corner of the large garage, she stepped into the side parking area and went in search of Gus. She'd asked for an SUV instead of a sedan because she wanted as much room between her and that slimy bastard as possible and remembering how annoyed Parker had been that she was separated from him when they'd drive in his big SUV, the choice seemed logical.

"Hiya Gus," she tittered when she caught sight of the older gentleman who managed the entire Justice fleet of moving objects. "Whatcha got for me?"

Approaching the kindly gray-haired man who was smiling warmly at her, she saw Ben was also there. Angie loved Ben. He was a piece of work—same for his wife Ria—but he was the loyal, dependable right-hand that her brother counted on. And his presence meant that her activities this fine morning were not flying under the radar.

Seriously. It was a wonder that Alex didn't come thundering down the path right behind her. Aunt Wendy would call how the men around here acted as being in cahoots. Angie wasn't sure of the origin of the word, but it sure did express a certain cowboy flair that fit perfectly.

Throwing Ben some humorous side shade, she snarked, "Do you have to fingerprint me or tag me with a GPS before I can take the leash off?"

He had the look of a man wishing he could be anywhere but there with her having this conversation. She was a Marquez, after all, and saying no to her or butting into her personal business was hard for him.

"Aw, come on, Miss Angie. That's not fair. You know all he cares about is your safety. We all do," he added with a nod at Gus.

They were cute, but she didn't have time for any of this. She had something to do. "Relax, Ben. I'm just yanking your chain." Seeing that Gus was standing beside the open driver door to a large white Explorer, she walked up to him and put out her hand. "Key, please."

The two men exchanged a silent look, but she stood her ground and waited them out—her hand hanging in the air, palm up, waiting.

Four minutes later, she was pulling up to the business center where the employee apartments were. So far, so good. Now for the fun part. Flipping the visor down, she peered into the mirror. Smartly remembering to bring along a lipstick, she pulled it from her pocket, checked the color, and immediately laughed. It was called *No Mercy*. How appropriate!

Applying the vibrant red color until her mouth rivaled the most perfect Hollywood pout, she winked at her reflection, muttered, "Showtime," and pushed open the car door with her booted foot. Desert Angel was on the scene and ready to fuck shit up.

Stomping angrily up the stairs to the second level, she made sure to make as much noise as humanly possible on her way to the apartment at the end. That was all the warning she was giving.

At the door, she stopped, made sure she had a plan, and then went for it. Swiftly pushing, she barged straight in as the wood slammed heavily against the inner wall with a loud thud.

Hehehe. Sound effects were so awesome sometimes! Angry boots, slamming doors. And she was just getting started.

When she burst into the room, Aldo jumped up from the sofa with a startled yelp. Seeing her coming at him, he started speaking rapidly in

Spanish, but she didn't bother to listen. Finding him on his cell phone had been a stroke of pure luck. While he yelled and waved his arms, she made straight for the phone, snatching it out of his hand before he could stop her.

Though he'd disconnected the call, the screen hadn't timed out yet, essentially giving her an unrestricted all access pass to his sordid little life. When he tried to grab the phone back, she deflected the attempt with a vicious slap, turning away and quickly putting half the room and all the furniture between them.

First, she checked his call log. Call after call after call, all to the same number, filled the screen. Baby mama? Probably. Or maybe the fuckwad was cheating on her, as well. Wouldn't be surprised if that were the case.

Then, for shits 'n' grins, she started scrolling through his photos, and holy crap, what a goldmine of douchebaggery was on display there. There were dozens of photos of him with countless women, all in seriously questionable circumstances, including a couple that told Angie he found someone willing to whip his sorry ass. *Ewwwww.*

But the absolute best part? The sleazy little fucker easily had a hundred truly captivating shots of what's called a Dick Pic. Jackpot! In seconds, she'd forwarded two dozen or so of the most incriminatingly embarrassing photos to her email for safe keeping. Damage control. She wanted to laugh but knew she couldn't. It would ruin the kickass performance she was putting on.

"Querida, I can explain."

Was he still talking? Sheesh. You'd think there was somebody wanting to listen to his sorry shit, but that person wasn't her.

Ignoring him completely after throwing the big iPhone at his head and secretly hoping the screen cracked, she stormed into the bedroom and went in search of his bags.

While Aldo ranted and raved, alternating between lame threats and pathetic whining, she gathered his crap and stuffed everything into a suitcase. In the bathroom, she used a sweeping arm gesture that she remembered seeing in a movie once to dramatically force his toiletries into a travel case. Was all sorts of fun, especially with him getting more frantic and crazier by the minute.

It was abundantly clear to Angie that he knew damn well the jig was up the minute she burst in on him. What a dick.

Lugging his big bag and the four or five smaller ones he traveled with to the door, she kept right on going, grunting and chugging as she dragged the heavy cases along the outside balcony to the steps, and from there, with much banging, she pulled everything down the stairs to the waiting car.

Throwing everything into the SUV almost wiped her out until she spied that rat bastard gawking at her from the top of the stairs and an instant spike of anger fueled adrenaline raced through her system.

"Get your ass down here, Aldo. If you're not in this car when I pull away, I'll have the local authorities arrest you for stalking and harassment and don't think for a second that I won't do just that."

He stood still, a stunned expression on his face. *Whatever.* She had better shit to do. He either heeded the threat or forced her to follow through. His choice.

Whirling away from him, she marched to the driver's door and yanked it open. Glaring back at a man she now realized she never knew at all, Angie barked, "What's it going to be? The car or handcuffs?"

After a second of hesitation, the car won out. Trudging grumpily down the stairs, he glowered at her as he went to the passenger door.

"Oh, bite me," she bit out, climbing into the big car and strapping in. Ignition on and the car in gear, she drove away from the Villa as she told him derisively, "Buck up, Daddy. You've got a plane to catch."

Chapter Sixty

"ALL RIGHT, KIDS." MEGHAN LAUGHED. "That was Betty on the phone. Even though it's Sunday, she was in the office taking care of some time-sensitive thing she said you knew about," she told a bemused looking Alex who nodded his awareness.

Parker just sat there looking like he couldn't form coherent sentences if he tried.

"Anyway, she heard a scuffle and went to check it out. The way she tells it, Angie kicked open Esperanza's door and then yelling started in Spanish. Not long after, your sister," she mugged comically at the Major, "hulked her way through dragging a bunch of suitcases to a car. There was more yelling and she thought maybe she heard something about catching a plane."

"*Whaaaat?*" Parker growled as he jumped to his feet.

Oh, so he actually was still alive. Well, finally! Meghan had begun to wonder if he'd lost it completely because she'd never seen him look so absent and confused.

"All right," Alex muttered darkly. "I've had enough. Hand me my phone, babe," he told her.

"What are you going to do?" she asked after handing it over.

He started tapping then lifted the phone to his ear. "Whatever the hell this is, it started with a phone call from Sophie. I'm going to the source to find out what's really going on."

Watching him march away, she swore there was smoke coming from his exit. Alex didn't like messes. They fucked with the natural order of things. Serving under him must have been challenging for the dramatically inclined. He had no time for divas. Especially when they drew bullshit like a magnet.

Leaving her to deal with Parker, she looked him over and wondered how she could help. He looked so unlike the dynamic guy she'd come to know. Meghan wondered if this was how Alex was after she'd returned to Boston.

"Did you two have a fight?" she asked softly.

Swinging a pained expression her way, he shook his head. "No, it's not like that."

"Oh, good," she stammered. "So . . . did you . . ."

He cut her off so fast, she got verbal whiplash.

"It wasn't me who . . ." He scowled. "*Ugh.* Forget it."

Reading the tea leaves wasn't all that difficult. Knowing Angie as she did and understanding Parker's idiosyncrasies, due in no small measure to how similar he and Alex were, Meghan had a pretty good idea what was causing the lawyer's funk.

Not specifically but she wasn't blind. Parker showed all the signs of a disgruntled alpha after being forced to jump through some relationship hoops.

Nice work, sis.

They turned together toward the archway when Alex's voice became louder the closer he got.

"Drae. Sorry for the Sunday interruption but I've got a mess on my hands up here and I need your help."

Meghan rubbed a hand over Parker's back to comfort him when he groaned.

"Who do we have at the main airport? Anyone?"

Alex glanced at them as he made his way into the kitchen, heading straight for a covered platter stacked with shortbread chunks. She'd converted him, converted all of Family Justice, into an appreciation of the buttery cookie masquerading as a pastry. Ria couldn't make enough to satisfy the demand.

Alternating between stuffing his mouth while crumbs fell onto his shirt and grumbling into the phone, she listened as he told Drae exactly what to do. From what she could gather, he wanted someone to run interference at the airport when Angie arrived.

And why was Angie at the airport? The tension radiating off Parker's torso indicated he had the same question.

Thank god Alex started explaining before the disconnect button got pushed. "According to Soph, little sister is, and I quote, *taking the trash out.*"

Meghan chuckled at the expression. This was going to be a great story one day.

Furiously scrolling, swiping, and tapping on Meghan's iPad as he talked, Alex frowned so hard his face looked like a mask on fright night. "Ah, here we go," he was muttering followed seconds later by a tersely ground out, "Asshole."

Shoving the device under Parker's nose, he grunted, "Get a load of this. It's started to gather moss all over the internet."

His reaction to whatever Alex showed him was instantaneous. "Motherfucker."

Parker repeatedly shook his head like he was trying to unscramble his thoughts, and Alex just growled. Meghan could almost smell the testosterone pumping in the air around them as she quickly scanned the blind item from a gossip site that made her wince. Oh, poor Ang.

Watching the two men side-by-side, while obvious indignation fueled their reaction, was enlightening.

"I'm going after her," Parker mumbled, but he didn't even get a chance to rise from his seat before Alex stopped him with a firm hand on his shoulder.

"Sorry, bud but that's a no. Let Angie take care of this. She knows what she's doing."

"But . . ." Parker protested.

He could say whatever he wanted. It wasn't going to make the Major budge. She knew that look. He was in Big Daddy mode and his word was his command. Period.

"Look, if you need a distraction, imagine what you know damn well she's putting that fucker through. Think about it, man. What she's doing is one hundred percent pure Grade-A top shelf Angelina. He crossed a line, fucked with her family, pissed her crazy, unpredictable ass off and what did she do? Immediately go rogue, commandeer a vehicle, clear his presence from the compound, and turbo-charge a drive to the airport. Bet she pulls in, kicks his ass to the drop-off curb, and leaves him coughing inside a cloud of desert dust."

His summary of probabilities was so funny and sardonic that Meghan snickered loudly as she imagined all the things Alex described. Desert Angel was not to be messed with.

"If he starts anything, I'll . . ."

"Yeah, yeah, yeah," Alex scoffed. "Get in line, man. Me first, and if there's anything left after I'm finished and my father kicks his ass, you're welcome to his sniveling ass."

In a perfectly synchronized pantomime, each of them noted the time. Meghan glanced at the clock on the microwave, Alex pulled up his wrist and consulted his watch, and Parker craned his neck to see what the big kitchen clock said.

"Luckily, we trained some of the airport security teams and Draegyn was able to get in touch with whoever is on duty now. When Angie gets there, she'll be met by security who will ensure that she makes a clean getaway. Once she's out of the mix, Ronald Esperanza will be put on blast. A little reminder not to fuck with her or Justice if he wants to keep his manhood attached."

"I want to know when she's clear," Parker growled.

Alex winked at Meghan then smirked at his friend. He was needling the man and she had to chew on her tongue to keep from laughing.

"Again, dude. Get the fuck in line. I'm responsible for my sister. Not you."

Parker looked like he wanted to strangle Alex. Being told he had no standing where Angie was concerned was a genius move on the Major's part. In Meghan's neck of the woods back in Boston, this maneuver would be described as a classic, *Shit or get off the pot,* move.

The atmosphere in the car during the long drive swung between tense silences and heated exchanges in a battle of wills that Angie won before the drive even began. Not that it mattered. In actuality, she was pretty much over all of it anyway.

Amazingly, she wasn't even mad. In order for that, she'd have to care and she didn't, beyond stressing over the cringe-worthy attention the family would endure once the salacious story hit the internet. But more than that? *Nah.*

When she'd railed at Aldo about being a snot, her outrage had been insincere. He'd always been that way—she just chose not to acknowledge it while they were together.

My bad.

Viewed in that light, she really had no one to blame for her part in his messy drama except herself. Lesson learned? Check.

It also saddened her that this lame excuse for a man was running off at the mouth, covering all his bases over and over, without ever once taking responsibility for the unalterable fact that there was a child in the middle of it all. *Ugh.* Aldo and his baby mama were going to make awesome parents.

Her plan was to pull into the airport, find the international terminal, push him out of the car, and drive off without a word or glance. Trash. Meet curb. Now get the fuck outta my life. She'd deal with what came next during the three-hour trip back to the Villa when, with only her thoughts for company, she could pick it all apart, decide how she wanted to continue, and then get on with it.

Used to the presence of heavy security at the international airports, Angie noted several large, black SUVs idling on the access road leading to departures and wouldn't have thought any more of them if one hadn't immediately slid into the slow moving line of traffic directly behind her.

That was odd, she thought. Checking briefly in the rearview mirror, she saw one person behind the wheel, talking. To who? He was alone. When he turned slightly to the side, she saw the telltale earpiece and microphone used by security for two-way communication.

Ooookay.

Aldo was freaking out big time now that he finally got it into his thick head that this was really happening. You'd think the endless drive would have clued him in. Nobody drove almost two hundred miles for no reason.

"Why are you doing this? Don't you see that I'm the victim here?

Losing you made me do dumb things but I can change. You are worth changing for, querida," he finished in an oily, smarmy sounding tone.

Creeping along through the congested travel gridlock, she spied Air France up ahead and started merging to the curb. Good enough.

Pulling swiftly into a spot being vacated by a taxi, she braked hurriedly bringing the vehicle to a jerking stop.

"Get out," she commanded. Unsnapping her seatbelt, she retracted it with a snap, pushed open her car door, and slid out. Stomping for emphasis, Angie moved swiftly to the rear lift gate so she could dump his shit on the pavement and be done.

It was while she was hauling his pretentious and probably fake designer bags out of the car when she noted that the black security SUV had pulled in directly behind them and the driver was still speaking to some unseen person, while looking directly at her. Feeling uneasy for half a second, she all of a sudden knew that her brother had something to do with this guy. The reach of Alex's protective arm was mind-boggling. And strangely comforting.

Aldo finally made his way to the back of the car, gesturing wildly and scolding her for tossing his precious Vuitton travel cases on the filthy ground.

Pussy. She snickered. The vulgar expression perfectly described the man she was seeing.

With his crazy unleashed, he was distracted enough that Angie had no problem reaching inside his jacket to grab his phone one last time. When he reached for it back, she jeered at him and did an impromptu version of a cowgirl drop and grind by slamming her booted foot, essentially the drop, onto his handmade Italian loafers and giving the heel a vicious grind that got exactly the reaction she wanted. Yelping in distress, he frantically backed away from her, forgetting the phone now that she'd mangled his foot.

Now Parker, mmm. There was a man who would *definitely* appreciate her take on the cowgirl maneuver which, in her active imagination, consisted of straddling a brawny cowboy with huge muscles and an even bigger dick. Who, in this case, would be Parker. Then dropping onto his challenging staff and furiously grinding them, western style, to a thundering climax. Ride 'em cowgirl!

Whew. She got all hot and bothered just thinking about it. That was a thing, right? The drop and grind? God, she hoped so. If it wasn't, she really needed to own that bitch. Maybe rename it Angel Descending. The delicious thought made her shiver with excitement.

With heat pouring into her center, she used his phone for the ultimate in fuck you's, holding it high and snapping an outrageous selfie showing most of her outfit as she smirked into the camera and flipped him off. For extra giggles, she kept pressing the camera button taking hundreds of meaningless, blurred shots of nothing. Ha! He was going to spend quite some time cleaning all that up. Jerk.

Tossing the phone back, she was disappointed when he caught it. The time had come to end this farce. Fixing her former fiancé with a caustic glare, she spat words at him that were mild compared to the bitchy tirade happening inside her head.

"You made a mistake messing with my family, Ronaldo, and will have to deal with the consequences of your foolish actions. Come anywhere near Valleja-Marquez again, or as much as look in my family's direction, and you will be feeling wrath like nothing you can imagine. Do I make myself clear?"

"Angelina," he bit out snidely with a cold look.

"Oh, fuck you, Aldo. Tell it to someone who cares. Go home and clean up the mess you made," she yelled.

The second her voice raised, he took a couple of menacing steps toward her, but the guy in the SUV appeared in time to put a forbidding hold on his arm. The instant outrage that anyone dare to touch him flashed on Aldo's face.

SUV man didn't give him a chance to say anything. He just held on, looked at her, and said, "Don't worry, Ms. Marquez. I'll take care of this."

Aldo's eyes literally bugged out of his head. Her answering look was little more than a withering sneer.

That's right shithead. Mess with any of Family Justice and this is just a tiny taste of the crapstorm coming your way. Hundreds of miles from the compound and yet the long reach of Justice could still be felt.

"Thank you," she drawled as if she was used to a bodyguard shadowing her every move. "I think I'll be going now."

Aldo lurched at her. He wasn't finished being a dick but her protector held him fast then told him in a plain-spoken voice that was tinged with the suggestion of threats that if he didn't get on the first plane overseas and promptly forget he ever knew the Marquez family, he was prepared to make him regret that decision. Forever.

She'd remember forever that her last glimpse of Aldo Esperanza was of him gulping, pale and wide-eyed at a brick wall dressed in full tactical gearwho was detailing the many ways he could fuck with him. She believed one of those ways had something to do with a certain someone's genitals returning to Spain in a paper bag.

And that, she thought derisively, was the end of her Spanish imbroglio. Good riddance—bad rubbish. *And dammit if imbroglio wasn't a five dollar word that didn't get enough use!*

Laughing, she drove away, made haste to the main highway, and turned north—back to her beloved red rocks and the only man she could ever love.

Chapter Sixty-One

Haunting the driveway and the front door to the hacienda, Parker survived the long stretch of anxious waiting by pacing back and forth—without pause. If he was still for too long, his mind started cranking and that wasn't necessarily a good thing.

Knowing he really should have told her why he was so bent this morning instead of pulling a silent act brought him the most illuminating 'ah-ha' moment of all times. He saw it so clearly—the thread that wove through everything. *He hadn't said this, he should have told her that. She didn't know, he hadn't said.*

It hit him like a lightning bolt. As someone who spoke for a living and had a more than adequate grasp on how to move people with words, none of that had ever been part of his behavior with Angie.

How stupid could one guy be? It was a good question he couldn't answer.

Nice going, shithead.

All that stopped right fucking now. The girl was his, and while she knew it and even encouraged him, she still didn't fully understand *why* she belonged to him. In that light, he was staggered that Angie yielded to him at all.

He was also going to have a serious talk with her when she got her ass back here about not taking matters into her own hands and going off on her own.

Pfft. Who the hell was he kidding? This was Angie he was talking about and she'd handle him laying down the law like that just exactly as he knew she would—with a kick in the shins and some haughty dismissal.

Goddammit. He'd take the shin kick and come back for more if she'd just come home. It was killing him that he couldn't get to her and she'd switched her phone off so all calls dumped into voicemail which just amped him up more.

Oh, yeah . . . and then there was Alex and his terse reminders that as of now, Parker didn't really have a say in anything that concerned Angie. He was a lawyer, for Christ's sake, so he knew when he was being played. The message inside his friend's actions was loud and clear.

What was that obnoxious expression people used in these situations? Something about putting a ring on it? If he wanted to be lord and master, which he did, all the proprieties must be observed. Until he did that, Parker was relegated to the cheap seats and could pretty much eat his boots before he'd get a say.

Angie was starting to feel the energy crash now that her adrenaline wasn't spiking all over the place. Washing her hands of Aldo's crap freed up a lot of space inside her—enough to carefully weigh and scrutinize what she had before her so she could get busy making the future she wanted.

From a corner of her mind, she heard the voice of her mother reminding Angie that *everything happens for a reason.* She'd heard the statement a hundred times, but it never resonated with her until now.

Everything happens for a reason.

Painful truth number one . . . no doubt about it, she'd been way too young before and no amount of loving Parker was going to change that fact. She was barely twenty at the time, and laugh all you want, but Britney still said it best about that holding pattern between being a girl and becoming a woman. Worst possible time to do what they did.

Could they have made it work with the age difference? Back then? Probably not. She wasn't mature enough on her own to be the partner he needed or the woman she wanted to be. But now? Now was a different story.

Another painful truth was that though she knew Parker loved her, she wasn't entirely sure he was *in love* with her, and for Angie, those two things could not be more different or more vitally important.

Everything happens for a reason.

Breaking up with Aldo, leaving Spain, and returning home? Each of those things seemed like the movement of pieces on a chess board or better yet, a puzzle that had her searching for connectors, jagged edges, and corners looking for the perfect fit.

And for her, Arizona was that fit. Something ridiculous to deny as she barreled along in a big SUV dressed like a boot scootin' cowgirl as the striking southwestern panorama sped by. This was her heart's home. Where she could fly free.

Everything happens for a reason.

Being at the hacienda and seeing firsthand the love her brother had for his bride-to-be was another milestone on her journey. Even the most jaded of skeptics couldn't deny that those two gave new meaning and life to outdated concepts like chivalry and the union of souls. And not just Alex. All around her were these amazing examples of love and how it came in all shapes, sizes, forms, and fashions from Cameron and Lacey to Draegyn and Victoria, and though she hadn't met her uncle's lady yet, she didn't doubt that when she did, Calder and Stephanie would take their place on the lover's podium with everyone else. She wanted that, too. With Parker. So much so that it scared her.

And then there was uncomfortable truth number three hundred and seven. She'd pushed him out of his comfort zone last night and though that could sometimes be a good thing, it took her hours and hours of silence and worry to understand that where honor, integrity, and respect among men was concerned, she'd fucked up.

There was no damn way he could have stopped her and she took advantage of that fact instead of thinking it through. The man had a conscience, thank god, since seeing Aldo again rather bluntly brought home what her life would have been like had she given herself to a man who couldn't find his fucking conscience with a detailed map and a homing device.

Angie shifted uncomfortably in the leather seat. Her own conscience was being a pain in the ass right now. What she'd done had been all about control and, in all honesty, a bit of payback. She stormed him and took what she wanted, rather like what he'd done to her years ago.

Had she been horny as fuck and ready to jump his bones? Oh, god yes. Coming out of a sleep-induced erotic dream lit the match that set fire to her desires and that, as they say, was that.

Until she saw him hours later and was forced to deal with his obvious turmoil over building a steaming tower of poop on his best friend's floor by having gotten down and dirty with her, she hadn't understood how vital those concepts were to both men.

Well, dammit, enough was enough. They were just going to keep screwing up this second chance to get it right if they didn't slow down and use their heads. Hard to do when the attraction was so overwhelming.

Alex and Meghan had been where she and Parker were and probably so had every other couple—maybe even her mom and dad. It was part of the journey and if they expected to make it, the first thing they had to do was be honest with each other.

That decided, Angie vowed to lay it all out when she saw him. She loved him and even if he didn't feel the same, there was still something there. Was it enough to build on? It was time she found out, wasn't it?

"Hey, babe. Look what I found," Alex boomed as he bounded into their bedroom like an overly excited puppy looking for its master. Carrying a stack of old photos he'd discovered crammed into a brown envelope that fell out of a box shoved to the back of a cabinet in his study, he was eager to share his extraordinary find.

"Where are you?" He laughed loudly when he didn't immediately see her.

"I'm in here," she hollered from the huge walk-in wardrobe they shared.

Dashing into the closet, Alex stumbled to a halt when he found her, not rifling through her stuff, but decisively sorting through his.

"Uh . . . what's this?" he asked bemused by her efforts.

She skipped over and plastered her body against his, kissing him sweetly. "Honey . . . you didn't think I was going to let you dress yourself for our desert date, did you?"

Swatting her butt playfully, he pushed her back and *tsked* a couple of times as he shook his head and sighed.

"Woman," he growled in his best alpha voice, "did you just insinuate that I am clueless in the fashion department?"

She laughed in his face. "You know damn well I did!"

This point was one of endless amusement to them. Before she came along, it wasn't even slightly unusual for him to throw on an ugly shirt and some equally fugly golf pants covered in beer logos for a jaunt around the local course and then come home and change into whatever his hand touched with no regard for fit, color, or suitability. Had he been a mess? Yep. A certifiable one.

Lightheartedly shoving her away from his side of the wardrobe, he scolded her with a lopsided grin. "I got this, babe. Relax."

"*Mmmm hmmm,*" she snickered. "I've heard that before."

Eh, she had a point. No way was he ever living down showing up in a pair of sloppy jeans and a NASCAR t-shirt at a church event Carmen dragged them to that he assumed was weekend casual when everyone else was dressed for a garden party. Funny now, but not so hilarious then.

"Seriously, bride . . . Daddy's got this."

Meghan laughed so hard that he had to laugh, too. "I'm making a new rule about you and that *Daddy* bullshit. Maybe points for each time you say it?" Her mocking simper cracked him right the fuck up.

Openly leering at her, Alex chuckled. "Yeah, about the point thing. That's getting a little out of hand don't you think?"

She grinned. "Did you hear me complaining?"

"No," he answered with a deep chuckle, "but don't you think we should discuss what happened."

Whoa. Instant serious. She lowered her eyes a moment and chewed on her lip but quickly recovered and even smiled.

"You mean the kidnapped and fucked thing or the tied up and flogged thing?"

"Both."

She hadn't shied away from talking about what they did that day, which was a relief, and she even managed to surprise him by actually saying out loud what he'd worried was a step too far for her.

Not a day went by when he didn't find more reasons to worship this remarkable woman who meant more to him than air to breathe and what she said next pretty much wrote that sentiment in stone.

"Make sure you pack that thing for the honeymoon."

Holy. Fucking. Shit.

"Any other requests?" he asked softly.

"Yeah." She giggled with a furious blush that shot into her face. "Bring the princess plug, too."

The TSA screeners and customs agents were going to have a field day with their luggage when they hopped continents for their honeymoon. Fun times.

Growling lustfully to her blushing request, he told her quite bluntly, "You do know we're going to fuck on the plane, right? We're not shelling out that kind of money on a private charter to haul us over the Atlantic and not mile high ourselves into a sex coma."

"God, that was *sooo* romantic," she teased. Her smirk was pure ball-busting bitch, and he loved the sight.

"What am I to do with you?" he quipped.

"*Ahahahaha.* You seem to be doing okay, Major."

He kissed her soundly then eagerly pulled her toward their enormous bed. "Come look at some pictures I found. Old photographs of the Villa before the restoration. Mostly post-war stuff when the place was crumbling. Wanna see?"

Crawling onto the mattress, they got comfortable and started going through a treasure trove of family history. Lost in their own little world, they happily looked at memories of the past while mapping out their unlimited future.

It was sunset. The perfect time to leave the highway and make those last winding turns that led Angie home. Sky blazing with a palette of colors that boggled the mind, she took it all in and let the power of nature fill her up. This was one of those times when she gave thanks that her hippie wild child mother had dropped everything to dance with her girls under a moonlit sky and who never failed to stop and quite literally smell the flowers.

Just before the final turn onto the long drive leading up to the hacienda, she stopped the car and sat quietly for a couple of minutes. This was it. Whatever happened once she got back to the house was only the most important moment in her whole life this far. No more rehearsals or script revisions. She got one shot, one performance, this night only.

No pressure, right?

About an hour ago, when she'd stopped to pee and grab something disgusting to eat from a convenience store, she'd considered turning her phone on but quickly nixed that idea. Her brother running interference at an airport hours away was quite the reminder of the reach Justice had in apparently every damn out-of-the-way corner. Also meant everyone at the Villa was well aware of what she'd been up to. Turning on her phone would no doubt result in finding her voicemail overflowing and a gazillion text messages pending. There weren't a lot of secrets with Family Justice.

No . . . she was going to do this head-on and simply drive back to the compound and face whatever waited for her.

Habit made her flip the visor down and open the mirror so she could check her appearance—not that she could do anything if she needed to. When she'd stormed after Aldo, all she took was what fit in her pockets. Her little wallet containing ID, some dollars, and credit card. The basics. Oh, yeah, and that tube of lipstick.

One glance at her reflection confirmed that she'd chewed all of the colored gloss off her lips a long time ago. The face looking back at her was completely natural. This was who she was—boots, cutoff jeans, a flannel shirt, no make-up, and running free. Everything else was window dressing.

Angie wasn't nervous as she drove the last stretch. Frankly, it was too damn late to be nervous. Then, an unexpected calm descended. As the Explorer swung into the constantly cluster-fucked driveway, she wasn't going to bother driving down to the garage, a rushing sensation echoed in her head and sped like a wildfire through her the second she caught sight of Parker prowling the front gate.

He was waiting for her. If anyone else was around, she didn't know, or care, because everything faded away at the sight of him.

They had locked eyes before she'd even gotten the car parked. Turning off the engine, Angie pushed the car door open as he moved in her direction. The closer he got, the more aware of him she became. It was this connection that never went away—a current arcing back and forth between them—even when they were apart.

Dropping onto the drive, she didn't hesitate, her boots pounding out a rhythm as she went to claim her destiny.

Parker's expression looked intense. Worried and relieved at the same time. His mouth in a grim, taut line, he reached out to her while he was still several feet away. "Angel," he growled, and with that one emotional cry, her life changed forever.

She ran the last couple of steps and went straight into his embrace. Wrapping her arms around his neck, she choked up and barely got out, "Oh god, Parker," before he crushed her body to his and went to her mouth.

Standing there, her feet no longer on the ground as she clung to him, Angie gave herself up entirely. There was passion in his kiss, but that was just a part of it. She prayed to all the angels up in heaven above that he loved her the same way she loved him.

It took forever for the kissing to slow down, not that she was complaining. When he eventually let her slide down his front until her feet hit the ground, he took hold of her face with both hands and looked into her eyes.

Would he scold her for being reckless like he had when she was a kid? Was he mad at her? Unhappy with her spur-of-the-moment behavior? His kiss hadn't seemed that way.

Expecting some sort of alpha reaction to her antics, Angie was stunned when he finally spoke. When he didn't bark commands—she knew immediately by the sound of his voice that he was really upset. Besides the time she saw him barely maintaining when Uncle Matt was in the hospital, she'd never known Parker to be bothered by much of anything.

"Please," he ground out. "Please, baby girl. Do not *ever* do anything like this again. You scared the shit out of me, Angie."

That was quite the admission coming from him.

"I'm sorry," she muttered. "Everything happened so fast." Shrugging, she grasped his forearms and gazed lovingly up at him.

"Are you okay?" The question was not much more than an anxious whisper.

"You were worried." Her answer was more an exclamation than a question.

There was crushed and then there was *crushed*—which was how it felt when he gathered her close.

Mmmm. He smelled good. A little sweaty maybe. Probably from being outside in the sun but the subtle earthiness of his natural scent was an instant turn on.

He said something, but with his face pressed into her hair and her focused on inhaling his essence, she completely missed whatever was said. Not really concerned about it, she went back to snuggling into his wide chest. *Mmmm.*

Chapter Sixty-Two

Would it be a bad thing if he threw up on her boots, 'cause that was how he felt. She was either trying to kill him or he'd totally misread the situation. One of the two. Was the only way to explain her silence. Wasn't she supposed to react when he told her he loved her? How come she didn't as much as sigh?

Aw, shit. If she didn't love him back the same way—it really would kill him. No joke. Prepared for her to shoot him down, Parker swallowed against the thickness in his throat that signaled approaching tears. He let her go suddenly and pulled away to search her face. She had a radiance about her that he'd miss every day for the rest of his life if she said no.

Her hand reached up and pushed the hair off his forehead. It was such a small, loving gesture that it stopped him cold. Maybe everything was going to be okay after all.

"I have something to tell you," she said.

Oh, my god. She was returning to Spain, wasn't she? He felt sick. Puking on her boots became a distinct possibility.

Trying for stoic, Parker hung on as best he could, waiting for her to decimate his heart.

"I'm *in love* with you," she whispered, her eyes bright and shining.

Waiting for the sword to drop on his neck, he wasn't prepared to hear those words and when she said them, he frowned deeply. Had he heard her right? Maybe if he just stood there and stared at her long enough, what was happening would start to make sense.

The longer he stared, the heavier the awkward silence became. When he didn't respond, she looked away and muttered, "Oh."

Not having any idea what he was saying, Parker echoed her, "Oh?" only making it a question.

"It's okay if you don't feel the same." Her voice sounded thin. "I get it."

Huh? Time out, time out, time out. They needed to get on the same page.

"What do you get?" he asked.

Quirking one shoulder, she crossed her arms in front of her—a defensive move that bothered him—murmuring, "Not being in love. You know. With me."

Goddammit. What the fuck was she talking about?

"I could say the same to you," he groused.

"No, you can't," she bit out.

"Can, too," he countered, and just like that, the years melted away and it was him and a spunky Angel hurling 'nah-nahs' at each other.

"How ya figure, counselor?"

She was kidding with that outraged tone, right?

"I said it first." His mom would call the way he answered his *sulky little shit* act. Moms always knew how to go right to the core of things.

"Did not!" she shrieked.

"I *sooo* did," he growled.

"When?"

"Just now."

Her expression mirrored his confusion. How the fuck could two people who were so connected be this clueless?

His inner lawyer *tsked* a couple of times and figuratively pushed his sorry ass aside. Get the facts, clean up loose ends, connect the dots. "You asked if I was worried about you and I answered."

"Ooookay," she drawled.

"Said I loved you." Her eyes went wide. "You didn't say it back." Then, her jaw hit the floor. "Next thing I know, you said it, too. At least I think you did. I don't know, Angie. Fuck!" he roared. "Did you say it or not?"

Wow. He could almost hear her brain working.

"You . . . *love* me." She sounded, *astonished.*

He shook his head no and she looked like her world ended.

"No. . . . I'm *in* love with you. Helplessly. Hopelessly. It's only ever been you, Angel."

"Oh, Parker," she cried with a little sob. "I've loved you my whole life, and I will love you with my all my heart and every bit of my soul until forever."

He thought about kissing her or perhaps dropping her to the pavement to make love to her where they stood, but there was still one thing that had to be settled before they went any further.

Taking her hand, he kissed it gently, and then twined his fingers through hers. The simple gesture felt damn good, her small hand in his.

"Come on," he urged as he started walking toward the house.

"Where are we going?"

"There's something I need to do," he told her brusquely as he hurried them to the door.

"I suppose my brother is waiting for an explanation, huh?"

"Nope. Team Baby Girl the whole way. He spoke to Soph."

She giggled at his side. "That explains the terminator-looking guy at the airport who duck marched Aldo into the terminal."

He chuckled. *Justice. Go figure.*

Inside the house, they were met with quiet. Neither Alex nor Meghan was anywhere around and with dinner over and cleaned up, they could be almost anywhere. Doing anything. *Shit.* If his timing sucked, he'd just have to deal with it. Wouldn't be the first time he'd broken up a make-out session.

Suddenly, he was in his man-of-action character and couldn't move, talk, or act fast enough. As he pulled Angie across the entryway toward the big staircase, Parker was belatedly conscious that he was actually dragging her, but instead of slowing down or backing off, he kept stomping along. Something about the whole setup struck him as funny and unusually primal. Her two or three boot steps sounding to each of his better be included on the alpha soundtrack. A couple of tracks after the little noise she had made right before she came and the big Kahuna . . . her telling him she *wanted* him to master her.

Dropping her at the landing, he told her to "Sit," which was met with a husky giggle.

"Yes, sir," she purred with just enough mockery to make him grab her by the neck and furiously kiss that wicked mouth. Afterward, she wasn't laughing, but she did wipe the corners of her mouth before pointedly lowering her butt onto the next to last step.

For good measure, and because he liked fucking with her, Parker started up the stairs then turned back, barking, "Stay!"

After that he took the stairs two at a time. Just as he hit the top, he heard her chuckle and say, "Woof." He grinned. The girl needed a good spanking.

Taking a deep breath, he straightened, thought about what he was doing, then kicked off and went down the long hallway to the master suite.

"Why has no work been done on the old homestead?" Meghan asked him. "From these pictures, I can see how it once looked. It's such a shame that it's crumbling to nothing."

Alex agreed. Restoring the homestead was at the top of his bucket list. The opportunity to do it the way he wanted just hadn't materialized yet—but he'd know when the time came. Sooner or later, he'd find someone to realize his unique vision for the ancient structure.

"The Villa was such a shit show that it wasn't a priority. As it was," he told her, scooping the photos together into a pile, "renovating the hacienda and outbuildings took nearly a decade. Was my grandparents' life work to restore the property."

She smiled warmly, looking around their bedroom and sighing. "I love it here." Her shy smirk told him there was more to that statement. "Did you know the first night I spent in that cozy guest room, I thought it would be the most wonderful thing in the world to wake up every morning and see those old ceiling beams."

Meghan had a way of expressing her emotions that sounded like poetry no matter how simple the sentiment. Old ceiling beams—the most wonderful thing in the world.

"It's a lot different than how you grew up."

Alex had stopped worrying that she might miss her old life in Boston. Having her family nearby, her friends and work colleagues . . . she said those things paled next to being here with him. Her love for the life they were creating was absolute. Meghan O'Brien was his for all time and would take her place in his family's history with all the grace, charm, and sweetness people loved her for.

She smirked slyly. "It was the cowgirl boots that sold this place, you know."

He smiled, remembering Meghan's cheeky delight in her first pair of boots. She'd been a cowgirl, *Boston style,* ever since.

"That and the adorable-as-fuck absentminded professor thing you had going on."

As she teased him, her hands reached for his head, scraping back and forth, making his hair an even unholier mess. "You're just lucky that whole Major Marquez thing gets me wet."

"Bah!" he bellowed with glee, taking her by surprise and hauling her so swiftly over his knee, she grunted out an, "oomph," as she landed.

"Getting you wet is my life's mission, baby," he teased seconds before his hand swung and smacked her bottom soundly.

Her yelp of feigned distress was comical. Just as he was about to swing again, he heard a decisive knock rapped out on their bedroom door. *What the fuck?*

Meghan scrambled off him as if they'd been caught by the police doing something criminal, squeaking, "Who would be knocking on our door?"

Regretting the loss of so perfect an opportunity to dominate her magnificent ass, he grunted furiously, "What?" pretty much at the top of his lungs.

Parker's voice came from the other side of the door. "Can I speak to you a minute, Alex?"

They looked at each other in mild surprise. "What do you think that's all about?" she whispered.

Ah, crap. It all came back to him. Angie. Maybe she was finally back and that was why Parker wanted to talk. It was highly unusual for him to come knocking on their door so something had to be up.

"Probably my sister," he assured her. Dropping a quick kiss on her lips, Alex slid off the bed and headed for the door. "I'd like it very much if when I came back, you were naked and bent over on the bed."

"I'll see what I can do." She giggled. "And be nice, Major. That nonsense was us not that long ago."

She had a point.

He found Parker in the hallway outside their room, not quite pacing but not exactly still either. Energy was bouncing from his friend to the walls, the ceiling, everywhere.

My, my, my, how the mighty have fallen. Looked like old Parker Sullivan, valedictorian, rocker, all around shitkicker, was in the obvious midst of a come to Jesus moment that had Angelina Marquez etched all over it. *Hehehe.*

Should he yank his chain? Maybe give him an emotional wedgie that'd have him grabbing for his balls? Both sounded like fun—this was Parker, after all—but Alex remembered with searing, painful clarity the awful time preceding his and Meghan's engagement when he'd probably looked exactly as his old friend looked right now. Frantic. Slightly shell-shocked. Definitely unhinged. Whatever was driving the man was as serious as a heart attack.

What would his dad do? After all, if this conversation went where he suspected it might, this was really something his father should be handling. Recalling his own Jesus moment when he sucked it up and let Meghan's father, mother, and brothers read him the riot act before consenting to their marriage, he decided to cut the poor sucker some slack. If he knew his sister, she was probably finding more hoops for Parker to jump through, a thought that made him smile.

"Okay, um . . ." Parker stammered, his brows bumping together. "Um . . ."

And this tongue-tied nitwit argued before the Supreme Court? Alex was enjoying this more than he should.

The brain dead mumbling continued. "Right, um . . . Alex."

Oh, good. He knew who he was talking to. That was encouraging. And . . . ?

Parker took a deep breath. "Fuck. This is harder than I thought."

Hmmm. "Which part?" He wasn't going to like it much if Parker was hesitating. Enough already. Either claim the girl or let it go.

Parker groaned. "The part where you tell me that I'm not the man for your sister."

Alex couldn't believe he'd said that! Good lord. He was further gone than he imagined. Good for little sister. She'd gotten herself a keeper.

"Hang on," he grumbled to his friend, holding up his hand indicating he should wait there. Walking halfway down the hallway until he could see the top of the stairs because he was certain Angie was hovering nearby, Alex stopped and hollered, "You in love with this jackass?"

The sound of Angie's little girl giggle washed away the years, reminding Alex how long they'd been this odd little unit. Him, Parker, and Angie.

"Yep!" she hollered back gleefully followed quickly by a sisterly admonishment, "Be nice, Alexander."

He strolled back to where Parker stood frozen in the hallway, a look of pure, dumb shock on his face.

"Okay," Alex told him. "I'm listening."

This whole thing was surreal.

He and Alex facing each other in the hallway outside his friend's bedroom, where he knew a sexy Irish beauty waited for his friend's return.

Angie sitting at the foot of the stairs. Also waiting, although she had no idea for what.

Parker's heart was pounding so hard he felt it in his throat. He and the man staring him down knew each other too well. They'd helped bury each other's skeletons. If anyone had the right to object, it was Alex. In a way, he sincerely wished he was having this conversation with Uncle Cris.

As earnestly and straightforward as he could, Parker told him what was on his mind, starting with, "Man, I have done nothing for the past week except explain your fucking behavior and our friendship and let me tell you . . . that shit's not easy."

Alex's smirky eye roll pretty much said it all. He knew what a pain in the ass Angie could be once she got stuck on something. And since he'd done his own fair share of groveling over their Stifler's mom fuckery, he knew damn well what Parker had probably been through.

"If that's not the most fucked up backdrop to this conversation, well . . . I don't know what else would be."

Funny. They each nodded at the same time.

"So, that being said," he continued gravely, "there's something I need to say, and I hope you'll give me the chance to finish without putting me on the floor before I'm done."

"Before you start your opening statement, I want to respond to what you said earlier. About me not thinking you were the man for my sister."

Oh. Parker's heart dropped into his stomach.

"Dude. You've always been my brother. When I fill out stuff that asks for family, I have to stop from listing you that way. As my brother. I've known since Angie was a teenager that this day was a possibility. In a way, we've all been waiting for her to catch up and make it official."

Parker was having a hard time breathing. *Was he saying what I think he is?*

"You wanna marry the girl, I suppose?"

"I don't remember a time when I didn't love her. That's the given. It's the being *in* love with her that's changed everything."

Alex nodded with a rumbling grunt. "Understood."

Yeah. He bet.

"I can't sleep for dreaming about her and don't be a pig . . . I'm talking about a minivan, a dog, and a pack of kids dreaming. I'm distracted at work. My fucking stomach is in a perpetual knot worrying about whatever crazy fuckery she's likely to create or get drawn into. Today being a perfect example. Quiet has become my enemy 'cause all I do is remember how I fucked up and she got hurt. Thinking about her being upset or crying because of something I did, well . . . I can't . . ." He couldn't even finish. He wasn't fucking kidding. Those thoughts gutted him.

This was it. It all came down to one thing.

"I won't make it without her. I'm almost forty fucking years old and for the first and only time in my life, I know what's missing. It's her, man. It's always been her."

To his utter amazement, tears welled in his eyes and his nose stung like a son-of-a-bitch.

"Please tell me that I have your blessing, Alex. You know who I am and you know I wouldn't shit about what's in my heart. I swear to god she'll be safe with me. Whatever it takes to make her happy, I'll do. Fuck, if she wants to go back to Spain, I'll go with her."

Alex started and murmured, "Wow."

Parker held his hands up. "What else could I do? She owns my heart."

The answer came simply. Alex extended his hand. He took it in a firm grip.

"I'll be honored to call you my brother-in-law. Now, go get that troublemaker I'm saddled with as a sister and teach her some damn manners."

A handshake wasn't enough. Would never be enough. Going in for a hearty bro-hug, they slapped each other soundly on the back, ending with a fist bump and a second or two of throat clearing. Manly throat clearing.

"Tell Irish I'm sorry for interrupting your evening."

Parker wasn't an idiot. He saw something flare in his friend's eyes. The hacienda was going to be filled with lusty grunts and moaning whimpers tonight! Which reminded him . . .

"One last thing . . ."

Alex was chuckling. "As long as she says yes to a proposal, I won't object to you defiling my baby sister under my roof."

"Fuck, dude," Parker griped. "Was that necessary? I had something a little more romantic in mind than a defilement."

They laughed. Their relationship reset. The grumpy older brother with a handy shotgun nearby vanished. Once again, it was him and Alex. Friends and now really and truly brothers forever.

Chapter Sixty-Three

Angie stretched her legs out straight and tapped her boots together. What was taking so long? She was getting restless and antsy waiting for Parker to come back.

Wondering what in the world he was doing, she concluded he was most likely getting Alex's permission to sweep her away for an overnight in Sedona. He'd suggested it before, after all. The thought made her giddy. *Damn.* And hot, too! She'd gladly walk to Sedona for a chance to finally be with Parker.

Okay. So now restless was moving the needle to bored. She never really was very good at waiting . . . or behaving. Especially not when Alex and Parker were nearby. Some habits never died.

Peeling off the flannel shirt, she tied the arms about her waist and fluffed her hair. Tapping her boots a few more times, she impatiently looked around.

Honestly. If he didn't come back soon, she was going after him.

Just like that he was at the top of the stairs, moving in her direction, an odd look on his face. Uh-oh. If Alex had been a dick, she was definitely ready to cause a scene.

Jumping up, she turned toward him and waited.

When he hit the last few stairs and was right in front of her, he surprised the holy crap out of her by scooping her up in his strong, capable arms. Instinctively putting an arm around his shoulders, she searched his face while he said absolutely nothing—just started walking toward the back of the house.

Through the kitchen they went, and then out to the patio courtyard, straight to her special spot . . . the alcove with the wooden swing. Lowering her gently, she sat on the swing, her booted feet dangling down. Her legs started to tremble from the fierce look on his face so she pressed her knees together hoping to stop the quivering.

And then, like a scene from a movie, her handsome rock 'n' roll prince slowly sank onto a knee and reached for one of her hands. She was shaking so hard it was a wonder he could hold on.

Above them, a million stars twinkled in the inky blue sky and the air they breathed was infused with the sweet smells of the desert at night. A more perfect moment there would never be. One little tear escaped the outside corner of her eye and rolled over her cheek.

"The first time I saw you, a bundle of sweet-smelling pink and white, my fate was sealed."

"Oh, Parker," she sniffled.

"My heart has been yours ever since, Angelina Marquez. I will, *simply put,* never love anyone but you."

Angie took a big breath to calm her wildly beating heart. She wanted to take all this in and remember it forever. The stars. The twinkle lights. His expressive eyes. The sound of his voice. How her small hand trembled in the grasp of his bigger one.

"Now, I didn't expect to be doing this tonight or I would have come prepared with some bling," he told her before pressing a soft kiss on her naked ring finger. "So, in a way—you get to hold me up for whatever your little heart desires because I didn't have my shit together."

She giggle snorted with delight. *Smart man.*

"But the lack of jewelry doesn't change the magnitude of this moment. Angel baby," he said in a voice that sounded heavy with emotion, "will you marry me?"

Parker Sullivan just asked her to marry him.

No. Seriously. Parker Sullivan, Esquire . . . was down on one knee, asking her to be his wife.

This was beyond her wildest dreams.

"Angie?"

What? Oh. Right. He'd asked her a question. Will she marry him.

She heard Sheryl Crow singing in her head. He was definitely strong enough to be her man.

She wanted to be looking in his eyes when she gave her answer. Gazes locked, Angie smiled. "I've loved you forever, Parker. Even when I didn't want to, I loved you. Being your wife is just something I never dared to dream of so hearing you ask . . ." Overcome with emotion she nodded. "Yes. I will marry you."

If she had anything else to say, it didn't matter because he grabbed her so fast and pulled her down to her knees she squeaked with surprise. And then he kissed her.

They didn't separate until being on their knees on a tile patio got to be a bit much. As he helped her up, she gasped when he tweaked a puckered nipple plainly evident beneath the thin white t-shirt and chuckled into her shocked face with a wicked leer.

"Just so we're clear about what's happening next, I have the master of the house's permission to defile you within the walls of your family home."

"Oh, well that's nice!" she mocked.

"I totally agree," he told her with perfect solemnity.

Giggling, she drawled, "I may have to rethink this. No ring and now a defilement. *Hmmm.* I just don't know."

She squealed with delight when he rolled a shoulder and deftly hoisted her, soundly smacking her butt in the process. She couldn't help but hoot with laughter as he carried her, caveman style, back through the house and up the wide staircase, turning left toward the old family wing where her little suite was . . . far from the master suite which anchored a whole other section of the house.

As he marched along, she found that she had a rather interesting view of his fine backside from her vantage point slung over his shoulder. *Dayum, son!* That was one mighty awesome ass. One she couldn't pass up fondling.

Sliding the steadying hands anchored on his back into his pockets, she filled her hands with his rock hard buns. This sure was fun!

In her room, he kicked the door shut and strode quickly to the antique four poster bed. She'd barely enough time to pull her hands from his pockets before he tossed her. One second, she was dangling over his shoulder, and the next, she was sailing through the air. When she thudded onto the mattress, he instantly gripped her beneath the knees and pulled her to the edge of the bed.

The playfulness vanished, replaced by a need so great it was hard to contain. His eyes were flashing and the ruddy glow of desire made the angles on his face sharper.

He slowly removed one of her boots. She barely registered the sound as it fell to the floor. Holding her foot and leg in his hands, he rubbed the sole of her foot then ran his hands up either side of her calf. He bent and kissed her knee then slid his hands up her thighs to the frayed hem of her barely-there shorts.

Angie had to remind herself to breath as she watched his every move. Not only were her nipples taut and throbbing with want, she was boldly aware of the wet heat rushing into her sex.

The other boot came off next, and this time, he held her leg aloft and licked the sensitive skin on the back of her knee. She whimpered as desperation took hold.

Had he heard the urgency in her cry? He must have. Stopping to stare at her, she saw his inner struggle. Last night it had been her with the need that simply had to be answered. Tonight, it was him. The thought was thrilling and made her pussy tighten.

He ripped the shirt from around her waist then tore open the button on her shorts and tugged at the zipper. Within seconds, she was naked from the waist down. Some instinct made her writhe on the bed, a full-body undulation that ended with Angie spreading her legs. The invitation could not have been clearer.

His low, husky growling never let up. It was sexy as fuck and so animalistic that she began panting, overcome with building arousal. The sweet, sultry scent of her desire hit them at the same time. He groaned and shut his eyes, breathing deeply. She let her knees fall open further.

When his eyes opened, he looked straight at her. "I should slow down. Take you sweetly and tenderly so you'll know once and for all what it means when I say that I love you."

Unf. Her pussy pulsed wildly at his use of the word *take*.

The air around them stilled. He fought for control; she saw it in his clenched fists and grinding jaw as he stared at her exposed and vulnerable flesh. If he was making up his mind, she was going to help him out.

Legs spread, feet dug into the bed, she rolled her hips. In sexual sign language, she was begging to be fucked.

His eyes swung to hers. Yeah. He heard her loud and clear.

"But that's not happening this time. Hold on to the *I love you* part because Angel baby, I'm going to fuck you dirty until your sweet nectar coats my dick and you come while I'm so deep inside you that we've become one."

Oh, my fucking god.

"Then, when you're totally spent, I will bathe your pussy with my hot seed and no, I don't give a flying fuck whether you're on the pill or not."

He waited for her reaction. This was what she remembered and knew so well. His primal beast. That part of him that demanded she satisfy his enormous desire for her. Only for her.

She bit her lip knowing it was a sign of submission and coyly shielded her exposed mound with both hands. There was no way he was going to pass up the chance to demonstrate his mastery over her. Her trembling was real.

His eyes glued to hers, he tore off his shirt and quickly divested himself of his boots, pants, and briefs. The sight of his erect staff had her melting down in seconds. Seeing his desire for her made Angie shake even more.

There really wasn't anything between him standing there nude, slowly stroking his cock while devouring her with his eyes, and him pushing her back on the bed as he climbed between her spread thighs.

Moving her hands to the side, he shoved his under her ass and lifted. "I love you, baby girl," he growled, the head of his demanding cock beginning to part the lips of her dripping wet pussy.

And then he lunged forward with a tremendous grunt. Her back arched at the manly invasion, she groaned wildly as he sank deeper until the whole of him was sheathed in her wet heat.

She couldn't move. Breathe. See. Hear. The sensation of him deep inside her body overrode everything else. Holding still, Parker waited for her to come back. "Are you ready for me, baby?"

Wrapping him in her legs and arms, Angie ground her pelvis, the movement causing his cock to swell more. She quivered all over. After that, he didn't hold back at all.

It got wild and furious immediately. He pulled out and slammed home, grunting deeply with each delicious plunge. Because she still wore the thin t-shirt, he simply bit her nipples and sucked on them through the fabric with a fierceness that brought a string of harsh, guttural grunts from deep inside her.

They kissed furiously. The whole thing was wild and raw. Her nails were scoring his back. His hands gripped her hips so hard, she was sure there'd be marks.

There was no way she was going to last much longer. The fluttering of a building orgasm fired off with his each mighty thrust.

"I can feel your pussy getting tighter," he husked. "Come on, baby. Squeeze my cock with those fierce muscles."

His wish was her command. She gripped him with all her might, surging upward with each of his downward thrusts, losing herself in the sheer carnality of his possession. Take her, indeed.

"Are you going to come for me, Angel?"

Yes. Yes, she wanted to. Wanted to give him all her pleasure. Whimpering, she urged him on, faster and deeper. He wasn't kidding about fucking her dirty.

He shifted slightly making the angle of his shaft rub against her inner walls in a way that made her lose all control. On the heels of a deep, keening moan, deep waves of orgasmic bliss burst upon Angie. She cried out and clutched at him.

Parker roared his approval as her pussy convulsed over and over. He never stopped hammering into her.

"Fuck," he groaned when the wild convulsions deepened instead of easing off. It was like a slow-motion climax that went on and on and on. Wet sticky heat flooded into her pussy, and as he churned his cock inside her, it spread, covering them both with her sweet nectar.

He was biting her neck. The twin sensations of her quivering pussy and his ferocious mauling sent Angie spiraling wildly into oblivion.

Her low, lusty moan split the air when he stopped moving. Deep inside her body, she felt his huge cock throb against the walls of her sex. His hands went back on her ass.

"Gonna come inside you," he growled. "Look at me, baby," he demanded. "I want to see your eyes when I fill your pussy."

Barely conscious, she opened her eyes. He looked so big and powerful on top of her. Angie quivered knowing his cock had her pinned to the bed.

"Ready?" he asked. She nodded; although, with all her muscles straining around his shaft, she could have imagined it.

He gave it all he had . . . and then some. As he thrust, he pulled her ass up and back creating a friction that re-ignited her passion. She knew he felt her response by his surprised grunt.

She heard his roar, but it sounded a hundred miles away. Succumbing to the blinding stimulation, she flew so high and so far, there didn't seem to be enough oxygen. She came with a fierce rush. Through eyes blinded by lust, she saw his head go back and the veins in his neck pulse in time to his cock releasing inside her.

The last thing she had known before the darkness overtook her was a sense of overwhelming completion. Not just because they'd made fierce, hungry love but because her heart and soul were finally free. Free to love and be loved.

They'd actually made it. Found their way back to each other. She smiled and drifted away.

Chapter Sixty-Four

BREAKFAST THE FOLLOWING MORNING WAS quite a production. With Meghan and Alex smiling at them, Angie perched on Parker's lap, having declared the spot her favorite place to *drop her ass* although why she giggled and blushed each time she said it didn't make sense.

Women, huh? Go figure.

When Carmen made her morning appearance, she took one look at the two grinning couples and launched into throwing together a world-class breakfast. Real buttermilk pancakes—made special for Miss Angie—an embarrassingly large pile of bacon, Meghan's favorite cheesy eggs, and the best damn country hash browns not made on a campfire. This was going to be a great day.

"Stop wiggling," he chided his lap passenger quietly. Luckily, Carmen was dithering away and making so much racket, no one heard him but Angie.

She glanced hurriedly to Alex and Meghan before leaning in to nip his earlobe. "Stop giving me something *hard* to wiggle on."

His heart tapped out a rhythmic happy dance. The face of the angel smiling at him was glowing and Parker knew a satisfaction that shot into his balls knowing he'd get to gaze into those pretty sapphire eyes until his eyes no longer saw.

"I bet you're hungry," she drawled. "Worked up quite a calorie burn earlier, I must say."

She issued the smug dig with a look of total innocence. Angel, indeed! Her smart-aleky mood scattered his brain so much that he couldn't access the *Star Wars* quote he mentally searched for. Something about being so hungry he could . . . *something*. Whatever. It was gone that quickly. The quote search was replaced in his thoughts with a detailed summary of their overnight activities.

Their first coupling hadn't exactly been pretty. No long, drawn-out sensual ballet that time. No, they started with a raw, barely controlled explosion of untamed lust that was more a choreographed street fight than a waltz. A good thing too because satisfying that initial intensity let them explore the depth of their passions long into the night. And early this morning.

Parker learned his lesson years ago endlessly regretting not having made love to Angie the way he felt she deserved. Women needed all that romantic shit. The whispered words. The long, slow possession. And he'd brought it all.

Ya' didn't wait a lifetime to pull an angel from the heavens and then not express every desire and want he carried in his soul. Things only she could satisfy.

Remembering her hushed cries and gasps as he feasted on her femininity made his dick throb. If it wasn't taking vulgarity and crudeness to new heights, he'd commission a portrait to be hung above the fireplace in his bedroom depicting them in his new favorite position. Angie arching her back, knees wide apart, his face buried between her legs while his tongue lapped at her pussy. He'd have his arms reaching up to fondle her glorious tits. One of her hands would be clutched in his hair, the other hanging onto the bed covers for dear life.

It had taken all night to come even slightly close to satisfying his hunger. And satisfying his cock? Not a chance. In fact, if they didn't have an audience, she'd be laid out on the table right now while he did all sorts of things to her delicious pussy. Now, there was a breakfast treat he could get down with.

"Hey, butthead," Alex was drawling. "Earth to Space Cadet Sullivan."

Fucking crap. He'd been so lost in his thoughts that he wasn't paying attention to what was going on around him.

Angie's soft, mocking chuckle wrapped around his heart but that didn't stop him from grabbing a handful of hair for a gentle tug.

"What?" he barked into Alex's amused faced.

"It's nine o'clock. If you plan on calling someone's father to inform him that you put a ring on it, you better get your ass in gear—is all I'm saying."

"Oh, crap!" Angie exclaimed. "He's right. It's nearly dinnertime for them." She reacted like the starting gun went off, scrambling from his lap to pull him up from his chair. With her hands pushing him along from the small of his back, she blurted a rush of nonsense about Uncle Cris that got his head shaking.

"Don't say anything about how crazy the constuction is. Alex wants to surprise them when they get here. And don't let him railroad you into setting a date."

Ah, he thought. *So this is how it was going to be.* He'd never seen her so bossy. Well, okay. That was certainly an understatement, a funny one, but the underlying sentiment was still true. She was a pushy little thing at times.

Parker chuckled to himself. Maybe he'd remind her later what a truly craptacular submissive she'd have been and make the point by letting her run the show. See what she had. The toe-curling blowjob was hardly her best move and since he hadn't let her lay him low with a repeat performance, despite the pouting and whining, she'd been sulking about it since. Every so often she'd frown at him and mutter, "Not playing fair," which only made him snicker.

"All right, all right, all right," he drawled. "I've got this, woman, so settle down. This is my uncle we're talking about. I think I know how to talk to him."

Alex bawled with laughter. "Oh, my god, you poor dumb fuck! Uncle shmuncle shithead. That's her *father,* man. Show some fucking respect and be prepared to sweat balls. My dad's not stupid. He knows what giving his baby away to an old pervert like you means."

"Gag on my cock, Alex."

Meghan snickered. So did Angie.

Glancing at his fiancée . . . holy fuck! He had a fiancée. Anyway, when he looked at her, she smiled and twinkled her fingers.

Great. Twinkle fingers. Muttering darkly, Parker left the room, fishing his iPhone out of his pocket. When he shut the door of Alex's study behind him and pressed the call button, he had to center himself as some uncharacteristic nerves assailed him.

The call was answered almost immediately.

"Hi, Uncle Cris. Parker here. Have you got a moment, sir? There's something I need to discuss with you . . ."

Meghan shot Alex a scathing look when she sat down at the breakfast table after going to the fridge for some milk. As her knees bent, she became achingly aware of her sore bottom and the reason why.

Last night, he'd told her to be naked and bent over the bed, waiting for him when he came back from talking to Parker. She hadn't complied, of course. Feeling flirtatious and wantonly frisky, the minute he left the room, she'd shot from the bed and run into the wardrobe, pulling open drawers in a hurried search for something specific.

When she hurried back to the bed a minute later, she was completely covered, neck to toe by a baggy old Boston PD sweatshirt and pair of sloppy sweatpants. And underneath that? The ugliest, most unsexy sports bra she had and a pair of granny panties that had seen better days.

The expression on his face when he came back, fully expecting her naked ass to be on display, was nothing short of priceless. Chasing her around their room while she shrieked with laughter, Meghan gave him a decent challenge, not surrendering until he'd finally cornered her in the wardrobe and she'd had nowhere else to run.

She'd wanted to throttle him though when he grabbed the neckline of the frayed sweatshirt and dramatically ripped that shit in two with one mighty pull.

"Hey!" she yelled. "You can't do that." Bah! His fierce leer told her that he could do any damn thing he wanted. *Swoon.*

"Next time, do as you're told."

She wanted to answer, *Make me,* but this was working out pretty well so far so Meghan just pouted. He was doing fine!

"You're fucking joking," he snarled when the unsexy, gray sports bra came into view. "Take that off." His horrified expression told her what he thought of her underwear.

This time, she did simper, "Make me," and got exactly the reaction she hoped for. Was her bottom still a warm pink? Probably. But fuck ... had it ever been worth it!

Pouring the milk onto her cereal, she jumped with surprise when he leaned close and chuckled wickedly. "Bet that smarts, huh?"

Scathing look with the flash of a smile—take two.

"Be a good girl and Daddy will rub your tushy with lotion later."

Oh no, he didn't! Settling back heavily in her seat, she crossed her arms and sniggered. "Five points to the ledger of Major Marquez."

Alex roared with laughter, earning them an amused glance from Angie.

She was surprised when he changed subjects, babbling about the upcoming St. Patrick's Day get-together she was planning.

"So, I checked with Cam and he's all hooked up and set to go with streaming video of the Boston Parade. Ten o'clock our time so he'll record and we'll watch the playback before dinner. Okay?"

Of course, it was okay. Meghan couldn't believe all the effort Alex was making to celebrate her Irish heritage. It was sweet as a mountain of chocolate and just as decadently satisfying. He really would do anything for her.

"Can't wait," she assured him. "Ria's been face chatting nonstop with Ma. Cooking lessons from the old sod."

"So I'll finally get some of that brisket you go on and on about?"

"Indeed," she drawled.

"What's the matter? Something's not right. I can hear it in your voice."

Damn, he was good. Evasion was not an option. He'd drive her mental until she shared. Shrugging nonchalantly, Meghan swept her hair aside and spoke quietly. Carmen was still bustling in and out and she didn't want her to hear and get her feelings hurt.

"It's nothing ... I'm just not used to having other people take over. Ria had a shit attack when I said I wanted to cook. Made me feel like I'd just stabbed her with a fork."

He took one of her hands and squeezed it reassuringly. "It's just her way. She sees taking care of all of us, and especially you, as some sacred vow to the memory of our ancestors."

Awww. Meghan liked that he included her in that sentiment—calling them *our* ancestors.

"You're a Valleja-Marquez bride, my wild, Irish goddess. It's her privilege to take care of your every whim."

"I know. And she's over the moon planning and organizing everything with Carmen. We'll start here, of course. Maybe watch the parade playback on the big screen and hang out on the patio. Early dinner and then head down to the Camerons—take over the theater room for my favorite movie."

"And then, the next day . . ."

Meghan lit up with happiness. Yeah. The next day. She couldn't wait.

"Well? Did he say it was okay?"

"He wants to talk to you," Parker told her gravely, handing over his phone.

Eeek! Really? Hours ago during a pre-dawn bathroom run, Angie had seen when she glanced at her phone that her mom had left a message, *Call me.* So she had. Seemed her mother's quirky extra sense had picked up an energy flutter as she called it and she wanted to know if her baby Angel was all right.

She'd confessed it all. Aldo. The madcap airport run. Parker. Alex. Her mom had laughed with glee. When she hilariously shrieked, "Oh, my god! I'm going to be the mother of the bride!" they'd dissolved into happy tears and giggles. Her mom was the best.

And then she'd smirked—Angie could hear it in her voice—and asked her not to tell Daddy that they'd talked. She'd jumped the gun and called when she should have let him have his Father of the Angel moment. It was a husband and wife thing, she explained. Telling his wife of forty years that he'd given their blessing for a daughter's marriage was one of those moments she couldn't deny him. It was so sweet and loving, she'd teared up.

Taking the phone carefully, as though it was either dangerous or ridiculously expensive, Angie cleared her throat, then chirped happily,

"Hi, Daddy!"

Their part of the conversation was brief, direct, and to the point. No fucking around with Cristián Valleja-Marquez. Not when it came to his family.

"So . . ." he stated rather drily. "Tell me little one, are you really in love with this man?"

This man? *Sheesh.* Alex hadn't been kidding. Her father's gruff tone referring to his godson was chilly. Daddy first. Uncle and godfather a distant second. She got serious in a hurry.

"Yes." Her answer was definitive and forceful. "Yes, Daddy, I do."

"Do you want to marry him, Angelina? And do you know what that means?"

"Yeah, I do. He'll take good care of me, Dad. Please say it's okay."

"Are you absolutely sure this is what you want?"

"It is."

He sighed. Angie wondered if this was hard for him. She'd never thought about how her dad would feel about being supplanted in her heart by another man and wondered if Meghan's father had similar feelings.

"Your mom and I love you and just want you to be happy."

She nodded, not that he knew that from a phone call, but words weren't possible while her throat was thick with emotion.

"Hand the phone back to Parker, sweetie."

"Okay," she croaked as snot began seeping and tears burned in her eyes. Giving Parker the phone back, she wiped the back of her hand back and forth across her top lip. "Here."

Everything after that was half a blur. She heard him mutter a few words, say, "Thank you, sir," then a brief silence before Alex and Meghan along with Carmen and a just arrived Ben started screaming enthusiastically—rushing at them as shouts of 'congratulations' filled the air.

She would have liked a hug from her official fiancé. Maybe a kiss, too—but they get swept up in every else's enthusiasm.

What a glorious day!

Chapter Sixty-Five

STANDING IN THE SHOWER, ALEX reviewed a thousand small details that needed his attention. He was amazed at how much thought and planning had gone into the special day he had in store for his lady love. Hell. It seemed like there were as many factors to consider, if not more, than what he'd dealt with putting together mission plans during the war.

It wouldn't have been possible to pretend nothing was going on so, on the one hand, Meghan was well aware of and in on planning the St. Patty's Day celebration with Carmen and Ria. What she didn't realize though was that Family Justice also had some surprises in store.

And as if that wasn't enough, their secret plan for tomorrow was giving him nightmares. Again—she didn't even know the half of it.

The agency plane was going to be busy over the next few days and he had a few last-minute requests that only his personal pilot could help with, so making a mental note to have a talk with Captain Sawyer later, he startled when his lovely Meghan appeared out of thin air, alongside him in the shower. If her expression gave anything away, it was that she was in her Irish fuck goddess mood.

Flattening his big body against the tile wall warmed from the steaming shower, she rather aggressively grabbed hold of him. Thank god she was a natural athlete because she left her patience at the door, demanding he take her with a desperation he had to answer. Their shower gymnastics were so frenzied, he supposed at the end of it all he should thank Christ they hadn't ended up in the emergency room.

She was wiped out afterward so he tucked her back into their bed, kissed her forehead, and left her to a short nap. Closing the door quietly, he then sprinted to his tech cave where he could bring up his checklist on the computer, see what still needed handling, and get the ball rolling.

"You're glowing," Meghan teased Angie. She was, too. It was great seeing her looking so blissfully happy.

"It's the nonstop sex," her soon-to-be sister-in-law stated with a completely serious face. "Good for the skin."

Tori burst out laughing. "Well, if that's true, this whole place is a walking skincare ad!"

Even Betty chuckled although she made sure to punctuate her merriment with a motherly *tsk* or two.

"At first, I thought it was something in the water," Angie continued in that completely serious tone. "But apparently, I was wrong. It's not the water."

"What is it, then," Lacey asked.

Meghan couldn't help but laugh. Lacey was so adorably clueless sometimes.

"It's all that testosterone and shit like that! Did you know sperm have a five-day shelf-life?"

Meghan, in fact, did know that. Being a health and phys ed teacher had its advantages. Shrieks of laughter and shouts of, "Ewww, gross!" and, "Alrighty then," filled the air.

Lacey blushed several shades of red and murmured, "Good to know."

Oh, really? She and Tori exchanged a look.

"Raise your hand if you're trying to get pregnant," Tori quipped.

Angie shrugged.

Carmen and Ria *tsked*.

Betty snarked, "Gals, that ship has done passed."

Tori shoved her hands under her legs and sat on them with a chuckle.

Meghan glanced at Lacey, who was worrying the crap out of bottom lip with her teeth.

Feeling giddy, she pretended to raise her hand into the air with an invisible crank which was met with cheers and laughter from the women present. Finally, Lacey giggled shyly and ducked her head but her hand went up. Bravo, Mrs. Cameron!

They were all gathered on the patio which looked like a mischievous leprechaun threw up everywhere. There was so much green happening, it resembled the damn tropics. Green balloons tied together in huge bouquets weighed down by miniature pots of gold were spread around. Green four-leaf clover decorations were all over the place. Everyone had gone all out to make her day Irish special.

Cam brought a rolling big screen from the business center and put it in a corner of the patio, replaying the colorful St. Patty's Day parade from her hometown. There was more in the way of snack foods and munchies laying around than was necessary.

Meghan got a huge kick out of watching Parker and Angie tossing Irish Potatoes candies into each other's mouth from ever increasing distances. She didn't have the heart to tell them that until Betty produced the container of homemade confections, she'd never seen one before in her life. Definitely not a Boston thing or even an authentic Irish tradition.

But the definitive high point of the day? All of the men, including both babies, were outfitted in kilts and Doc Martens. Some of the kilts were camouflage, others were plain. Not a tartan in sight. The women hooted and hollered when the guys burst onto the patio singing a horrendously off-key rendition of O' Danny Boy, bare-chested wearing only the kilts. Seeing Drae and Cam carrying their sons was just the sweetest thing ever.

And Alex, her Major—he of the manly chest and buns of steel? Oh, dear god. He looked so damn hot strutting around dressed like that. She intended to blow a bit of sunshine up his skirt later.

Oh, and good lord! Draegyn had made her the most amazing wooden chest, this huge thing that Alex placed at the foot of their bed. Her ma had a hope chest that was a veritable treasure chest stuffed with family memories. Knowing she and Alex would fill the beautiful trunk with the memories they would create touched her deeply.

Everyone had the best time and most of Family Justice was there except for Brody. And Calder. Meghan missed both men. And Stephanie, too. She couldn't help but think of the wedding in Boston when they all be together again.

After an early dinner, the entire group decided to stroll instead of drive down the lane to the Cameron's for more fun and a showing of an Ireland themed movie that was a favorite in the O'Brien household.

What a funny group they made. A bunch of serious alpha men, dressed in kilts, a couple of babies in strollers, two rambunctious dogs, and a gaggle of chatty women—laughing, joking, Frisbee throwing—holding hands and telling tall tales as they walked along.

The best damn support team anywhere—Carmen, Gus, Ria, Ben, and Betty—saw them off with a round of hearty congratulations for Angie and Parker plus a flurry of hugs and kisses for everyone else.

Meghan was so happy she couldn't contain all the joy.

"Yeah, okay," Cameron quipped in that dry but terribly witty way he had. "That movie's a keeper, Red. Thanks for sharing!"

Tori yelled from across the theater room as she bundled Daniel into his stroller. "Who knew John Wayne was so damn hot? Was he like the first alpha or something?"

Parker enjoyed the easy way this group of unique but very different people connected with each other. It was refreshing, the bone-deep loyalty and caring that came naturally to all of them. Maybe it was true what they said about people of like interests and temperaments being inextricably drawn together.

Feeling close to Alex was one thing—they'd known each other since forever. But he had the same sense of absolute trust with Cameron and Draegyn. Sometimes, he wondered if he hadn't met the other two men in another time when death and terror were part of every day if they'd have such an instant connection.

He'd been with them when they were warriors . . . serious, sometimes scary, and always badass shitkickers who knew crap, saw stuff and did things that could haunt a man until his dying day. Parker respected each of them enormously.

Draegyn came over to him and shook his hand for the tenth time. Several fucking cases of Guinness, spread over an entire afternoon and evening, had a way of catching up with even the most adept beer drinker.

"That girl's a fucking handful," Drae teased looking at Angie. "You sure you're not too old for that shit?"

Motherfucker. At some point everyone, even Betty, goddammit, had something to say about their age difference. Why they all found it so hilarious was beyond him. Was it because Angie had been handing him his ass from the moment she arrived? No doubt.

"Yeah, well, she was mine first, a long time ago and maybe waiting around for her to no longer be actual motherfucking jailbait—*that was the Guinness talking*—was what the universe had in mind all along."

"Counselor," Draegyn smirked. "You fucking dog. Did you just admit what I think you did?"

Um . . . huh? What? *Hmmm.* Oh, shit. Yeah. Maybe he had.

"Fuck you, St. John. You've had it the easiest so maybe shut your damn mouth."

"You've met my wife, right?" Drae chuckled. "If that's what you call easiest . . . you're insane, dude."

Parker fake punched him in the gut. "I'm referring to you guys eloping. No months-long planning. None of that hearts and flowers shit. If you don't see how easy that was, you're the one who's insane."

Angie's small hand slid up his arm and pulled lightly on his earlobe. "Don't give Draegyn a hard time, sweetie. It's not easy being Studly Do-Her-Right."

Next, Victoria joined in the teasing fun. "Did you just refer to my husband with a sexual term?"

"That I did," Angie assured her seriously. "We've all seen those gossip rag stories about him, you know."

Drae growled hilariously, winking on an aside to Parker. "The only *her* this *stud* is doing right is standing right here."

Angie smacked Parker in the center of his bare chest. "Why can't you say romantic things like that?"

Eh . . . er . . . what?

"Oh, my god. Quick!" Drae chortled. "Someone get a shot of his face!"

Angie flung her arms about his waist and giggled into his shoulder. *This must be some traditional engagement rite of passage,* he figured. That was the only way to explain the constant ribbing he was getting.

Alex pounded him on the back. "Get used to it," he grunted.

"Yeah, funny shit. I know. Have done my fair share of messing with you three but fuck, man—I don't get it. The bullshit about our age." Parker was sulking and he knew it. "No one gives Cam shit and Lacey's the youngest one in this room except for the kids."

Angie was still plastered against him, her arms holding him tightly around his waist. She "*Hmmph'd*" and look up at him, her chin resting on his chest. "Word," she drawled.

Cam stepped in then and flat-out mocked him. "What you say is true. Except in our case, I hadn't changed my wife's diaper as a baby."

Everyone gathered around laughing and elbowing each other. Hurling randy comments about butt creams and baby wipes that quickly devolved to a triple X-rated giggle fest.

Lacey, dear sweet Lacey, who had Dylan half asleep on her shoulder, threw him a lifeline. "What did you give Angie for her sweet sixteen?"

Angie's sharp gasp and the speed with which she turned to look at her new friend set his awareness to high. Her sixteenth birthday? No way was that a random question. Lacey was trying to make a point.

Okay. He could do this. Her sweet sixteen. *Hmmm.* He would have been in D.C. by then while Alex had been doing his thing. What had he given her? Parker searched his memory, wishing the Guinness fog wasn't so thick.

And then he remembered. Holy fuckballz. Of course! Angel's sweet sixteen.

Uncle Cris and Aunt Ashleigh had thrown a fabulous party and his parents were right there in the thick of things. He couldn't get away from work for a trip home so he'd sent a present to his mom and asked her to see that Angie got it.

That was the first and only time, aside from anything having to do with his mom, that he'd walked into a jewelry store and bought a gift. The salesman had dazzled him with all sorts of crazy stuff until he'd glimpsed a dainty pair of ruby and diamond earrings that he just had to give her. Ruby was her birthstone and the diamonds, well . . . he remembered thinking with her coloring, that she'd look outrageous in diamonds.

Lacey was smiling at him. To Angie she said, "Do you remember? What did he give you?"

Before she could answer, he hugged her tight and kissed the top of her head. He *totally* fucking had this and he *totally* fucking knew exactly what Lacey was doing.

"Ruby earrings. I gave her ruby and diamond earrings that I bought myself from a small jewelry shop in Georgetown."

Angie was positively beaming at him. Did she think he wouldn't remember? Maybe he hadn't exactly forgotten but until Lacey brought it up, he hadn't seen how important the moment had been for them.

"Even then, you knew." No question. Lacey Cameron. One smart lady.

Parker gulped. Yeah. Even then.

"You guys have something none of us will ever have. A history that probably starts long before either of you were born. I think they call that destiny."

He wanted to kiss her. How could one so damn young be so damn wise?

"I heard Ben needling you earlier about the lack of bling."

Hmph. He remembered. Pissed him off—everyone making it seem like he'd let her down by not coming prepared with a ring. For Christ's sake! He'd just asked her. You'd think he could be cut a little slack. It was not like there was a jeweler out here in the middle of nowhere.

"Angie," Lacey said. "Still have those earrings?"

"I do indeed."

"Don't suppose you have them with you?"

Angie rocked against him, her whole body saying, *yes.*

Parker put his fingers beneath her chin and urged her to look at him. "Really?"

She nodded. They stared at each other. He didn't know what to say. Even though he'd hurt her so badly that she couldn't let him put so much as a toenail in her life, she held on to those tiny jewels. *And,* she brought them halfway around the planet when she knew, at some point, they'd have to confront their past.

Wow.

Like the waves that moved upon the shore that had no beginning and no end, Cam and Lacey, Drae and Tori, Alex and Meghan . . . they moved in and surrounded him and Angie with a force field of love that staggered him.

Theirs wasn't a conventional romance and thank fucking god for that. With so much history between them, it was inevitable that sometimes they got ahead of themselves before either was ready for the consequences of their actions—but with just a few words from Lacey, Parker saw so clearly that, even though those starts and stops were painful, maybe what was actually happening was flashes of their future coming through. Just at the wrong time.

Alex had the last word . . . as it should be.

"Family is all about connections. Everyone here understands that in their own unique way. We made a family together in the middle of a war," he said with a nod to Cam and Drae. "We call ourselves brothers but that word can't do justice to our connection."

They each fist bumped.

"And it can't really explain our connection either, can it?" he asked Parker. "Brothers, but not. Totally weird, man."

Angie blurted out, "I love you, Alexander."

"Love you too, little sister."

Alex looked around at all of them. You could see the emotion on his face.

"We're making something fucking special out here in the desert. It's not always about blood, is it?"

Every head in the room shook.

Alex extended his hand, palm down. "Family Justice," was all he said.

Drae put his hand on top of Alex's. Followed by Meghan, Tori, Cam, and Lacey.

Parker took Angie's hand in his and kissed it softly. "Family Justice," he murmured into eyes that looked upon him with amazing love. Still holding tight, he joined their hands to everyone else's.

"To the future," Alex said with a strength that resonated through the room.

"Family Justice!" they all boomed.

On cue, Daniel let out an impressive burp-fart to which Drae drawled, "That's my boy!"

"And on that note," Tori laughed, "I think it's time to call it a night."

Alex was on a high. When you have a lot of shit in your head from the past, it was good to have these palette cleansing times. Family Justice was solid. Things were back on track. Relieved, his thoughts instantly moved to his Meghan.

Today's family get-together might have meant more to him than to her. Hell, he would never get enough of surprising her or planning things, big and small, that were expressions of how much he fucking adored her and the balls out, day-long celebration, a tip of the hat to her Irish heritage would definitely end up being an annual thing.

One by one everyone drifted away. Drae and Tori called for Raven, then with Daniel in the stroller, set out for home.

When Angie kissed him good night and reminded him that she was going home with Parker, he almost said, *over my dead body,* before remembering the two were now engaged.

He and Meghan, along with Cam, Lacey, and Dylan, waved them off at the front door as they too started off on the walk back to the hacienda where Parker's SUV was parked.

"I think they're gonna make it," Cam told him. "I've never seen Parker so . . . undone."

Happy to hear it, Alex put out his hand. "Thanks for all you did today. Meghan and I appreciate it."

Cam leaned in and gave Meghan a kiss on the cheek. "My pleasure, Red. And just so you know, loved the movie. I'm adding it to my classics library."

A few more minutes went by while they chatted but all Alex was aware of was the hand he held in his. Suddenly, he couldn't get her out of there fast enough.

They were halfway home, walking silently side-by-side, their hands clasped, when he mumbled, "I don't think we should sleep together tonight."

Meghan stumbled and almost went down, but he caught her and helped her steady.

"*Whaaat?* Why?" she whined.

He'd been thinking about this all day but didn't know the right way to say what was on his mind so he went with the obvious.

"Aren't the bride and groom not supposed to see each other the night before they marry?"

Her disappointment when he stated his case was palpable. "Oh."

They walked on a little further. "I had Carmen fix up the casita."

This time she didn't stumble. Instead, she came to a complete halt and yanked on his arm.

"Excuse me?" She sounded incredulous. A little like he felt. Alex couldn't believe he was buying into this wedding folklore nonsense.

They'd just passed the turn to the St. John's and were headed straight for the winding path that snaked behind the hacienda where the casita sat halfway between home and Drae's house. He could see the soft lights coming from the little bungalow.

He didn't respond to her question, just urged her to, "Come on," and kept walking.

By the time they reached the casita door, Meghan was openly fretting.

"Alex, no. Don't. Please." She rushed him and tried to wind around his body. "I need you."

That almost undid him.

He called Zeus to his side and scratched her head when she came dutifully and sat next to him.

"You take care of Mommy, okay?" he told the dog. "And don't let her sulk too long."

A side of his fiancée he'd never seen before made an appearance. Stomping her foot like a frustrated kid, she got angry and pushed him away.

"Fine. If that's how you want to do this." Her flash of Irish fire fueled by irritation and what he suspected was a bad case of the boo-hoos was something to behold.

Smacking her hand against her leg, she motioned for the dog to follow and turned on her heel to go. Alex shook his head. Like he was going to let her get the last word and stomp away!

Before she finished even one step away from him, he grabbed and spun her around, moving her quickly until her back was against the front door.

He could have spent the next twenty minutes trying to cajole her into a better mood, but Alex knew exactly what she needed.

Cupping her face in his hands he looked deep into her eyes.

"I love you. Tomorrow, I make you my wife. Mine," he whispered just as his lips met hers.

Kissing her tenderly, he knew the second her upset crumbled to dust.

When he pulled back, he arched an eyebrow at her and waited. She nodded after a minute and swallowed heavily.

"Yours," she murmured.

He smiled. "Go home. Crawl in our bed and dream about the next time we make love. As husband and wife."

"Oh, baby," she sighed.

"I'll come for you at eleven. Be ready."

And with that, he shooed her along, patting her bottom gently, gesturing to Zeus to follow along.

She went because she knew that was what he wanted, but her steps were heavy and slow. Right before she turned toward the big house, he called after her, "And no playing with yourself when I'm not there!" he yelled.

Now that got a laugh—something he heard carried on the nighttime air for long moments after she disappeared.

"Tomorrow, my love," he said quietly out loud. "Tomorrow you become Meghan Valleja-Marquez."

Above him, the sky twinkled as the stars shone their approval.

Their future began tomorrow.

Epilogue

MEGHAN'S HEART WAS OVERFLOWING WITH love and happiness. At the stroke of eleven, she left their bedroom and made her way through the hacienda, with a wink to Abuela's portrait as she passed by and stumbled to an astonished halt when Alex came into view. Having never seen him in a formal dress uniform, she was completely unprepared for the emotional wallop that struck her and built with each step she took down the long staircase.

When her dashing Major came to the foot of the stairs, offered his arm, and looked into her eyes, her soul took flight. The love shining back at her was big enough to get lost in. It was a moment to be frozen in time that she could replay in her heart, over and over.

They didn't say anything. No words were necessary. Plenty of time for that later. Right now, she just wanted to take in how handsome he looked and how damn lucky she was that he looked at her the way he did.

As they bounced along in the truck, she smiled so big that her jaw ached. Zeus, her faithful companion and ally, sat proudly between them, just like she had the first time Meghan had ridden out into the desert with Alex in this very vehicle. A rapid, heated rush crept up her neck remembering what else happened that day in the front seat, and she found herself biting back a giggle.

Beaming at her hunky fiancé, she almost lost the battle of staying still and if not for the dog blocking her way, would have been all over

Alex like a rash.

Oh, my lord, he looked so fucking hot and sexy in his uniform. She truly had no idea how turned on seeing him like this would get her. There was something hugely impressive about the dress uniform and the colorful bars, medals, and insignias. Of course, the really impressive thing was the brawny, solid body beneath the immaculate military costume. *Have his thighs always been that muscular,* she wondered.

Alex glanced her way and smirked, almost like he was picking up on her private thoughts. Laughing, she did absolutely nothing to disguise the look of hungry desire she was sure was shining in her eyes.

"You look ravishing," he murmured with an appraising drift of his gaze to her outfit. She'd thought of everything, right down to the beautiful western boots that she jokingly said came from the Cowgirl Bridal Collection.

The simple white dress was dignified but sexy with a flared skirt and lace draping around her bared shoulders. She'd piled her hair on top of her head and let auburn tendrils fall all around, adding tiny crystal studded pins for some bling. She wore no jewelry except the magnificent diamond and emerald ring that marked her as his.

And she also wore no panties—but he didn't know that. Not yet. The sheer white scrap intended for her special attire was pretty. But let's face it, sometimes it was smarter to go au naturel. He wouldn't be able to remain still or concentrate if he knew she was naked beneath her dress, so she said nothing. Just sat there with a sly smile, totally aware of her bare bottom in the fancy dress.

Ahead in the distance, Drae's beautiful pergola came into view. The closer she got, the more excited she became because, even at a distance, she could see that the tall wooden structure had sheaths of white draped all around.

Amor Vórtice. *Awww,* Alex had really gone all out. How sweet was he? Then she noticed a big SUV was parked nearby.

That was Calder's car. Oh, my god. Wait a minute! Calder? Meghan had assumed they were headed into the desert for a private moment, just between her and Alex. The scenario she pictured in her mind seemed so romantic. Alone, surrounded by nature's simple solitude—saying vows and making promises. The ones that would count. That was all she ever really wanted. The privacy to make their sacred commitments to each other in a meaningful way minus everyone else's potential bullshit clouding her joy.

Why was Calder here? She honestly had no idea. Besides, wasn't he supposed to be in Atlanta begging Tori's mom to take him on?

"What's going on, Major?" she asked breathlessly as they drew closer.

Zeus noticed something was up because she started fidgeting and making little doggie noises.

They were on the final approach to their special spot when Alex slowed to a crawl.

"There was no way I was letting you fly out of here—away from me—even though it's only for a few weeks, without us being truly married first. You belong to me, Meghan. I want the words said before you leave."

"Oh, Alex," she murmured softly.

"My uncle is here because he loves you almost as much as I do. I asked for his help and you won't believe he did this, but Calder's solution was fucking epic. He got ordained as a minister and can legally perform weddings. What we start here today, Uncle Eduardo and the church can sanctify later."

Meghan almost shot from her seat and jumped in his lap. If the dog hadn't been in the way, that was exactly what would have happened. "For real? Calder can marry us?"

"Yep, yep," he drawled. "And to save my eardrums from the excited squeal I know is coming, I'll tell you now that Stephanie is with him. She's agreed to be our witness, and like my uncle, has sworn a vow of secrecy. No use in hurting anyone's feelings. Your family's or mine."

"Stephanie?" Meghan screamed as Alex laughed at her reaction. "Does Tori know she's here?"

"No. Not yet. Cam and Drae are in on what we're doing, which is why the Camerons and the St. Johns chose today to take the boys on an outing. The ladies have been distracted and no one knows a thing. This is about us, Meghan. You and me. It's what you wanted, right?"

Tears stung at her nose and swam in her eyes. They were getting married. Him in his magnificent dress uniform and her in some sexy cowgirl boots and no undies. Could anything be more perfect? She didn't think so and giggled at the thought.

"Did I do okay, baby?" he asked. The uncertainty she heard in his voice was so fucking cute.

"Did you do okay?" she barked happily. "Did you do okay? Oh, my fucking god, Alex."

Meghan searched for the right thing to say. Something profound and eloquent so he'd know how much his efforts touched her. In every way. A naughty grin lit up her face when just the right thing came to mind.

Shimmying around the damn dog who she made switch places with her, Meghan leaned into Alex's solid body and sent a hand onto his thigh where sliding it toward the bulge in his slacks was an easy move.

"You are too good to me, Major," she purred close to his ear.

With only a minute or so before they'd be at their spot, she palmed the hardness and smiled with satisfaction when she felt his flesh surge against her questing fingers.

"If we didn't have an audience, I'd be sucking your cock right fucking now to let you know just how good you did!" Her laughter was naughty and joyous because, as vulgar as that sounded, it was the damn truth.

His sharp hiss sent molten desire flooding into her core.

"But since that's not possible, I'll leave you with this . . ." Sucking his earlobe into her mouth, she nipped it hard and whispered, "I don't have any panties on."

The truck slowed to a halt. As he put it into park, Alex turned her way and husked, "You always know the right thing to say, and since you just pleased me very, very much, in honor of your bare ass and the vows we're about to say, I'm going to wipe out what's left of your naughty points. Think of it as a bridal gift."

Forgive the points? Was he insane? Those damn points were sexy as shit and no way did she want to give them up.

"What? Shut up!" she drawled dramatically as she slapped him on the shoulder.

Alex threw back his head and barked a tremendous laugh. "Insatiable wench," he teased. "Okay, wife." His eyes blazed as he said the word. "Five points on your side of the leaderboard and we'll negotiate terms later."

She high-fived him with glee.

"Let's get married, baby," he exclaimed with a face-splitting grin. She'd never seen him look happier.

THE END

You Are Cordially Invited

To the Very Special Family Justice Wedding of

Alexander Valleja-Marquez

and

Meghan Elizabeth O'Brien

This Fall 2015

SANCTUARY

A FAMILY JUSTICE NOVEL

Other Books by Suzanne Halliday

The Justice Brothers
Broken Justice
Fixing Justice
Redeeming Justice

Family Justice
Always

Wilde Women
Wilde Forever
WIlde Heart

Acknowledgments

Ella Fox
I know it's getting old for me to keep saying this but you really are my sunshine!

Jenny Sims
Thanks for explaining the difference between crumble and crumple. Next we'll work on grey and gray.

Author K Webster
What you did with the book teasers completely rocked my world. Thank you seems like so little. . . .

Stacey Blake
Champagne for everyone!
These stories aren't complete until you make everything look so nice.

Ashley Bauman
Once again—you bring my Justice visions to life

Jennifer G. Wenstad
Thank you for handling the social media while I'm writing!
Carpe Diem

Cheryl Stork
Desert Thunder thanks you

About the Author

Suzanne Halliday writes what she knows and what she loves—sexy adult contemporary romance with strong men and spirited women. Her love of creating short stories for friends and family has developed into a passion for writing romantic fiction with a sensual edge. She finds the world of digital, self-publishing to be the perfect platform for sharing her stories and also for what she enjoys most of all—reading. When she's not on a deadline you'll find her loading up on books to devour.

Currently a wanderer, she and her family divide their time between the east and west coast, somehow always managing to get the seasons mixed up. When not digging out from snow or trying to stay cool in the desert, you can find her in the kitchen, 80's hair band music playing in the background, kids running in and out, laptop on with way too many screens open, something awesome in the oven, and a mug of hot tea clutched in one hand.

Visit her at:

Website:authorsuzannehalliday.com
Facebook https://www.facebook.com/SuzanneHallidayAuthor
Twitter@suzannehalliday
Check out the Pinterest Boards for my stories:
http://www.pinterest.com/halliday0383/
I love getting feedback from readers!

Printed in Great Britain
by Amazon